Probability Sun

BY NANCY KRESS

NOVELS

Prince of Morning Bells

The White Pipes

The Golden Grove

An Alien Light

Brainrose

Beggars in Spain

Beggars and Choosers

Oaths and Miracles

Beggars Ride

Maximum Light

Stinger

Yanked!

Probability Moon

Probability Sun

STORY COLLECTIONS

Trinity and Other Stories

The Aliens of Earth

Beaker's Dozen

Probability Sun

Nancy Kress

TOR®

A Tom Doherty Associates Book

New York

PROBABILITY SUN

Copyright © 2001 by Nancy Kress

This book is printed on acid-free paper.

Edited by David G. Hartwell

A Tor Book
Published by Tom Doherty Associates, LLC
175 Fifth Avenue
New York, NY 10010

www.tor.com

Tor® is a registered trademark of Tom Doherty Associates, LLC.

Library of Congress Cataloging-in-Publication Data

Kress, Nancy.
    Probability sun / Nancy Kress.—1st ed.
        p. cm.
    "A Tom Doherty Associates book."
    ISBN 0-312-87407-3
        1. Human-alien encounters—Fiction.   2. Life on other planets—Fiction.
    3. Space warfare—Fiction.   I. Title.

PS3561.R46 P78 2001
813'.54—dc21   2001027119

First Edition: July 2001

Printed in the United States of America

0 9 8 7 6 5 4 3 2 1

For Charles Sheffield, founder, The Charitable Foundation for the
Promotion of Scientific Literacy Among People Purporting
to Be Science Fiction Writers

ACKNOWLEDGMENTS

This novel owes a large debt to Brian Greene's fascinating *Elegant Universe*. Greene's explanations of superstring theory provided the bases, both factual and speculative, for the even more speculative and eccentric theories of my character Dr. Thomas Capelo.

I also owe gratitude to my husband, Charles Sheffield, who went over the manuscript carefully and made many valuable suggestions about both science and plot.

Probability Sun

PROLOGUE

GOFKIT SHAMLOE, WORLD

The farewell burning had reached its unfolding. Standing at the edge of the circle of mourners in her black robe, Enli held her breath. This was the moment she loved, the moment of joy.

The procession had left Gofkit Shamloe at sunrise. Four moons had still graced the sky: Lil, Cut, Ap, and Obri. The entire village, including ancient Ayu Pek Marrifin carried on a litter and the two tiny Palofrit twins, just past their Flower Ceremony, walked slowly behind the farm cart. It was pulled by Tiril Pek Bafor's two oldest grandsons. The old man, chief gardener to the village for as long as Enli could remember, had been laid, unwashed, in the cart the night before and buried under mounds of flowers: huge bright red jellitib, cluster-blossoms of pajalib, fragrant waxy sajib.

The priest stepped forward, the servant of the First Flower, and raised her hands. The subdued crowd turned toward her. Behind the priest the fire, started last night, leaped higher than the holy one's head. Its crackling was the only sound.

"Now," said the servant of the First Flower, a short dumpy middle-aged woman whose neckfur was prematurely sparse.

Tiril Pek Bafor's grandsons pulled the cart through a narrow lane among mourners, to the very edge of the fire. They tipped the cart forward. The wood had been highly waxed; the body slid effortlessly into the flame, mostly hidden by flowers. And everyone in the entire crowd, the grieving and the old and the halt and the lame, simultaneously threw off their thin black robes and shouted loud enough to wake the dead.

It was a shout of pure joy. The dead man was returning to his ancestors.

The village chanted and sang. Under their black capes they all wore brilliantly-colored short tunics sewn, festooned, and entwined before dawn with fresh flowers. Each bloom represented some facet of the wearer's relationship with the soul now so jubilantly released to the spirit world, where every flower bloomed forever.

Everyone began to dance. People sang; the fire jumped and shouted; the air filled with the rich fragrance of the oil the priests used to make Tiril Pek Bafor's passage smell sweet. Amid the dancing and rejoicing, the sun rose, red and warm.

Enli danced with Calin Pek Lillifar, round and round . . . it wasn't only the dance that made her head whirl. She had known Calin since childhood, but this felt like a new way of knowing, a different sharing . . .

Her sister Ano tapped her on the shoulder. "Enli . . . come with me."

"Later," Enli said. Calin was a good dancer, and Enli, helped by a generous swig of pel from the jug passed around by Pek Bafor's daughters, even felt graceful herself. This was a rarity; Enli was a big, plain woman with no natural grace, and knew it. But Calin didn't seem to mind. Round and round . . .

"Come now," Ano said.

"What is it?" Enli said crossly, after following Ano away from the fire. "And why can't it wait? I want to enjoy the farewell burning!" She glanced back at Calin, not yet dancing with anyone else.

Ano's skull ridges creased in worry. "I know. But there's a government messenger to see you. He's waiting in the hut."

"A government messenger? For me?"

Ano nodded. The sisters stared at each other. There was no reason for a government messenger to seek Enli. Her old trouble was past, atoned for, finished. And to interrupt her during a farewell burning!

"Thank you," Enli said to Ano, in a tone that let Ano know not to follow. Enli walked among the revelers, increasingly drunk on pel, and back along the path, bright with morning flowers, to the deserted village.

The messenger was young enough to still relish formality. "Enli Pek Brimmidin? May your garden bloom. I am come from the capital city, Rafkit Seloe. I bring a message."

He carried no letter. Enli heard her voice come out too hoarse. "May your blossoms flourish. And your message is what?"

"That your presence is required at Rafkit Seloe, at the office of the Servants of the First Flower. The Sun Blossom himself wishes to talk to you."

"About what?" Enli said, knowing that whatever it was, the messenger would of course know. Shared reality.

The boy couldn't help himself. He was young, and excitement won out over dignity and formality. He shook his neckfur and said, "About the Terrans!"

Terrans. Some Terrans had come to World three years ago, from some place unimaginably far away, in a metal flying boat. They had disrupted everything. But then they had gone away again, leaving three graves, and World had returned to sweet peace. Enli got out, "The Terrans left."

The boy shook his neckfur again and, in sheer exuberance, rose up on his tiptoes.

"Yes. But, Pek Brimmidin—they have come back!"

Enli's headache began, the sharp boring pain between the eyes. No, no, not again . . . in the name of the First Flower, not again.

"Yes," the messenger said, when Enli didn't respond. "And this time we know they're real! The priests made their decision last time, remember? We can trade with the Terrans again and . . . and everything. They came again from all that way out there beyond the stars. They have come back!

"Isn't it wonderful?"

ONE

LOWELL CITY, MARS

General Tolliver Gordon looked up from the holocube in his meaty hands. "Who else has seen this?"

Major Lyle Kaufman, standing at attention, permitted himself a wintry smile. "Practically everyone, sir. This civilian Dieter Gruber has spent two years trying to get someone from Alliance Command interested. Anyone."

"Stefanek?"

"No, sir." It was not lost on Major Kaufman that a general had referred to the supreme commander of the Solar Alliance Defense Council without his title, and to a junior officer. For the first time, Kaufman felt a twinge of hope. He could never get in to see General Stefanak. Gordon could.

"General Ling?"

"Yes, sir."

"Ling saw this, and dismissed it?"

"He said there's no hard evidence, sir."

"Hard evidence isn't the only kind worth considering." Gordon stood, a big man in a small room. He handled the gravity of Mars easily. Born here, decided Kaufman, who had not been. That would help, too. In theory all nation members, and all service branches, of the Solar Alliance Defense Council were equal. However, some were more equal than others, especially in wartime.

Gordon walked to a small shelf on one wall of his underground bunker/office. On the shelf stood a mesh cage about a meter square, filled with plastic "shavings." He picked up a watering can, poked it through the mesh, and filled a water bowl just inside the cage. "All right, Major, I've viewed the cube and read the report. Now tell me in your own words what this scientific quest is about, why you think it's important, and why I should think so."

This was his chance. Everyone had told him that if he got this far, Gordon would really listen. Kaufman cleared his throat. "Two years ago, sir, on a routine recon, the one military officer on a scientific expedition to a new planet discovered that one of its moons was an artificial construct with the same kind of markings as the space tunnels. The war was going badly then—"

Kaufman broke off. A mistake: The war with the Fallers was still going badly, worse than ever, but he had never met an officer in High Command who appreciated being reminded of it. Gordon, however, merely picked up a bag of small seeds and began filling a clear plastic tube leading inside the cage.

". . . And so we launched a secret expedition to see if the moon was, or could be, a weapon. That is, the expedition wasn't secret, it looked like just another bunch of anthropologists, but it included a team of unacknowledged military scientists led by Colonel Syree Johnson, retired. The ship was the *Zeus*, under Commander Rafael Peres. Johnson discovered that the moon would indeed make a formidable weapon. It released a spherical wave that destabilized all nuclei with an atomic number greater than seventy-five. While they were still testing the artifact, the Fallers showed up and wanted it, too. Johnson and Peres tried a race for the system's only space tunnel, #438, towing the moon—"

"Towing it? How big was this moon?"

"Almost twenty times the size of the *Zeus*, sir. Mass of nine hundred thousand tons. Just short of the tunnel, Peres engaged with the enemy. The next sequence of events isn't clear, but either the *Zeus*, the Fallers, or the moon itself blew up all three. Colonel Johnson's previous reports suggest that it might have been the artifact that caused the blow-up. Its mass was too great to go through a tunnel, but she tried to send it through anyway, into our space, to keep it from enemy hands."

"So everything blew up. And that was the end of it, from High Command's point of view."

"Yes, sir." Kaufman felt more and more hopeful. Gordon's tone conveyed clearly his point of view about High Command's point of view. "But not the end of it to the surface team. That included a geologist with enough physics to follow what Johnson was doing. Dr. Dieter Gruber, Berlin University. The anthropologists had some sort of trouble with the natives on the planet—"

"Industrials?"

"No, sir. Artisan-level at best. Gruber led his team to safety inside a cave-ridden mountain range, where the natives won't go for religious reasons. He says that in there he discovered a second alien artifact, potentially of inestimable scientific and military value. Shortly afterward, a rescue effort lifted him out along with the two remaining anthropologists—three more humans died on the planet— and ever since, Gruber's been trying to convince the High Command to go back and dig up the second artifact."

Gordon finished filling the seed tube and set the package on the shelf. "And?"

This was the tricky part. Kaufman proceeded carefully. "Gruber says that at the moment the artifact-moon exploded—the *very* moment—the artifact buried in the mountains was affected. He argues for the same kind of macro-level quantum entanglement that we think might be the principle behind the space tunnels." The words were chosen deliberately; no one knew what was the actual science behind the space tunnels, those enigmatic remains of a vanished civilization that would have dwarfed any human one.

Gordon said, "But . . ."

"But Gruber has no direct proof. Nothing documented."

"Still, you believe him."

"I don't know him well," Kaufman said quietly. "But I served under Colonel Syree Johnson in the action at Edge. She was the finest and most committed scientist-officer I've ever known. It's not always an easy combination, sir."

Gordon looked at him penetratingly. "I can imagine. Pressure from science to find objective truth, pressure from the military to deploy pragmatic necessity?"

"Yes, sir. Syree Johnson, too, thought there was some connection between the alien construct in space and the buried one in the mountains. She told Gruber so just before she died."

"A recorded conversation?"

"No, sir. Unfortunately not."

"And there's no direct proof."

"No, sir. But scientifically—"

"Wait on the scientific 'buts.' I'll hear them in a moment. Tell me what you're going to want if I find the science convincing, and what we stand to gain from following your recommendations."

Kaufman took a deep breath. "I think we should send a scientific team to dig up and examine the second artifact. It would require a ship routed through Caligula space, that's Tunnel #438, with military escort and two flyers permanently attached for tunnel communications. You'd need a good political team to handle native relations, but the crucial thing is the scientist aboard. There's only one that, in my opinion, can do this. We stand to gain a possible weapon—only possible, of course—related to the moon/artifact that blew up. Gruber says they're made of the same material, and it's also the material of the space tunnels. Syree Johnson's reports say the destroyed artifact affected radioactivity levels in a controlled way, which implies it affected the probability of atomic decay. Anything that affects probability has to be related to the Faller beam-disrupter shields that are letting them attack us with impunity. We could gain a counter-weapon to the Faller shields, sir."

Kaufman paused. He'd just fired his biggest gun. If it didn't hit, nothing would. The beam-disrupter shields had only recently appeared on select Faller ships. Anything fired at such a ship-proton beam, laser cannon, any sort of beam at all—simply disappeared. Gone. Not even an energy trace left behind.

Gordon left the mesh cage and sat down again behind his desk. His eyes were shrewd.

"Big promises, Major."

"Not promises, sir. But definite possibilities. And we need those. In my opinion, General, the chance is worth the cost."

"Even though this geologist, Gruber, has no documentation?"

Kaufman kept his face blank. "Nothing new starts with documentation, sir. By definition. Especially not in science."

"I suppose not. All right, the costs. I listen well, Major, and I heard two worms in your carefully polished apple. First, why would we need 'a good political team to handle native relations'? Why not just the usual anthropologists?"

Yes, Gordon did listen well. He was good. Kaufman said, "The planet's proscribed by the Solar Alliance, sir."

"A fairly large worm. Why?"

"The natives don't want us. They've decided we lack souls. In their parlance, humans are 'unreal.' "

"Interesting," Gordon said. "And why didn't you name the 'one scientist' that, in your opinion, can do this job? Is the job of digging up and investigating an artifact that difficult?"

"This one is, sir. Syree Johnson didn't get it figured out, and she was damn good. She got blown up instead. You need someone with both experimental background and theoretical brilliance, and not many physicists ever are both. I want Dr. Thomas Capelo, sir."

He could see the name meant nothing to Gordon.

"He's probably on the short list for the Nobel, sir, although he hasn't won yet. He's still young, physicists usually do their most innovative work young. He *has* won the Tabor Phillips prize. His work is on the relationship between quantum events and probability."

"Quantum events and probability?"

"Yes, sir. We know that certain quantum-level events are probabilistic. They may or may not occur. We also know that some events have measurable probability—that is, we can say there's a seventeen percent chance that x will occur, or a thirty-four percent chance, or whatever. What we can't do yet is say *why* this event occurs seventeen percent of the time and that event thirty-four percent of the time. We have equations for the wave functions of quantum-mechanical probability, but no causals for the phenomenon of probability as a whole. That's the area of Capelo's work. He theorizes that a particle, or a virtual particle, is involved."

Kaufman could see that this meant nothing to General Gordon. He added, "I'm not a scientist either, sir. Just a very interested amateur. But let me go out on a limb and say that if you don't send Dr. Capelo, I'm not sure the expedition is worth doing at all, given the awful political beating we'll take from invading a proscribed planet."

Gordon shifted in his chair. " 'Invading' is a pretty strong word, Major."

"Yes, sir."

"And why wouldn't this Capelo be everybody's obvious choice? What's the other shoe here?"

Kaufman said, "He's not military, sir. Harvard University, United Atlantic Federation. And he's reputed to be . . . eccentric. Not everybody likes working with him." Kaufman paused, considered, decided on honesty. "In fact, hardly anybody likes working with him. He's sarcastic, and he's always convinced he's perfectly right."

"And is he?"

"Usually, sir."

"I see. Major, you've handed me a stinker."

"Yes, sir."

"All right. Let's hold our noses while you explain this science to me. Do it slowly, do it clearly, and show me why you think it might lead to some counter-device to the Faller shields. And don't overstate your case, Major. I probably won't be able to detect if you're doing so now, but I'll find out eventually."

"Yes, sir," Kaufman said, and had to hold still a moment before he began again. His head felt light. The science wouldn't be easy to explain, but that wasn't the problem. Nor was obtaining Gordon's consent. Kaufman knew that he, like Gordon, was a good judge of men. Gordon had already decided to chance the expedition. No, Kaufman's light-headedness wasn't because he was nervous about Gordon's refusal. He was nervous about Gordon's acceptance.

And of what train of events he, Lyle Kaufman, had just, finally, got out of the station and into motion.

TWO

THARSIS PROVINCE, MARS

When the comlink shrilled in his brother-in-law's comfortable living room, Tom Capelo said, "If that's for me, I'm not here."

"Incoming message in real-time from Earth, United Atlantic Federation, for Dr. Capelo, priority one," the house system said.

"I'm not here. In fact, I'm not anywhere. I've vanished from timespace."

"Tom," Martin Blumberg said with weary patience.

"System, tell them I'm caught in a space tunnel."

"It won't do that," Martin said. "Only *your* system will do that. This is a normal system. House, put the call on screen."

Capelo's younger daughter said, "Daddy, you're not really in a space tunnel." After a moment she added, "Are you?"

"Caught with all my molecules dissassembled."

"Oh, he's just acting stupid again," the older daughter told her sister, with enormous disgust. "You're such a baby."

"I am not! I'm five!"

"So what? I'm ten, and that's twice as old."

"Transferring message," the house system said. A section of the living room wall, which had previously shown the Martian sunset outside the room, darkened briefly, then brightened into an image of a sharp-featured man in a darkened bare room. The image said formally, "This is Dr. Raymond Pellier at Harvard University, UAF, calling for Dr. Thomas Capelo. Please activate two-way visual and audio. There will be a six-minute delay between transmission points. Acknowledge immediately."

"Asshole," Capelo said, into the six-minute delay.

"Daddy said a bad word," said Sudie, the five-year-old.

"Frozen star," Capelo said in a heavily fake Russian accent.

"Stop acting so fizzy, Daddy," ordered Amanda. "You always embarrass us."

"I'm not embarrassed," Sudie said stoutly. "What's embarrassed mean?"

Martin stood. "Girls, your father is receiving an important message from his department chair, and I think he needs to do it in private. Let's go find Aunt Kristen."

The two children, unmoving, looked at their father. Capelo said, "You might as well go. I'm only going to tell the frozen star that I'm disassembled."

"Daddy—"

"All right, all right, I'm not disassembled. You two never let me be anything fun. House, activate two-way visual and audio. Ray, you're acknowledged. 'Give sorrow words.' "

Martin took his nieces by the hands and led them away, closing the door behind him. Capelo waited the twelve minutes for his message to be received on Earth and responded to. While he waited, he paced restlessly around the room, touching objects. Bookshelves with actual books, a vase of genemod flowers from the garden at the far side of the dome, a severe metal table topped with a severe slab of red Martian stone—why did all of Kristen's furniture look so austere? His sister used to have a healthy sense of excess, back when they were kids. But now look: books lined up neatly, flowers sedate in a severe vase. Somehow excess had vanished when she'd married Martin, that most sensible of men. Patient Martin, putting up with his crazy brother-in-law. Although probably it was for the sake of the girls. *Give them a sense of family*, Kristen probably said to Martin, *poor things*. Well, that was all right, Capelo himself would put up with anything for Amanda and Sudie, even Kristen's ugly furniture. Even Mars, with its too-close horizon and grossly inadequate gravity. Even Raymond Pellier. Even—

"Dr. Capelo," the image of his department chair said, "I have just received a message from the Solar Alliance Defense Council. A representative is currently on her way to see you in person, and will probably arrive shortly after this message does. I'm calling you first to let you know this representative is on her way so you may prepare yourself. Also, to tell you that I'm arranging indefinite leave of absence for you from the university so you can accept the mission the council is sending you on."

"*What?*" Capelo said, although of course the image wouldn't hear him for six minutes. "Mission? What mission, Ray? I'm not a fucking soldier!"

"I know you're always interested in your graduate seminar, so I want to reassure you that Dr. Gerdes will be covering both that and your thesis advisees."

"Gerdes? *Gerdes?* He can't advise the way across campus!"

"Let me just add, Dr. Capelo, the department and the university's congratulations on your being tapped for an assignment vital to the war effort. Transmission finished."

"House, turn off the system," Capelo said.

He poured himself another drink. "*Assignment vital to the war effort.*" What crap. The council had probably concocted another of those exploratory committees of scientists they were always putting together to forecast what the Fallers would do next and what protocols should be designed to meet it . . . as if anyone knew what the bastards would do next. But undoubtedly the council had requested "a top Harvard physicist," good window dressing for PR purposes, see if you can dig up a Nobel winner or at least a short-list candidate, and just look, citizens of the Solar System, at the efforts we're making to protect you! And Ray, that pompous bureaucrat, had jumped at the chance to unload difficult touchy Capelo somewhere beyond a distant space tunnel so the physics department could have some peace.

Well, forget it. Capelo wasn't going. Let someone else enact the farce that there was any way to protect citizens from Fallers. If anybody had reason to know better, he did.

The door opened and Martin stuck his head in. "Tom . . . you have a visitor, from the Solar Alliance Defense Council. Do you want to see her in here or—"

"I don't want to see her at all."

"I'm afraid that's not a choice, Dr. Capelo," another voice said, and a woman pushed past Martin into the living room. Tall, outwardly sixty-ish (always hard to tell with genemods), with short gray hair, she wore a crisp Alliance Army uniform. "Thank you, Mr. Blumberg. Please leave us."

And Martin meekly went, ordered out of his own living room, quietly closing the door behind him.

Capelo said, "Hello, and good-bye. You're here to request my inclusion on a scientific war committee; my department chair just called to tell me. But I'm not interested. Sorry."

"Yes, you are interested," the woman said. "I'm Colonel Byars, Dr. Capelo. I'm here on the direct authority of General Stefanak."

"Very impressive," Capelo said. "And so are you, Colonel. You positively exude authority, your own and the general's. Unfortunately, I'm not intrigued by authority. And the last time I looked, the military was not drafting civilians for its exploratory committees. I'm flattered as hell by your wanting me and all that, but no thanks."

"May I sit down?"

"If you insist."

"Will you sit down, too?"

"Certainly. I can say no just as well sitting down as standing up. It's an inherited family ability, passed along for generations."

They sat. Colonel Byars pulled her chair uncomfortably close to Capelo's and said calmly, "This assignment is not an exploratory committee, Dr. Capelo. And you are not just any civilian—you're a scientist with irreplaceable and non-duplicatable skills needed for this project, which is priority one, Special Compartmented Information clearance carrying 'most vital to war effort' status. You *can* be recruited for a project with that status, and you are being so recruited. Now."

Capelo said, "You're wearing a portable communications shield. With a Faraday field big enough to encase these chairs."

"Affirmative. Your SCI clearances are already in process, and until they come through, I can't give you all the specifics on the project. I can say that it's one worthy of your prodigious talents, as they've been described to me. Of course, we can't forcibly carry you off and make you do physics for us, but if you absolutely refuse to serve the Alliance, we can find you a willful obstruction to the war effort."

"And send me to prison," Capelo said. "My God."

"And send you to prison," Byars agreed. "But we don't expect that to happen. First, there's nothing in your record that indicates you oppose the war, and at least one personal reason to think you have an interest in defeating the Fallers who—"

"Stop," Capelo said. "Stop right now."

"As you wish. Second, the project is one with genuine and major scientific interest, one that we think will hold authentic fascination for you. Real physics, at the experimental and theoretical edge."

"You're not a physicist," Capelo said. "Not even a minor one. You wouldn't know the theoretical edge if it sliced you in half."

"No. I'm proceeding on the words of people who are physicists."

"And you'd really send me to prison if I say no."

"We would indeed. We don't like doing it this way, Dr. Capelo. A reluctant scientist on a military mission is nobody's conception of ideal. Especially not mine. If this were up to me, I'd choose somebody else."

"Points for honesty, Colonel. But not many. I don't like being pushed around."

"I don't like doing it. But apparently you, and only you, are needed for this."

"And from the way you're studying me, you can't imagine why."

She didn't answer. Capelo got up and strode around his sister's sensibly decorated room, fighting the impulse to throw something. The bastards. The fucking imperial bastards. High-handed, dictatorial . . . Abruptly he flung himself back into the chair that stood too close to Byars's.

"I'm going to astonish you, Colonel. I'm going to accept."

"I'm pleased."

"No, you're not. You wanted me to say no, that's why you presented this as autocratically as possible. Your starched little military soul really does want somebody else. But somewhere above you there's a military physicist who knows better, and I think I can guess who. He's worth listening to. So I'll accept, with two conditions."

Byars said levelly, "The Solar Alliance Defense Council doesn't accede to conditions, Dr. Capelo."

"You will this time. This little recruiting session is being recorded, isn't it? Of course it is. I already called you on your overall approach. Don't add to it unreasonable obstruction of a war effort on *your* part."

Byars was good. She didn't retort, didn't move even a facial muscle. But Capelo saw the anger in her eyes.

He said, "First condition: You confirm for me that the military physicist who wants me is Vladimir Cherkov. Confirming that surely doesn't violate security."

"Affirmative. It is Dr. Cherkov, responding to a request for recommendation from non-scientist officers."

"The opinions of non-scientists don't count. Second, no matter
where this project is, anywhere in the galaxy, my two daughters and
their nanny go with me."

"Unacceptable."

"Then I'll go to jail."

For the first time, Byars's expression changed. "You'd take two
children into a war zone?"

Capelo threw back his head and laughed.

The laughter—sharp, bitter—finally seemed to disconcert Colonel Byars. But she said nothing until Capelo turned on her.

"Take two kids into danger, you mean? Where the enemy is?
Let me finish what I wouldn't let *you* finish before, Colonel. You
said I have at least one personal reason for wanting to see the Fallers
defeated. You meant the death of my wife in the Faller raid on New
London. Were you there, Colonel? No, you probably weren't. New
London is a peaceful colony—*was* a peaceful colony—with no military presence whatsoever, on a peaceful planet beyond Space Tunnel
#264, where my wife was surveying alien fishes. She was a xeno-
biologist, as your briefing undoubtedly told you. The Fallers attacked
and she died, just as they've attacked numerous other human settlements, military and civilian. With no apparent obstruction of their
war effort by the Solar Alliance."

"Their beam-disrupter shield—"

"Is impenetrable, I know. We all know. And if I can do anything
real to crack the science of that bugger, I will. Because that's what
this project is connected with, isn't it? Has to be. I'll do it. Just don't
sit there and try to tell me that there's anywhere I could go that's
more dangerous than anywhere else for my girls. Because I know
better. Where I go, they go. They've already lost one parent—they're
not going to lose the other. I'll go to prison first, and make sure
they're housed right outside the walls. Do I make myself clear?"

"Perfectly," Byars said. She stood. "I'll report your answer."

"And hope it disqualifies me, right? It won't. Not if Vladimir Cherkov wants me. Make reservations for four, Colonel. Table near the war."

"I'm turning off the communications shield now."

"Fine by me. Have a good trip back. Stay in touch."

She walked out of the room, back stiff with disapproval. Or with military uprightness. Or with something—who the hell cared?

A moment later, Amanda and Sudie burst into the room. "Your company's gone! Can we make a fort?"

"Sure you can. Upend the furniture. Puncture the dome. But first come give your daddy two kisses. Oh, hell, you taste of crabbiness! You've been swimming in the underground Martian sea again!"

Sudie giggled. Amanda said with disgust, "You're being fizzy again, Daddy."

"Always."

"Why can't we have a normal daddy, like other kids?"

"You were born lucky. I knew it the minute I saw all those angels singing in the sky."

Kristen entered, looking vaguely worried. "Tom? What was it?"

"Nothing, sis. But we may have to cut our visit short a bit." Howls of protest from the girls. "Yes, we may. The university is sending us all on a nice paid vacation."

THREE

LUNA CITY, LUNA

Major Kaufman walked in his spacesuit from the shuttle to the clear piezoelectric plastic dome on Luna. These days he spent all his time under the hazy red-dust sky of Mars; he had almost forgotten how a sky looked without an atmosphere. Black, cold, pricked with diamond-bright and diamond-sharp stars. Beautiful.

He wasn't here to admire stars. He was here in his professional military capacity, to recruit a civilian. It was to be, *had* to be, recruitment through persuasion only. Dr. Thomas Capelo, Kaufman had heard, had not been persuaded so much as bullied. However, bullying was out of the question here, even if he'd been good at it, which he wasn't. But he was pretty good at persuasion, especially for a soldier. To recruit Marbet Grant, he'd have to be.

Lyle Kaufman had never wanted to be a soldier. This was not something that a major in the Solar Alliance Defense Army, attached to High Command of the Solar Alliance Defense Council, could admit to anyone. Kaufman never had.

His family was military, all of them, UAF Army. When the time came for seventeen-year-old Lyle to choose a college, no one had ever asked him if he wanted to go to West Point. It was assumed he was going, even if West Point wasn't what it had been, was in fact only the heavy-gravity training arm of the SADA Military Academy on Mars. Lyle Kaufman, intelligent and hard-working but with minimal genetic enhancements, could not aspire to the Martian Academy. Even acceptance at West Point was not assured, although only Lyle seemed to realize this. His parents, uncle, sisters, and brother never questioned his going, and Lyle never discussed it with them.

He knew, somewhere in the recesses of his orderly and conventional mind, that the reason he was going to West Point was that he had no particular desire to go anywhere else, study anything else, become anything else. He also knew that wasn't a good reason for becoming an Army officer. But he ignored the knowledge. He was seventeen, amiable and calm by temperament, and he had not been brought up to think very much or very deeply. Certainly not about choices in life. A good soldier did what was expected.

By the time Lyle Kaufman did get around to thinking about his choices, he was a captain. To his faint surprise, advancement came from doing what he was told to do as well as he could do it, without either opposition or self-interest. This held true in combat as well as out of it. At some level, that didn't seem right. Surely he should feel more involved with the decisions he made, decisions which affected other men's lives as well as his own? But he didn't. He proceeded with whatever task was at hand to the best of his ability. Other officers, he saw, seemed to respect this, although Lyle could not shake the feeling that he was on autopilot, not all that different from a very sophisticated computer. After his tour of combat duty, he was promoted to major.

The rest of his life seemed to possess the same mild, competent tone. He dated women, slept with them, grew fond of some, married none. He enjoyed reading physics journals, but not enough to study physics seriously, even if he had possessed the necessary aptitude for mathematics, which he knew he did not. His post on Mars, in the Solar Alliance Defense Council Military Advisory Committee, was interesting enough. He explored and recommended, with level-headed judiciousness, diplomatic options among the sometimes fractious member nations of the council and military options in the war against the Fallers. He played politics, of course—in his position it was inevitable—but not for partisanship, revenge, or self-aggrandizement. He expected to make colonel in due time.

The first time Lyle Kaufman had ever stepped outside the expected was to champion Dr. Dieter Gruber's passionate desire to return to the planet he called "World" to dig up the object he called "an alien probability machine."

Gruber himself didn't move Kaufman. In fact, he found the German geologist to be the sort of man Kaufman didn't much like: noisy, one-sided, bull-headed. Nor did Gruber's passion impress Kaufman. The military was full of passion, especially in wartime. No, what impressed Kaufman was Gruber's story. The fascinating physics of it. The possibilities for a new weapon. And the desire, which Kaufman hadn't even known he possessed, to forward, in some small behind-the-scenes way, a major scientific find. For Lyle Kaufman, science had always been a spectator sport, but the only sport that interested him, however moderately.

Now on Luna he was about to meet one of that sport's . . . no, not major players. Perhaps major outcomes. It was hard to tell.

She was waiting just inside the dome, beyond the airlock, alone. Kaufman removed his helmet. "Hello, Ms. Grant."

"Hello, Major Kaufman."

She matched the space under the dome. All the living and working quarters on Luna were below ground, safe from meteor bombardment. The dome served as elevator exit-point, observatory, visitor reception, and garden for Luna City's eight thousand inhabitants, who were mostly scientists, technicians, military, and their dependents. The number was low enough that the dome could be small and still contain separate areas: some shielded bunkers, a play-ground for kids, a sports field (for what?), and the "garden" where Marbet Grant greeted him.

Like it, she was pared-down and stylized. The garden consisted of raked smooth sand set with boulders, benches, and the occasional bed of genetically modified flowers developed from low-light fungi. Marbet Grant, short and slim, wore a white tunic and pants with no adornment except her own beautiful bone structure. Her cheekbones cut like knives above a wide, soft nose. Her skin was chocolate brown, her eyes emerald green, her short curly hair auburn. Never had Kaufman seen anyone so aggressively genemod. She was wholly artificial, as artificial as human habitation where there was neither water nor arable soil.

He said, "Thank you for agreeing to see me."

"Would you like to go below, or sit out here? You've never been to Luna City before."

How did she know that? It seemed as good a place to begin as any. "May I ask how you know that, Ms. Grant?"

She smiled, and he had his answer.

"Let's sit out here. You're right, I haven't ever been to Luna City. But I don't want a tour. I'd rather just tell you why I've come. Unless you already know that, too."

He said it with deliberate playfulness, but she didn't take the bait. Instead she led him to a bench made of laser-carved lunar rock. Kaufman's suit had adjusted for the heated air under the dome, but he still found the gravity, one-half of Mars's, unsettling. Marbet Grant obviously did not, lounging with her legs curled under her, a small graceful figure against the stone.

She began, "No, Major, I don't know what you're thinking. I'm not telepathic in the slightest degree. You're safe from mental eaves-dropping."

"From what I've read, that's only half true. The mental inevitably gets mirrored in the physical, except for good actors. I'm not that."

"No." She smiled again. He liked her honesty.

"So does my physical presence tell you that I want something from you?"

"Oh, yes."

"But not what?"

"That would be a lot to ask from body language."

They studied each other frankly. Kaufman knew that she was seeing more than he did — oh, so much more! — and tried not to mind. That was her gift. It was why she had been created.

Throughout history, there had always been people who were unusually sensitive to others, unusually adept at reading others' states of mind. Historians claimed it was a survival necessity of the underclasses: serfs, slaves, women, subject peoples. Life itself might depend on correctly reading the mood of the masters.

Evolutionary biologists pointed out that this fit well with Darwinian theory. Survival of the most accurately perceptive, those who could adapt to others because they perceived accurately what they must adapt to.

Social researchers documented the tiny, unconscious clues that signaled emotion and intent: minute facial changes, shifts in body distribution, voice intonations, rise in skin temperature. Crosscultural anthropologists traced the existence of people good at perceiving these clues, almost always without knowing how they did it, in all societies.

But it was the genetic engineers who tied this perceptiveness to specific genetic patterns, subtle but identifiable combinations of otherwise disparate genes. And it was a single group of geneticists who engineered for it, starting with the most available research subjects, their own children. The geneticists had believed themselves to be giving their children a survival advantage, not much different than the augmented muscles, boosted intelligence, or enhanced beauty common to the rich. It hadn't quite worked out like that. Instinctively understanding your neighbor might aid you, but it disconcerted the neighbor. Many, many people do not wish to be understood. They would rather that their feelings and intentions remained hidden.

When the "Sensitives" encountered notoriety, job discrimination, and the inevitable hate crimes, most of them reacted to the news frenzy by disappearing into anonymity. Marbet Grant, daughter of the brazenly publicity seeking Dr. Eric Grant, had merely moved to the moon.

She said, "Major, let's not fence. What do you want me to do?"

"I want you to go on a scientific expedition to the far end of the galaxy. A military science expedition. There's something there that we're interested in, and we're putting together an expedition to study it."

"But you don't need a Sensitive for that."

He noted that she used the word, an ordinary one turned pejorative through prejudice, without irony. "No. But there's a chance, not certain but definite, that the expedition may also capture the first live Faller ever. If so, we want you to be there to help interpret whatever it says or does."

He had succeeded in astonishing her. She said, "I thought that in twenty years of war, no one has captured a live Faller."

"No. Not even a Faller ship. At the mere possibility they blow up themselves, their crafts, their colonies, and their civilians. If they have civilians."

"And no one has communicated with the Fallers, either, have they?"

"No." Humanity didn't even know why it was at war. The Fallers didn't negotiate, warn, convey terms, or surrender. To humans, they had exhibited only two behaviors: killing and dying.

"Then how—"

"I can't tell you that. There's a plan, and it may or may not work. But if it does, and we get a live Faller, we want you to be there. To give us an edge in communicating with it."

"I'm sure you already know, Major, that communication signals are always species-specific, and usually culture-specific. What I do is interpret *human* behavior. Also, after direct observation of them and many trials and errors, the behavior of alien species. But those alien species have all been DNA-based, and remarkably similar to our own. The 'galaxy-seeding theory,' in fact. An enormous amount of behavior grows out of genetic imperatives. We know from charred corpses that the Fallers are not seeded from DNA like our own. And there is no reason to think I would be any better at reading Faller behavior than would any other random human. You, for instance."

Kaufman smiled. "Thank you. But we will provide direct observation for you to build on, plus trial-and-error. It should be, if nothing else, a fascinating experience for you. Can you pack and leave with me now?"

She laughed, a laugh full and deep for that slight frame. "You knew I would say yes. You're something of a Sensitive yourself, Major."

"No, Ms. Grant. I have no particular talents."

She studied him for a long minute. "You actually believe that."

Kaufman didn't answer. She might be a Sensitive, but he was better acquainted with the recesses of his own mind. All she could read was the outer packaging. Still, with the Fallers, perhaps that would be better than nothing.

Perhaps.

FOUR

ABOARD THE *ALAN B. SHEPARD*

Who's arrived on Mars so far?" General Gordon asked. He was again feeding and watering whatever lived in the mesh cage in his underground office. Lyle Kaufman wondered what animal actually lived under all those artificial plastic shavings. So far, the shavings hadn't as much as rustled.

"Dr. Capelo's arrived, with his children and their nurse. Marbet Grant. Dieter Gruber and his wife, Dr. Ann Sikorski, expedition xenobiologist. She too was a member of the previous expedition, and speaks the native language extremely well. Far better than her husband."

Gordon grinned, watering can in hand. "You don't like Gruber."

"That's irrelevant, sir," Kaufman said primly.

"Yes, it is. But since the planet's proscribed and we're unwelcome on it, there's not going to be a great deal for a non-military xenobiologist to do anyway." Kaufman caught the distinction. If the doubly secret part of this mission succeeded, the capture of a Faller, the military would provide its own xenobiologists.

Gordon continued, "The orders—grudgingly obtained, I might add—are minimal contact with natives who don't want us. You keep away from them, and you keep them away from the mission."

An uneasy feeling started in Kaufman's stomach. He ignored it. "Sir, I'm told that at least one native will need to be located and talked to. She had extensive contact with the previous anthropological team, especially Ann Sikorski. She—"

"I'm only telling you the official position, Lyle. You'll rule on exceptions as they come up."

"But I'm—"

"Who else has arrived?"

"Marbet Grant. Also another physicist whom Dr. Capelo requested, Dr. Rosalind Singh from Cambridge University, UAF. We're still waiting for the military physicist that High Command assigned to the project, Captain Harold Albemarle, and the spelunking tech. And the warship shuttle has docked. They've given us the *Alan B. Shepard*, under Commander Matthew Grafton."

"Good man."

"The ship is awaiting completion of weapons inspection. Commander Grafton has an appointment with you at fourteen hundred hours. After that, he can be underway whenever you want."

"You mean, underway whenever *you* want."

"Me?" Kaufman said. The uneasy feeling returned to his stomach, this time not ignorable.

"You. I've got you appointed as expedition leader."

Instantly Kaufman said, "I don't want it."

"I know you don't. And I don't blame you—it's a bunch of goddamn cowboys and misfits, and if Dr. Capelo comes up with nothing or fucks up that primitive native culture while digging around in it, your career is over. Sorry, Lyle. It's a rotten shame to do this to you. But you're the best man for the job."

"Sir, with all due respect, I don't see how you could have decided that. I'm not at all qualified. I'm not even command rank!"

"You are now. I put in for you for colonel this morning, battlefield processing. Lyle, you have three qualifications for this post.

First, you actually believe Dieter Gruber's story that there's something of value on World, which is more than anybody else on Mars does.

"Second, you understand more physics than anyone but an actual physicist, and from what I can see, they're all nuts.

"Third, and most important, you see all sides of issues. To some, that might make you look wishy-washy. I suspect that to yourself it makes you wishy-washy. But to me, it looks exactly like what that bunch of wild people are going to need out there. You'll keep the entire quixotic affair from going over the top in any way."

Kaufman said sourly, "I never knew a general before who could use the word 'quixotic.' Sir."

Gordon threw back his head and laughed. "You're probably right."

"What's in that cage, sir?"

"What do you think is in there. Colonel?"

"I think nothing is in there. I think you feed and water nothing just to keep your visitors wondering what you've captured, and so a little bit off-balance."

"Right again. See, Lyle, I knew you were the correct choice for this job. Now get yourself up to the *Alan B. Shepard* and plan your team quarters. Oh, and one thing more —"

"Yes, sir?" Kaufman said unhappily.

"Good luck."

The first night aboard ship, Kaufman arranged for a Special Project Team get-acquainted party. Commander Grafton made available the services of the ship's galley, the observation deck, and a spectacular view of Mars as the *Alan B. Shepard* pulled away from orbit. She would proceed at top speed toward Space Tunnel #1, that enigmatic object silently circling the Solar System out beyond Neptune.

The space tunnels had been discovered fifty-six years ago. A flexible, mappable network of wormholes, they made the galaxy into a giant instantaneous bus system. All you had to do was get your bus to the nearest tunnel, drive it through, and you emerged at another station at the edge of another star system. Double back through the same tunnel and you emerged at your place of origin—*if* nothing else had gone through that tunnel in the meantime. If something had, you emerged in the same place it did. The bus system kept rerouting its vehicles.

Some systems had three or even four tunnels in orbit around them, although Sol had only one. Evidently whatever long-vanished race had constructed the tunnels had not considered Sol an important nexus.

It was now. Exploring the space tunnels, humans had made two astonishing discoveries. One was that the other races in the galaxy and even most (not all) of the other vegetation in the galaxy shared basic DNA with humanity. Somewhere there had been a common "seeding" of an enormous number of planets—by whom? Unknown.

The second discovery was that humans were the most technologically advanced of all species—until the Fallers emerged from their own space tunnel to make swift and uncommunicative attacks.

The discovery of Space Tunnel #1 had rocked the struggling solar civilization. New disciplines sprang up: xenobiology, interstellar treasure hunting, holomovies shot under pink or yellow skies. Serious thinkers pointed out that humankind was scarcely ready to colonize the stars, having solved none of its problems at home. Nobody listened. The rich flourished on the new investments; the poor remained poor; Earth went on lurching from one ecological tragedy to another. Everything was the same, and nothing was.

The first years were filled with triumphs and disasters. Experimentation proved that a ship—or any other object—put through a space tunnel for the first time went to wherever the directly previous ship had gone. A ship that had gone through a tunnel and then went through it from the other side was automatically returned to its starting point, no matter how many other ships had used the tunnel in the meantime. Somehow—that most operative word in human understanding of tunnel technology—the tunnel "remembered" where each individual ship had entered tunnel space. It was an interstellar "Chutes and Ladders" composed of all chutes.

After fifty-six years, science still knew almost nothing about how space tunnels actually worked. The physical objects, panels floating in space in the general shape of a doughnut, were completely impenetrable. The science was too alien. The best guess was that the panels created a field of macro-level object entanglement, analogous to the quantum entanglement that permitted one particle to affect its paired counterpart regardless of distance, thus eliminating any spatial dimension to the universe by treating it as a single point. But this was merely a guess. Achieving entanglement for an object the size of a warship—let alone *controlling* the phenomenon—violated so many cherished principles that the feuding in physics journals resembled gang warfare. But the bottom line remained: The tunnels worked.

It would take the *Alan B. Shepard* several days to reach Space Tunnel #1 and less than twenty-four hours to go through the rest of the tunnels that would bring her to the "World" System. And, of course, the Special Project Team would be together for weeks after that. Kaufman hoped the first-night celebration would provide a pleasant, relaxed atmosphere for the all-important initial sizing up of each other.

The party was a disaster.

Dr. Rosalind Singh, Capelo's choice as back-up physicist, was the first to join Kaufman on the observation deck. She was a short, gray-haired woman in her sixties, robust enough to suggest health genemods but obviously possessing no appearance modifications. Based at Cambridge University, UAF, she had never before been out of the Solar System. She seemed to Kaufman very civilized. He liked her precise, musical British accent and her low-key manner. They chatted about the view, about music, about anticipated living conditions on World.

Capelo arrived next, a daughter on either hand. Kaufman hadn't realized he was bringing them to the party; he'd assumed they would stay in their quarters with their nurse. He didn't approve of Capelo's having dragged his daughters on a military mission, but he had of course not said so. Kaufman didn't much like children, another fact he kept to himself.

"Colonel, these are my daughters, Amanda and Sudie. Girls, say hello."

"Hello," said the older girl, a tall skinny child with long fair hair.

"I don't want to say hello," whined the younger. She looked unlike both her sister and her father. She shared Capelo's dark hair and sallow skin, but while he was thin, short, and nervous, the little girl was a round, pink-faced lump of dough.

"I'm pleased to meet you both," Kaufman said, insincerely. "May I present Dr. Singh?"

The older girl smiled and returned Dr. Singh's handshake; Kaufman thought she might be tolerable, for a child. The younger stuck out her lip and scowled.

"Hello, Tom," Dr. Singh said to Capelo. "It's good to see you. I'm glad we'll be working together again."

"I am, too, Roz," Capelo said, and seemed to mean it. Kaufman was pleased. Maybe Rosalind Singh would be a calming influence for the famously frenetic Capelo.

Marbet Grant walked up to them. She was the only one besides Lyle, who had put on his dress uniform, in evening clothes. Her gown was made of some wispy green material, the same color as her startling eyes, and it floated around her when she moved. Capelo's daughters reacted instantly.

"Oh, you're so pretty!" Sudie burst out. She stopped scowling and touched Marbet's gown.

"Sudie, don't do that," Capelo said.

"I don't mind," Marbet said gaily. "You must be Dr. Capelo. And this is Sudie and this is Amanda."

"How did you know?" Sudie said. "Daddy, I want a dress like this!"

Kaufman made all the introductions, but of course the others already knew of Marbet. The entire Solar System knew of her. Kaufman was particularly interested in this first meeting between Marbet and Capelo. He introduced Marbet as "project psychologist."

"I don't believe in psychology," Capelo said flatly.

Marbet remained unruffled. "Even that based on physiology?"

"If it's based on chemistry, with replicable results from controlled experiments, then of course I believe in it. That's science. Literary theories about the mind are not."

"Ah," Marbet said.

"Fairy tales, all. From Uncle Droselmeyer Freud to Lady Godiva Jennings, undressing some poor sap's mind 'consciousness layer' by 'consciousness layer.' All for a large amount of money, of course."

Amanda said to Marbet, "You shouldn't mind Daddy, ma'am. He's always horrible to people he likes."

"Unmasked by my own child. Amanda, you know that's a fib. I'm horrible to everybody, whether I like them or not. Roz will confirm that."

Marbet said to Amanda, "Is he horrible to you?"

"*Awful*," Amanda said, grinning. "He just torments my life out."

"Yeah," said Sudie, the five-year-old, holding Capelo's other hand.

"Unmasked by both my daughters," Capelo said. "Okay, into the airlock with both of you. I was never meant to be a father."

The girls ignored him. Amanda said to Marbet, "You're famous. I saw you on the Net."

"Have a little dignity, girls," Capelo said. "Don't crumble in the face of notoriety. Remember that you come from a long line of proudly independent nonentities."

Marbet laughed. She hadn't stopped studying Capelo, and suddenly Kaufman wondered what she saw. He saw a man feeling uncomfortable under scrutiny and covering his discomfort with mockery and sarcasm. On the other hand, since mockery and sarcasm were the physicist's constant mode, perhaps they couldn't really be called a response to Marbet's attention.

The remaining three guests appeared, along with the steward's mates serving dinner. Kaufman moved everyone to the table, set with white damask and wardroom plate service. There were oohs and aaahhs.

Dr. Ann Sikorski, the xenobiologist, sat between Marbet and Kaufman. Her husband, Dr. Dieter Gruber, the cause of this entire expedition, sat opposite, beside the Capelo children. Gruber was a big blunt man to whom somebody had given the genome of a magnificent Teutonic warrior. Blond, blue-eyed, theatrically muscled. Sudie Capelo took one look at Gruber and burst into tears.

"I don't want to sit next to that Malor!" she cried.

"She's been cranky all afternoon," Capelo apologized. "Come here, Sudie, sit on my lap."

"Nnnnooooooooo!" the child wailed.

Gruber looked bewildered. "What did I do? And what is this 'Malor'?"

Tom Capelo's lips twitched. "The evil warlords on her favorite Net program. Too bad we can't all be physically appealing, Dieter."

Sudie clung to her father's arm, sobbing as if her world had been shattered. Snot ran from her nose. Gruber, looking repelled and determined, leaned toward the little girl and said with forced heartiness, "Don't cry, Liebchen! See, I don't bite, not pretty little girls."

Sudie screamed harder. Capelo said to Amanda, "Call Jane to come get Sudie. She's just tired; she'll be fine once she calms down."

"I always thought," Hal Albemarle said, "that the Victorians were on the right track. Seen but not heard. Especially not on a Navy warship, which is no place for children anyway."

Capelo's face turned ugly. Before he could answer, Marbet Grant said swiftly, "Hal, you don't know what you're talking about. Just because you had an unhappy childhood is no reason to pick on poor Sudie, who's just having a normal overtired mood."

Everyone stared at Marbet, who went on calmly buttering a piece of bread. Hal said, "How the hell do you know if I had an unhappy childhood? Oh, I get it . . . you're trading on your famous sensitivity to impress Capelo. Well, it just so happens you're wrong."

"No, I'm not," Marbet said. "Please don't try to lie to me."

Albemarle rose. "Excuse me, please, Colonel Kaufman. I have some unfinished work in my quarters." He stalked off the deck.

"Oh, I shouldn't have said that," Marbet said. "How about I go tell him I'm sorry? Lyle?"

"Give him time to calm down first," Kaufman said, wondering what he had just witnessed. She was too socially adept for him to take the scene at face value.

Tom Capelo didn't, either. "Very nice, Marbet. Deflect Albemarle's attention to yourself and provoke him to leave before he and I can come to serious blows. Do you always interfere in other people's confrontations? Are you that most dangerous of all people, a peace-at-any-price meddler?"

"No," Marbet answered, nibbling at her bread.

Capelo gazed at her a moment longer, then laughed. "Don't try to stage-manage *me*, Lady Meddler."

"Daddy," Amanda said, "don't be mean to Ms. Grant. I like her."

Capelo turned to his older daughter. Amanda looked steadily back, her small face determined. "A quisling in my camp," Capelo said. "Defeated again by the solidarity of women, damn it. All right, honey, I won't be mean. Ms. Grant, I'm sorry you meddled with me and Albemarle."

"I'm not," Marbet said, so serenely that Capelo's eyes widened and he gave another short bark of laughter.

"No, I'll bet you're not. Kaufman, I don't envy you managing this team."

"I didn't want the job," Kaufman said truthfully, and everyone laughed again. The tension eased. Rosalind Singh left and quietly brought back Hal Albemarle, who nodded stiffly first to Kaufman, then to Capelo. For the rest of the meal, he had the air of a man deliberately trying to be pleasant, but Kaufman doubted he was enjoying himself very much. He wasn't sure anyone else was, either, except possibly Amanda, who seemed fascinated by Marbet Grant. Still, everyone talked animatedly, first names were introduced, and anyone looking on would have thought these were, if not old friends, at least cheerful acquaintances.

Afterwards, as small groups stood around admiring the receding planet, forming and reforming small groups, Kaufman steered Marbet out of earshot.

"Quite a maneuver you brought off at dinner. *Did* Albemarle have an unhappy childhood?"

"No more than anybody else. But he thinks he did."

Kaufman considered that. "He's going to be a difficult team member, isn't he?"

"I think that under ordinary circumstances, Hal would work to fit himself in. But these aren't ordinary circumstances. He's not very sure of himself, and it can't be easy to be a third-rate scientist working with a more-than-first-rate one who doesn't bother to hide his opinion of other people's talents. Why did you include him on the expedition, Lyle?"

"I wasn't given a choice. He's Navy, you know. I'm Army. The Solar Alliance balances out the services as carefully as a cook making a soufflé. You think that in wartime we'd let all that go, but we never do. And I'm told that as a scientist, Albemarle is more than competent."

"But not a Thomas Capelo."

"No, not that. Not to be expected," Kaufman said. "Are you going to apologize to Albemarle?"

"Oh, yes. Fulsomely. He's feeling very upset about his own reaction, which surprised even him. I don't want him to blame me for his losing control like that."

"Is he going to blame Tom Capelo?"

"Yes, but he was prepared to dislike Tom anyway, even before dinner."

"And what do you think of Tom?" Kaufman had been contemplating the question throughout dinner.

She answered indirectly, watching Rosalind Singh talk with Capelo and Amanda. Rosalind said something that made Capelo laugh, momentarily lighting up his dark, thin face. "I'm glad Dr. Singh is on the team. She doesn't feel competitive with Tom, and she's compassionate about his bitterness."

"Do you see him as bitter, then?"

"I think he is the bitterest man I have ever met."

Kaufman was silent a moment. "His wife died two years ago. Killed in a Faller raid."

Marbet said, "He must have loved her unto distraction."

An odd choice of words, Kaufman thought. "Dieter seems to get along with Tom."

"Yes. Dieter is insensitive to mockery, sarcasm, nuances, and insight. Tom may find that restful. At any rate, Tom will never upset Dieter. Only Dieter's wife can do that. I like Ann, incidentally. Such a gentle person."

"Yes," Kaufman said. They went on discussing the team members. Her eyes, however, never left Capelo, now clowning with Amanda and Dieter Gruber at the far end of the deck, and Kaufman couldn't read her expression at all.

•   •   •

The next day, Capelo ambushed Kaufman before breakfast, in the corridor outside Kaufman's quarters. "Lyle, I need a favor."

"Good morning, Tom. I hope you're comfortable in your quarters."

"That's the favor."

"You don't like your quarters?" Kaufman said pleasantly. Capelo should like them. He'd been given the VIP stateroom for the children and their nurse, a room big enough to function as bedroom, schoolroom, playroom, and whatever else children needed. Kaufman didn't want them roaming around the ship, irritating Commander Grafton, who hadn't wanted children aboard any more than Kaufman did. Capelo had a small room next door.

"The quarters are fine. But Sudie doesn't like not being able to get to me without going out into the corridor and through my door. She doesn't even know if I'm there until she does that, which scares her. She's a bit nervous, and she's entitled."

It was the closest Kaufman had heard him come to mentioning his wife's death. Kaufman said, "I'm not sure what you're asking. Do you want another bunk put in the stateroom?"

"No. I work at night, and anyway Amanda's going through a super-modest phase. No, I want you to have a little door cut in the wall between the girls' room and mine."

Kaufman stared at him. Evidently Capelo didn't realize that Army officers didn't just go around cutting holes in Navy ships. "Tom, I don't think that's possible."

"Just a small door, big enough for me to crawl through. Under my bunk, and we'll push furniture in front of it on the other side. Sudie just wants the reassurance that she can get to me anytime she needs to, and she likes the idea of a tiny secret door."

What Sudie liked wasn't the point, Kaufman thought. Grafton wouldn't like it at all. Kaufman had told Marbet the truth: Balancing Army and Navy was a delicate act. Kaufman was Special Project Team head, with considerable powers to direct where the *Alan B.*

Shepard went, when she went, and what she did when she got there. But she was still Grafton's ship.

"Tom—"

"Please, Lyle. I really need this."

Kaufman studied him. Army/Navy wasn't the only balancing act here. Capelo was as difficult as everybody had warned, judging from his effect on Albemarle, and even on Marbet, last night. Granting this favor might go far in making him willing to work with Kaufman. Capelo stood now with a most uncharacteristic look on his face: humble waiting. That was too much credit in the bank to throw away.

Kaufman calculated rapidly. Grafton would never agree. But Kaufman hadn't been in diplomacy as long as he had without learning how to make detours around immovable objects. "All right, Tom, I'll see what I can do. But neither you nor your daughters can say anything, not to anybody."

"Wonderful! I'm really grateful, Lyle."

Which was the point.

Kaufman found the correct form on ship's computer: Work Form for Alterations to Bulkhead, Non-Operational and Non-Secure Areas. He filled it in, printed a flimsy, and summoned Carpenter's Mate First Class Michael Doolin, whose name was on ship's roster.

"Doolin, here's a work form. Carry out the assignment and return the flimsy to me. I'll enter it in the records myself."

"Aye, aye, sir. Only, sir . . . this form ain't signed."

"Yes, it is. See, there—'Colonel Lyle Kaufman, SADA.' "

"Supposed to be a Navy officer's signature, sir. Captain or exec or OOD."

"Doolin," Kaufman said, with all the quiet authority he'd learned to project in twenty years, underlaid with the subtle menace he'd also learned, "do you understand my position on this ship?"

"Yes, sir," Doolin said unhappily.

"Do I outrank the OOD?"

"Yes, sir."

"And the exec?"

"Yes, sir."

"Then can you explain the nature of your problem with this direct order?"

"No, sir. Do it right away, sir." Doolin took the flimsy and set off, his gait expressive of everything he wasn't saying.

Kaufman deleted the completed work form from the computer. When Doolin returned the flimsy, Kaufman would destroy it. Of course, scuttlebutt would go around about the "tiny, secret door." But Kaufman doubted it would reach any officer. It was too trivial, and Grafton ran too much of a by-the-book ship. Crewmen and officers didn't fraternize. Also, the crew on this particular expedition had been carefully selected for trouble-free service records and consistently reliable performance of duties. No one aboard, not the lowest crewman third class, had ever had so much as an official reprimand logged anywhere in the SADN records. Kaufman was pretty sure nothing would come of the hole in the stateroom wall, which he would have Doolin restore when the ship returned to Mars.

All the same, Capelo had, after less than twenty-four hours aboard, already caused Kaufman to move outside the rules. Kaufman wondered how many more times the physicist would do so, and how far he, Kaufman, was actually prepared to go on behalf of Thomas Capelo.

FIVE

ABOARD THE *ALAN B. SHEPARD*

There it is," Capelo said, "the most fried object in a thousand star systems. We who are already dead salute you."

"There wasn't any life on it anyway," Hal Albemarle said.

"Do we know that? Do you know that? Are you holding out on us, Hal? Give, give, share the wisdom of the ages."

Albemarle glared. Kaufman, gathered with the rest of his team on the observation deck of the *Alan B. Shepard,* suppressed an impatient twinge. The relationship between Capelo and Albemarle had not improved since their first encounter, and neither one bothered to hide his dislike. Fortunately, Albemarle and Commander Grafton seemed to be the only ones that challenged Capelo's sharp mockery. Rosalind Singh indulged it; Ann Sikorski tolerated it; Dieter Gruber was oblivious of it.

Gruber was the only one missing from the preliminary survey of Nimitri, sixth planet from the star in the World System. The geologist had taken ill the day after boarding. Ship's doctor determined that Gruber had contracted a virus, one of the nasty mutated strains appearing so frequently on Earth; that the virus was laterally transmitted; and that nobody on the *Alan B. Shepard* possessed immunity. Immediately she slapped Gruber into quarantine, where he remained, querulous at being able to participate only virtually in the project team's discussions.

The ship had journeyed at top speed from Mars to Space Tunnel #1, and then through several more clustered tunnels to reach this remote system at the far edge of the galaxy. After emerging from the system's only tunnel, #438, the *Alan B. Shepard* took another three days to reach orbit around Nimitri, a bleak, frozen, atmosphereless globe that was the closest planet to Space Tunnel #438. Long before their arrival in the star system, Commander Grafton had turned over the observation deck to the project team, who had set up their data-ports there. Now Capelo, Albemarle, and Rosalind Singh studied the displays, which coordinated data from the ship's normal sensors from those added to her for this expedition, and from the two probes sent down to the surface.

Rosalind said, "Radioactivity is twenty-nine times what would be predicted. Spectography results . . . high concentrations of iridium, platinum, thorium, moderately high amounts of uranium . . . Hal, run an Auberjois test on that data, please."

Capelo said, "Looks like Syree Johnson called it."

"I told you so!" crowed the voice of Gruber, following the proceedings from quarantine.

Dr. Singh said, "Hal?"

Albemarle said, "The numbers correlate. A huge leap in the rate of decay occurred two-point-one E-years ago, and no rate change since."

Marbet said, "For us non-physicists, what does that mean?"

"It means," Rosalind Singh said in her precise voice, "that what Dr. Johnson said in her preliminary report fits the facts as they exist now. It's at least possible that her 'wave effect' hit Nimitri and caused its massive radioactivity by destabilizing the nucleus of every element above atomic number seventy-five. In other words, the probability that each nucleus would emit a radioactive particle increased enormously. Of course, that doesn't provide the cause of the phenomenon."

Gruber's voice said, "The moon they towed to the tunnel was the cause!" at the same moment that Capelo said, "That's why I love you, Roz. You keep us honest. No prematurely ejaculated conclusions for you, no matter what Gruber says *in absentia*. But I'll bet my nonexistent soul that our sneezing geologist is right. Ol' Syree's wave effect was real, and it hit Nimitri, and it rolled on outward to hit World. Had to."

"Ja!" Gruber said.

Kaufman said, "Much weakened? Did it obey the inverse-square law?"

Albemarle said, "No way to tell until we take measurements on the rest of the system and compare them with the initial data from the *Zeus*."

Kaufman nodded. He was surprised at how interested he was in the answer.

Marbet said to him quietly, "Fascinating stuff, isn't it?"

"To me, yes. To you?"

"Not the science," she admitted. "But the team interactions certainly are."

Again he wondered what she saw. He'd avoided asking her; her mission here wasn't with the humans.

"Lyle," she said, as the others became involved in some debate about mathematics, not one word of which was intelligible to Kaufman, "we're now in the World System. Don't you think it's time you told me about this Faller I'm supposed to be presented with?"

"Not yet," Kaufman said, "because so far there's nothing to tell. The moment there is, I'll put you in the data chain, Marbet. I promise."

"All right." She went back to watching the mathematical debate.

Kaufman didn't know whether to feel piqued or pleased. She seemed to have no interest in him apart from her mission here. Or was it just that she trusted him to communicate anything important without her having to press?

He studied the curve of her brown throat, pure and strong. In profile like this, the startlingly high, sharp cheekbone made a clean plane below one emerald eye. Soft auburn curls clustered over her small ear. On the lobe was a jade earring. She looked as precise as if she were carved, and yet the flesh on that perfect genemod throat moved in and out with the breath of warm life.

Lyle Kaufman suddenly hoped she hadn't caught him staring.

Albemarle finally said huffily, "Well, naturally, if you think that, there's no point in arguing."

"That's true," Capelo said, "because whatever I think must be right. I came eighty thousand light years for no other purpose than to be right when you're wrong. I live for the pleasure of flattening stupid mathematical theories, and you're supplying me with food and drink. Isn't that right, Roz?"

"You are correct on this one mathematical point," Dr. Singh said, "but no, you are not always right. Now leave Hal alone, Tom, so he can do the analysis I've requested of him."

"You sound just like my daughter," Capelo said, "ordering me around. I'm surrounded by bossy women. Lyle, remind them who's in charge here."

"I am," Kaufman said mildly, and was rewarded by Marbet's turning to him with her amused, full-lipped smile.

"Dinner, sir," announced a serving cart, entering with a full, fragrant tray. And that was another problem. Except for sleep, the team now pretty much lived on the observation deck, working and talking and eating there. They had all been invited to take their meals in the wardroom, but this had not worked out very well. The officers of the *Alan B. Shepard* were the usual mixed lot off-duty, ranging from the sophisticated, music-loving executive officer to the communications officer, who had the foulest sense of humor Kaufman, during a long Army career, had ever encountered. Despite the differences among them, they were all Navy officers, military men and women first. They found Tom Capelo just too weird, and the presence of his little girls too inhibiting. Marbet Grant clearly unnerved them. Everyone knew who she was. Kaufman saw the officers gazing at her sideways when they thought she wouldn't notice, and he knew they were wondering what she noticed about them that they would rather keep hidden. Most of them didn't meet her eyes.

So a few days out from Earth, the project team had begun having its meals brought to the observation deck. Hal Albemarle dined in the wardroom occasionally, when he couldn't stand Capelo any more. But Albemarle was always drawn back, afraid of missing something important. Kaufman felt the same way, but he scrupulously divided his meals between the wardroom and his fractious team.

Two days later they went into orbit around the star system's next planet, another lifeless rock. At the same time, Dieter Gruber was released from quarantine. Kaufman was glad to see him. Gruber's enthusiasm for the project and his obliviousness of social tension were equally welcome.

The fifth planet from the system's star also proved to be highly radioactive. In fact, it was just exactly as radioactive as Nimitri.

"Run the data again," Capelo said flatly.

"I already ran it twice!" Albemarle retorted.

"Then run it three times."

Albemarle did. It came up the same. *#5 NOT NEC, FARTHER FROM WAVE SOURCE –*

Rosalind Singh said thoughtfully, "So the wave effect did not obey the inverse-square law. Interesting."

"More than that!" Dieter Gruber said. The big man was so excited he could not stay still. He prowled the observation deck like a huge golden cat, stopping every few minutes to stare at the dead planet rotating beyond the viewport. Gray and airless, it looked much like a smaller Nimitri.

Kaufman wanted to be sure he understood. Only the five of them were on deck. Capelo, Singh, Gruber, and Albemarle were scientists. He was not. He said, "Does that mean that when the artifact that the *Zeus* was towing exploded, or was shot down, it gave out a different kind of wave than Syree Johnson reported finding when she examined the thing in orbit?"

Rosalind Singh said patiently, "Yes, Lyle. Or, rather, not different in effect, because the data showed that all three times, the wave destabilized atoms with an atomic number above seventy-five. It happened in orbit, it happened at Nimitri, it happened here. But when Dr. Johnson deliberately activated the artifact in orbit, she did so at the lowest setting. It was marked in primes with the addition of the integer 'one,' you know, the way the space-tunnels are. On that occasion, the wave obeyed the inverse-square law. The data from her, the shuttle, and various orbital sensors are quite definite about that.

"But when that same artifact 'blew,' it apparently set off a much stronger wave, perhaps at the strongest setting, and that wave does *not* seem to have obeyed the inverse-square law. It affected this planet just as strongly as it affected Nimitri, although they are fifty-six million kilometers apart."

Kaufman said, "So . . . does that mean it would have hit World just as strongly?"

"Yes!" crowed Gruber. "And yet World did not go radioactive! That was because of the buried artifact! It was at the exact moment of explosion that the artifact reacted! The exact moment, with no delay for light-speed! Because they are entangled!"

"You cannot know that yet, Dieter," Rosalind Singh said mildly.

"No? What other theories do you have, Dr. Singh?"

"I won't have any theories until I can include the fall-off as well."

Kaufman said, "And fall-off is . . ."

"It describes how an effect weakens until it's undetectable. It must fade away with distance eventually, or it would affect the entire universe. We launched probes in the opposite direction from the planets, you remember, and they show a very abrupt fall-off of radiation at about six billion kilometers from the star. That's a very strange decay. We have no equations that can account for it."

"We will get them," said Dieter, the optimist. His blue eyes sparkled.

Kaufman turned to study Capelo, who appeared oblivious of the entire conversation. He paced, thinking, his dark thin face taut with concentration. Seeing Capelo like that, Kaufman realized how different the man looked when he was thinking deeply. For the moment, all bitterness and mockery had vanished from his face. It left Capelo looking both younger and, curiously, more mature, capable of intense mental exploration from which he would not be distracted. There was something impressive in his constantly moving figure. Even Albemarle did not interrupt.

Gruber said, softly for him, to Kaufman, "You will see when we dig up the buried artifact, Colonel. It, too, alters probability. Like the exploded artifact altered the probability of any given atom going radioactive at any given time. The brain, too, is a probability field, and the buried one affects brains. I know, I felt it. You will see."

Kaufman had studied carefully this part of Gruber's report. It was the part that had made High Command dismiss Gruber as a crackpot. The buried artifact, according to the geologist, affected the release of neurotransmitters in the brain, and, by existing on the planet for eons, had affected the mental evolution of the natives. More alarmingly, it had affected the brains of the human research team when they entered caves too close to the buried object.

With such a claim, it had been all too easy to ridicule Gruber's entire story. Yes, his brain *had* been affected. He'd been gassed by some hallucinogen, said one military doctor after another, or brainwashed by natives, or sent over the edge by some psychotropic he'd eaten.

Kaufman had spent days poring over data cubes about the brain, trying to evaluate Gruber's claim. Yes, there was a probability component to the release of neurotransmitters in the brain. For reasons no one understood, transmitters were not released each and every time an electrical impulse traveled along a brain nerve. The release rate varied from 17 percent to 62 percent, depending on the kind of nerve — *even though the electrical impulse in each case was the exact same voltage*. A single atom triggered or did not trigger the release of packets of transmitters. Whenever single atoms were involved, of course, you got quantum effects . . . and that brought in probability.

Looked at that way, Gruber's theory made sense.

But no one had ever defined, measured, or created a "probability field." It was a blue-sky concept. And even assuming such a thing existed, the idea of one that could be controlled violated practically every known idea of physics. At least, the level of physics that Kaufman could understand. On the other hand, so did the space tunnels, and they clearly existed. On the third hand, so did Tom Capelo's ideas on probability, which some considered as crazy as Gruber's. Capelo, however, was a figure not easily dismissed.

As Kaufman understood contemporary physics, subatomic particles, however they were referred to, were not actually particles but tiny vibrating threads. That had been conclusively proven by the great Elisar Yeovil in 2041, building on work stretching back almost a century. All "particle" properties — charge, spin, mass — arose from differences in vibrational patterns of the fundamental threads. Spacetime was a rich fabric of threads twisting and vibrating throughout its four familiar dimensions and the six less familiar, tiny, curled-up dimensions that adjoined length, breadth, and height at every point in the universe.

With the discovery of the graviton in 2052, gravity had finally been fully integrated into human understanding of the forces controlling spacetime. Gravitational fields were encoded into the warpings of the spacetime fabric, as an enormous—but not infinite—number of threads all vibrated in the same "graviton pattern." The graviton—massless, spin-2, a perfect fit into the equations of both relativity and quantum mechanics—joined the gluon, the photon, and the gauge bosons as a "messenger particle," a transmitter of a basic force.

What made Tom Capelo look like a lunatic to so many of his fellows was his desire to account for probability amplitudes the same way: through an as-yet-undiscovered messenger "particle," a new vibrational pattern, which Capelo dubbed the "probon." Not only was the probon undiscovered experimentally, Capelo could not account for it mathematically except in the most obscure and roundabout way. Nor did he have any sort of coherent model. Capelo's argument for the existence of the probon depended on equations too difficult for Kaufman to follow, equations ancillary to the existence of the six curled-up spatial dimensions conclusively proven to exist by the great Yeovil. The dimensions were usually called Calabi-Yau spaces, named for a particular class of geometric shapes. These tiny dimensions existed at every single point in spacetime. What Capelo had done so far was use the Sung-Rendell transformation equations to—

"Colonel." Commander Grafton stood by his side; Kaufman hadn't even heard him approach. Kaufman couldn't help smiling inwardly. Did that mean that he himself was capable of the same deep, unconscious-of-surroundings thought as Tom Capelo? Hardly to the same brilliant degree. He looked up at Grafton and saw what he should have noticed instantly.

The Navy commander was taut with excitement. Being a Navy commander, his excitement had none of Gruber's bluster or Capelo's inward focus. Grafton stood straight as always, contained and military. But the line of his jaw, the look in his eyes, told Kaufman what must have happened.

My God. They did it.

But all Grafton said was, "Will you come with me, Colonel? There's a message for you from the flyer."

"Yes, of course." Kaufman rose and let himself be led from the observation deck. Capelo still paced, oblivious to everything but whatever rolled through his head. The other three speculated softly among themselves.

In the corridor, Kaufman couldn't wait. He said to Grafton, "They've captured a Faller, haven't they? It worked. They've got one alive."

"Yes," Grafton said, "alive," and something in his tone made Kaufman remember reading Grafton's personnel file as part of the preparation for this expedition. Grafton had had a brother killed in the battle with the Fallers in Quatorze system.

He followed Grafton to the shielded communication room, where the encoded message from the flyer stationed at the space tunnel would have been received. The flyer itself would take days to catch up to its lightspeed message. But another ship must be enroute to World, carrying the first enemy alien ever captured in this long and inexplicable and unwelcome war.

And then . . .

"Send for Ms. Grant, please."

"She's already on her way," Grafton said. "There are datacubes for her to look at in the comm room."

"Good," Kaufman said, and hoped it was. His breath came faster.

Maybe humanity had a fighting chance after all.

SIX

FALLER SPACE, UNNAMED STAR SYSTEM

Nothing about the plan had been simple. Thus, everyone was astonished when it actually worked. Some, in addition, felt a little ashamed, since the plan depended on the death of a child.

The project team had arranged everything else ahead of time. All sat in readiness until the right child could be found. Two children were found suitable, but their parents refused. More than refused—they recoiled in horror when the plan was explained to them. One of the fathers struck Project Leader Colonel Ethan McChesney in the face, a blow of pure grief and rage. McChesney understood.

Then, two and a half weeks after the *Alan B. Shepard* had flown into Space Tunnel #1 and left the solar system, Katrina Van Rynn fell off her brother's power scooter in the colony of De Kooy, on New Holland. Katrina should not have been on the scooter. Her brother Michael, thirteen, had been warned that Katrina, four, was too young to ride behind him. She might get scared, and he wasn't yet experienced enough with the scooter. He took her for a ride anyway, because she begged and because he loved showing it off, even to a little sister. He belted her in securely and they set off over the low purple hills where Dutch settlers were recreating a mode of religious life that had all but vanished on Earth.

Michael flew the scooter too high, and Katrina did get scared. She panicked, unlocked herself (Michael had not realized she knew how to do this), and climbed off. The scooter was thirty feet above the ground. The little girl died three hours later in the De Kooy medcenter.

McChesney was already there. His intelligence network was among the best in the galaxy. Despite their terrible grief, the Van Rynns agreed to McChesney's plan. They were patriots. They also hoped that the use McChesney would make of Katrina's body might help Michael. The boy was wild with guilt. The family needed to salvage something, anything, out of what had happened to them all.

Katrina's body was flown by flyer to Space Tunnel #86, one of several that orbited the New Holland system, at the maximum speed the flyer and the corpse could sustain. Katrina wasn't frozen. It was important that nothing be done to the body that would change its composition in any way.

Seven tunnels later, the flyer reached Mowbray Base, a brand new military space station beside Tunnel #472. Orbiting beside both of them was another tunnel, #473, that gave onto an obscure Faller colony. Mapping tunnels was an intricate task. A ship that flew through a space tunnel and then eventually went back through the same tunnel would be returned to its place of origin—*if* nothing else had gone through the tunnel in the meantime. If something had, the first ship emerged in the same place the second one had. Much-used tunnels were thus fluid, requiring complex central routing in order to keep them focused on a given system.

Tunnels #470 through #473, however, were not much used. Newly discovered and remote, they had been explored by only one human flyer. It had passed through #473, discovered the small Faller colony on the system's single planet, and immediately popped back through the tunnel. The colony had not been military. It was possible the Fallers did not yet know that the star system had been discovered or visited by humans. McChesney gambled on that.

Katrina's body was strapped into a small two-person personal flyer, of the kind that rich people and commercial explorers used. In the pilot seat was strapped the body of a young soldier who had died that same day of a brain virus, one of the virulent strains that demolished entire cerebral centers in hours. The flyer was loaded with provisions, including toys and holos suitable for a four-year-old girl. Except for the usual civilian light arms, the craft was defenseless.

The computer, preset, flew it through Space Tunnel #473, shut down all engines, and let the flyer drift in space.

McChesney and his team waited on the other side of the tunnel. They were effectively blind. No probe could go with the flyer, no signal could be sent back; the Solar Alliance had ample evidence that the Fallers were well able to detect anything electromagnetic. Their detection technology seemed to be equal to humans'. So did their weaponry. And their defenses, since they'd acquired the mysterious beam-disrupter shields, were infinitely superior. A proton beam fired at a Faller skeeter, the equivalent of a human flyer, simply disappeared. No scientists had been able to discover where the beam went, or why the conservation of matter/energy had not been violated. McChesney didn't concern himself with the physics problems, which he knew he wouldn't understand.

He didn't understand nanotechnology, either, but the science advisors told him that might be the one area in which humans were ahead of Fallers. No one knew for sure. No Faller had ever been captured alive, and no skeeter had ever been taken as anything other than a melted hulk unsuitable for reverse engineering. However, neither the charred dead Faller bodies nor the charred dead Faller craft had shown, as far as the science advisors could guess, any signs of nanotech.

"How long?" McChesney said, on the human side of Space Tunnel #473, although of course he knew the answer.

"Forty-seven E-hours," said his aide.

"Fuck it. We're going in."

The aide stared at him. "Supposed to be two more hours, sir."

"Now." And then, by way of feeble explanation, "It feels right. Now!"

"Yes, sir," the aide said, her voice expressive of reservation, and they had gone in.

And hit the goddamned jackpot. Caught the Fallies un-fucking-believably in the act. Actually aboard the human flyer.

Wait forty-nine hours, the intelligence guys had said. We know that Fallers often wait twenty E-hours from the point of detection to the point of action. Their home planet has a twenty-hour day; maybe there's a hard-wired circadian rhythm that affects social decision making. Maybe not. At any rate, it's definitely nine hours up to the tunnel from the surface of their colony planet, given the planet's position when you send the flyer through, and given the speed of their civilian skeeters. We're assuming they have no military craft in the colony. No telling how long it will take them to notice the drifting flyer. They might even detect our flyer the second you send it through the tunnel, if they have a probe in orbit around the space tunnel.

"Then why didn't the probe detect our original flyer?" Mc-Chesney asked.

"Maybe it did. Or maybe there's no probe because this is such a small colony and not military. We're flying blind here, Colonel. Just go in at forty-nine hours and see what you catch. Twenty hours from the time they detect the flyer to decision to go up. Nine hours up. Another twenty hours to contemplate the flyer and probe it with sensors. Then you go in."

But McChesney had gone in two hours early, and caught the bastards in the act.

The colony skeeter had matched trajectory with the drifting human flyer, five clicks away, when McChesney's first military flyer erupted from the space tunnel. The skeeter was better armed than humans had expected. It opened fire immediately on the flyer and destroyed it. But McChesney had four other flyers and a warship. He blasted the skeeter before it could annihilate anything else. The skeeter, unequipped with the new Faller shields that could render a particle beam useless, exploded.

The warship carried the most advanced sensors humans could devise. They picked up the two heat signatures inside the drifting flyer, where only two unheated dead bodies should have been. The sensors also registered that the heat signatures were not moving.

McChesney moved faster than safety regulations permitted. In seven minutes he had suited Marines aboard the flyer. The Marines were unnecessary. For once, the science brains had actually understood a military situation.

The Fallers had undoubtedly subjected the drifting human flyer to every sensing device they could before they boarded her. Their sensors told them there were two dead humans aboard, one a child. Maybe the Fallers had been able to tell that the man was damaged in the brain, a father who had abruptly died while taking his child somewhere. Maybe not. Maybe they had been able to tell that Katrina Van Rynn's body included broken and reset bones. Maybe not. But they had never, to human knowledge, had the chance to examine a human child. Their blitzkrieg approach to attack had not included taking prisoners. They had taken possession of dead adult soldiers before now — but never a child. An alien species would want to know how their enemy developed — wouldn't they? And they would reason that this probably wasn't a military craft, not with a child aboard. Surely the Fallers had learned by now that humans did not take their offspring to battle. Katrina Van Rynn in her helpless, utterly threatless flyer, had been good bait.

A single Faller had boarded, accompanied by a robot probe capable of detecting any trap known to Faller technology. It couldn't, however, detect the unknown. If the boarding Faller had stopped breathing, it would probably have blown up the Faller, the ship, and itself. It would probably have done the same if its master had told it to, or if the Faller's suit had signified any breach, or if any machinery aboard the flyer had suddenly activated.

None of those things happened. The tiny nanos that the robot probe didn't know how to detect clung to the bottom of the Faller's suit as soon as he crossed the threshold. The nanos never punctured the suit. Instead they moved through it, one molecular layer at a time, mindlessly destroying a molecule and then immediately rebuilding it behind them out of the same atoms, as they had been programmed to do. Neither robot nor Faller detected a breach because there never was one. When the nanos reached material giving out the heat signature of living flesh, their program changed.

The nanos entered the Faller body and began to paralyze it slowly. Human biologists had learned enough from the few badly charred Faller bodies they'd salvaged to analyze the genome. It wasn't DNA-based. Thus, almost anything biological added to it could be fatal. But nanos weren't biologics; they were tiny machines. Their programming determined easily what gas the Faller breathed inside his sealed suit: the species' medium for energy transport. Then they began to absorb the supply of it, replicating rapidly at the same time. The Faller, never realizing it, slid easily into the equivalent of oxygen-deprivation (it wasn't oxygen) and fainted. Or perhaps fell asleep, or whatever the alien equivalent was of reduced conscious activity. The nanos stopped replicating. They kept the Faller unconscious but did not deprive his brain of all energy. The probe did not register anything wrong; every complex species sleeps.

By the time the Marines entered the ship, the probe couldn't register anything. Other nanos it had never been built to detect had inactivated it, atom by atom.

The Marines carefully bound the sleeping Faller's limbs and carried him, suited, to the warship. McChesney immediately took off through Space Tunnel #473, followed by twelve other tunnels, some of them highly fluid. There was no way he could be followed. Xenobiologists aboard ship began careful analysis of the gas mixture inside the Faller's suit before they removed it, as well as every other variable they could think of. By the time they let the alien wake up, their knowledge of Faller biology, until now minuscule, had increased by orders of magnitude.

The alien awoke inside an environment constructed to his exact biological needs. Atmosphere, humidity, temperature, all matched what had been inside his suit. He also woke bound to the back wall, gently but inexorably. Small capsules had been removed from various parts of his body. Maybe they were the equivalent of tooth fillings, but maybe not. McChesney and his medical team were not going to allow the first Faller POW ever to turn suicide.

Nor were they going to let him starve himself to death. The xenobiologists weren't exactly sure what liquids would nourish the alien, but they'd analyzed the contents of his stomachs (two) and put together what they hoped were reasonable synthetics. The synthetics would be delivered by forced feeding tube. By the time the prisoner regained consciousness, his only options in his padded prison were to communicate or not.

By that time, McChesney's warship was in World's remote star system, ready to transfer cell, prisoner, and xenobiologists to the *Alan B. Shepard*. After the transfer, McChesney flew back to Space Tunnel #438 to take up position in orbit around it until further orders. The warship carried every weapon known to human military. Nothing was coming through Tunnel #438 and advancing toward World without going through McChesney.

The Fallers may or may not have realized that one of their own, instead of dying with the colony skeeter, had been captured alive. But if they did, they weren't getting him back.

.   .   .

"Tell me again," Marbet Grant said to Lyle Kaufman as they waited at the security checkpoint in the deep gut of the *Alan B. Shepard*. She closed her eyes.

Watching her, Kaufman understood. It wasn't that Marbet wanted to hear the information again because she hadn't understood it. She wanted to hear it again as a mantra, a calming device, a stream of known words. After this last checkpoint, nothing would be known.

He said, "The theory—and it *is* only theory—is that the Fallers have a strong, overriding instinct to eliminate any 'others' that could present any danger to themselves. It's an evolutionary strategy that may have worked and been reinforced over eons on their home planet, which we know has high cosmic bombardment and thus may have yielded many, many mutations. They simply wiped out anything, including their own children, that were too different.

"At the first sign of any otherness, a Faller seems to go into something like human instinctive fear of falling—a xenophobia way beyond what humans usually feel. Although nobody is sure, there may be only one surviving, genetically similar group of Fallers. No races, few permitted variant alleles. Anything else arouses hostility, including us."

"The ultimate committers of hate crimes," Marbet murmured. She still had not opened her eyes. After a moment she added, "I've never met any alien."

He shouldn't be surprised, Kaufman thought. She'd never been out of the Solar System, and no other aliens in the known galaxy except Fallers had invented space travel. Or even the steam engine.

"All right," Marbet said, opening her eyes, "I'm ready."

Kaufman thumbed open the door.

The Faller's cage was ten meters wide by twenty meters long. The length was divided by an invisible, two-molecule-thick plastic sheet separating the Faller's atmosphere from the human one. The barrier conducted sound almost perfectly. Behind it the Faller was bound naked against the far wall, which was padded so that the alien could not injure itself, no matter what it did.

Not "it," Kaufman reminded himself. The xenobiologists, none of whom at Marbet's request were present, had decided that the Faller was male, although not for any reason apparent to Kaufman. The alien was about a meter and a half tall, covered with hairless tough hide of deep brown. Short powerful legs. An equally powerful tail on which he balanced at rest. A torso like a barrel, with three incongruously slim "arms" that seemed all flexible tentacle, each ending in a hand with three fingers and an opposable thumb. No claws or nails. The head, although roughly the size of a human head, was far more cylindrical. Two eyes, no visible nostrils (they were located under the chin), a large mouth.

At first sight of them, the Faller bared sharp long teeth.

Marbet did not react. She walked to the barrier and sat down cross-legged in front of it, looking upward at the alien. A posture of submission, Kaufman decided, and wondered if that was a good idea with a species that wiped out anything it didn't like.

"You can leave if you like, Lyle," Marbet said over her shoulder. "I'm going to be here for a few days, and there won't be anything to see."

A few *days*? "You mean . . . sleeping and eating here?"

"Yes. And I'll need a chamber pot." And then, not rising, Marbet began removing her clothes.

"Do you . . . do you want me to take those away?"

"No. Leave them right here, along with everything else you bring me. Food, utensils, bedding. Also an erasable tablet and pen—not a computer or holostage, please—and a music cube."

"All right," Kaufman said. Marbet was now removing her underclothes. Her body, genemod perfect, gave Kaufman a sudden lamentable erection. The alien was still baring its teeth. Kaufman left to find the things Marbet wanted.

When he returned, he had controlled himself again. He laid the things beside her and then seated himself, cross-legged like her, against the back wall of the room.

Marbet drew squares on the tablet, then laid it beside her in easy view of the Faller, who did not react. Although how could you tell? Maybe it was reacting all over the place. Kaufman craned his neck to see the tablet:

Primes. Well, that made sense: The one thing in common between humans and Fallers was the space tunnels, which were marked in primes. Although the tunnels, inexplicably, included "one" along with the primes. Kaufman would have to remember to remind Marbet of that.

Marbet held up both hands, fingers splayed. She held up one finger, waited. Two fingers, waited. Three fingers, waited. Five. Seven. Eleven.

The alien did nothing.

Marbet repeated the pantomime several times, got no response, then stopped. After that she just sat, watching.

An hour passed. Somewhere in it, the alien stopped baring his teeth, perhaps because his facial muscles got tired. He did nothing else. Neither did Marbet, except watch.

Eventually, to Kaufman's surprise, she curled up naked on the floor and went to sleep.

He watched her a while. She was so lovely. But watching even a beautiful woman sleep, and an alien do nothing, could only hold his attention so long. Kaufman left. It was all being recorded anyway, with flag programs to alert him to anything interesting.

Kaufman felt pessimistic as he went to report by comlink to McChesney, now en route to the space tunnel. No response to something as basic as primes. How were they ever supposed to wrest from this enemy any knowledge as complex as the physics of the beam-disrupter shield? It seemed hopeless.

Maybe Gruber's buried artifact would somehow help. Tomorrow they would make orbit around World.

SEVEN

WORLD

don't want to go down to the stupid planet," Sudie said. She stuck her lip out at her father. "I want to stay on the ship with Marbet."

"Where is Marbet, anyway?" Amanda said. "I haven't seen her for two days, and she promised to help me with my math."

"Life is a vale of tears," Tom Capelo said. "Why don't you ask me to help with your math? I'm a world-renowned physicist, after all, available to you at one-half my usual price."

"You don't explain things clearly," Amanda said.

"Yeah," Sudie echoed. "We want Marbet."

Capelo pushed back his irritation. He couldn't afford it, not today. He needed all his concentration for the job ahead. He looked at his daughters. God, they were so beautiful. Amanda, with her mother's blonde calm. And Sudie, a miniature of himself, now working up to what he had to ruefully admit could be a Tom Capelo tantrum if it weren't squashed now. He tried again.

"Sudie, Jane is going down to the planet with us." And where *was* Jane? She was supposed to be getting the girls ready. Sudie's hair was still a snarl, Amanda's bag stood open but unpacked. Now Capelo had an appropriate outlet for his irritation. "Jane!"

"Don't bellow, Daddy," Amanda said. "Jane's in the toilet."

"I'm not going down to that stupid old planet!" Sudie said. "I'm not! I want Marbet!"

"Jane!"

Jane Shaw came out of the bathroom. Capelo was even more annoyed to see that her short gray hair was neatly combed, her coverall spotless. While Sudie sat in a dejected tearful untended lump. He repressed this annoyance. Jane was a treasure, the one tutor-cum-nanny who had not quit within one month of being hired, and Capelo needed her too much to rile her.

"Jane, we have insurrection. We have mutiny. We have limp pajamas, and I have to be in shuttle bay in five minutes, all of us leaving in forty-five. I am clay in your digits."

"Go on, Tom," Jane said. "We'll be there on time. You just go."

"May your blossoms bloom forever," Capelo said, and Amanda smiled. They had all been reviewing the datacubes on World culture, but only Amanda had been truly interested. Sudie had not. She started to wail again, "I don't want to go to the planet! I want Marbet!"

"Isaac Newton never had to put up with this," Capelo said, and escaped.

Two corridors away, he turned back. A passing crewman flattened herself against the wall. Capelo barely saw her. He yanked open the door to the girls' quarters. Poor Sudie, poor baby, she'd been through so much already, her little tearful face . . .

Sudie sat on the floor watching a holoshow, laughing at the antics of a green hippopotamus and packing her toys into a plastic case. Her hair bounced in neat shining ponytails. Jane, helping Amanda pack, smiled at him and made a go-away gesture.

Meekly Capelo closed the door and went to shuttle bay.

•   •   •

Sergeant Karim Safir, Specialist First Class, SADA, stood with Dieter Gruber, studying the flimsies of the Neury Mountains. Capelo hadn't had much contact with the tech specialist, who had bunked and eaten with the crew and who had not, until now, been made aware of his duties beyond being told that there were caves to explore on a new planet. Presumably Safir was used to such assignments. He was supposed to be the best Army spelunker on several worlds.

Safir was small and slim, but he looked strong. He had a thick head of black curling hair and a dapper, very anachronistic mustache. He and the enormous blond Gruber made a comic contrast.

"So how does it look?" Capelo asked. "What's the first step when we get down there?"

Gruber handed him a flimsy. "The shuttle brings us to just beyond this side of the mountains—here, see?—and the shuttle becomes base camp. Then we go right in. This time I have such good sonar maps that we know exactly where to go. Not like last time, but then I didn't know I would need such maps. We go in here, through these tunnels, to—"

"We can't land in that little upland valley you told us about? The one right above the artifact?"

"No, the shuttle is too big. But the digger is hovercrafted, and after we land, Karim will fly it up and over to the valley, with the other heavy equipment. The rest of us walk. What's the matter, Tom, do you not like caves?"

"I'm going to be underground a long time when I'm dead. I don't want to start now."

Gruber laughed. "Don't worry, these are easy tunnels, big enough to walk upright, mostly dry. And after the nanos finish their smoothing, it will be like walking through the ship, only with more interest on the walls. The site is very complex, you know. Quite a history. There was underwater volcanic activity originally, then the impact of the artifact striking, then tectonic plate subduction and more hot-spot stress . . . marvelous! The result is different kinds of caves, some chimneys, lava tunnels . . . and wait till you see the vug!"

"The vug," Capelo said. He didn't want to admit that he didn't know what a vug was.

"I will not tell you in advance. It is amazing! You will want to bring your children in to see it."

"Yes," Capelo said. "Which reminds me—where's Marbet?"

"She is not going down yet," Gruber said.

"Why not? I thought she was native liaison. What if natives show up?"

"They will not," Gruber said. His joviality had abruptly faded. "We will set up an electronic perimeter."

"Because to them we're 'unreal,' " Capelo said. The natives didn't interest him, but of course he knew the situation. Part of Gruber's theory—the crackpot part—concerned finding one specific native. A woman, Only or Anly or something like that, who had been Gruber's main contact on the last trip. Gruber believed that this alien might have had her brain somehow affected at the moment that the first artifact, the one that Syree Johnson had been towing toward the space tunnel, blew itself up.

Capelo considered this idea actively silly. If the two artifacts had indeed been linked in an entanglement of unknown type, that was fascinating. It was also explorable: through the radiation increase on the outer planets, through direct experimentation with the buried artifact itself. An undocumented and subjective "brain event" two E-years ago in an alien brain, on the other hand, was not documentable or explorable, especially not mathematically. It was not science.

"Ms. Grant, she comes maybe in shuttle journey number two," Safir said, the first time he'd spoken. The words were spaced and heavily accented. Capelo's respect for him rose. The Solar Alliance Defense Council had wanted this tech badly enough to teach him, an enlisted man, drug-augmented English. Safir must be exceptional.

The first trip down included Capelo, Singh, Albemarle, Safir, Kaufman, ship's doctor, Gruber, and essential specialists with huge

amounts of equipment. The digger alone took up over half the shuttle space, crowding everybody. Support crew would come later, including Jane and the children.

Capelo looked back at the ship as the shuttle left it. He didn't
like leaving Amanda and Sudie behind for even a few hours. No
matter what the "psychologists" had said after Karen's death.

*"You're overcompensating, Dr. Capelo. Not letting your children out
of your sight cannot make up to them for the death of their mother."*

"They're not going to lose two parents. Where I go, they go."

"Even into danger?"

*"Their mother was killed in an act of war while doing a peaceful job
on a peaceful planet. You tell me where there's no danger."*

"You're not making sense, Dr. Capelo."

*"I'm making perfect sense, based on empirical experience. You, on the
other hand, are talking squishy psychological cant."*

"I know an irrational position when I see one."

"Mirrors must drive you crazy."

The shuttle landed on a flat plain beside the Neury Mountains.
Capelo, no geologist, was surprised at how abruptly the plain turned
into hills and the hills into low mountains. No snowcaps. Also no
villages, although he had clearly seen settlements from the air. In
turn, the shuttle must have been seen, a great bright hunk of metal
screaming through an atmosphere devoid even of prop planes. Well,
that was somebody else's headache. Capelo himself didn't expect to
so much as glimpse a native.

As soon as the sensor readings had been taken, the tech crew
was out setting up the electronic perimeter. They worked under the
capable, dour direction of Security Chief Captain Thekla Heller, who
appeared to have done this a thousand times. Perhaps she had.

Capelo stood to one side of the bustle, trying to clear his mind.
Gruber and Safir unloaded the digger, checking equipment and safe-
ties. When they were done, Safir would lift the craft over the mountains and set it down in what Gruber had described as a "small

upland valley, directly above the buried artifact." Then the others, crew and scientists, would go in through Gruber's "easy tunnels, big enough to walk upright, mostly dry."

Capelo hoped Gruber knew what he was talking about.

Lyle Kaufman trudged through tunnel after tunnel behind the scientists. He had had to go planetside with the first team; there'd really been no choice. But he'd hated to leave Marbet Grant and the Faller in their secret quarters aboard the *Alan B. Shepard*. Watching them was too fascinating.

Not that there had been anything much to see. Marbet had spent most of her time watching the alien, who had watched back. Except when the Faller was being force-fed, there had been very little to observe. Occasionally Marbet repeated her prime-signaling, both on erasable tablet and with raised fingers. She also played music, sang to herself, danced a bit. The Faller had not responded to any of it, as far as Kaufman could see.

What had Marbet seen? He hadn't wanted to interrupt her to ask.

Most recently Marbet had called for a full-length mirror to be brought to the cell anteroom. She spent time making faces in front of it. Duplicating the minute facial and body changes that she had registered and he had not, Kaufman guessed. He had become accustomed to the sight of her nude body, but he knew he wasn't nearly as unconscious of it as she was. She was working. He was infatuated.

The infatuation would pass. It always did, with every new woman. It was merely a matter of not letting it interfere with his work.

The tunnels, lit by Gruber's powertorches, were not a hard climb. Everyone wore s-suits, including helmets, since parts of the mountains had intense radiation and other parts, according to

Gruber, almost none. Some of the radiation was natural, some was caused by the buried artifact. Periodically Kaufman's suit informed him that he was in a dangerous area of x number of rads. He ignored it. The suit was safe.

"We are almost there," Gruber said encouragingly, after the long line of humans had slogged through a jagged, twisting tunnel filled thigh-high with brown water. Snake-like things swam through the water, many of them looking deformed. "That was the worst. From here, smooth going! And by tomorrow, the nanos will make this all so different, you won't recognize it."

One of the crewmen somewhere behind Kaufman gave a short derisive laugh.

However, the geologist told the truth; a few minutes later they emerged, one by one and ducking low, into the upland valley. It was small, no larger than a sports field, surrounded by looming rocks with overhangs, tunnel openings, and shallow alcoves. A stream babbled through the middle of the valley before it disappeared underground. Flowering plants dotted the undergrowth, some of them beautiful colors. Kaufman found himself wondering if Marbet would like them.

Put Marbet out of mind.

The digger had already arrived. Hal Albemarle began directing the set-up of sensing equipment all over the valley. Crew checked the huge digger. Gruber and Safir, both strapped about with climbing equipment, unrolled a flimsy in front of Kaufman and stabbed a finger at it.

"Here, Colonel, is the chimney I went down last time. It gives direct access to the artifact, and it is the only direct access. Karim and I will go to make sure nothing has changed in two years. It is not an easy descent, so the rest of you wait here."

"I'm going, too," Capelo said.

Gruber said, "You should not, Tom. I have done much spelunking, and Karim is the best in SADA. It is too dangerous for an amateur."

"You don't understand," Capelo said, with what Kaufman recognized as willed patience. "I have to see the artifact before you disturb it. It may not be the same afterward, or behave the same. I need baseline comparisons. The measurements we're taking up here aren't enough. Besides, for all you know, the second you move the thing one millimeter, it may vaporize. It may be designed to only function when buried under a quarter mile of dirt and rock."

"It has undoubtedly been moved before," Gruber said dryly. "After all, it has been there for perhaps three million years. Quake activity is what set off the destabilizing of atoms that has produced all the radioactivity in the first place."

"But quake activity *in situ*, packed into rock and dirt," Capelo said. "I'm going down with you."

"You don't know how," Gruber said flatly.

"I'm a quick study."

"It is not only mental, like mathematics," Gruber said. "It is physical experience."

Kaufman intervened. "Dieter, I'm afraid Tom is right. He has to examine the artifact before you move it, or move anything else."

Gruber was capable of yielding without resentment. "All right, ja, if you must you must. Get suited. Karim, Dr. Capelo goes with us." He said the last sentence slowly and clearly. Safir nodded, unperturbed. Kaufman wondered if anything perturbed him. The little spelunker seemed to have no nerves.

The three of them moved off. Kaufman watched the shouting, swearing techs unload digging equipment, then looked for Hal Albemarle.

"We have all the baseline measurements we can take from here," Albemarle said. "Sonar, radar, neutrino flow, everything matches what Gruber got two years ago on his handheld. Actually, it's amazing he got as much as he did. As far as we can tell, during the last two E-years nothing has disturbed whatever's down there."

"Gruber said the radiation field was strange," Kaufman said. "Like a flattened doughnut."

"Yes, a torus. Look."

Albemarle did something to his equipment, and a three-dimensional holodisplay floated above it. It showed a doughnut made of dots, thickly clustered in some places and thinly in others.

"Look, there's a dead 'eye,'" Albemarle said, "like in a hurricane. No radiation there, or only what might occur from natural pressure and decay. Then, around the 'eye,' this toroidal field of radiation surrounding the artifact. That's not natural. And it doesn't match what Syree Johnson told us about the other artifact, the one that exploded and killed her."

"In what way doesn't it match?" Kaufman asked. He knew the answer; he had studied all this data intensely before the expedition even left Mars. But Albemarle needed to shine, away from Capelo's withering glare. Kaufman would let him do it.

"You have to understand what radiation is, Colonel. The binding energy of atomic nuclei holds the nucleus together, within an 'energy barrier.' But nobody can predict exactly where subatomic particles are—that's implied in the Heisenberg Uncertainty Principle. You can only say where they probably are. And part of that probability field lies outside the atom. So quantum events being what they are, sometimes radiation is emitted from an atom despite the constraints of the binding energy. Are you with me so far?"

"Yes," Kaufman said. He let Albemarle patronize him. This was elementary physics.

"One way to look at radiation is to say that a nucleus temporarily destabilized, so an alpha particle escaped. The big artifact that Syree Johnson found in orbit, the one the natives thought was a moon, sent out some sort of probability wave that destabilized atoms with more than seventy-five protons and neutrons. At least, the number was seventy-five when it was used the first time, still in orbit, and killed that shuttle pilot from radiation poisoning."

"I see," Kaufman said. He kept his expression one of alert interest.

"Who knows what got destabilized when the moon went off at the end, at full strength, and killed everybody aboard the *Zeus*. But the point is, Colonel, that in both those cases, the wave was spherical. It went out in all directions equally, from what we know. This buried thing, on the other hand, is producing a toroidal wave. It's been *unevenly* destabilizing atoms and increasing the probability of their sending out an alpha particle. In a doughnut pattern."

"And what causes that pattern of radioactivity?"

"Nothing," Albemarle said flatly.

"Well, something is. There's the pattern, on your display."

"Yeah," Albemarle said. "It's a mystery."

He seemed more likable away from Capelo, despite his condescension. Kaufman could see that Albemarle, too, actually cared about this mystery. Kaufman said, "So you think that the strange wave has been emitted over the millennia whenever a quake jostled the artifact underground."

"Probably. Although maybe only on some low setting. If it had activated higher settings—presuming the thing *has* higher settings—the mountains would have blown like the *Zeus* did. Or at least become as radioactive as Nimitri."

"But instead the explosion of the other artifact killed the *Zeus*, fried Nimitri, fried the next planet, and did nothing at all to World."

"Yeah," Albemarle said. "And that makes no sense either." He stared at the holo doughnut.

"Thanks for the physics lesson," Kaufman said, as devoid of irony as he could manage.

"You're welcome," Albemarle said graciously. "Don't worry, you'll understand the basics eventually."

"Yes," Kaufman said.

His open comlink to Gruber said, "Colonel? We are at the first chimney. We go down now."

"Be careful, Dieter. And keep me informed of everything."

"*Ja,*" Gruber said cheerfully. "Don't worry, Lyle—we will not lose you your prize physicist. Tom, watch out there!"

"I see it," said Capelo's voice irritably.

Kaufman found a convenient rock, out of the way of the clamor surrounding the digger, to pay attention to Gruber's progress reports. But he had only been sitting there a few minutes when his comlink shrilled and said, "Sir, priority two message from base camp."

"On. Captain Heller?"

Kaufman's formidable security chief said, "Sir, we have the perimeter up and working. But there are natives clustered at it, a whole delegation of them. One speaks English. They want to talk to 'the head of our household.' "

"That's impossible," Kaufman said, stupidly. "The natives won't talk to us. They've declared us unreal."

"I don't know anything about that, sir. But they're here, they want to talk to 'the head of our household,' and the shuttle hasn't yet brought down Dr. Sikorski, the xenobiologist."

"All right," Kaufman said. "I'm on my way. Tell the natives that the head of this household will arrive soon." He could monitor Gruber's progress from base camp.

Why did the natives want to talk? The last time they'd seen humans, Gruber had said, they were ready to kill us all.

He said to Heller, "About half an hour, Captain. Anything else?"

"They have a lot of flowers with them."

"What colors?"

"Sir?"

"What colors are the *flowers?*"

"Uh, orange and yellow, sir."

Hospitality colors. So humans were no longer proscribed on

World. No longer unreal. All that political maneuvering General Gordon had done to get an expedition authorized to a proscribed planet—all unnecessary. But what had happened in the last two E-years, almost three years on World, to change the natives' minds? How could they decide that humans did after all possess souls, in the absence of all humans?

Kaufman hoped the answer wasn't going to make their job here harder than it already was.

EIGHT

THE NEURY MOUNTAINS

The electronic perimeter circled the base a quarter click from the shuttle pad, now empty since the shuttle had returned to the *Alan B. Shepard* for its second load of personnel. A small group of aliens milled around beyond the perimeter. One lay on the ground. As soon as Lyle Kaufman saw them, he knew what had happened.

"Turn off the perimeter," he said to Security Chief Heller.

"Sir, that isn't—"

"Turn it off."

"Yes, sir," she said unhappily.

The shock from the electric field was not enough to seriously hurt a human. But these were not humans, Kaufman reminded himself. Their physiology, although based on the same DNA as humanity, was nonetheless subtly different. Plus, coming up against an invisible source of pain would be a shock in itself for people who had not yet discovered electricity. Plus, they'd been coming in peace.

"May your flowers bloom forever," Kaufman said in English to the group as a whole.

"I rejoice in your garden," an alien said, also in English. She (he?) was large in size compared to the others. Next to him (her?), a little in front of the others, stood an even bigger alien whose skin gleamed with some sort of oil. Both of them scowled in what looked like pain.

"I am so sorry I bring no hospitality blossoms," Kaufman said, hoping the alien's English stretched that far. There hadn't supposed to be any need for him to learn World. Ann Sikorski and Gruber Dieter had been going to deal with finding Enli Brimmidin, and even they had not expected to talk to anyone else because humans on World were "unreal." But now here were Worlders talking, and Ann wasn't even planetside yet.

The big alien turned to the bigger one and spoke rapidly, obviously translating. The ridges on both their skulls wrinkled horribly. The translator turned back to Kaufman. "You are welcome to World. I am Enli Pek Brimmidin. This is Hadjil Pek Voratur, head of the Voratur household." The large native thrust his bouquet at Kaufman.

So this was Enli Brimmidin, the alien that Ann Sikorski sought, the one who had helped the previous team escape from Voratur's household with their lives after humans had been found unreal by the local priesthood. No, not local—nothing on World was local, not even Voratur's headache. Worlders "shared reality." The mechanism was physiological, Ann said. When their perceptions of reality did not match, they got terrible headaches. Culture on World, and nowhere else in the sentient universe, was monolithic.

Except for perhaps Fallers.

"I am Lyle Pek Kaufman, head of the Terran household on World. I am so sorry your householder was injured on our machine for bringing the flying boat down from the sky." God, that had better be convincing; he was flying blind here. He also hoped Enli Brimmidin's English extended past ritual phrases.

Apparently it did. Enli Brimmidin translated for both Voratur and the others. Frowns, grimaces, skull ridges eased throughout the crowd. Even the shocked man (woman?) sat up. It was just another

Terran machine; they had all seen or heard about the strange Terran machines. It wasn't any unshared reality, such as an attack by visitors.

Voratur said something, beaming, and Enli Brimmidin translated. "World welcomes the Terran traders who return to us. May your garden please your ancestors."

"May your garden bloom forever," Kaufman said.

"Are Peks Sikorski, Bazargan, and Gruber with your household, Pek Kaufman?" Enli asked.

"Pek Gruber is here. Pek Sikorski arrives soon. Pek Bazargan is not with us." Dr. Ahmed Bazargan, chief anthropologist on the previous trip, had declared himself unwilling to return to World, as well as unneeded. *"We are unreal there; you will not be able to talk to anyone. And I am too old for the danger of more field work."*

"May Pek Gruber's garden and Pek Sikorski's garden perfume the souls of their ancestors."

"May your garden bloom forever," Kaufman said, knowing he was sounding repetitious. What was expected of him next? Why couldn't they have come when Ann Sikorski was here?

"The household of Voratur invites Pek Kaufman, Pek Sikorski, and Pek Gruber to eat the sunset meal tomorrow," Enli Brimmidin said.

"We accept with pleasure," Kaufman said. "Pek Sikorski and Pek Gruber will want to see you and Pek Voratur again." At least he could ensure that Ann got to see Enli.

"And it may be that Pek Voratur and the Terrans will plant a bargain together."

So that was it. Kaufman suddenly felt better. Trade he could handle. Ann and Gruber could sort out the intricacies of reality, unreality, and how humans had apparently changed categories.

"Yes, we can talk trade."

"May your blossoms flourish in the soul of the First Flower," said Enli, with an abrupt return to polished ritual phrases.

"May your blossoms . . . uh . . . bloom forever." Kaufman was aware of not keeping up his end of flowery variations.

More flowers were handed to him and to the security chief, who took them only after Kaufman told her to. She had held a laser gun trained the entire time on the aliens, who apparently didn't recognize it as a weapon. Good thing. The alien lying on the ground stood up, and the group moved off.

"Captain Heller," Kaufman said, "new standing orders. Patrol the perimeter but don't fence it."

"Sir, I don't—"

"No fence, Captain. Double the patrol to prevent stealing." Worlders were a larcenous lot, he remembered from the datacubes. Apparently, transferring ownership of objects did not, in itself, violate shared expectations of reality.

"Yes, sir," Heller said. "Anything else, sir?"

"Yes. All personnel are to attend briefing sessions held by Dr. Sikorski as soon as she lands. *All* personnel."

"Yes, sir." Heller's tone spoke volumes. "What is the subject of the briefing sessions, sir?"

"Interaction with natives." Kaufman considered. "And the language of flowers."

"*Flowers*, sir?"

"Flowers," Kaufman said, and the security chief remained silent.

Tom Capelo gritted his teeth as he lowered himself down the narrow rock chimney. Karim Safir, below him, had used nanos to drive strong pitons into the chimney wall. Nanos could have widened the chimney, too, but Dieter Gruber, above him, was in too much of a hurry to use them. Gruber held the other end of a rope around Capelo's waist; a blazing powertorch illuminated every wrinkle in the rock; Gruber's ample body would cushion any fall. Capelo still didn't like it.

"Did Sir Isaac Newton have to go crawling around caves to

advance physics?" he called up to Gruber. "Did Einstein? Did Yeo-vil?"

"They were not so lucky as you," Gruber called back. "Do not land on Karim."

Safir wouldn't care if he did, Capelo thought. Nothing disturbed the young spelunker, and little disturbed Gruber. It made them easy to work with—unlike, say, that idiot Albemarle—but it also made Capelo feel tense by contrast.

The chimney was so narrow he scraped his elbow. How would the massive Gruber get down it? Not Capelo's problem. He felt with his boot for the next piton, and encountered floor. Grateful, he twisted his body to look for Safir. The sergeant was inserting himself into a small horizontal cave, one hand waggling behind for Capelo to follow.

"Down the rabbit hole. Oh, my ears and whiskers," Capelo said, but no one heard him. He wriggled after Safir, scraping the side of his face bloody, an event he noted in language foreign to Lewis Carroll.

But it was worth it when they reached the buried artifact.

Only one small section of it was visible, a curve of smooth metal rising from the floor of a small irregular cave. From the visible part, Capelo estimated that the artifact was a sphere twenty-five meters or so in diameter. He touched the metal reverently, then unbuckled his instruments from his suit. Safir watched him, faintly smiling, but Capelo was oblivious. He didn't even register that Gruber, unable to fit into the tiny space with the other two men, crouched in the mouth of the cave.

"Surface seems to be made of some allotropic form of carbon, like fullerenes," Capelo said for the benefit of his recorder. "No vis-ible markings, no burn or scorch marks, no discolorations. It is not presently emitting any radiation. Nor do the rocks in the surround-ing cave wall show any radioactivity—"

"I said all that in my initial report!" Gruber protested. Capelo didn't hear him. He went on taking measurements and recording everything he could think of, and only when he was done did he look up to see both men watching him in the uneven shadows from the powertorch, their faces as blackened with rock dust as he supposed his must be.

"All right," he said. "Let's get this cork out of its bottle."

The rest of the day, the huge digger destroyed the small upland valley. The stream was diverted into a new nano-dug hole to flow downward into oblivion. Flowers and foliage disappeared. Block after block of ground was sliced by lasers, grappled onto by nano-fasteners, and lifted by the hovering, workaholic digger. The problem was, there was no place to put the blocks.

The hole that Gruber was so carefully engineering would be forty meters in diameter and almost a quarter kilometer deep. The sides of the hole were being fortified with the same nanocoating that kept the lifted blocks of dirt-plus-boulders neatly together and securely fastened to the grapplers. The hole would not cave in, and the blocks would not crumble and rain back into the hole. But forty meters across pretty much defined the entire valley. The blocks had to be individually, slowly, lifted over the surrounding mountains and set down wherever there was room.

"This will take longer than we thought," Kaufman said, watching.

"Ja," Gruber replied, without regret, "but we will get there. We can work through the night, easy. Look, Lyle, at that striation. Ten thousand years of geologic history on the side of a cube of dirt!"

Kaufman couldn't find the rock strata as compelling as Gruber did. "How long do you think it will be before the natives notice that we're dicing and rearranging their planet?"

But Gruber seemed as little interested in native reaction as Kaufman was in hole digging. Kaufman sighed. Maybe, since the excavation was all occurring within the Neury Mountains where natives never went, they wouldn't ever know about the strip mining.

Another concern presented itself. He would have to walk back through the tunnels. Crewmen had begun widening the narrowest of these and draining the wettest, using nano and lasers under the supervision of an experienced mining tech. But the work was far from finished.

To Kaufman's surprise, Capelo walked with him.

"I'd have thought you would have slept right next to the hole," Kaufman said lightly. He wasn't driven into a rage by Capelo's abrasive remarks as Albemarle always was, but he couldn't say he liked the young physicist, either.

"My kids came down on the second shuttle run," Capelo said. "I can't supervise here without having dinner with them and saying good night."

"Of course," said Kaufman, who didn't have and didn't want children.

"By the way," Capelo said abruptly as they turned the corner of a smooth round lava tunnel, "where's Marbet Grant been lately?"

"Marbet?"

"Yes, you know—our diminutive, red-headed, over-engineered Sensitive. It's not like we have scads of them on board. Isn't she supposed to help Ann Sikorski play liaison with the natives?"

"She was," Kaufman said easily, "and she was scheduled to come down with Ann. But I got a comlink from the *Shepard* a few hours ago. Marbet's caught some sort of virus, and ship's doctor has quarantined her in orbit until he knows exactly what it is."

Capelo glanced at him. "That's funny. I should think any virus any of us had picked up on Mars would have shown up before now. Like Gruber's did."

"There are a lot of mutated viruses whose replicating behavior we don't understand yet," Kaufman said, hoping this was true. Biology was not his forte. "Why do you ask?"

"My girls asked. She played with them, and Sudie especially misses her."

"Well, there will be a lot of new things for them to see down here," Kaufman said.

"Yes. But I'm glad we have that electronic perimeter. These natives are the same ones that killed two human kids in the previous expedition, you know. Cut their throats. Bastards decided the kids weren't 'real.' "

"Yes," Kaufman said neutrally. He thought quickly. Would it be better to encounter Capelo's rage, or lose his trust through implied lies?

"Actually, Tom, we've had to turn off the perimeter. But we've doubled guard patrols and—"

Capelo stopped walking and turned to face Kaufman. In the tunnel shadows thrown by the powertorch his face looked eerily distorted. "Turned off the perimeter?"

"The Worlders have changed their minds and decided humans *are* real, after all. One of the aliens got badly shocked on the fence. It violates their shared perceptions of reality, which we can't afford, Tom."

Capelo said flatly, "Because it's their planet."

"Yes, it's their planet," Kaufman said, and waited for the explosion.

It didn't come. Capelo resumed walking, picking his way over a spate of rubble fallen from the tunnel wall. "In that case, I'm moving my kids to the digging site."

"To the site? But—"

"The natives won't go into the Neury Mountains at all. Religious taboo. Didn't you do your prep, Colonel?"

Kaufman didn't allow himself temper. "But if the artifact does send out a wave, or blow in some way—"

"If it blows like the first artifact did, the whole planet goes. And I think the possibilities of setting off a wave inadvertently are less than that of crazed religious aliens attacking my children. The first expedition set off that wave deliberately, you know. They didn't deliberately get their kids murdered."

"Tom, it isn't—"

"Listen, Lyle," Capelo said, stopping again, "I don't expect you to understand. I don't even expect you, or the entire Solar Alliance military that you represent, to protect me and mine. You've already amply demonstrated your failure at that. So I'm doing this my way. My kids go back with me tomorrow morning, and they stay locked in the shuttle tonight."

"All right," Kaufman said, because further opposition wouldn't get him anywhere anyway. "Will we get the artifact out tomorrow?"

"Sure. We're exactly on military schedule, where everything proceeds in a timely fashion."

"Do you really believe that?"

"No," Capelo said wearily, "but it sounds like the kind of thing a physicist on a military project should say."

They walked the rest of the way in silence.

At camp, the shuttle had just come down. Ann Sikorski disembarked into the red sunset, her long pale face both eager and apprehensive. Gruber, of course, was staying with his beloved dig. Kaufman moved toward Ann to tell her that humanity had been mysteriously restored to World reality, and that she had a dinner invitation for the following evening.

nInE

ABOARD THE *ALAN B. SHEPARD*

L yle," said Marbet's excited face on the shuttle's viewlink the next afternoon, "I think you should come up here, if you can." Something in Kaufman's chest lurched. Was it the words or the speaker? At least now, calling from the ship's heavily shielded comroom, she was clothed. He kept his voice steady.

"The artifact lifts out of the hole later today, Marbet. And we have dinner with natives, including Enli Brimmidin. She was easy to locate, after all. Can you make an oral report and then just send me the tapes?"

"Of course," Marbet said. "But I'd rather do it the other way around. You view the tapes and then we'll talk."

"I take it you've made progress."

"Oh, yes."

"Tom's daughters were asking about you. I had to tell him that you have a virus and are in quarantine."

"Give them my love. And now, what aren't you telling me, Lyle? It's something important."

He remembered that the viewlink was two-way, and that she was reading his body language and facial expressions more minutely and easily than anyone ever had before. For a brief instant, he understood why people feared and hated Sensitives. The instant passed, and he made himself smile.

He said, "Why? What are you picking up from me?"

"Frustration. Anxiety."

He laughed. Even to him it sounded forced. "Well, why wouldn't I be frustrated and anxious? I've got a three-stranded situation here—dangerous artifact, native traders, imprisoned enemy—and every strand includes a generous share of lunatics. In your strand that refers to the Faller, not you, Marbet."

"Tom Capelo giving you trouble?"

"Last night he and Albemarle actually swung on each other. If they were soldiers, I'd throw them both in stockade. If they were officers, I'd court-martial them. But they're essential civilian personnel I have to work with, and they have to work with each other, and I'm manacled by that."

"So what did you do?" Marbet said, with her quiet sympathy. Kaufman marveled at himself; he did not open up like this about difficulties, not to anyone. It was one reason he'd gotten as far as he had in the military.

"I grabbed Capelo—that skinny son-of-a-bitch is *strong*—and Gruber grabbed Albemarle. We dragged them out of sight of each other. Then Rosalind Singh talked physics to Capelo and Ann Sikorski talked data to Albemarle. Or maybe not. I didn't listen."

"Ah, the soothing power of us women," Marbet said, and he heard the edge in her voice: mockery, and more.

"Of those women, anyway. I wouldn't have sent Captain Heller to talk to either one of them. She's furious at me, too."

Marbet laughed. "You had to take down the perimeter."

"How did you guess that?"

"If you're having dinner with natives, then the Worlders must have declared humanity real again. If that's so, you can't risk violating shared reality by attacking them with painful shocks. You'd give everybody on the planet a communal headache, or risk being declared unreal again, or both."

"Yes," Kaufman said. How easy his job would be if everyone saw as clearly as Marbet Grant.

"No wonder Captain Heller is furious. Poor Lyle. But look at my tapes, they'll cheer you up."

"Marbet," he said quietly, "is the Faller talking to you?"

"Sort of. Not vocally, of course—neither of our vocal chords can handle the other's speech, even if he were inclined to talk to me. But we're communicating. But, Lyle, I'm warning you now: I'm going to ask for something big."

"What?"

"After you see the tapes."

"All right."

"Bye." The viewscreen blanked.

Kaufman sat thinking for five minutes. Communication with a Faller. There had been no communication with the murderous Fallers in twenty years. Only death and destruction and blood, more of it human than alien. It wasn't conceivable that the captured Faller would cooperate in reversing that bloodflow. Marbet might be the universe's best communicator, but she was not a soldier. She had never seen combat. She was unfamiliar with military treachery.

It was thirteen hundred hours. He called Capelo on his comlink. "Tom, this is Lyle. I have a scheduling decision to make, and I want to know if the artifact is lifting out early this afternoon or later."

"It's not coming out today at all," Capelo said.

"No? Why not?"

"Caution. You approve of caution, Lyle, don't you? We got the artifact uncovered and it has markings on it pretty close to those Syree Johnson reported on the first artifact."

"Go on." Excitement started in him like tiny bubbles.

"There are also protuberances similar to the pressure points she described. On and off switches, or at least that's what they were on her object. The original artifact required two points in opposition to be simultaneously activated to set off a wave, and this seems to be the same setup. Gruber and I don't want to set it off inadvertently. Might mess the whole place up."

"Yes."

"So we've got crew in the hole hand-brushing dirt away from the artifact as if it were a pottery shard from the early Paleolithic. That takes time. We'll lift it out tomorrow. The digger's busy preparing a place now. Sudie, not now!"

"Daddy!" the child's voice said excitedly, "come look!"

Kaufman said, more sharply than he intended, "Tom, are you trying to supervise a major military find and baby-sit at the same time?"

"No, no, their nanny is here. Sudie just escaped for a minute. Here, Jane, take her. Tomorrow, Lyle. Early in the morning. Then, when it's out, I can do the real tests."

"All right," Kaufman said, and broke the link before he said something to Capelo that he'd regret. Capelo was a lunatic, just as he'd told Marbet. Children at a weapon site! Arrogant individualist, assuming whatever he did had to be right, simply because he did it.

Arrogant brilliant individualist.

Kaufman called the shuttle pilot, who was off-duty and asleep. "Captain DeVolites, this is Colonel Kaufman. How quickly could you take me up to the *Shepard* and back down again?"

The pilot was instantly alert. "Under emergency conditions, sir?"

"No, we're not under attack." Kaufman explained no further. "Leaving as soon as possible."

DeVolites couldn't quite keep the curiosity out of his voice, although he tried. "Two hours up, sir, including docking. Less than two down." The *Shepard* was in geosynchronous orbit over the Neury Mountains, monitoring everything with sensors that could resolve an image to a few centimeters.

"Prepare to leave in fifteen minutes," Kaufman said, and went to tell Captain Heller that the shuttle was making an unscheduled liftoff.

Commander Grafton met Kaufman in the shuttle bay. Grafton did not look happy.

"Colonel, a word, please, in private."

"Certainly."

Grafton led the way to a shielded conference room off the shuttle bay. "Colonel Kaufman, I request clarification of the parameters allowed for Ms. Grant's interactions with the prisoner."

Grafton looked very stiff, very Navy. Kaufman relaxed. He had dealt often with outraged protocol.

"What has she been doing, Commander?" Kaufman asked, allowing the slightest hint of sympathy into his voice.

"She has activated the extensive holo library, which is of course acceptable. She has commandeered—" Kaufman noted the word "—enormous computer power, which is also within her charter, even if those uses seem offensive. But she has also interfered with the feeding and possible preservation of the prisoner, which infringes on my responsibility for this operation. And now she wants one of the prisoner's so-called 'hands' freed. One hand, Colonel, might be enough for a Faller to devise a method of suicide. That's their projected primary response to captivity, as you know. I cannot permit that to happen."

"No, of course not," Kaufman said. The chain of command here was tricky. Grafton was Navy, Kaufman Army. Grafton had final control of anything that threatened his ship, but Kaufman was in control of the "special project" involving the alien. However, both men knew that if the only Faller ever captured alive was allowed to kill himself on Grafton's ship, Grafton's career was over.

Grafton said, "So you agree that Ms. Grant's request must be denied."

"I'd like to talk to Ms. Grant," Kaufman said, "but it certainly sounds as if freeing the prisoner's hand could endanger him." A reply that actually said nothing, but denied nothing either.

Grafton was no fool. He recognized that was all he was getting at this point. He rose and said stiffly, "I'll take you to Ms. Grant."

Marbet waited for him in the anteroom to the prisoner's cell, an anteroom of amazing messiness. Computer flimsies lay curled on the floor, the table, the chairs. Three holo display stages—three!—crowded one wall, interspersed with full-length mirrors. Various uniforms crumpled themselves into fantastic shapes in every corner, along with what Kaufman at first thought were dead animals. He started. Closer scrutiny showed him the things were pieces of fur. Where had she gotten fur aboard ship?

"Hello, Lyle," she said when Grafton had left them. "The commander has been complaining about me to you."

"Don't tell me how my body language is revealing that," Kaufman said, smiling. She looked wonderful, green eyes alight and brown face glowing with excitement. Even her short auburn curls seemed to have extra spring. "Tell me what you've done."

She knew how to present information succinctly. "I proceeded in four stages. First, observation of the Faller, especially when he was being force fed, combined with preliminary attempts to communicate using prime numbers. He didn't respond. But my observations, combined with the computer analysis of the holo recordings of every session, gave me a feel for how his face and body express half the human primary emotions."

"Half?" Kaufman said. He noted that she hadn't used a personal name for the Faller.

"Anger, fear, and disgust. The others are pleasure, surprise, and lust."

"So next you went after those," Kaufman said. Lust?

"Yes. I used holos on the solidest setting to elicit surprise. Animals, mostly. I don't know yet if the Fallers have holo tech or if he thought the rabbits I pulled out of my hat were real, but I got surprise."

"I'll bet."

"Pleasure was a lot harder. I'll come to that in a minute. And lust, too."

"I'm fascinated," Kaufman said, without sarcasm.

"The second stage was learning to simulate the Faller's body language and facial expressions myself."

"You?" Kaufman said, startled.

"Well, yes, Lyle. He has no motivation to learn our communication."

"True enough." You didn't need to communicate to commit suicide.

"I used the same body language he did," Marbet continued, "and his body responses were surprise and disgust, without any reciprocation of communication. And even then I could sense that something else was going on here, although I couldn't put my finger on what. And neither could the computer. Why are you smiling?"

"At the idea of a computer with a finger." Even her metaphors were body-oriented.

She smiled, without stemming her tide of words. "Stage three was holo simulation of other Fallers, programmed with the body language I'd been able to classify so far. *That* was fascinating! The Faller seemed to understand right away that those holos weren't real, but body language is involuntary, Lyle. He couldn't help responding somewhat. And his responses were vastly different whether the Faller holo was naked, dressed in a uniform identical to the one he was captured in, or dressed in human uniforms."

"You projected holos of a Faller dressed in human uniforms?" No wonder Grafton had found Marbet's work "offensive."

"Yes. Also in imaginary uniforms, basically the Faller garment but with different looks based on human notions of decoration. At least, at first. And here's where I had the first breakthrough. The Faller's responses differed markedly depending on rank . . . even human rank. They know a lot more about us than we do about them."

"I believe it," Lyle said grimly.

"What I think is that Faller society is rigidly hierarchical. That makes sense, when you consider that they eliminate anything that looks like a threat. You'd have to have some mechanism to keep them from completely eliminating each other. I think that mechanism is strict and unvarying hierarchy, life-long. And I think that, unlike human societies that have done the same thing, the Faller mechanism is biological. Hard-wired in the brain."

Kaufman said slowly, "You mean, like the shared-reality mechanism of the Worlders is biological and hard-wired."

"Yes! Exactly!"

"The alien universe is turning out to be a very strange place."

Marbet laughed, a laugh so free and joyous that Kaufman was startled. This was more than just solving a scientific and military problem. Marbet Grant relished the strangeness that made him, Colonel Lyle Kaufman, a bit uneasy.

But, then, she had always been treated as a living strangeness herself.

"Yes. What emerged from the idea of ranking was a means to discriminate among the Fallers' reactions to different humans. The only ones he's seen, you know, are the techs who force-feed him, who are all three crew and who happen to all be men, and the xenobiologists, who are officers but not line officers with power. He's incredibly sensitive to the possession of power, you know, in ways we can't imagine. It's like a dog being so much more sensitive than we are to smells. What I had to find was a way to use that."

Kaufman had a sudden unsettling thought. "You got him to react to Commander Grafton, the highest-ranking officer aboard."

"Yes. It was a failure. The Faller's reaction was fear and anger, not increased willingness to communicate. We're the enemy, after all."

Kaufman couldn't resist. "What were Grafton's body reactions?"

Marbet laughed again. "The same fear and anger. Neither of them knew it, and if you ever repeat this I'll deny it, but that's actually the moment human and Faller most resembled each other."

I'll bet they did, Kaufman thought, remembering Grafton's stiffness and outrage at Marbet's work. But all he said aloud was, "So what was your breakthrough?"

"I went the other way. The Faller wouldn't communicate with human power. He disdained human inferiors. None of us could ever be equal to Fallers, in his mind. That left only one option."

All at once Kaufman knew what she meant. His stomach clenched.

Marbet said, "You don't like it, I can see. And nobody knows anything about Faller females, not even whether they're sentient. But I had the computer create various female holos based on the sex differences most common among galactic species, if not exactly universal. Smaller body. Softer wherever the Faller seemed hard. That sort of thing. I left the female holos unclothed, to eliminate rank considerations, and sort of blurry, since I had absolutely no idea what the sex organs themselves might look like. And the Faller responded, with the first body signs of pleasure I had observed. Fleeting, of course, and involuntary . . . he knows perfectly well that it's a holo. But enough reaction for me to build a partial vocabulary of pleasure and lust, and to see what bodily vocabulary on the part of the holo provoked it."

"And then you learned the vocabulary yourself."

"Yes."

Kaufman didn't like it. Marbet, presenting herself as a Faller female, or a slavish clumsy copy of one, probably naked . . . He strove to hide what he felt, and knew he failed.

She watched him keenly. Finally she said, "Grafton doesn't know I'm doing this part."

"No."

"He would react the same way you are, only more so. A lot

more so. But, Lyle, I'm not pretending to be a Faller female. The prisoner isn't stupid. I'm merely trying to present myself in the way that will least arouse his instinctive hostility, and most create a possible willingness to communicate. Animal handlers on Earth do the same thing, you know. In fact—" She hesitated, decided to go ahead "—so do you, in your work in diplomacy."

True enough. Kaufman nodded, reluctantly. "Did it work? Was he more willing to talk to you?"

"Yes. I'm still the enemy, of course, but I'm an enemy that arouses positive physiological responses rather than hostile ones. And make no mistake, Lyle—the instinctive physiological component in Faller behavior is much stronger than in humans. The Fallers are much less adaptable than we are. In a real sense, they're prisoners of their biology."

"Which is why they kill us without negotiation in the first place. All right, Marbet. What has he told you?"

"He hasn't 'told' me anything yet." She sounded exasperated. "I thought you understood, Lyle. It's a nonverbal channel of communication, and so far a tenuous one. But I'm using it to tell him things."

"Like what?"

"To convey that humans want to talk, to stop the killing. I use holos, pantomime, anything I can think of. In a few minutes I'll show you."

"Marbet . . ." Appalled, Kaufman couldn't think how to go on. "Marbet, you—we—aren't empowered to negotiate peace!"

"I know that," she said, with dignity. "I understand that I'm supposed to learn what I can of Faller culture and, by implication, Faller military strategy. And if I get really lucky, uncover the secrets of the beam-disrupter shield. Oh, and it would probably also be nice if I walked on water."

Kaufman tried to imagine what discussions had looked like between her and Grafton.

After a moment she said, "I'm sorry. Tension, I guess, plus lack of sleep."

"No, I'm sorry," Kaufman said. "You've done amazing work, Marbet, and of course you're right when you say there's no telling where it will lead. It's a stunning achievement, and a real contribution to both science and the war."

She said flatly, "You're very good at your job."

"I didn't mean—"

"Yes, you did. But I like you better when you're being straightforward. I'm going in to him now. You can observe on this viewscreen."

"All right," he said, but she'd already vanished through a side door. Kaufman stepped up to the viewscreen.

Behind it, the Faller looked as Kaufman remembered, a deformed log-like human with three tentacle-like arms, tied to the back wall. Kaufman studied the noseless face, but could see no change of expression. A door opened and Marbet entered the prisoner's cell.

For a suspended second Kaufman wasn't sure it was her. Or even human. But of course it was Marbet, a Marbet moving somehow differently, with an alien gait, her arms held at a peculiar angle and her fingers splayed. Bent-kneed, somehow fatter . . . she couldn't be fatter. It was an illusion. She wore nothing but a yellow strip of cloth around her hips, hiding her genitals . . . maybe the cloth was padded and that's why she looked fatter. No, it was something in the way she held herself, the way she moved. And what he'd thought was cloth wasn't. It was a blurred holo projection suggesting cloth without being specific about texture, composition, or draping.

Marbet moved very close to the Faller. She must be right up against the invisible barrier that separated her atmosphere from his. The viewscreen recorders were placed such that Kaufman had a clear three-quarter profile of her face. It looked even stranger than her body. She was moving her facial muscles in ways that looked grotesque to him, contorting her features.

The alien contorted his, although not as much as she did. Still, Kaufman felt his breath catch. He was seeing the first human-Faller conversation in twenty years of war.

No, he had to remind himself, not a conversation. No ideas were being exchanged, not even basic nouns on the level of "Me Tarzan, you Jane." Even as Kaufman watched, the alien's face returned to passivity. No, not completely . . . there was still something, some twitches, some meaning he had no way of beginning to read.

Then Marbet held up one arm and began to gesture.

A genuine shock ran through Kaufman's body. The angle Marbet held her arm, the way she splayed her fingers, the awkward way one finger remained folded back (the aliens were four-fingered) all looked strange and grotesque to him. But the movements he recognized. Between remedial genemods and nanomeds, there were no deaf people on Mars. But Mars was not the Solar System. In the slums of Earth, and on religious colonies where settlers forbade both genetic engineering and nanotech, Kaufman had seen deaf children do what Marbet did now. Marbet was teaching the alien American Sign Language.

Or a version of it, anyway. *I-want-not-hurt-you.*

The alien's face moved slightly, muscle shifts Kaufman could not interpret. Could Marbet?

She went on a few minutes more, then executed a sort of dipping bow. Something happened, then. A crest began to rise at the back of the alien's neck, a thin layer of flesh that rose rigid a few inches and then abruptly collapsed. But Kaufman had seen it, and seen things like it in other species, some of them Terran. It was an involuntary mating display, quickly suppressed.

Lust.

The alien missed the females of his own species.

Kaufman closed his eyes. When he brought Marbet Grant here, he'd never expected anything like this. Not that he'd had clear expectations, but still . . . alien mating behavior did not form a part of military weapons-project reports. They were a long, long way from beam-disrupter shields and probability wave functions.

Marbet stood beside him. She said quietly, "So you see how it is, Lyle. I wanted you to see for yourself. There's no way he can answer me with his hand tied like that."

Kaufman waited.

"You have to convince Grafton and his xenobiologists to let one of the Faller's hands go free."

There was no diplomatic way to say it, no quibbling or evasiveness that she would not see through. Kaufman braced himself.

"No, Marbet. It's impossible."

"But—"

"No."

TEN

GOFKIT JEMLOE

Enli Pek Brimmidin watched the Terrans walk toward the gate of the Voratur household and felt the headache begin between her eyes. They were not yet in hearing distance, and still the head pain began. That was what Terrans did to people.

No one else felt it, of course. Pek Voratur and his wife Alu Pek Voratur, their grown sons, the household priest—all stood calmly, smiling above their armloads of hospitality flowers. The servants of the First Flower had declared Terrans real, the possessors of souls, and so there was no unreality here to bring on head pain. All were in harmony, sharing reality.

Except Enli.

Enli, who had spent time alone with the Terrans of the previous expedition, who had learned their difficult speech, who had seen them at their worst, and their best. Terrans were so frightening! They could deny reality to each other, fight with each other, love those of each other they should not . . . all apparently without head pain. But only Enli really understood this, because one of them had died to save the others and to save World, and so the servants of the First Flower had declared all humans real. Thus, they *were* real. And they presented no break in shared reality for anyone except Enli, who had hoped to never set eyes on any of them again.

And yet—see what the Terrans did to people!—her heart leapt in gladness when she saw that Ann Pek Sikorski was one of the Terrans making their way to dinner at the house of Pek Voratur. Gentle Pek Sikorski, kind and soft-spoken, with the same long fair headfur looped in shining curves. Enli had always secretly liked the Terrans' headfur, weird though it was. And somebody—probably Pek Sikorski—had told the humans to hide their lack of neckfur. High curving collars—rather pretty—decently covered their naked necks.

"You are welcome to the house of Voratur!" boomed Pek Voratur, and Enli translated. Masses of hospitality flowers, orange and yellow, were exchanged. There were four visitors: Pek Sikorski; Lyle Pek Kaufman (they had such strange names!), the head of the Terran household who had spoken to Enli yesterday; and two servants, a man and a woman. The woman was the hard-faced servant who had pointed a *gun* at Pek Voratur yesterday. Only Enli had known the word, or the reality; she was the only person on World who had ever seen a Terran *gun*. Pek Voratur had not even recognized it as a danger.

The head pain grew worse.

But not intolerable. Enli had been afraid it would be, but something had happened to her during the Terrans' previous visit. They had changed her. They had shown her other realities than the one shared on World (who had imagined such a thing!), and made her live in them for a time, and left her knowing that she could tolerate the existence of those other realities if she had to. No one else on World lived knowing those things. Only Enli Pek Brimmidin, real and yet not of shared reality, because of the Terrans.

It was possible she would never forgive them.

·   ·   ·

"It is good to see you, Enli," said Ann Pek Sikorski, as the two walked side by side, a little behind the others. "How is your soil?"

"The soil is good today, Pek Sikorski."

"Ann. Please."

Enli did not want to call this alien by her childname. And yet Pek Sikorski asked her to, setting off mild head pain. See what the Terrans did to people!

"We have not seen each other for three years," Pek Sikorski said, sharing reality. She always did have the best manners of all the Terrans.

"Yes, three years," Enli said. "You will want to see David Pek Allen's grave."

Did Pek Sikorski look startled? Yes. Why? Surely she knew Pek Allen had died on World. And yet, the other Terrans had left so abruptly in their flying boat . . .

"Will you take me to his grave tomorrow?" Pek Sikorski said.

"If Pek Voratur wishes. I am temporarily in his household." Yes, and resenting it. She missed Gofkit Shamloe. She missed her sister Ano and Ano's children. She missed Calin, dancing with Calin, whatever else might have happened between her and Calin if she had remained a few days longer in Gofkit Shamloe . . . But the servants of the First Flower had seen that shared reality was otherwise.

"Does David's grave have a flower altar?" Pek Sikorski asked.

"A beautiful flower altar," Enli said, "as befits one who died for others."

"I would like to share that reality fully with you at his grave, Enli."

"We will share the garden of our heart," Enli said formally. They walked through an open arch into one of the tens and tens of rooms in the Voratur household. Pek Voratur gestured, and everyone sat down. Only Enli and Pek Sikorski spoke both Terran and World, however imperfectly, and Enli prepared herself to translate.

"This room is very beautiful," Pek Kaufman said.

"You are welcome to the best flowers of my household," Pek Voratur said, and indeed they sat in the loveliest and most expensive room Enli had ever seen. The curving walls represented the fullest bloom of the wallers' art, covered with thousands of preserved and flattened flowers faded to soft subtle colors. The flowing curves of the low wooden table, the rich embroidery on the floor pillows (they had to have come from the Seury Islands), the heavy pewter dishes — all created by master artisans. Nowhere was there a straight line, or an ugly blunt corner. And beyond the open arched windows flourished the magnificent Voratur gardens, famous for fifty villages around and even in the capital itself.

Rich dishes were served, foods Enli rarely saw in her own village of Gofkit Shamloe. How Ano would love this food! Greedy Ano, who ate and ate and never got fat. Well, Ano was beautiful anyway. Enli tried to eat, but found she could not. Being around the Terrans wilted her stomach.

They were polite enough, however, and the meal progressed with ritual exchanges and easy conversation. Pek Sikorski did most of this. Of course, she was the only Terran who could speak World. Pek Kaufman watched everything keenly and smiled often. A happy man, Enli thought, or a good trader. Only five sat around the table, Voratur having dismissed everyone except his oldest son, Soshaf Pek Voratur. This was, or would eventually be once the eating was over, business. The two Terran servants sat apart. Pek Voratur had seemed surprised that Pek Kaufman had not dismissed them, and the trader had ordered a second table, which was hastily erected. Enli was grateful to sit with her back to the Terran servants. Somewhere in her strange stiff clothing the woman, Pek Heller, carried a *gun*.

When the last dishes were removed, a little silence fell. Pek Voratur waited. Just as the first feelings of unshared reality were beginning, Pek Kaufman ran his hand over the gleaming table. "Beautiful wood," he said in World, the words obviously newly learned and laughably accented.

Pek Voratur relaxed. Business had begun as it should. He wiped his mouth on a food cloth, belched, and said, "My garden blooms anew because you admire this table. The artisan is Holit Pek Marrabilor. It may be possible that he would like to trade tables with our Terran visitors." Pek Sikorski translated this; her World was better than Enli's Terran.

"It may be possible that Terrans would like to acquire such tables in trade," Pek Kaufman said, in Terran. More translation.

"Perhaps in return for bicycles," Voratur said. "The Terran bicycles bloom in my heart."

"We have twenty bicycles to trade," Pek Sikorski said, this time without consulting Pek Kaufman. Well, the Terrans were like that. High members of a household could speak for the head, could even disagree with him or her. What a peculiar people!

Voratur's eyes gleamed in his well-oiled face. "Twenty bicycles are welcome in trade. Perhaps for twenty tables by Holit Pek Marrabilor, or by artisans as skilled?"

Pek Sikorski translated for Pek Kaufman, who surprised everyone by saying in World, "Yes. Trade. May your flowers bloom." Basic words and still that laughable accent . . . but yesterday Pek Kaufman had known no World words. Could all Terrans learn to speak so quickly? Then they were a brilliant people, as well as a dangerous one.

"It may be that larger trades also grow in this garden," Pek Sikorski said, and something in her voice, or the way her body leaned forward, made Enli suddenly tense. This was going to be one of the Terran different realities; she could feel it.

"Tell me of the flowers you smell in that garden," Voratur said.

"Once before, Pek Voratur, we made an unusual trade to you. We traded potions against the flower sickness."

"Ah, yes, the *antihistamines*," Voratur said; the word was Terran. "I have traded them well, Pek Sikorski."

He had indeed, Enli thought. Terran *antihistamines* had made Voratur one of the richest men on World.

"And in return for the *antihistamines*," Pek Sikorski continued, "you traded to us a picture of your brain."

A "*Lagerfeld scan.*" Enli had not felt the strange words sprout in her mind in three years. The Terrans had put a metal hat on Pek Voratur and asked him many questions. This was supposed to make pictures of how his brain worked, although Enli had never been shown such pictures. She was not sure they really existed. And yet, the Terrans had all been excited over the *Lagerfeld scan*. Perhaps the pictures did exist. After all, the Terrans had *antihistamines*, flying boats, *guns*, hurtful invisible walls, and other bizarre and mostly unnecessary machines.

"I remember the picture of my brain," Voratur said cautiously. Enli understood the caution. The scan had been a piece of unshared reality, although a minor one, and hence had cost him a thumping headache.

Pek Sikorski said something to Pek Kaufman in Terran too rapid for Enli to follow. She caught only the words "control data." What were the Terrans seeking to control now?

Cold seeped up her spine, and her neckfur bristled.

Pek Sikorski said, "We would plant a trade together with you, Pek Voratur, and may it bloom for us both. We would trade you this." She looked at Pek Kaufman, who drew from his pocket a piece of paper and unfolded it.

It was a very wasteful use of paper, that expensive stuff, Enli thought. Most of the paper was blank. Only the middle had drawing, a picture of a complicated machine. Pek Kaufman turned the paper toward Pek Voratur, and Enli could no longer see it.

"This is a steam machine," Pek Sikorski said. "We can show you exactly how to build it. Once you understand that, you can build many different kinds of steam machines, to do many different things.

Logs can be carried on carts that do not have to be pulled. Water can be brought from rivers to water fields and gardens. Boats can travel to the many islands where you trade, without sail or oars. Of course, it will take time to learn to do these things, maybe years, but their value will be very great."

Pek Voratur studied the drawing. "A steam machine?"

"Hot steam. It can move things. Here, let me explain." Pek Sikorski talked on, but Enli did not attempt to follow. She watched Pek Voratur's face, knowing what he would say.

"Yes, yes, I see," he said finally, without enthusiasm. "But why should we want such a machine?"

Pek Sikorski and Pek Kaufman looked at each other.

Soshaf Pek Voratur said, "What would we do with it?"

"We told you," Pek Sikorski said. "Carry logs, water fields, move boats—"

"If a machine carried logs, what work would there be for our woodsmen?" Soshaf said reasonably.

"Why would we need to water our fields when the First Flower always sends us the rain she wishes us to have?" Voratur said.

"And to move boats?" Soshaf asked. "Boats move downriver of themselves, and back upriver and over the sea by the efforts of wind or oarsmen. Would you put the oarsmen all out of work? How would they feed their children?"

"And if they could not trade their labor, to whom would I trade the goods on my trading fleet?" Pek Voratur said in bewilderment. Not only bewilderment. Enli saw clearly the start of Voratur and Soshaf's head pain. The Terrans must already see their objections; they were shared reality. Yet the Terrans did not seem to see. Unshared reality . . .

Pek Sikorski said quickly, "Yes, of course. Your trading would not be increased. Forgive us; our soil is poor today, and we imagine in bad dreams."

"May your soil improve and your gardens flourish," Voratur

said, without warmth. "But bad dreams do not help trade. It may be that we cannot bring a trade to flower between us, Pek Kaufman."

Pek Sikorski said, without translating. "I am sure we can plant a gloriously blossoming trade, Pek Voratur!" To Enli's ears she sounded desperate. Why?

"What did he say?" Pek Kaufman asked Pek Sikorski.

"Backing out," she said in English. "We misjudged. A steam engine won't aid productivity as much as disrupt economic stability."

"Damn," Pek Kaufman said. "Tell him we have something else to offer."

"Lyle, no!"

"Tell him, Ann." The tone of authority was unmistakable.

Voratur listened to all these words he could not understand. Enli saw his temper rise: disrespect on top of the imaginings of bad dreams. Offered to him, Hadjil Pek Voratur, the best trader on World! To him!

"Tell Pek Kaufman," he said to Enli, "that our trade does not bloom. May the First Flower bloom for him elsewhere." Voratur stood.

"Pek Voratur!" Pek Kaufman said, standing as well. "Look! Trade!" His accent had worsened even more and his words were barely recognizable, simple as they were. But the object he pulled from inside his bizarre clothing was recognized. Enli knew what it was, and from his face, Voratur did, too. Of course he did; the trader had let no tiny detail go unobserved when the Terrans had stayed with him on their previous trading journey.

"Enli, please translate," Kaufman said in Terran. "Pek Voratur, this comlink is a box to send messages over long distances. When your—"

"He knows what a comlink is," Enli said to Kaufman, and realized that for the first time in her life she had interrupted a Terran. She didn't need to look at Pek Voratur to know what he was thinking.

Voratur, like all traders, used sunflashers to send and receive messages from his trading fleet. The carefully spaced towers and skilled mirror users were a good way to ensure that any shared reality, trade or not, reached all of World in one day and one night. But only when the sun was shining. With four or five Terran *comlinks*, Pek Voratur could reach his fleet, his land caravans, his agents in the capital at any time, day or night, in any weather.

Pek Voratur said, "Please sit, Pek Kaufman. More pel?"

"Lyle," Pek Sikorski said in a low, urgent voice in Terran, "you can't. The steam engine is the next projected step in their industrial development anyway. But a *comlink*—"

Pek Kaufman said pleasantly, not lowering his voice, "They can't duplicate it. I am not an anthropologist, I am a military negotiator on a major war effort. Now please be quiet, Dr. Sikorski."

Even Voratur, ignorant of the words, understood Kaufman's tone. Pek Sikorski sank back on her pillow as if she'd been struck.

Voratur said briskly, "Six comlinks, Pek Kaufman, in return for pictures of my brain and Enli Pek Brimmidin's. Enli, for each year the comlinks work, there will come to you every third share of my increased profits over my profits for this past year. Do you wish to plant that trade with me, Enli?"

Enli didn't look at Pek Sikorski. She didn't understand why Pek Sikorski didn't want Pek Voratur to have the *comlinks*, but Enli didn't like it. Why should Pek Sikorski say what Worlders could or could not have in trade? Was Pek Sikorski trying to keep useful things away from World because she thought Terrans were of more value than Worlders? Well, Pek Voratur should have whatever he could make a fair trade for. That was shared reality, and this was not Pek Sikorski's world, but Pek Voratur's.

And Enli's.

She said, "I wish to plant that trade with you, Pek Voratur."

"May it bloom and flourish. Tell Pek Kaufman 'yes,' in his Terran words."

"Tell Pek Voratur," Kaufman replied easily, "that I am delighted we will plant a trade together. Will he come tomorrow afternoon to our household to make the brain pictures and receive the comlinks? And you, too, Enli?"

Enli translated. "We will come," Pek Voratur said, but even as Enli took the celebratory glass of pel from Soshaf Voratur's triumphant hand, she felt the strength go out of her legs so that they trembled and ran like water.

ELEVEN

THE NEURY MOUNTAINS

insist," Dieter Gruber said, his blue eyes cold. "Tom comes, too. This is critical."

"This is irrelevant," Tom Capelo said, mimicking Gruber's accent accurately and cruelly. "Unmeasurable subjective feely-squirmy stuff."

Lyle Kaufman looked from one man to the other. Gruber, tall and implacable, a Teutonic warrior issuing battle orders. Capelo, short and disheveled, the scrawny foot soldier somehow, incredibly, in charge of the battle. Both of them gleaming with the dangerous mad irritability of men short on sleep.

"If you call yourself a scientist, you will come."

"Because I call myself a scientist I don't base hypotheses on tickles in my brain. Or yours."

"All right," Kaufman said. "All *right*."

They stood at the edge of the massive hole in the upland valley. A quarter-mile below them, Albemarle directed a crew of techs in the minute mapping of the exact position of every newly exposed protuberance on the artifact. Tomorrow it would be lifted free. The sheer drop at Kaufman's feet, kept vertical and solid by nanotech supports, was dizzying. It didn't seem to bother either Gruber or Capelo, however, who went on arguing about Gruber's foot expedition into another part of the mountains.

Gruber said, "Lyle can simply order you to go."

"I wouldn't order Tom to do that," Lyle said quickly. Direct orders were the very worst way to manage a man like Tom Capelo. Gruber was no diplomat. "Tom, tell me again why you don't want to go."

Capelo said with exaggerated, sarcastic patience, "Because I am already juggling four sets of real data. One, the neutrino map of the Neury Mountains. Two, our data readings here. Three, the readings in Syree Johnson's report about the other artifact that exploded in space. And four, everything we know—which isn't much—about the Faller beam-disrupter shield. Four real, measurable sets of data. I don't need to take time from them to crawl through irradiated tunnels to some spot that supposedly will create subjective little diddles in my brain."

Gruber said, "He is afraid of the tunnels and radiation. You are a coward, Capelo."

Such an ugly look flashed into Capelo's eyes that Kaufman had to stop himself from taking a step backward. Before Capelo could speak, Kaufman said quickly, "Be careful, Tom. Your children are watching."

Capelo spun around, so that for one heart-stopping moment Kaufman was afraid he would fall into the hole. The two little girls, tended by their nurse, played under a rock overhang as far away from the hole as the tiny valley allowed. At that moment Sudie happened to look toward her father. She waved happily. "Hi, Daddy! I'm a rock doggie!"

"Arf, arf, sweetheart," Capelo called, and when he turned back to Gruber, the worst moment had passed. It was the first time that

Lyle had found any reason to be glad the children existed. Nonetheless, he gave Capelo no chance to speak before castigating Gruber himself.

"Dieter, that's slanderous and untrue, and you know it. If you call yourself a scientist, stick to facts in presenting your case to Tom. Ja?"

"Ja," Gruber said. "I am sorry, Tom. You are not a coward. But you still must come experience this spot in the field."

Kaufman said, "I'm going on the expedition, Tom. After all, you told me yourself that scientific data are often preceded by phenomena nobody knows how to measure yet. Today's truths were yesterday's scientific heresies."

Capelo ran a hand through his dirty, already disheveled hair. He glared resentfully at Gruber; unlike the stolid geologist, Capelo remembered slights a long time. A grudge holder on a galactic scale: witness his frightening hatred for the Fallers, still white-hot three years after his wife's death. Kaufman, a military man, knew better than to waste his energy hating the enemy. Much more productive to put the energy into defeating them. Capelo was incapable of that sort of practical detachment.

But he was fair. "All right, damn it, I'll go! In the interests of completion, if not rationality. But if we all get killed when a non-nano-coated tunnel falls on us, remember at your dying moment that I said 'I told you so.'"

"I'll remember," Kaufman said. "But there will be nanos reinforcing just ahead of us, so it doesn't seem likely."

"There are no chimneys or hard climbs," Gruber said. "It is an easy spelunk."

"Pierre Curie was killed by a beer wagon during an easy walk," Capelo said.

"Because he wasn't paying attention," Kaufman answered.

"And he wasn't paying attention because he was thinking about a far more important scientific problem," Capelo retorted, and Kaufman knew enough to let him have the last word.

Suited but not helmeted, the three men walked through tunnels deep in the Neury Mountains. Walked, crawled, scrambled, waded . . . Capelo hated it. At least the damn suit kept him warm, dry, whole, and warned about radiation levels. Gruber was an idiot, and he was a bigger one to have agreed to trail along.

The geologist led, carrying a powertorch and guided by sonar and radiation maps created from satellite information. The maps were remarkably detailed. There was no chance of getting lost, merely of getting stuck in some rocky hole-turned-tomb. Idiots all. And the supreme idiocy was the rock-climbing cord that bound them all together. Coated with nanos like minute ball-bearings so that the cord was virtually frictionless, its handled end was held by the smiling Karim Safir. Gruber had carefully stationed Safir in a cave that looked to Capelo like every other cave, but whose location apparently had significance to Gruber.

"Everybody all right?" Gruber called back cheerfully. Why wouldn't he be cheerful? He had the sensitivity of a water bucket, and he'd gotten his way about this stupid expedition. "Watch out ahead, it gets a little damp."

Wading through knee-high brackish water, his hand groping along the tunnel wall to keep himself upright, Capelo said, " 'A little damp'?"

"Professional understatement," Kaufman said. "Gruber cuts rocks a lot of slack."

"He doesn't . . . Lyle! Was that a snake?"

"I don't think they have snakes on World," Kaufman said uncertainly.

"Then an alien analogue!"

"Don't mind that small swimmer," Gruber called back happily. "Ann says they are harmless."

Then let Ann encounter them, Capelo thought savagely. But, no, the project biologist was off on some errand involving natives, while the project physicist sloshed through alien reptiles. Idiocy, stupidity . . .

His nerves were too frayed. Nobody ever did any worthwhile science in this state. All right, then, he would calm himself. Don't think about this exercise in geologic futility. Think instead about the data, clean and rational.

Four sets of real data, he'd told Kaufman, and that was right. When all four were as complete as the team could make them, it was Capelo's job to integrate them, to find the connections and hypotheses that would make mathematical sense out of what seemed to be happening in the quantum-level universe.

First, the neutrino map of the Neury Mountains. That was easy, known and understood. Neutrino detectors on the *Alan B. Shepard* and on geosynchronous satellites had measured and plotted the unusually large neutrino flow from this section of the mountain range. The result was a map of radioactive activity centered on the buried artifact. The map showed a clear hole, fifty meters in diameter, of no unusual radioactivity directly around the artifact. It was the hole at the heart of the toroid. It was also the reason why everyone could work unsuited in the upland valley.

Beyond that grace area, radiation increased dramatically and irregularly, then tapered off. A whole lot of nuclei around the artifact had destabilized. Which was another way of saying that, at the quantum level, a lot of matter had exceeded the usual probabilities that alpha particles would be emitted from nuclei. Nuclear particles, and the tiny vibrating threads that composed them, like all matter, had a probability field, the sum of wave functions, where they could be found. Part of that probability field lay outside the binding energy barrier. Quantum determinism decreed the probability that any particular event will occur at some chosen time in the future was fully determined by knowledge of the wave functions at any prior time. In the Neury Mountains, that equation did not hold.

Was time the disrupting factor? Nothing in quantum physics mandated a distinction between past and future. But Capelo could see no way to fit that into the data he had.

"Almost there!" Gruber called to his struggling, roped-together team. "Pay attention to your thinking!"

The second set of data was the readings he, Rosalind Singh, and that pig-fat Albemarle had made at the site. These data were more ambiguous. The artifact was made of the same material as the space tunnels. Its interior, from what the team could tell, seemed to feature shadowy folded structures of no mass whatsoever, an impossibility. The buried artifact had the same markings as the much larger artifact Syree Johnson had investigated. Most pertinently, it had the same protuberances, marked in primes. Now, while he was slogging along on this moronic underground trip, Rosalind and Albemarle were setting up computer programs to compare the location of the protuberances with variations in rock radioactivity, adjusted for probable shifts over geologic time.

Syree Johnson's data about the other artifact, the much larger one that had exploded when she tried to send it through a space tunnel, had indicated . . . had indicated . . .

Syree . . .

Sudie . . .

Sudie and . . . and . . . there was another child . . .

Karen, help me . . .

He was falling, upright on his feet. Falling into a blank whiteness. Then there wasn't even the whiteness, there was nothing, not even time.

·   ·   ·

"Tom."

Whiteness.

"Tom."

Blankness.

"Tom."

Whiteness.

"Tom!"

The voice had been saying his name for a long time, he thought confusedly. Who was it? Who was he?

"Tom."

"Yes," he finally said, and the word sounded strange, from another language, or possibly another person.

"Keep walking. Come on, walk."

He had no choice; a rope pulled him forward. Another few steps, and the confusion lifted slightly.

"Walk!" The voice was . . . Lyle. Kaufman. Yes. And he was Tom. Capelo.

"That's better. You're almost out."

Another few steps, and the confusion disappeared.

"Jesus Christ! What just happened to me?"

But Kaufman kept pulling on the rope, helped by the smiling Karim Safir. At the end of the rope Gruber stumbled forward like a sleepwalker. Capelo abruptly sat on the tunnel floor. He had been . . . empty. Mind-blind. Unable to think, or with thinking slowed so much that it felt like the same thing. He watched Gruber being pulled forward, watched consciousness return to Gruber's glazed blue eyes.

Safir said something in Arabic and kept pulling. The other three stumbled through the rest of the tunnel into a larger, comparatively dry cave. They slumped on its floor in the eerie shadows thrown by Gruber's powertorch.

Kaufman spoke first. His voice sounded hoarse. "All right, Gruber. Tell me the theory again. What *was* that?"

"The thickest part of the toroidal field," Gruber said. "Ach, I wish Ann were here. She can explain it so much better."

"You try," Capelo rasped. He heard the panic still inhabiting his own voice. Nothing like that had ever happened to him before. To lose his mind, the only thing he possessed that justified his existence, his only real identity . . . Despite himself, a deep shudder shook him, and he glared at Gruber in embarrassment.

Gruber, of course, didn't notice. He said, "We stumbled into it on the last expedition. No rope to pull us out then, but Enli was with us—she's a native, Tom, and apparently they are not affected as we are. Enli pulled us out. She—"

"Forget Enli," Kaufman said jaggedly, utterly unlike his usual smooth speech. "What just happened to us?"

"Ann can explain it better than I can," Gruber repeated, "but I will try. Syree Johnson's artifact made all atoms with an atomic number over seventy-five destabilize and emit radiation, *ja*? It affected their probability fields. And we think the buried artifact does that, too, maybe. But the brain, too, operates on probability at the quantum level."

"It does?" Kaufman said.

"Yes. The electrical impulses in the brain travel to the ends of cerebral nerves, which then release neurotransmitters into the synapses. But not always. The probability of the exact same voltage causing a release varies from seventeen percent to sixty-two percent. The release is caused by a single atom, so it is a quantum event.

"In fact, more and more it looks like that is how consciousness is born. Through altering probability. There is no other way to explain how a purely mental event, like deciding to stand up, can produce an effect in the material world."

"All right," Kaufman said, "the brain operates on probability. Then—"

"Partly on probability," Gruber corrected.

"Partly on probability," Kaufman repeated. "But why should an artifact that destabilizes atoms to produce radioactivity also wipe out my ability to think? Tom, you aren't saying anything. Are you all right?"

"Yes," Capelo said, unwilling to reveal how shaken he felt. Shattered. What had just happened should not have happened, not by any laws of physics he understood.

Kaufman turned back to Gruber. "Dieter? Why should an artifact that destabilizes atoms to produce radioactivity also wipe out my ability to think?"

"I don't know," Gruber said. "I have only a theory."

Capelo said, more harshly than he intended, "Let's hear it."

Gruber said, "I think the artifact creates also a second kind of probability field. That's the one that affects quantum events in the brain."

"What's your proof?"

"Only what happened to us. And that Enli, whose people evolved here, was not affected at that spot. I think the artifact must generate some sort of field of varying strengths that envelops the entire planet. Ann believes that accounts for the evolution of the shared-reality mechanism in Worlders."

Capelo exploded. "That's not a theory! It's a crackpot lunacy!"

Gruber spat, "Can you do better?"

"Not the point. You don't have any data, or any way to test the data you don't have."

"Yes, I do," Gruber said. "Two ways to test. First, Ann is making Lagerfeld scans of two native brains to compare with our earlier ones. To see if there was any effect from the moment the buried artifact saved World from the wave effect that irradiated Nimitri."

Capelo got to his feet. A familiar rage was starting in him; its very familiarity was comfortable. It was anger at the morons who desecrated science. Who wandered into universities with pathetic "theories" recorded in cheap school computers. Who put out popular flimsies, available for a fee of course, that "explained" the origin of the universe in terms of astrology or numerology or the course of ancient rivers. Who claimed that the existence of angels could be proven mathematically.

"So this buried artifact does everything," he said to Gruber, not hiding his contempt. Why bother? "It destabilizes atoms with an atomic number over seventy-five. It stops other destabilizing waves cold in their wavy tracks. And it generates a secondary probability field that affects brain activity. Can it also conduct an orchestra and take out the trash?"

Gruber rose, too. Before the idiot could answer, Kaufman said quietly from the ground below both of them, "Tom, the destabilizing and wave deflection and mind-blanking were all quantum events. And they all happened."

Capelo looked down at Kaufman's mild, practical, effective face. The man never looked angry, or even annoyed. He never even looked surprised. Kaufman's clear brown eyes held steady under Capelo's gaze.

"Yes, Lyle," Capelo said bleakly. "They're all quantum events, and they all happened."

"Let's head back," Kaufman said.

At the hole, Albemarle, Rosalind Singh, and the techs were still at work mapping exactly how the most radioactive parts of the Neury Mountains compared with the positions of the protuberances on the artifact. The task required computer simulations of fifty thousand years of geologic activity, along with analysis of satellite imaging of the present patterns of radioactivity. Capelo couldn't face any of it just yet, especially Albemarle.

Nor did he want to see Amanda and Sudie. The girls were getting tired of camping out in the cave. Jane Shaw had performed miracles of instruction and amusement, but they were kids, and kids didn't like being cooped up beside an excavation site they were forbidden to go near. Capelo couldn't blame them; he just didn't want to hear any more complaints about it.

He wanted to be alone to think.

The problem was, it was difficult to be alone in the upland valley. Too many people doing too many things. Base camp was worse, and the tunnel system between them had more traffic than New York maglevs. If he wanted to be alone, he would have to hike out of the valley.

It wasn't hard to do. These mountains were low and shallow, with few peaks and many rifts and passes. Capelo put on his hiking boots and took the easiest one upwards, hoping his daughters didn't spot him going and set up a clamor.

After a half hour of climbing, he was breathing hard. The sun beat down on him, and he sat on a convenient boulder, took off his shirt, and panted at the mess humans had made of the Neury Mountains.

The enormous amount of dirt and rock from the excavation site—a quarter-mile down!—had to go somewhere. The digger had simply lifted it out, flown away from the valley, and dumped. The mountainsides, upland meadows, and ravines surrounding the site were smothered in raw rubble. It was ugly and depressing, and Kaufman's only defense was that the natives, who had strong superstitious taboos about the mountains, would never see it. The place looked like a war zone.

The real war was inside Capelo.

Four sets of data. No, five now; what Gruber had made him experience could not really be left out, although calling it "data" was ludicrous. Five sets of information, with no way to integrate them. And possibly the outcome of the war rested on that integration.

He tried to let his mind drift. It was a trick he sometimes used: focus on something irrelevant or empty your mind, and an insight may float up into the emptiness. Henri Poincaré had done it, and Roger Penrose, and the great Salah Majoub.

Capelo focused on a red flower growing on a patch of mountainside that had somehow escaped being dumped on. He let the red flower fill his mind, and then let his mind slide away from it and just drift.

The sun slipped down the sky.

Time slipped by unnoticed.

No insight came.

"Tom?"

Capelo jumped. Kaufman, creeping up behind him. "Don't do that!"

"Sorry. Shall I leave?" Kaufman the considerate, the urbane.

"No, might as well stay. Nothing going on here. What's happening at the hole?"

"Rosalind and Hal want you. The simulations are done. The protuberance marked as setting one seems to match up with the simulated history of geologic shifting of the radioactive veins. The artifact is a directed-beam destabilizer, just as you thought."

Two sets of data integrated, Tom thought, but it brought him no pleasure. He said to Kaufman, "I suppose that means the artifact will make an invaluable weapon."

"Yes."

"One that justifies this entire expedition."

"Oh, yes."

"I'm glad."

Kaufman said, "You don't sound glad, Tom."

"It's a result, Lyle, not a cause. The physics are just as obscure as ever."

Kaufman sat, uninvited, on the rock beside Capelo. "Tell me in simple terms what the physics problem is, please."

Capelo looked at him in frustration. Laymen were always asking for simple explanations of the complex, a vital part of which consisted of math they couldn't follow. This was the same reason Capelo didn't like teaching. Or half his colleagues.

"I know I'm asking a lot," Kaufman said, so humbly that Capelo was trapped.

"All right," he said. "We have four — no, five — sets of data. First, the patterns of excess radioactivity in the mountains, now known to be caused by the artifact. The thing alters the probability that certain nuclei will destabilize. All quantum events can be viewed as changes to topological surfaces created by the vibrating threads that make up the fabric of spacetime. The artifact affects the probability amplitudes, which are computed by summing over all possible topological surfaces.

"In other words, our muddy ball drastically increases the chance that the emitted particle will be found in that part of its probability field outside the energy barrier of the nucleus."

Kaufman said, "So a 'probability amplitude' is just the area that a particle might be found, given the Heisenberg Uncertainty Principle."

There was a lot more to it than that, but Capelo decided to let it go. "More or less. It's clear from Syree Johnson's report that the other artifact, the big one, did the same thing as our smaller one, except that it emitted its destabilizing effect in a spherical wave, not a directed beam. And when it blew, it destabilized a hell of a lot more than atoms above atomic number seventy-five. It blew up Johnson's ship, the enemy's ship, and a few unlucky flyers. And it sent out a destabilizing wave through this entire star system. A probability shockwave, you could call it, since it changed the probability of all sorts of nuclei destabilizing."

"I'm with you," Kaufman said.

"No, you're not, because already I'm not even with me. Or with the physics we know. There's no such thing as a probability shockwave, and nothing in our physics permits the possibility of controlling such a thing if it did exist."

"Well, the space tunnels aren't in our physics, either."

"True enough," Capelo said. "Anyway, the wave hit Nimitri and the next planet, and it did its job there. It rolled on toward World. And then . . . nothing. The wave caused absolutely no measurable effect on World. *Nada.*"

Kaufman said, "Because World is so far away?"

"No. Don't play dumb, Lyle. You already know there was no weakening of the wave effect between Nimitri and the next planet." What was that planet's name? No matter. "World should have been fried. And it wasn't."

"So your working hypothesis is that the artifact buried on World set up a planet-wide probability field of its own that neutralized the wave effect."

This was why he hated talking to laymen. Capelo tried to control his impatience. "That's not a hypothesis, Lyle. That's sheer speculation, expressed in gibberish. It says nothing. What forces are involved? What happens at the level of vibrating threads? What is the mechanism and where is the math? What in hell *happens*? And how does whatever happened fit with the Faller beam-disrupter shield, which also appears to alter probability?"

Kaufman said, "Tell me about that."

Jesus Christ, the man was obtuse. But what better did Capelo have to do? He certainly wasn't getting anywhere with his so-called "work" on the problem.

He said, "The Faller shield does something we also think of as impossible. We fire a beam of protons at a Faller ship. The beam is made of particles, but of course it's also a wave. The ship has the shield. Syree Johnson thought that before the proton beam hits the ship, the shield somehow alters the wave function of the proton beam, making its phase complex just before it hits."

Kaufman echoed stupidly, " 'Makes its phase complex'?"

"The proton beam is supposed to resolve itself into particles the second it hits the observer, which is the ship. As particles, the beam blows the ship to smithereens. But the shield somehow resolves the beam into a wave, according to Johnson. Plus it alters the wave phase to a complexity that doesn't interact with ordinary matter. How does it do that, Lyle? Where does the beam go?"

"I don't know," Kaufman said humbly.

"Nor do I. Nor do I know how this same versatile handy-dandy artifact affected the probability amplitudes of neurotransmitter release in my brain this morning. *If* that's what it did. Haven't a clue."

"Which means you don't have a clue how the artifact will react if we take it away from World entirely."

Capelo turned to gaze full at Kaufman's face. "No. And that's what concerns you, isn't it? You already understood as much physics as I've explained to you. You're too sharp not to have. You got me talking to focus me on your concern, which is using this damn thing as a war weapon."

Kaufman said quietly, "I thought that was your concern, too, Tom. For personal reasons of your own."

Capelo was horrified to feel his eyelids prickle. God, wouldn't this grief over Karen ever lessen? That's all he asked: lessening, not going away completely, which he understood to be impossible. He turned away so that Kaufman wouldn't see him blinking hard.

"Yes, that's my concern, too. If this artifact will blow the Faller bastards out of the sky, I want it to do that. More than you can know. But I also want to know *why* it does that. For physics, but also for control. You can't control your new weapon, Lyle, unless you understand it. You don't know what the hell that thing will do in actual battle conditions. You don't even know what will happen if you try to take it through a space tunnel."

"Neither do I know what will happen to the brains of a planet full of aliens if I remove the artifact that's shaped their brains."

"I haven't even considered that," Capelo said.

"I have," Kaufman said.

"Next to a war involving the future of our own race, I don't think it matters," Capelo said. "We're talking about the future of humanity! This is a war—you're supposed to be the soldier!"

"I am," Kaufman said, but Capelo didn't, or couldn't, hear the complexities in his voice.

TWELVE

BASE CAMP

Kaufman arrived at base camp at the same time as Ann Sikorski, Enli, and four soldiers. He emerged from the tunnels under the mountains; the others approached across the grassy, fertile plain that remained untilled only because as yet World did not need the space. The soldiers were led by Captain Heller, looking even grimmer than usual.

Although how would you tell? Even for a security chief, a notably suspicious lot, Heller was pessimistic. She had not wanted Ann to visit David Campbell Allen's grave, a visit that the aliens apparently considered absolutely necessary. Kaufman had not disagreed; he wanted to do nothing that would hint to Voratur, or to the shadowy priest "Servants of the First Flower," that humans were not completely of the same mind as Worlders. Shared reality.

Captain Heller, on the other hand, had objected strenuously to permitting a key member of the project team to leave the immediate area of the base and venture into totally unscouted habitats. She did not, she had informed Kaufman, "give a three-handed fuck about shared reality."

After Kaufman had mildly forced her to accept that Ann was

going, Heller had next wanted a dozen conspicuously armed soldiers to escort her. They had compromised on four soldiers, unobtrusively carrying laser pistols, tanglefoam, and nervewash. Kaufman failed to convince Heller that the natives were unarmed, unbellicose, and unsuspicious of humans now that humans were real again.

" 'Unsuspicious?' " Heller had said, suspicious.

" 'We see the universe not as it is, but as we are,' " Kaufman had quoted, but this had been lost on Captain Heller.

Now she approached with an apparently unharmed Ann, who trudged along tiredly. Kaufman had vetoed the use of land mobiles as too alien to Worlders, and Heller had vetoed the use of bicycles as leaving her soldiers too vulnerable. Kaufman suspected that Heller did not know how to ride a bicycle, an antiquated artifact even on Earth. Heller had been born in the Belt.

From the opposite direction, Voratur and his son sped along on what were clearly Terran bicycles from the last expedition. Both groups arrived together.

"Pek Voratur!" Ann called. "May your blossoms flourish in sunlight!"

"May your garden delight the First Flower," Voratur answered. "And yours, Pek Kaufman!"

"May your garden bloom," Kaufman said, in his carefully memorized World. It seemed to him that Voratur looked nervous, although Kaufman wasn't familiar enough with alien expressions to be sure.

How was Marbet doing with the Faller's expressions? All Kaufman had had from her since his visit were short, curt reports in routine language. He hadn't had time to review the holorecordings of her sessions with the prisoner.

Hospitality flowers were exchanged: pajalib and allabenirib. Kaufman was learning the strange, all-important names. Then Ann led them all into the foamhut where her equipment for the Lagerfeld scans was already set up.

Voratur said something, and Kaufman looked at Ann. She translated. "He says he remembers this metal hat from last time. He's
nervous but willing. Enli, don't be afraid."

The female alien said nothing.

Ann switched back to World, and Kaufman could not follow.
Voratur sat on a low pillow with his back to the equipment. Carefully
Ann lowered the helmet onto his head. It adjusted itself to fit snugly
over his scalp, neck, and forehead, leaving his face clear. Ann began
to ask Voratur questions in her low, soothing voice. At least it
sounded soothing to Kaufman; he had no way of knowing how it
sounded to the alien.

Kaufman did know roughly how the Lagerfeld scan worked.
Hundreds of minute electrodes were sliding into place on Voratur's
bald head and through his neckfur. Tiny needles carrying their own
anesthetic would also sample blood, cerebrospinal fluid, even sweat.
But the most useful data would come from the MOSS component
of the Lagerfeld.

MOSS—"Multi-layer Organ Structure Scan"—delivered almost
neuron-by-neuron detail of the brain in action. Which cells were
activated, which neurotransmitters were released, which neuron-
firing patterns emerged. Receptor-cell docking, transmitter reuptake,
enzyme cascades, substance breakdown and by-products . . . MOSS
captured it all, analyzed the data in multiple ways and delivered equations and formulae to explain them. It did everything but synthesize
pills and put labels on the bottle. The result was a virtual fingerprint
of the workings of an individual brain in reaction to various stimuli.

The stimuli were the questions Ann asked Voratur. Think about
a beautiful garden, about a good meal, about falling off your bicycle
and breaking your back . . . on and on. Ann had all the data from
the earlier scan of Voratur's brain for comparison.

Soshaf Voratur and Enli chanted fervently, words meaningless
to Kaufman. On the Lagerfeld display screen, graphs flickered, also
meaningless. Sweat broke out on Voratur's face. Evidently he found

this very stressful, perhaps even dangerous. The alien was a brave man.

Next Ann offered him concrete items to react to: food, tools, flowers. All trace of weariness had vanished from her face. After fifteen minutes she smiled brilliantly and removed the helmet from Voratur, who sprang up as if made of rubber.

Enli took his place. For the first time, Kaufman wondered about Ann's insistence on including a brainscan of Enli in their bargaining with Voratur. Ann had no base data for Enli. What was she looking for?

Now it was Soshaf and Voratur who chanted, swaying on their pillows. Kaufman found his mind moving away from what Ann was saying now to what she was going to say later. It would not be pleasant. Kaufman hadn't told her about the findings at the excavation site. She didn't yet know that the buried artifact was most likely a directed-beam weapon. Or that it would probably be taken off-planet.

What if she and Gruber were right, and it somehow created a secondary probability field that had shaped these aliens' brains?

Only a theory. No data.

God, he sounded like Capelo.

What was Marbet doing, aboard the *Alan B. Shepard*?

"We're finished," Ann said in English. She removed the helmet. Unlike Voratur, Enli did not bounce joyfully off the floor pillow. She rose slowly, gravely, and the flesh between her eyes wrinkled. Her skull ridges creased. Now that Kaufman looked, he saw that Voratur's smooth, oiled flesh wrinkled in the same way.

Head pain. The Lagerfeld scans represented some sort of un-shared reality, however minor, and that had given the two aliens — no, three, Soshaf also had creased forehead and skull ridges — massive headaches. They must have known it would. Bravery indeed.

Or greed. Voratur said something to Ann, then put his hands to his head. Ann turned to Kaufman.

"Give them the six comlinks, Lyle, so they can leave. This is very painful for all of them."

Despite his head pain, Voratur's eyes gleamed as Kaufman handed him the small black boxes. He expected to show Voratur how they worked, but Voratur didn't ask. He said something to Soshaf, who took one of the boxes and moved outside the hut. Expertly Voratur opened the link and spoke in World. Soshaf's voice sounded back, and Voratur broke into a huge grin that needed no interpretation by anybody.

In thirty more seconds, with only minimum flower exchanging, the three aliens bicycled away.

"Well," Kaufman said, "speedy diplomacy, at least."

Ann said stubbornly, "They should not have those comlinks."

"Then you would not have your Lagerfeld data. And the comlinks won't affect their overall society very much. Really. If they take the comlinks apart, they won't discover anything useful to them—these people are centuries from microchips." He considered this, wondered if it were true, and changed the subject. "Tell me what you learned at David Allen's grave."

Ann was clearly impatient to get to her data. But she sat down on the pillow Enli had vacated. "What do you know about David Allen, Lyle?"

"That he was the graduate student with the previous expedition. That he got the position only because his very influential father pulled strings. That when all of you were hiding in the Neury Mountains because the Worlders had declared you unreal, David Allen took Gruber's gun and kidnapped Enli, and neither of them was ever heard from again. A few days later a flyer picked up you others and lifted you off-planet."

"Yes. And so we still believed humans were thought to be unreal," Ann said. "But it turns out we were real again to Worlders. Because of what David did."

"What did he do?"

She pushed back a few strands of the long fair hair that had come loose from her topknot. Not really pretty—her face was long and her features too small—Ann Sikorski nonetheless had one of the most attractive faces Kaufman had ever seen. For its kindness, for the steady integrity in her pale eyes. Precisely the qualities he was going to have to outrage a few minutes from now.

She said, "When David took Enli and left us in the middle of the night, we all knew that Tas—the artifact Syree Johnson had moved out of orbit—might blow if Johnson tried to take it through the space tunnel. The mass was too great. Gruber worked it out for us, because Johnson was giving out minimum information to us anthropologists on the planet. Like most military."

Kaufman didn't reply to the dig, but he noted it. It wasn't like Ann. She was really upset about the comlinks.

"David was . . . in an excitable state," Ann continued. Again Kaufman said nothing. The planetside team leader, Dr. Bazargan, had said in his report that Allen had developed a full-blown grandiose paranoia.

"He took Enli to the closest village and together they told the villagers that a 'sky sickness' was coming. That's how he described the wave effect. He said he'd been told about the sky sickness by the First Flower while he was in the Neury Mountains."

"Why did they believe him?"

Ann smiled wanly. In that smile Kaufman saw that she had liked David Allen, no matter what he had been. She said, "It's a paradox. They believed him because Enli had also been in the Neury Mountains and yet wasn't sick, which was clearly a miracle from the First Flower. And also because David *was* sick, sick enough from radiation poisoning that he died, and so clearly he gave his life to warn everyone else. Anyone who dies for another is real. And so, by extension, are the rest of us humans."

"I see."

"The Worlders listened to him. They sent word around the

entire planet, using their sunflasher network, and by twenty-four hours later they were all holed up underground. Eventually they came out, found themselves unharmed, and made Enli real again and David a hero. I saw the flower altar they erected to him."

It made sense, given the Worlder beliefs. They wouldn't know about the s-suit that had protected Enli from radiation in the mountains, or about David's mental state, or about the wave effect's mysteriously not having any effect whatsoever on World, aboveground or below.

He said, "The outcome was fortunate for this expedition, anyway. Worlders have let us come in peace."

"Yes," Ann said, "and in return you're going to destroy their entire civilization."

So here it was. Kaufman had hoped to postpone this discussion, but he realized now how stupid that hope had been. "You talked by comlink to Dieter."

"Of course I talked to Dieter. He's jubilant that the mapping of the radioactivity patterns match the simulated seismic shifts of the artifact's protuberances. It's a directed beam destabilizer, isn't it? Or can be used as one?"

"Yes," Kaufman said.

"And so you're going to take it to a war zone."

"Probably."

"At the very least," Ann said, "you're going to remove it into space to test it, aren't you?"

Kaufman evaded. "That's not clear yet. We may do some on-planet tests. And, of course, we may be wrong."

"You *are* wrong," Ann said bitterly. "You're wrong to think you can just remove at your pleasure something that's holding together the entire fabric of Worlder society!"

"You don't know that."

"Yes, I do!" She jumped up from her pillow, forcing Kaufman to also stand. They stood facing each other, inches apart. "The shared-reality mechanism has evolved here and nowhere else in the galaxy. When Enli was in the dead 'eye' of its field, right above it, she had no head pain no matter how many unshared concepts were discussed. When you went into the thickest part of its field, your brain stopped thinking entirely—yes, Dieter told me that, too. The buried artifact affects thinking, Lyle! And these people have had it affect theirs throughout their entire evolution. What will happen to them if you remove it, and they no longer have operable shared-reality in their brains?"

They'll get fewer headaches, Kaufman thought, but didn't say it aloud. Ann Sikorski had genuine empathy. She cared what happened to the aliens.

He suddenly wondered what Marbet would be feeling about them if she were planetside.

"Ann, let me just make two points," he said quietly. "First, let's assume you're right and the aliens have evolved their shared-reality mechanism because of some planet-wide field generated by the artifact. If it's truly an evolved brain pattern, then it's in their genome and will continue just as if the artifact were still there."

"No! It's an evolved mechanism designed to operate only in the presence of the field! Otherwise, Enli wouldn't have felt no head pain in the field's eye!"

"Second, if what you just said is true, then removing that field will have no more effect on all the Worlders than it did on Enli. She wasn't harmed in what you call the 'eye.' She merely didn't have head pain. But she still felt healthy, acted normal, thought without difficulty. She wasn't harmed, and neither will the rest of the aliens."

Ann's pale face flamed with anger. "You're being deliberately obtuse, Lyle, and you know it. It isn't their individual selves that will be destroyed if you remove that artifact, although I'm by no means convinced that they're all as mentally resilient as Enli. What will be destroyed is their entire society. Every single one of their social patterns is built on shared reality. *Every single one*. If you remove shared reality, you destroy their patterns of interacting, of trading, of raising children, of mating, of all economic and political structures. Violence will emerge, with no social controls on it, because none were ever necessary before. Can you imagine what that will mean?"

"Nothing happened to Voratur when the first wave effect, the one that destroyed Nimitri, hit World. You just told me that at least at first look, Voratur's Lagerfeld scan matches the one you took of him on your first expedition."

"If they match, it's because the artifact was there! It protected the Worlders from the wave effect!"

"Now *that* you don't know. That's speculation. We have no proof it was the buried artifact that resulted in no change in brain scans."

She was silent; he was right about that. Kaufman pressed his advantage. "Have you discussed this with Dieter?"

She said, so bitterly that Kaufman knew husband and wife had quarreled over this, "Dieter's not an anthropologist. He's a geologist."

And I'm a soldier. "Ann, we're at war. And we're losing."

"Does that justify destroying another race's entire civilization?"

"Yes," Kaufman said, and knew he believed it, and disliked himself for believing it and Ann for making him aware of the fact. He looked at her with distaste.

"You're finally registering emotion, Lyle. Look at you. You don't think removing the artifact is right, either."

"I think it's necessary."

"It's not ours! It's theirs!"

There was no answer to that, and nowhere else for the discussion to go except into personal acrimony. Kaufman turned to leave. But Ann surprised him.

"Wait. I want to make a request."

He turned back to face her. "What is it?"

"Before you remove the artifact, let me take Enli, Voratur, and at least six other Worlders away from the field, to see what happens to them. For at least twenty-four hours, so I can observe their interactions when they no longer have shared reality. Let me take them up to the *Alan B. Shepard*."

It was the last thing Kaufman had expected. "It's against all regs. And a full-scale contamination of their society, too. You even objected to giving them comlinks."

"That was before I was sure you were going to do far worse damage by removing the artifact."

Kaufman was thinking fast. Grafton would have a fit, of course. But this clearly came under Special Projects authority. If the aliens came up out of their "field" and didn't kill each other, it might get Ann on Kaufman's side. On the other hand, if they *did* end up killing each other, he would definitely lose support. How would it play at Headquarters? Probably that he had gathered all possible information before making his decision, which was always good.

Stalling, he said, "You suspected this might happen, Ann. That's why you bargained for a Lagerfeld scan for Enli as well as Voratur. You wanted additional baseline data."

"Yes."

"To get—how many?—eight or ten aliens to agree to go into space, we'd have to give Voratur . . . I don't know what. A lot of trade goods. I thought you didn't want to further contaminate their culture."

"Better to contaminate it than wipe it out completely," Ann said. God, she was stubborn. One of those people who lose all mildness when they believe they're on the side of the angels.

"Besides, Lyle," she said, and now she looked not furious but shrewd, "don't you want to know how the Worlders will react? In the name of science? Aren't you the big science worshipper?"

She had let shrewdness slide into sarcasm. But she was right; Kaufman wanted to know. And if he lifted the artifact into space with no human observer on the planet (no reason to leave anyone behind), he would never know.

"All right," he said. "If you can get the aliens to agree, a maximum of ten of them can be lifted to the ship for an observation period of no more than thirty-six hours, confined to a secure area that has been cleared of all advanced technology."

"Thank you," Ann said, and from her smile, Kaufman saw suddenly that he had made a bad mistake. She was certain that if the Worlders were badly affected by being away from their artifact, Kaufman would change his mind about removing it from World. She was wrong. Kaufman knew he would not change his mind.

He didn't tell her that. Never enrage an ally—even a deluded ally—until you absolutely had to. Instead, he went to comlink Grafton that there were going to be more aliens aboard his strictly regulation, severely Navy ship.

THIRTEEN

IN THE NEURY MOUNTAINS

apelo didn't know what to do with Amanda and Sudie while the artifact was being lifted out of its hole.

Even he recognized that this was a bizarre reason to hold up the greatest scientific find in human history. But the problem was real. He couldn't keep them with him in the valley; nobody knew what this alien son-of-a-bitch would do when they hoisted it. Even base camp was too close, not to mention having its perimeter down. That left only sending them back up to the *Alan B. Shepard*, which would move to the relative safety of the other side of the planet. Just in case. But Capelo cringed at asking Kaufman to send the shuttle up just for Sudie and Amanda. Kaufman, who didn't have kids and didn't like kids and had told him not to bring his kids down from the ship in the first place.

Nonetheless, Capelo had no choice. He comlinked Kaufman. "Lyle? I have a favor to ask. I don't want my daughters here for the artifact hoist tomorrow, or even at camp. Can they go back up on the shuttle?" More curt than he'd intended. But Capelo hated asking favors.

To his surprise, Kaufman said, "Sure, Tom. The shuttle's leaving anyway in a few hours."

It was? That was not according to plan. But Capelo was too tired for questions. He hadn't had a good night's sleep in days. Well, the plan was to get one tonight and then hoist the artifact out of its hole tomorrow morning. And he'd certainly sleep better if he didn't have to worry about the girls. Still, it wasn't like Kaufman, that supreme diplomat, to simply agree to requests without negotiating something in return.

"Thanks, Lyle. We'll be there."

Now all he had to do was stay awake long enough to walk the girls through the tunnel system to the shuttle. He shambled to the shallow cave which camping out had made their temporary home. Amanda sat at the cave mouth working on her schoolscreen, her shadow long from the lowering sun. Sudie, farther back with Jane Shaw, was playing some kind of game with glittery rocks. Capelo knew what those were. The girls' possessions lay scattered all over the ground.

"C'mon, Mandy, we're moving house. Pack up your old kit bag."

Amanda looked up. "Moving? Where, Daddy?"

"Back to base camp."

"Why?" Amanda said. Always the logical child. Capelo looked with exhausted love at her smooth fair braids. The older she grew, the more she looked like Karen.

"Back to base camp. And then on the shuttle up to the ship."

Jane Shaw had heard. She looked inquiringly at Tom. "For safety?"

"Yes."

Jane—what would he do without Jane?—immediately began gathering up clothing and toys. But Amanda said, "I don't want to go up, Daddy. I want to see the artifact lifted out of the hole."

"It's too dangerous, honey. You'll be safer aboard ship."

"Safety is not the primary fact of a scientific life."

It was something he had said to her. Pride fought with irritation. "You're not a scientist."

"I want to be one someday!"

"Well, you're not one now. Pack up."

Sudie started to cry. "I want to stay with Daddy!"

"Sudie . . . not now, for the love of God!"

"You don't believe in God," Amanda said primly.

"I want to stay with Daddy!" Sudie rushed forward and threw her arms around his knees, almost knocking him over.

Capelo glared down at the top of her head, which was dirty. Sudie had taken to camping out like the small savage she was. She'd exuded hectic, extravagant squalor. In the last light of the sun, her springy filthy hair stood out from her head, glinting like iron filings.

Amanda said, "I know! We could stay in the vug!"

"The vug! The vug!" Sudie cried. "I want to stay in the vug!"

"You can't stay in the vug," Capelo said firmly. The vug had already caused enough problems.

Gruber had discovered the vug on his first expedition. He offered to lead them to it, promising a fairly easy trip through ample tunnels and a spectacular surprise at the end. Capelo had agreed only because Amanda and Sudie had been so bored, confined to their camping cave in the upland valley. He hadn't expected much.

Gruber had kept his powertorch trained unusually low until they were traversing a medium-sized cave. Then he abruptly stopped, turned the torch to maximum light, and swung it toward the ceiling. "Look!"

Capelo gasped. The children screamed with delight. Jewels sparkled on the cave ceiling, on the walls, in heaps on the floor. As his dazzled eyes adjusted to the bright light, he saw that the jewels were millions of gold crystals. Spattered among them were glowing flakes of pure gold as big as thumbnails. Gold nuggets glittered on the floor. Piles of white quartz sand glowed like spun glass.

"This is the vug," Dieter said happily. "The biggest one I have ever heard of!"

"What . . . how . . ." Capelo sputtered.

"It is the inside of a geode. There must have been the caldera of a volcano right here, once. The gold precipitates out from circulating water heated by magma."

Capelo touched a wall. Gold flaked over his fingers like shining rain.

"It's incredible."

"Is it not?" Gruber said, swinging his torch proprietarily around the walls.

Amanda and Sudie raced to the walls. Gruber was so pleased with the effect of his surprise that he let the girls stuff the pockets of their miniature s-suits with gold and jewels.

Capelo said, "How long has this been here? When did it form?"

"Hundreds of thousands of years ago."

"And the natives haven't ever found it and mined it?"

"It is forbidden for them to enter the sacred mountains. Also, they would have learned centuries ago that the mountains gave them radiation sickness. A good example of religious taboo guarding health!" Gruber laughed.

"That's enough, girls," Capelo said. "Don't be greedy." But he had taken a sparkling diamond for himself. It would be valuable on Mars, but not as valuable as the glittery gems were right here on World. They kept Amanda and Sudie absorbed, inventing endless games that occupied them and saved Jane Shaw's sanity.

The problem was that ever since that trip, the girls had begged constantly to return to the vug. Kaufman, mildly tight-lipped, had vetoed this. "Tom, Dieter never should have taken you three there in the first place. We're trying to physically disturb World as little as possible. Certainly not to thieve from it."

"We've strip-mined their so-called sacred mountains!"

"I know," Kaufman said wearily. "Unavoidable necessity. Carrying off native wealth is not. Your daughters can keep their gems, but no more trips to the vug. I've told Dieter so."

Sanctimonious hypocrite. Capelo had been half tempted to take Amanda and Sudie back anyway, by himself. But he'd been too busy, and he wasn't sure of the tunnels, and the faithful Jane had been the one to take the brunt of Sudie's wheedling and begging.

Now Jane said briskly, "We're going on the shuttle, girls, just as your father said. Sudie, are you forgetting that Marbet's aboard the ship? She's been there all this time. I wonder what she's been doing?"

Sudie instantly unclasped Capelo's knees. "Marbet?"

"Do you think she's programmed that halo lion she promised you?"

"I want to see," Sudie said, and began picking up her things and stuffing them in her bag, a model of obedience.

"I'll go," Amanda said, "but I don't like it."

"Understood," Capelo said, somewhere between gratitude and exasperation.

The trip through the mountain tunnels was uneventful. By now the route between valley and base camp had been used so much that it had developed litter and graffiti, both against orders. Capelo passed a scrawl that said PHYSICS AIN'T PHYSICAL ENOUGH FOR ME. He grinned; no wonder he liked crew better than officers. The crudely scratched grumble cheered him up.

The cheer faded when they emerged from the last tunnel, walked to the shuttle area, and found Ann Sikorski and Lyle Kaufman inexplicably standing beside the shuttle with nine aliens.

With nine aliens.

"Wait here," he snapped at Jane. "Kaufman! Wait!"

The colonel turned, spotted Capelo, and hastily walked toward him and away from the aliens.

"What the hell's going on here!"

Kaufman said, "These natives are going up to the *Shepard* as part of Dr. Sikorski's research."

"Boarding a Navy ship? What kind of research is that?"

"Dr. Sikorski's. Tom, stop shouting."

"My kids are going on that ship!"

"And so are the aliens, and Ann, and me, and a security team, and you, if you want to. The shuttle will return in plenty of time for tomorrow's hoist."

"I don't want my daughters traveling with a bunch of aliens nobody knows anything about."

"Then leave your daughters here," Kaufman said. "And as it happens, we know a great deal about Worlders, including the fact that they're peaceful. Aboard the shuttle they will be strapped in. On ship they will be segregated from everyone but Ann and her security team. And if you don't like it, Tom, either stay here or stay quiet. I have enough to contend with without flack from you. And the natives are nervous enough already."

Rage filled Capelo. He struggled to hold it in check, to speak calmly. "But why are they going up?"

"To see how they behave away from the buried artifact. Out of its field."

"Oh, God, not this again. Not the undetectable-field-affects-all-Worlders'-brains theory again."

Kaufman said nothing. Capelo said, "Then how do you know the absence of this hypothetical field won't drive them all berserk? God, I can't believe I'm even discussing this lunacy."

"Then don't discuss it. I didn't come several hundred light years to argue with you."

"I did. Arguing was my sole purpose in coming to this rat's ass end of the galaxy. Okay, Kaufman, you win. But let me know that the aliens are all strapped in before I bring Amanda and Sudie aboard." These same aliens had once slit the throats of two human kids.

"Of course," Kaufman said. A gracious winner. Damn him.

Capelo walked back to the girls. "There are going to be aliens—
natives—going up to the ship with you."

"Really?" Amanda said. "Great! Can I talk to them?"

"They don't speak English." Was that true? Of all of them?

"Come on, Daddy, let's hurry up!"

He held them back, with Jane's help, until Kaufman signaled
from the shuttle ramp. The aliens filled the passenger chairs, grim-
acing horribly, wrinkling their bald skulls, and *singing*. No, chanting.
Capelo kept a firm grip on Sudie, who wanted to rush over and
make friends. Amanda studied the aliens carefully. Capelo let Jane
do all the work of strapping the kids in. He was so tired.

"They're chanting a ritual song requesting strength in undertak-
ing some dangerous task," Ann Sikorski explained.

"I thought there was no danger among the ever-peaceful Worlders," Capelo retorted.

"It applies to dangers such as climbing down cliffs after bird
eggs."

Capelo lay back in his own chair and strapped himself in. Bird
eggs. The artifact like a huge egg, ready to be lifted off a cliff, although of course these primitives didn't know that. The artifact
marked in primes, protuberances marked in primes, probability amplitudes that—

He was asleep.

Exhausted past any normal meaning of the word, Capelo slept
through the alien chanting, the shuttle takeoff, its docking with the
Alan B. Shepard, the transfer of passengers, and Amanda and Sudie's
light farewell kisses. He slept through the trip back down, awaking
only when the shuttle screamed its way back into the atmosphere
and landed beside base camp. By then it was morning, a bright cool
morning of the day they would hoist the artifact, wrench it free from
the secret dark place where it had lain for fifty thousand years.

· · ·

Kaufman's nerves had been fraying since Grafton's comlink, an hour before shuttle departure. Kaufman knew they were fraying. He knew, from long practice, how to compensate. So there was no reason for him to have been so peremptory and antagonistic with Tom Capelo.

Fortunately, the physicist was always so peremptory and antagonistic himself that he seemed not to have noticed.

Grafton had not even offered any greeting. "Colonel Kaufman, I require your presence immediately aboard ship."

"Are we under attack?" A not-so-subtle reminder to Grafton that under any other circumstance, Kaufman was still running this show.

"We are not. But your 'researcher,' Ms. Grant, has violated military orders. Since she is a civilian and I am not allowed to throw her in the brig for anything less than treason, I require you to come up and discipline her."

"What has she done?"

"She has freed one hand of the prisoner Faller. Against, as I understand it, your express orders."

It took Kaufman's breath away. He hadn't expected it of Marbet, hadn't seen it coming. "Is she physically unharmed?"

"Yes."

"Has anyone else been harmed?"

"No."

"Has the Faller attempted to kill himself?"

"No."

"What is the Faller's current status?"

"The hand has been retied. Despite Ms. Grant's threatening to physically attack any tech who tried to resecure the prisoner. Which she tried to do, until restrained by MPs."

Oh, Lord. Kaufman said, "Thank you, Commander. Please leave the situation at status quo until I arrive. ETA available from Captain DeVolites."

"As you wish." Grafton's voice could have frozen glaciers. It hadn't seemed the right time to tell him that the shuttle was bringing nine natives up to his ship.

As soon as docking was completed, Kaufman was through the lock. Grafton was not on hand to meet him. Kaufman gave orders to the gaping OOD about housing the Worlders according to Ann Sikorski's instructions. Then he went straight to the closed bay where the Faller was imprisoned, looking for Marbet Grant.

FOURTEEN

ABOARD THE *ALAN B. SHEPARD*

They had left at dusk for the Terran camp, pumping away on the best bicycles Enli had ever seen, or ridden. Two moons were already up, Cut and Obri, and the sun set in a clear cool sky. Flowers lined the road. In Gofkit Jemloe they were garden flowers, lovingly planted: showy red jellitib, lacy trifalitib, the cluster blossoms of orange allabenirib, the hospitality flower. Later, in the farmlands, came wildflowers, the ubiquitous mittib and, in the shade, vekifirib in all the colors of World. Enli saw how the others drank up the sight of the flowers. She knew what they were thinking: This might be the last time any of them ever saw flowers.

She could have told them different.

Terrans may or may not fully share reality (head pain: don't think about it). They could *lie*, that difficult act for which there was no good word in World. They could die, or be killed, or kill. But their machines didn't fail. If they said the metal flying boat would take them up in the sky and bring them back safely, then it would.

Earlier that day, Pek Voratur had called together his entire household in the great central garden. A gardener, covered with good loam and smelling of rosib, asked Enli, "Do you know why he wants us?"

"No."

"Have any more of those big Terrans come today? They look so strange, without even decent neckfur! And they smell odd. When they come, I try to plant in a different garden."

"No more Terrans came today," Enli said.

"Good. But they do grow lovely flowers, I will say that for them—look at those rosib they traded Pek Voratur!" He gazed admiringly at the red, pink, and white blooms on their long thorny stems, which he himself had probably nurtured.

"People of the household of Voratur," Pek Voratur said when everyone was present. His large bulk balanced, Soshaf beside him, on an upended vegetable crate. Alu Pek Voratur was still in childbed. "I bring you here to share reality of a trade with the Terrans."

People glanced at their neighbors; traders did not inform every servant in the household of their trading bargains.

"The Terran head of their household, Lyle Pek Kaufman, has called me on my *comlink*," Voratur said importantly. "He offers to plant a trade with me. He would like ten people today to travel in their metal flying boat up into the sky to a larger boat, stay two days, and come back home."

Loud exclamations broke out in the crowd: "To the sky!" "By the First Flower—what will those people do next!" "I'm not going!" "Ten people! Why?"

Voratur flapped his arms for quiet. "One of the ten will be me. Another place is already claimed. Soshaf Pek Voratur will stay here." *In case I die*, he didn't say, but everyone heard it anyway. "The others must choose to go."

"What will they trade us for going?" someone called.

Voratur smiled. "Ah, that is the best part. I have told them I will not plant a bargain with them until I see what trading goods they have in the larger flying boat. We will bargain then. But whatever bargain I plant, there will be profit for all who go. One-half for the household of Voratur, the other half to be divided equally among those who make the journey."

The crowd buzzed. Half the profits to be divided equally among the travelers! Voratur was the best trader on World; one eighteenth of whatever bargain he planted might be more than anyone had owned before, or his mother before him. But to go into the sky . . .

"I will go," a woman called out from the back of the crowd.

"And I," said Telif Pek Forbin, Voratur's head gardener. The undergardener standing beside Enli stared incredulously.

"Let me go!" cried a child, to nervous laughter.

In the end, there were seven volunteers, not eight. The Terrans would have to make do with that. Enli waited quietly for Pek Voratur to turn to her. When the others had been sent to the bicycle shed, he did.

"Enli . . . the last place on the flying boat . . . Pek Kaufman said it must be yours, as translator."

"I know," Enli said, and Pek Voratur nodded. There was no need to discuss the decision; it was shared reality. That satisfied Voratur. Only Enli wondered how long reality would continue to be shared with the Terrans.

Head pain.

She went to choose a bicycle for the trip to the Terran camp.

"All right," Ann Pek Sikorski said in World, "come with me, please."

The nine Worlders huddled together, singing the request for the protection of the First Flower. The beautiful chant quieted Enli a little. She had never seen the flying boat so close up. It was not as big as the family wing of the Voratur compound. A ramp, like those used to help farmcarts up slippery slopes, led to a shadowy inside.

A short distance away, Lyle Pek Kaufman stood being shouted

at by a Terran whom Enli had not seen before. The man was shorter than Pek Kaufman, very dirty, and very angry. With him stood a woman and two female Terran children, eagerly watching the Worlders. Enli stopped singing long enough to risk smiling at them. The older one smiled back.

Pek Kaufman finished arguing and walked up to Ann. "All right, take them aboard."

"What did he say?" Pek Voratur demanded of Enli.

"We go into the flying boat now."

The singing grew louder. Holding hands, skull ridges creased and neckfur bristling, the nine Worlders stumbled into an alien machine. Enli felt her stomach clench.

The inside of the flying boat was much smaller; evidently most of the space lay behind doors. The flying boat was lit inside, although Enli saw no lamps. Seats were arranged in straight ugly rows. In the center seat of the first row sat a man with utensils and moving pictures in front of him like those on the Lagerfeld machine; he must steer the boat. But how? There were no oars, no wings, nothing to navigate the currents of the wind. Which the flying boat was far too heavy to sail on anyway.

"This is Nick Pek DeVolites," Ann said in her accented World. What strange names Terrans had! Pek DeVolites held out a yellow hospitality flower. He did it more awkwardly than anyone Enli had ever seen. Pek Voratur presented his gift flowers, his fleshy oiled hands visibly shaking.

"Sit here," Ann said, "and here . . . and here . . . that's good. Are you comfortable? I must lock these straps onto you, for safety . . ."

The head gardener, Pek Forbin, said, trying to mask fear, "Will the currents of the wind be rough sailing?"

"We hope not," Ann said. "There . . . are you comfortable? Enli?"

"My soil is good," Enli answered.

When everyone was tied in, the shouting man came into the

boat with the older woman and the two little girls. Up close, the man looked even dirtier and wearier. The little girls looked as if they wanted to talk but had been told not to. The younger was very small, and almost as dirty as the man. The older girl had smooth fair hair like Pek Sikorski—her niece, perhaps? Ann did not introduce any of them, bad manners that Enli had never seen from her before. The older woman tied the children down, and then herself. That made the Worlders feel better; the tying must be all right if the Terrans did it to their own children.

Ann and Pek Kaufman took the seats on either side of Pek DeVolites, who said, "We're away." The door closed, there was a noise like a hundred bicycle wheels grinding, and the boat began to move, faster and faster, until it rose into the air.

All the Worlders fell silent, too frightened even to chant.

Beyond the window in front of Pek DeVolites was sky. Then clouds. The metal boat screamed—surely it was coming apart! Then the boat flew through the clouds—to be above the clouds!—and Enli closed her eyes. When she opened them again, the black sky was full of stars, and the moons Cut and Obri glowed larger and brighter than she had ever imagined. Obri, first home of the First Flower, who had unfolded her petals to create World. Reverence swept over Enli. She began to chant the creation song, most sacred of the holy chants.

Pek Voratur began to sing a sky-watching song.

The gardener resumed chanting the First Flower protection tune.

Asto Pek Valifin, a cook's assistant, started a work song.

Everyone fell silent. They twisted in their straps to look at each other, eyes wide. Neckfur bristled. This was not possible. Songs always began together, or just a few notes after each other, the same songs, the song right for the occasion. The song that, once heard, felt right. Shared reality.

Pek Valifin sang another few faltering notes. No one followed. She stopped.

There was no head pain.

Enli saw Ann watching closely. Was this, then, why the Terrans had brought the Worlders here, far into the sky? To break shared reality? The Terrans had always been fascinated by shared reality, especially Pek Sikorski. But of the nine Worlders aboard, only Enli knew that, and the unshared reality should have been giving her terrible head pain.

There was no pain at all.

She grappled with this, saw the others doing the same thing, saw the fear on their faces. This could not be. No one spoke.

Finally a high clear voice said, "Hi. I'm Sudie Capelo. I'm five."

"Sudie, Daddy said—"

"Daddy and Jane are asleep," the child said, and all the Worlders turned to look at her desperately, the smiling dirty child, bouncing a little in her straps, the most solid thing in a world suddenly as insubstantial as empty air.

"We are dead," the head gardener said. "And this is the world of our ancestors."

"No," Ann Sikorski said gently, "you are not dead. Truly."

"Where is shared reality? I am unreal!" He began to wail. No one joined in, which only made their numb terror worse.

The flying boat had stopped. It was now joined to a larger flying boat, one as huge as a village, but only Enli had noticed this. The others were too terrified.

Ann said, "You are not unreal. None of you are unreal. When we go back to World, shared reality will return to you. I promise this."

Voratur said, "Reality cannot 'return'! It does not come and go!

It always *is*, or it is not reality." Sweat beaded on his oiled forehead. "Why do I feel no head pain at this unreality here?"

Ann said, still in that same kind voice, "Shared reality, complete with head pain, will return to you on World. I promise this. Nick," she added in Terran, "switch the viewscreen direction to show the planet."

Pek DeVolites did something to the window, and it suddenly faced in a different direction. Another impossibility.

"Look, Pek Voratur," Ann said. "Look at your World."

It lay as if just beyond the window, filling it, indescribably beautiful. Clouds, seas, the dull purple of land . . . the sweetest blossom of the First Flower, as no Worlder had ever seen it before. Even the hysterical gardener stood still, his mouth open.

"Why did they all stop talking?" the younger child said.

The older one answered, "Because they never saw their planet from space before."

"It's just a planet," the child said. "I'm hungry."

"Shut up, Sudie."

"Don't say shut up to me! Daddy, Amanda said shut up to me!"

The Worlders went on gazing at their home, where shared reality still lived, while the Terrans did incomprehensible things to the flying boats.

Eventually the Worlders were led through a little metal hallway into the larger boat, then to a big room with no windows and nine pallets on the floor. Not really pallets, just piles of Terran blankets, but they would do. Ann stayed with them, talking softly in World, soothing fear. The other Terrans disappeared. Food was brought, good familiar food from World, Enli saw with relief. People ate, and then most escaped from the terrible strangeness into sleep. It was very late at night, except that night was down below, in the lost reality.

Enli could not sleep. She lay on her blankets in the faint light— there was still no telling where it came from, everywhere and nowhere, like her thoughts. This was truth, then. Shared reality was only one reality. The Terrans had a different one. She had known that before—she, and only she of all World had known that—but not in the stone-solid way she perceived it now.

Suddenly Enli knew why she and Pek Voratur were going to each have another brain picture tomorrow. That was part of the bargain. Pek Sikorski wanted pictures of their brains away from World. She wanted to see if the pictures were different from the ones made in shared reality.

And the Terrans—Pek Sikorski and Pek Kaufman and the dirty man and his children—moved in and out of realities as if realities were bicycle sheds. *"It's only a planet,"* the grubby little girl had said, in the Terran only Enli had understood. Many, many realities, and this was the first time Enli had ever been able to think about that without head pain.

She was afraid. Not of the many, many realities—although that she was not afraid was probably proof that she was crazy. No, she was afraid of something else. A feeling that, she recognized, had been a long time coming. A feeling she could not have if she hadn't known the Terrans before, and journeyed with them, and learned their speech. Certainly a feeling she never could have on World, with the head pain of World.

The feeling was curiosity. It was *interesting* to think about many, many realities. To wonder what they were like. Terrifying, but also interesting. And that was the strangest reality of all.

She lay awake a long time, in the alien ship flying through the sky among stars.

Kaufman confronted Marbet in her quarters. She opened the door heavy-eyed with sleep, draped in a white nightdress, her auburn curls tumbled. He would not be distracted. He pushed past her into the tiny cabin and closed the door behind him.

"Lyle! What are you doing on ship?"

"What are *you* doing is a better question. Grafton tells me you untied the prisoner's hand. Against my specific orders."

The sleepiness left her eyes. "Don't get huffy, Lyle."

"I am not huffy. I am extremely angry."

"You don't have the right to be angry. You told me to get this job done and I'm doing that."

"I do have the right to be angry. I told you to do the job within specific parameters, and you've violated those. If you were military, I would have you court-martialed. As it is, you've imperiled yourself, the med techs, and the project."

Her eyes widened. "I didn't think of it that way."

"Why not?"

"I got so caught up in the progress I . . . oh, Lyle, I didn't mean to imperil the project. Or your career. I'm sorry."

She spread her hands, palms up, in appeal. Her shoulders drooped. Lyle felt his anger lessen. "At least no one was hurt."

"Yes. I'm glad of that. But I really didn't think about your career. You have a lot riding on this."

Her distress erased the last of his anger. She was a civilian, after all. He said, "All right, no real harm done. I'll square it with Grafton."

"Thank you." She looked at him so gratefully that he said, "Maybe he can be convinced, since nothing negative resulted, to try the experiment again, under more controlled conditions. Tell me, what progress have you made? What did you learn?"

All at once Marbet changed. Her shoulders straightened and her face lost its pleading look. She stared at him. "More important, what did *you* just learn?"

"What?"

"You heard me. You were hostile, and by being submissive—standard pack behavior, incidentally, and doubly effective when coming from a female—I defused your hostility. I even got you to the point of cooperation. That's exactly what I'm trying to do with the Faller. And I was succeeding until you soldiers interfered."

A different anger swept Kaufman. "You were using me."

"No. I was demonstrating to you. Big difference."

"And you have no compunction about using your femininity to manipulate me. There's a name for that, Marbet."

To his angry surprise, she laughed. "Do you think I have to deny being female to function professionally? Or to prove anything to anybody? If so, you're wrong. I'm a woman. Sometimes it works against me, sometimes for me, like being short, or brown-skinned, or Martian. None of it outweighs with anybody the fact that I'm a Sensitive. That's the single defining fact about me, and the rest I use as I have to in order to do my job."

"Including manipulating me."

"Listen to me, Lyle. I wasn't manipulating you, *I was demonstrating to you*. And you can't tell me that my demonstration was all that different from what you do in the diplomatic."

No. He couldn't. She was good, and he'd hired her to be good, and anything personal should be left out of it. It was unlike him to have to make an effort to remember that fact. He said, with effort, "I'm sorry. Tell me what you've learned."

"You don't have to be stiff-neutral with me, either. I'm glad to tell you. Sit down."

A tiny table was jammed between the bunk and the wall. Lyle sat on one of its two chairs. Marbet took the other, looking more at ease than Kaufman felt.

"What Grafton probably told you is essentially true. I put on a helmet with air supply, went into the Faller's space through the tech airlock, and untied the Faller's hand. He didn't try to attack me or to kill himself. He didn't answer my signing, either, although everything I know about his nonverbal signals says that he understands my signing. I sign from a submissive posture, as I understand it to look to a Faller. But the main thing is hard to explain, Lyle. He wasn't answering me, but something has shifted between us. There's a . . . not a rapport, that's too strong. But an increased receptivity."

"Do you think he'll answer soon?"

"Yes, although I can't offer you any objective proof."

Kaufman smiled thinly. "Nothing about your work is objective."

"True enough. But the work was progressing until Grafton retied the Faller and barred me completely from seeing him until you ruled on the situation."

Kaufman said nothing.

Marbet looked at him directly, without coyness or submission or anything but professionalism. "Lyle, I need access to the Faller, I need him to have one hand untied, and I need the freedom to work unhampered by Grafton's notions of Navy security. Otherwise, I won't ever get to a point where I can learn anything from the Faller about why his people are destroying ours."

"All right," Kaufman said. "You have it."

"All of it? All three things?"

"Yes."

"Thank you, Lyle." She stood, forcing him to do the same. "I'll reestablish connection with the Faller—if I can—tomorrow morning. I'll also show you the tapes from the last sessions, if you like."

"I can't," Kaufman said. "Send them to me planetside. I have to go back down almost immediately. We're lifting the artifact out of the hole tomorrow morning."

Interest sharpened her gaze. "Tell me what's going on."

He did, throwing in Ann's experiment with the natives. Marbet exclaimed, "Nine Worlders? Aboard ship now?"

"Yes. I have to explain that to Grafton, too, as well as your carte blanche."

She grinned. "I don't envy you that. But you'll pull it off. You always do."

"Not always." Nonetheless, he was warmed by her praise, at the same time as he suspected it. Always she confused him. "Good-bye, Marbet. Keep me posted on progress."

"I will." She opened the door for him, waited until he was out of it, and then said, "Lyle?"

"What?"

"I would kiss you if I didn't think you'd think it was professional manipulation. But it wouldn't have been." Quickly she shut the door.

He stood in the night-dimmed ship's corridor for a long moment, and then went to wake up Grafton.

FIFTEEN

IN THE NEURY MOUNTAINS

Capelo, standing by the hole, said, "Galactic trashmen here, planetside service. One load of alien junk for recycling."

Rosalind Singh looked at him with amusement, Albemarle with dislike. Lyle Kaufman looked only at the scene, which seemed to him ominously weird in ways he could not have explained.

The digger, reconfigured by the techs for its new role, hovered above the hole in the tiny upland valley. Almost filling the sky in the narrow place between mountain cliffs, the digger dwarfed the humans standing below. The powerful electromagnetic field that kept it there did not extend into the hole. The artifact had been tested with such a field while in the hole, producing no observable effect, but that was no guarantee there would be no effect outside the hole. Capelo was taking no chances. The artifact rested in a net of dislocation-free monofilament cables strong enough to tether a small moon.

Into his comlink Capelo said to the digger, "All right . . . lift."

Slowly the digger increased elevation in the air, and the artifact rose out of burial for the first time in fifty thousand years.

Kaufman peered at the artifact's sides as they rose past him, at its inward curvature, and finally at its underside. As it rose, the artifact shed rock and dirt like hail, sending everyone running into the ubiquitous caves for cover. Whatever the thing was made of, at least it didn't fuse to rock, apparently not even under great heat. That was a stroke of luck. They would have to brush the artifact clean, of course, but at least they were spared laborious, and possibly damaging, rock chipping.

The digger lifted the artifact clear not only of the hole but of the entire valley. Much debate about where to put it down had finally ended in the choice of the best available mountain meadow, about a half click away. Techs had flattened the site with nano and lasers and had built a thin, strong ring to hold the artifact three feet above the ground. At roughly twenty-five meters in diameter, the artifact would look like an enormous antique floor globe from the library of a giant.

Here be dragons, thought Kaufman. Two techs climbed into the elevator to go down into the hole, in case the artifact had left anything of interest behind. Capelo had told him this was a long shot but that he didn't want to overlook anything.

As soon as the giant ball had carried its hail of dirt and rock away from the valley, the scientists all ran out of their natural caves and into the artificial cave dug by nanos. Techs had burned and lit an entirely new tunnel system to the meadow. This path sloped sharply upward. Kaufman turned back to accompany Rosalind Singh, who would never admit that her age slowed her down but who always thanked him anyway for waiting.

"Thank you, Lyle. Don't we look silly! Do you know what I. I. Rabi said about physicists?"

"No," Kaufman said, although he did. He'd done a lot of reading about physicists.

Rosalind panted slightly. "Rabi said that physicists are the Peter Pans of the human race, never growing up."

"Second tunnel to the right and straight on till morning," Kaufman said, and she laughed.

They emerged, twenty minutes later and behind all the others, into bright sunlight. Albemarle, Gruber, and Kaufman swarmed around and under the artifact on its giant ring. Already they were cleaning it of the remaining grime with stiff-bristled brushes. Kaufman, too, ducked underneath, wishing he knew what he was looking at.

"Don't be so rough, Hal," Capelo said acidly to Albemarle. "It isn't going to rust, you know."

Albemarle ignored him. Probably hadn't even heard him. Albemarle, Kaufman saw, was filled with his own absorbing scientific excitement.

Kaufman studied the curve of dirty metal . . . no, not metal, it was some sort of fullerenes. As far as he could tell, the protuberances that Capelo had shown him on the sphere's top and sides continued their equidistant equatorial march underneath. The protuberances totaled seven. Each was marked with a cluster of raised dots: one dot, two, three, five, seven, and, presumably under the dirt, eleven and thirteen. Primes, except for "one," although everything the master makers had left included "one" along with primes. Because of some totally different approach to mathematics? The project team had gone along with the vanished creators. On World, "one" was a prime.

Away from the artifact, Rosalind began the non-invasive tests they had already performed a half-dozen times. Just to make sure that moving the artifact hadn't changed anything detectably significant about it.

"Oh my dear gods," Capelo said. He stared at the patch he had just cleaned.

Instantly Kaufman was beside him. "What is it, Tom?"

"That protuberance . . . Rosalind! Come here! Look at this!"

She, Albemarle, and Gruber crowded close. Capelo pointed.

Each of them inspected the protuberance, then looked at each other wild-eyed. *"Mein Gott,"* Gruber breathed.

"What?" Kaufman said. God, it was humbling being the only non-scientist. *"What is it?"*

Rosalind took pity on him. "Look, Lyle, at this protuberance over here. Do you see, it has two deep dimples in it, about six centimeters apart, with nipples in the bottoms. We think that sets off whatever that protuberance does, and that both nipples must be depressed to do that. At least, that was the system on Syree Johnson's larger artifact, although there the depressions were on opposite sides of the circumference, and much bigger. In one of the protuberances that we already cleaned off, we found a rock fragment wedged in one dimple, depressing the nipple deeper than the other. Nothing happened when we removed it. But this protuberance here, prime five, has *both* nipples depressed already! Look . . . they're barely visible!"

Kaufman said, "How? What did it?"

"No way to tell," Gruber said. "Maybe it has been that way since the original impact. Maybe it was created that way. How can we know?"

"Listen," Capelo said. He wore his intent, focused look. "Here's what we have. From the mapping to the radioactive rock distribution, we hypothesize that protuberance setting prime one is a directed beam destabilizer, and that various seismic events have set it off over the centuries. We hypothesize from the same data that protuberance setting prime three may be a spherical wave-effect destabilizer like the one Syree Johnson reported on her artifact, at its lowest setting. If so, the spherical wave effect should follow the inverse square law. And that's all we know so far. Just speculation."

Gruber said thoughtfully, "I offer another hypothesis."

The others turned to look at him, and suddenly Kaufman thought how they would look from above, or from a little distance away. A tense knot of serious people standing and pontificating beside a giant alien sphere in an alien meadow.

Gruber continued, "If protuberance prime five *is* working, as the two depressed nipples say it is . . . ja?"

"Get to the point," Capelo said.

"Then protuberance prime five is generating the probability field that affects brain probabilities. In us in the tunnel, maybe in all of World in the shared-reality mechanism, if it has been switched on for fifty thousand years, since the original impact. Maybe these things are only side effects of whatever protuberance prime five was designed to do, but they come from it anyway."

Capelo said abruptly, "When Syree Johnson's artifact—Tas—blew up, the wave effect that destroyed Nimitri should have reached World. It didn't. That's hard data, not speculation about brain events. Maybe what protuberance setting prime five was designed to do was provide planet-wide protection against a planet-wide version of the destabilizer wave."

"Yes," breathed Rosalind Singh, *"yes."* Her placid face suddenly blazed.

"Ja," Gruber said. "That would fit!"

"It's only a guess," Albemarle said. "Where's your data? You're the one that's always talking about data."

"Oh, we'll get data," Capelo said.

Kaufman said, "How?"

Capelo said, "Empirically. We set the thing off."

That was the answer Kaufman had expected, had known was inevitable, had feared. It was the only practical option: Their mission was to investigate this find with regard to possible military use. For that, testing was essential. Even though there was no way to predict what the tests would do to the artifact, the testers, the natives, or the planet. On the other hand, there was no one to organize any protest against whatever the tests would do.

All at once, Kaufman was glad that Ann Sikorski was safely stowed away on the *Shepard*, forty-eight thousand clicks out in space.

But it was another day before they made the first test. Rosalind Singh wanted far more complete analyses of the artifact than she could make while it had been underground. More large items of equipment came down on the shuttle from the *Alan B. Shepard*. Kaufman used the delay to return to base camp and review the constant stream of data coming from both Ann Sikorski and Marbet Grant. For different reasons, he chose not to contact either of them directly, even though Ann had been trying to reach him for several hours now.

Marbet Grant's recordings required no response, largely because they were incomprehensible. He watched the real-time recordings inside the prisoner's cell, sampling them at random. The Faller's "left" hand was again untied, his other two still manacled to the soft wall behind him. Marbet went through various grimaces and body shifts and hand signings with him. In return, he made several involuntary grimaces and body shifts—at least, Kaufman assumed they were involuntary. His free hand made no signs. None of it conveyed any meaning to Kaufman.

Ann, too, had real-time cams covering the nine Worlders in their sequestered quarters aboard ship. Kaufman watched the first hour, skipped an hour to watch fifteen minutes, and kept to that interval until he had caught up to the present. Then he accessed Ann's recorded summaries, watching her face grow more and more haggard with each one. Finally, he ran the computer sim results she'd sent him, worked out by the sophisticated near-AI on board.

All this took most of the day. When he was finished, Kaufman went outside. The sun was just setting. He walked to the edge of the patrolled perimeter, and by then it was dusk. Three moons shone, one of them the small, close one—he'd forgotten its name—that

?.? moved so fast (it looked retrograde) in the sky. There were no clouds. The air had the lively, faintly sweet smell peculiar to World; maybe it came from the superabundance of flowers. Kaufman thought of Voratur's magnificent, carefully tended gardens. Of the well-ordered Voratur household, everyone accepting his place and none of those places wretched or abused. Of Worlders' pleasure in their fully shared rituals, where priest and rich merchant danced beside gardener and chamberpot cleaner. Shared reality.

Kaufman stared into the sweet-smelling dark a very long time.

When he arrived back at the meadow site, where the scientists and techs had camped all night, he found everything ready for the first test of the artifact. He'd almost missed it.

"Why are you so far ahead of schedule? And why wasn't I told?" Kaufman demanded.

"We tried to comlink you; you were in the tunnels," Rosalind Singh said. "It was a quick decision, Lyle, caused by the loss of an orbital probe. A meteor took it out. So we had to recalibrate to use a different probe, and it will be in position much sooner."

"I see," Kaufman said. Why did they need an orbital probe?

"Put on this s-suit," she said, and so he did.

At least he understood the planned first test. The radiation maps and geologic computer sims had showed, or seemed to show, that setting prime one was a directed beam destabilizer, operant outside of a "dead-eye" area directly surrounding the artifact. The project team had taken detailed radiation readings of a cliff face across the meadow from the artifact, beyond the "eye." Then they rotated the artifact so that setting prime one was in direct line with the cliff face. Robots were set to simultaneously depress both nipples in prime setting one, at whatever force was necessary to get a reaction.

Kaufman said, "What if the cliff face is too far away for the beam to reach?"

Capelo glanced at him impatiently. In his s-suit, helmet on, he reminded Kaufman of a thin hopping insect. "Then we set up closer targets, which we'll do anyway to verify the inverse-square law attribute."

"Of course," Kaufman said.

Rosalind added kindly, "Elevation and horizon curvature mean that if the beam has deep penetration and very long range, it will pass through the cliff and then encounter nothing but space. Nothing else on World will be affected."

"I see."

"More—the timing has been determined exactly, so that if the beam travels at light speed, and if it does go through the cliff, and if it does have a very long range, it will hit an orbital probe. The probe will send back radiation measurements. But we don't expect that to happen, because we think the directed beam has a short effective range."

"All right," Capelo said. "Three, two, one . . . now!"

Kaufman saw nothing—no shaft of light shooting out from the artifact, no sudden explosion on the cliff face. But the sensors and displays in front of the scientists went crazy.

"Got it!" Albemarle shouted. "Got the son of a bitch, by God!"

Capelo didn't even answer with sarcasm. The four scientists immediately fell into excited chatter, most of which was gibberish to Kaufman. Capelo was running equations on his handheld. Rosalind captained her large equipment, re-running the tests she had done yesterday. Kaufman waited patiently.

This time it was Gruber who remembered him. "It *is* a directed beam destabilizer, Lyle, just as we think. A narrow conical beam following the inverse square law. The close rock is fried. The sensors in the cliff face show the beam reaches that far, but weakly, although with no loss of effect from passing through the first rock. A meter into the cliff there is no effect at all, and also none on the orbital probe."

"So as a weapon," Kaufman said, "it has a very limited range."

Clearly Gruber had forgotten the beam was being considered as a weapon. He was caught up in pure discovery. "Ja, ja, limited range. And not acting instantaneously. You can see from the displays — see? — that the radiation does not emit instantly. There is a time lag, and a rise, and a faster fall."

Kaufman could see no such thing from the jumble of data before him. He considered the information carefully. Gruber jumped back into the argumentative chaos of the scientists.

Rosalind Singh was easier to distract from her data; she and her techs stood in front of more incomprehensible displays. She actually looked up as Kaufman approached. He said, "Is there any change in what you're measuring, as a result of the test?"

"None." She looked at him shrewdly. "Did any of those bloody sods tell you what I'm measuring?"

He smiled at her uncharacteristic language. She was just as excited as any of them. "No."

"Then I will. We know that the inside of the artifact is mostly hollow. But there are unidentifiable structures somehow suspended inside in an extremely complex but partial manner, without direct connection to each other. These structures seem stable. They also seem to be without any mass, which seems impossible.

"The mathematical analyses describe the suspensions as a . . . a sort of complicated web. Each curve folds back on itself many times, a sort of multidimensional fractal. Computer breakdown further suggests a strange attractor — do you know what that is, Lyle?"

"No."

"A region in which all sufficiently close trajectories are attracted in the limit, but in which arbitrarily close points over time became exponentially separated." Rosalind looked as if she realized this was no help, but didn't stop to explain. "The Hausdorff dimension of the suggested fractal is one point two. That's the same dimension as the galactic filling of the universe."

"What does it all indicate?" Kaufman asked.

"We haven't the faintest idea."

"None?"

"None. This is science so different from our own that we are in pitch black. We are, as Darwin famously said, like dogs speculating on the mind of Newton. All I can tell you is that my measurements today after the test are the same as those yesterday before the test, and that both match the measurements Syree Johnson made on the first artifact. Adjusting for scale, of course."

"Do you think moving the artifact into space will alter those measurements?"

"The first artifact was found in space. The natives thought it was a moon."

Which was no more definite an answer than any of the others had been.

The team spent the rest of the day confirming their data about setting prime one. Capelo assured him that they wouldn't be ready to test setting prime two until the next day, and that they wouldn't start without him. Kaufman didn't put much faith in Capelo's assurances; the physicist looked more and more like a grasshopper, thin and brown and hopping with inhuman impulses. In the heat of science, Capelo was quite capable of forgetting that Kaufman existed.

He felt a twinge of unmistakable envy.

Rosalind Singh also assured him that they would not test setting prime two without him. Rosalind he believed. So Kaufman again started back to base camp. Ann was bringing the nine Worlders back down this afternoon and he wanted to be there when the shuttle landed.

SIXTEEN

ABOARD THE *ALAN B. SHEPARD*

The "sky" of the big room brightened, and Enli realized it was "morning." Whatever that might mean on a metal flying boat in space. She didn't think she had slept at all.

Sitting up, she studied her fellow Worlders. Four lay asleep. Pek Voratur, on the pallet in the corner, sat with a fixed expression that frightened her a little. His fleshy oiled face was gray as rain clouds. She approached tentatively; he neither moved nor spoke.

"Pek Voratur?"

Nothing.

"Pek Voratur!"

Slowly his head swiveled, his eyes focused. "Enli?"

"Yes." She took his hand, marveling at her boldness. This was the richest trader on World. But at the moment he reminded her of her small nephew, Fentil, scared from a bad fall while climbing high in a tree.

"Enli . . . what has happened?"

She considered what to say. On the next pallet Asto Pek Valifin, cook's assistant, listened intently.

"I think, Pek Voratur . . . I think reality has shifted up this high in space."

"Highness does not shift reality. It is shared on the mountain villages of Caulily and deep in mines of Neerit. My agents have told me so."

"Yes. But we are much higher than the mountains of Caulily. We are off World, you know." She hesitated, unsure of how much to say. "Shared reality happens in our brains, you know."

"The brain is the home of the soul, by the blooming of the First Flower." He said it eagerly, seizing on the familiar. Enli had a sudden inspiration.

"Yes. And when the First Flower came down from Obri and unfolded her petals to create World, she created our souls. Our brains. And our shared reality. But now we are away from the World she unfolded for us. So reality is different."

"Reality is reality! As well say that a stone is a flower!"

"Reality is different away from World," Enli repeated. "World was unfolded by the First Flower. This place was not."

She watched him consider this. It made sense to him . . . as much as anything here could.

He said, "Then if reality is different away from the gift of the First Flower, what is this reality here?"

"It is not shared."

The listening Pek Valifin abruptly sat up on her pallet. "That is not possible!"

"It is so," Enli said. "We are each alone in our reality here." But that far, she saw, neither of them could yet go.

Pek Voratur had recovered himself. He was naturally a bold man, a great trader. He said to Enli, with all the tentativeness of a child testing the strength of sand houses, "I am Pek Malinorit, who keeps the pel house in Gofkit Jemloe."

Enli understood. "No. You are not."

They looked at each other. No head pain at the differences in their words. No head pain at Voratur's saying what was not so. No head pain in Enli's hearing it.

"Aaaiiieeeeee!" the cook's assistant wailed. "We are unreal! We can never join our ancestors in peace and flowers!"

Ann Pek Sikorski suddenly crouched beside the terrified woman, holding her, addressing the entire room. "You are *not* unreal. Reality has shifted here. Enli understands. Say again what you said to Pek Voratur, Enli."

How did Pek Sikorski know what Enli had said? Pek Sikorski had not—Enli was certain of this—been in the room then. She had entered later, and yet she knew what Enli had said to Pek Voratur. Enli felt no head pain over knowing this.

Enli said loudly, "When the First Flower came down from Obri and unfolded her petals to create World, she created our souls. Our brains. And our shared reality. But now we are away from the World she unfolded for us. So reality is different. World was unfolded by the First Flower. This place was not. In this place, away from the gift of the First Flower, reality is not shared."

"Say it again," Pek Sikorski said.

Enli repeated her words. She saw them bewilder everyone. Then make sense to everyone. Then bewilder them again, although this time without as much panic.

Was that not a kind of shared reality, too?

For many hours, people were afraid to do anything. They sat on their pallets. They ate the food Pek Sikorski brought, thanking her timidly. Occasionally someone exchanged a remark with someone else, commonplace remarks that spoke of what was clearly held in common: "The flying boat does not feel like it's moving." "The light comes from everywhere and nowhere." "Tomorrow the Terrans will take us back to World."

Finally, Pek Voratur stood. His face glistened, but his eyes in their folds of flesh were determined. "Pek Sikorski!" he called.

She had told them to simply call her name if they wanted her. Immediately a door opened and she was there. "Yes, Pek Voratur?"

"We have come very far to this flying boat of yours. We . . ." he faltered, went on, ". . . I would like to see more of it."

"No!" cried the nervous gardener. "We must stay together."

Pek Voratur's hands trembled. "I would like to see more of the flying boat."

Pek Sikorski looked surprised. "More? I . . . it isn't . . ."

"There are trading bargains to be planted," Pek Voratur said.

"Let me . . . let me talk to the head of the flying boat household. I will be back very soon."

Into the silence of her departure Pek Voratur said, "Who will go with me to see more of the flying boat?"

No one answered.

"Who wishes to smell the blooms of this . . . this different . . . reality?" He got the words out, face still glistening with sweat, hands still trembling.

The cook's assistant lay back on her pallet and pulled the blankets over her head.

"I will go," said someone Enli had hardly noticed, the youngest of the eight Worlders, barely out of childfur. She wore the tunic of an unskilled cleaner, a short girl with lank brown neckfur and a too-round skull. But her black eyes sparkled.

"And I," said Enli. Where did the girl get her courage? Enli herself had had so much time with the Terrans, so much time to grasp the idea of many unshared realities, an idea as slippery and odorous as fish. Yet here was this girl, with her eyes sparkling.

"I have forgotten your name," Voratur said.

"Essa Pek Criltifor."

"Anyone else?" said Voratur, too loudly. No one spoke. A

woman put her hand to her head, wonderingly, as if she could not believe there was no head pain. Probably, Enli thought, she could not.

Pek Sikorski returned. "Come with me, Pek Voratur. And anyone else . . . Yes, Enli and . . . Essa? Come with me."

She led them through the door, into the corridor Enli remembered from last night. It was very ugly: all straight lines and dull metal. They went through another door into a room so small that Enli thought there must be some mistake. This was an empty storage shed.

Pek Sikorski said, "Now, please, don't be startled or frightened. This is just an *elevator*. A machine to move us. We will only be in it a few moments."

The *elevator*—the word was Terran, of course—closed its door, trapping them in a windowless box. Then it began to move sideways. Pek Voratur clutched at the smooth wall. Essa Pek Criltifor's eyes widened. Then she smiled. "Why, it's just a cart."

"A cart with no one to pull it," Voratur said, nervously jaunty. "How interesting a new thing!"

The elevator stopped and opened its door. The three Worlders exclaimed aloud.

They stood in a garden—a garden aboard the flying boat, a garden in the sky. There were plants under glass, and small plants in bubbling vats, and beds of flowers. Strange, beautiful, perfect flowers never seen on World, all heights and colors, their petals shining with dew and perfuming the air. The beds surrounded small village greens set with chairs and little tables. The flowerbeds and greens, unlike anything else on the flying boat, curved into pleasing shapes. A few Terrans sat at these tables, drinking from plain cups; more Terrans tended the flowers. Everyone stopped to stare at the Worlders.

Voratur boomed, "May your blossoms rejoice the souls of your ancestors!"

Pek Sikorski said to the Terrans, "Our guest says hello."

"Hello," the closest Terrans responded, smiling, and Pek Sikorski said to Voratur, "They welcome you to our garden." She broke off a yellow flower and handed it to Pek Voratur. A Terran gardener looked as if he were going to protest, but at a look from Pek Sikorski, did not.

She said, "Our blossoms rejoice that you visit us."

"We praise the blooms of your heart. May we walk in the garden?"

"Yes, certainly."

The three Worlders started timidly forward. They stopped in the middle of the first village green. Enli was wondering how there could be village dancing in it, it was so small, when the two human children they'd seen before ran out from between trees. The smaller threw her arms around Pek Sikorski's knees. "Dr. Ann! Marbet's here!"

A Terran followed the children, a small brown woman with short red headfur that curled prettily. She was much closer to the size of Worlders than any Terran Enli had ever seen. Her eyes were a startling color, the green of glassy rocks worn bright and smooth by river water.

Pek Sikorski said in World, "Pek Voratur, this is Marbet Pek Grant. And these children are named Amanda and Sudie." She switched to Terran. "Marbet, three of our guests: Pek Voratur, Pek Criltifor, Pek Brimmidin. Pek Brimmidin speaks and understands English."

Pek Grant said in World, "May your blossoms flourish." Pek Sikorski looked surprised. Pek Grant added in Terran, "Learned it from Lyle."

Sudie said, "You have hair on your necks!"

"What did the child say?" Voratur asked Enli, who hesitated before answering.

"She says that Worlders have neckfur and Terrans have headfur."

"True enough," Voratur said.

Amanda said with childish formality, "Would you like to tour the garden?"

Enli translated, and Voratur agreed. They began a slow walk through the garden in the sky. Pek Grant and Pek Sikorski walked beside Pek Voratur, with Pek Sikorski translating. Enli saw that his fear had lessened; he appraised everything with the shrewd eyes of a trader. Enli walked beside Amanda, talking with the pale human girl, who had beautiful manners.

Not so Sudie. No Worlder child would have behaved, or been permitted to behave, as she did—not even those too young to be real. Sudie ran ahead, hid behind bushes, climbed trees, lagged behind, called, "Come find me!" And to make it worse, the girl Essa Pek Criltifor began to do the same thing. Here she was, a guest and a few years older than the well-behaved Amanda, and she was disgracing them all. And Pek Voratur, whose household she belonged to, was too preoccupied to even notice!

Finally Enli caught Essa's eye and frowned. Essa stood still for a moment. And then she crinkled her skull ridges at Enli and scampered after Sudie.

Essa had disobeyed her elder. And there was no head pain to stop her.

For just a moment Enli glimpsed what the loss of shared reality could mean.

"Enli," Pek Voratur said, suddenly beside her, "we can plant a very profitable bargain for some of these flowers and the healing doses that are made from them. Pek Grant tells me that garden there"—he pointed to a covered glass bowl inside which grew tall plants dense with brown pods—"contains plants which have been manufactured by seed-altering machines. The seeds contain tiny potions that will dry up many body growths people now die of."

Manufactured plants? Seed-altering machines? It made no sense to Enli. Pek Grant was now in earnest conversation with Pek Sikorski. Enli saw Pek Sikorski's eyes grow wide and her face even paler than usual. What was Pek Grant telling her?

Voratur said, "I want you to translate when I plant the bargains for the flowers and other things I want in exchange for coming here," Voratur said. "You, Enli, not Pek Sikorski. How do I know she translates the same words I say?"

Enli stopped watching the Terran women's intense conversation. Pek Voratur had her full attention. He was saying that he believed the Terrans might not be sharing reality . . . and yet he was still willing to trade with them. He had not instantly decided they were unreal.

Voratur caught her intense gaze. Quickly he said, "And you will get your share of the bargain, of course, Enli. So we want to make it a profitable one."

"All of us who came here will get our share."

"Yes, of course. Although . . ." he suddenly looked thoughtful. "Up here, the others do not know how much we will plant in our bargain . . . and it was, after all, only you and I who gave brain pictures. There isn't as much reason to share with the others, who only came and sat like logs in that bare room. Not as much reason to share at all."

Enli stared at him. "Pek Voratur . . ."

"Yes, yes, you're right. We will have to share. As soon as we return to World, shared reality will return to us. We will have to share."

He closed his eyes, calculating silently. Enli went on staring at him, while Essa ran past, searching for Sudie, who erupted in a flurry of noise from behind the low bushes beside Pek Sikorski and Marbet Pek Grant.

SEVENTEEN

IN THE NEURY MOUNTAINS

Captain Heller reported to Kaufman by comlink the return of the shuttle to base camp, even though Kaufman had just heard it screaming through the atmosphere overhead. "Shuttle has returned, sir."

"Thank you, Captain." Just now he didn't want one of the military briefings so dear to Heller, status quo report and procedural report and deployment report. The second test on the artifact would begin any moment.

"Disembarking were nine natives, who will be immediately escorted to the perimeter, and—"

"Give them a minute to recover, Captain. They're not used to hurtling on and off their planet."

"Yes, sir," Heller said frostily. "Also disembarking were Dr. Sikorski and Ms. Grant."

Marbet? Why had she come down? No point in asking Heller, who had started on her meticulous reports.

"Lyle!" called Dieter Gruber. "Come, we are ready to begin!"

"—No signals received of any—"

"Yes, thank you, dismissed," Lyle said, and broke the link.

At the edge of the meadow the scientists waited impatiently. Again the detection equipment had been set up, including the robot to depress setting prime two. Boulders and other objects, of various compositions, sat at various distances from the artifact. Sensors had been programmed in orbit. The difference was that setting prime one had produced a phenomenon predicted to a fairly high confidence level. No one had any idea what setting prime two would produce. Nor what would be required to shield against it, although they had done their best.

Shields up, the small group waited tensely. When the orbitals were in the right position, Capelo said, "Now!"

Nothing happened.

"No changes in radiation level at any detection site," Albemarle said, studying his displays, and one by one the rest of the detectors reported the same thing.

"No change anywhere," Gruber said. "Why not?"

Rosalind Singh said, "I doubt they'd build in a setting with no effect."

"How do we know what they'd do?" Albemarle said. "Maybe the setting's broken, somehow."

Gruber said, "Nothing has ever malfunctioned anywhere in any space tunnel. Their equipment does not seem to break."

"But there's a first time for everything, Dieter."

Only Capelo said nothing. Kaufman watched him curiously. The physicist stood with his eyes closed and his arms crossed on his chest, the same posture Kaufman had surprised him in before. A black hole . . . everything about him seemed concentrated inward, cut off from communication with the outer world. Albemarle was watching Capelo carefully, and it seemed to Kaufman that Albemarle's expression was a strange combination of curiosity, disdain, and wistfulness.

The others resumed running programs that might find some

change in something, somewhere, as a result of activating setting prime two. Capelo abruptly came out of his trance and walked rapidly away. Kaufman didn't try to stop him.

It was half an hour before he returned, dirty from climbing rocks. Without preamble he said, "Set up to test setting prime three."

Albemarle said, "Without knowing what prime two does? Why? To go to a greater strength because you can't crack a lesser one is—"

Kaufman said, "What are you thinking, Tom?"

Capelo said, "I'm not sure yet. But we need to test setting prime three first."

"Why?" Rosalind Singh said.

"I can't tell. But I've been going through the situation . . . there's a gap. No, not a gap, a . . . an unmade connection. It feels right to test prime three now."

"Oh," Albemarle said, with a flash of the old jealousy, "if we're going by *feelings* now . . . I thought we were doing science."

Kaufman studied Capelo. After a moment Kaufman said to the others, in the voice he reserved for situations requiring unarguable authority, "Do it. Set up to test setting prime three."

Rosalind Singh began giving orders to the techs. Kaufman waited until everyone else was similarly occupied to say quietly to Capelo, "Is it like chess, Tom?"

With effort, Capelo focused on Kaufman. "Chess?"

"I'm not a scientist," Kaufman said, "but I play a fair game of chess, and I've read about the great players. They don't logically reason out the possibilities as much as see them whole . . . no, not see, apprehend them in some inexplicable way, all the possible outcomes a few moves ahead. Do you do something like that with the physics of the artifact, with the equations?"

"Something like that," Capelo said. All at once he smiled, the kind of smile Kaufman had never seen from him. Not sardonic, not bitter, not amused. Happy. "We'll get them yet, Lyle." He walked off.

"Them?" Kaufman wondered. The equations? The doubters like Albemarle? The builders of the artifact? There was no way to tell.

Setting up for test three didn't involve much work; the remote robot was repositioned and the calculations done to receive feedback from different orbital sensors. When you don't know what you're doing, Kaufman reflected, you can easily recycle from other efforts where you also didn't know what you were doing.

There was a two-hour wait for the orbitals to reach position. In the middle of it, Ann Sikorski and Marbet Grant, clad in s-suits, emerged from the tunnel into the meadow. Marbet walked over to Rosalind, and Ann made straight for Kaufman.

"Ann, I—"

"You can't do it, Lyle."

"Do what?" he said, although he already knew. He'd watched Ann's recordings, and Ann had obviously talked to Marbet.

"You can't remove that artifact from World. Not to test it in space, even. It generates the shared reality mechanism. Without it, Worlders can't share reality. Their entire society will fall apart. On ship—"

"Slow down a minute, Ann. Just listen a minute. You found out that something on World generates some sort of mechanism that enables shared reality. You don't know that something is the artifact."

"Come on, Lyle! What else could it be?"

"I don't know. But you don't, either. You're proceeding on assumptions, not facts."

"Marbet told me you'd discovered a prime setting already permanently activated! That's a fact!"

Kaufman had obviously told Marbet too damn much, without specifying that she keep the information from Ann. Which, since Ann was a member of the team, wouldn't have occurred to Marbet. Anyway, Ann would only have learned the same thing from Dieter.

Ann said, "You're planning on experimenting with these people's *brains*, Lyle. They evolved in this probability field. You don't know what will happen to them physically if they lose the field permanently, or even for longer than the nine Worlders spent aboard ship. You're experimenting with a whole planetful of people's brains!"

"I don't have any choice."

"Of course you do! You have total discretion on this project!"

"I have military objectives."

She stared at him. "You're really going to do it, aren't you? Take the thing first into space, and then if it's useful enough, out of the star system entirely?"

"Yes. If I can."

She gazed at him a moment longer, then turned and walked away. Kaufman hadn't thought her gentle face could look like that.

He didn't want to talk to Marbet, now inspecting the artifact up close with Rosalind. He said abruptly to a tech, "Sergeant, clear the field immediately of nonessential personnel."

"Yes, sir."

When the orbital sensors registered proper position, Capelo said, "Now!" The command was unnecessary; everything of course was preprogrammed. But Kaufman saw that Capelo couldn't help himself.

This time the displays registered all kinds of results. When Kaufman could sort out the technical discussion among the scientists, he said, "It's the same effect that Syree Johnson got when she activated setting prime one on the bigger artifact, isn't it? A spherical wave destabilizing everything above atomic number seventy-five, and obeying the inverse square law."

"That's what it is," Gruber said happily. "Two down, five to go!"

Capelo had not gone into his black-hole thinking mode. Kaufman said to him, "You expected this for setting prime three."

"Not expected. But when we didn't get this for setting two, I hoped we'd get it for three."

"So what is two?"

The others, alerted by some shift in the experimental weather, stopped talking to listen.

"I don't *know* what two is," Capelo said, with all his old irritability. "I just have a theory. I think it's a shield. Against setting one, and maybe against other things, too."

"A shield!" Gruber said.

Albemarle snapped, "With what evidence?"

"None, Hal. None whatsoever."

"Then pardon me for not being impressed. We activated setting prime two and nothing happened. A difference that makes no difference is no difference."

"You've never bought artwork, have you?"

Albemarle looked peevishly puzzled, but Kaufman couldn't help smiling. Original oil painting versus forged copies so good that the difference was undetectable. Until the right expert came along, anyway.

Capelo explained the problem. "We need to fire a destabilizing beam from setting prime one, reflect it back to the artifact, and see if setting prime two is automatically activated. It would have to be automatic—there's no use in having a defense that can't intercept an unexpected attack at light speed. But there are two problems. First, the beam goes through everything, so what are we going to reflect it back off of? And since the beam fades out over such short range, how far away does the reflector have to be to still be outside the shield range?"

"If there is a shield range," Albemarle muttered.

Rosalind said, "What are you implying about the dispersion relationship?"

The three physicists fell into argument that Kaufman couldn't follow. S-matrices, modes of resonance, J constant, infinite malleability. Finally he grasped that Capelo was arguing that the destabilizing beam manipulated probability by exchanging virtual particles with other Calabi-Yau dimensions in the spacetime curvature.

Rosalind had an objection to this that Kaufman couldn't follow, and Albemarle objected to it from, it seemed, instinctive opposition to Capelo.

"All right," Capelo finally said, "we'll try it."

"Try what?" Kaufman said.

Rosalind said in her clear, precise voice, "If setting prime two is a shield against the destabilizing beam, we would need to test it by firing a destabilizing beam at it. But we have no idea how to create such a thing, or even any idea of the principles behind it. But Tom thinks setting prime two might also be a more generalized shield, against a variety of weapons."

Kaufman got it. "You think that's what the Fallers are using for their beam-disrupter shield. That they've cracked the same principle employed by the artifact. That they're using it to deflect our proton beams."

"We can't know that yet," Albemarle said. "But Dr. Capelo here wants to test it anyway."

Kaufman stood very still. The principle behind the beam-disrupter shield. An artifact that duplicated the Faller shield. If he could bring that back to Mars . . . And then the thought, clear and hard, *Ann just lost any chance at all of leaving the artifact on World.*

"Start with a simple laser gun," Rosalind suggested. "You'll want Carlington sensors," and the three were off again, discussing ideas Kaufman could not follow. At least now Gruber, too, looked left out. The geologist's knowledge of physics did not extend to whatever rarefied heights the others trod.

An artifact that duplicated the Faller shield. Right in front of them, here, now.

Rosalind and Capelo were giving orders to techs, who then started attaching sensors to the artifact, near the artifact, at various distances from the artifact. Kaufman's comlink rang. It was De-Volites. "Major, are you authorizing the shuttle return to the *Shepard?*"

Kaufman stopped himself from saying, *what return?* He waited.

DeVolites finally said uneasily, "Ms. Grant has requested being taken back up. She said it was all right with you."

"Yes, it is," Kaufman said, broke link, and pushed down his anger at Marbet. She took enormous liberties. A civilian project specialist did not give orders to a military shuttle pilot. He punched at his comlink to tell her so, but stopped himself before the link was completed.

She would only say that of course Kaufman would have authorized her return on the shuttle. Her work was on board ship with the Faller. And she would be right.

Kaufman canceled the comlink. He told himself that her work was too important to interrupt with procedural complaints. But he realized, with dismayed honesty, that he also didn't want to tangle with Marbet just now. She was too disconcerting, reading his intentions from his voice or body language or minute facial movements or whatever the hell she read. He was too transparent to her. He didn't like it.

Even though, under other circumstances, he had welcomed it.

When everything was ready, a tech fired a laser handgun directly at the artifact from various distances. No one had expected this to affect the artifact, which had once survived a high-speed collision with the planet, and it didn't. But it did affect the scientists.

"Amazing," Rosalind Singh said, and from her it was the most profound awe. "Nothing. No reflection, no scattering, no residual heat, no atmospheric resonance, nothing. The laser beam has just disappeared."

"Try it again, at a different angle," Albemarle suggested. Once again, curiosity seemed to have overcome his dislike of Capelo. Albemarle was a scientist at his core.

Capelo said nothing. To Kaufman, the physicist seemed different now. His biting sarcasm had all but disappeared, as if burned off in the furnace of scientific intensity. Kaufman saw that Capelo was thinking, and that this thinking was different not only in degree but in kind from what the rest of them did when thinking.

For the rest of the day they hit the artifact with beams of electromagnetic energies in various wavelengths. None of them affected the artifact. All of them seemed to vanish with no trace whatsoever, except for macro-scale material missiles. Those simply ricocheted.

Finally Capelo said, "I want a beam of proton particles. Bring the ship around."

"You'll blow apart the mountain," Kaufman said. "Proton beams are a major offensive weapon, Tom."

"I want it. We'll dig the artifact out of the rubble afterward."

"No," Kaufman said, for the first time, and prepared for Capelo's explosion. It didn't come.

"You're right, you're right," Capelo muttered. "It wouldn't work. I'm not thinking about this right. There's something missing. Something I'm not seeing . . . but I need the proton beam. We'll have to move the artifact out into space."

Everyone looked at Kaufman. It was almost dark; they had worked straight through the day without food, or thinking of food. The photosensors had activated the lights that turned the alien meadow into a human outpost, filled with human equipment. Only the smells were still alien. That, and the four small moons among the strange constellations in the sky. Kaufman thought, irrelevantly, of Hadjil Voratur, eating his evening meal amid his flowery gardens and his shared reality.

"Lyle?" Rosalind said. "Tom wants to move the artifact off-planet in the morning."

"Yes," Kaufman said, and opened the link to the *Alan B. Shepard*.

•   •   •

Sometime much later, when Kaufman had finally drifted toward sleep, his comlink rang. It was Marbet. As soon as he heard the tone in her voice, something in Kaufman's chest kicked him awake.

"Lyle. Come up right away. I did it."

"Did what?"

"I got the Faller to respond. Large scale. And what he's telling me could change everything."

EIGHTEEN

ABOARD THE *ALAN B. SHEPARD*

I t was ridiculously easy to steal a piece of a planet.

Kaufman had studied Syree Johnson's accounts of moving the first artifact from World to Space Tunnel #438. But that artifact had been in orbit, an artificial moon that the natives called Tas. It had been four kilometers in diameter and had massed nine hundred thousand tons. Colonel Johnson had moved it one point two billion kilometers, accelerating it most of the way by pushing it with the starship *Zeus* on full power. The effort had taken over five days, and by the end the *Zeus* was being fired on by a Faller warship, until both ships and the artifact were annihilated in the desperate effort of trying to force nine hundred thousand tons through a space tunnel that, Johnson had known, could handle no more than a hundred thousand tons.

In contrast, Kaufman's artifact was only twenty-five meters in diameter and massed less than a hundred tons. Kaufman merely had to lift it forty-eight thousand clicks to orbit. No one was shooting at them. The entire operation took one morning, with the artifact secured in its monofilament-cable net and carried up on the same trip that returned the scientists to the *Alan B. Shepard*.

All except for Ann, who had refused to go.

"I could order you aboard," Kaufman said. They faced each other a little after dawn at base camp. Around them, crew loaded equipment and baggage onto the shuttle for the first trip up. People snapped into comlinks and shouted to each other. The foamcast huts, soon to be abandoned shells, shone with reflected light from the rising sun. Ann's long, pale face looked gaunt.

Ann said, "It won't make any difference if you order me. I'm staying. I'm not military, remember."

"You're still under my command."

"If you take that artifact off this planet, you're not fit for command."

She couldn't enrage him the way Marbet could. He said gently, "I understand your viewpoint, Ann. But I can't share it, and I don't think you can expect me to. All right, you can stay even after the last shuttle departs. But you realize that you don't know how long you'll be here. World isn't going to be of interest to Mars anymore, and there may not be another expedition for years. Or ever."

"There'll be another expedition. You think so narrowly, Lyle — as if military expeditions are the only possible kind. Anthropologists and biologists are intensely interested in Worlders. Maybe even more so after you wreck their society. And you will, you know."

Kaufman was silent.

"Look at what happened when the nine Worlders went aboard ship. In only thirty-six hours away from the artifact and shared reality, all the accustomed restraints on rebellion and greed started to fray. What do you think will happen on World itself, with nothing in place to substitute for the traditional social restraints?"

Kaufman said only, "Is Dieter staying, too?"

"No," she said, so bleakly that Kaufman saw that husband and wife had seriously disagreed. Gruber had sided with military necessity over anthropological compassion, and Ann could not forgive him. Or Kaufman, for causing the break.

"Good-bye, Lyle," she said abruptly. She mounted a bicycle, already laden with her personal belongings, and started toward the native village, Gofkit Jemloe.

"Ann," Kaufman called after her, "are you at least armed? It may not be safe for you . . . afterwards."

She didn't even turn her head to look at him. Kaufman watched her until the bicycle was a slowly moving speck on the rolling plain.

"Colonel, we're ready to go," DeVolites said on comlink.

"I'm there," Kaufman answered. Once aboard, he avoided looking at Gruber. His first concerns now were Capelo's tests on the artifact and Marbet's revelation, whatever it was.

She waited for him in the anteroom beyond the Faller's prison. On the viewscreen Kaufman saw the Faller looking the same as always: a short leathery stump with three arms, a powerful tail, and an utterly alien head. Most of his body was still secured to the padded back wall, but one hand hung free. The Faller's face was as unreadable as ever.

Marbet turned as Kaufman entered. She wore a robe knotted loosely at the waist. Kaufman saw what she held in her hand and stopped dead.

It was a model of the artifact.

"Lyle," Marbet said, but he hardly heard her. He stared at the model. Made of hardened foamcast, he guessed. Colored accurately, faithfully reproduced surface sheen, about thirty centimeters in diameter. Detailed with all seven protuberances, each with depression and nipples to scale.

"You showed it to the Faller," Kaufman said.

"Yes."

"And no one stopped you?" He heard his voice scale upward.

"The security team didn't know what it was."

Of course not. Information about the artifact was given on a need-to-know basis; the security team aboard ship for a POW and his interpreter had no need to know about a secret alien artifact on the surface of the planet. Not what it looked like, nor what it allegedly did. But Marbet had come down to the surface with Ann, deliberately, to see the artifact that Ann had, as a fellow project-team member, described to her. Marbet had listened to the techs and scientists in the upland meadow. She knew as much as they did about what the artifact was and what it could do.

Kaufman said, "What have you shown him?"

"This. And—"

"What else?"

She didn't flinch at his tone. "This." A portable holostage sat against the wall; she turned it on. She'd programmed it well. A simulation of the artifact floated in one corner. It emitted a beam, traced only in dots. The dots struck a simulation of a human shuttle, and after a few moments—she'd even learned about the time lag, probably from either Rosalind or Albemarle—the tiny shuttle began to glow. Radioactivity. At the bottom of the stage flashed clusters of dots in consecutive order: one dot, two, three. All the clusters above seventy-five glowed the same as the shuttle. The hologram repeated, on a continuous loop.

"You're off the project," Kaufman said. "As of now. Permanently. And you're under arrest."

She didn't react at all. "Lyle, you have to see the recordings. He *recognized* the artifact. It was implicit in his entire body language, his expression . . . he recognized it! The Fallers must have one, too!"

"Marbet, did you hear me? You're under arrest for treason."

"Lyle, didn't you hear *me*? The Fallers already have an artifact like ours!"

And that was how they'd derived the principles to create the beam-disrupter shield. From setting prime two. Capelo needed to know that. But first, Kaufman did what was necessary. He opened a comlink. "Commander Grafton, this is Colonel Kaufman. We have had a serious security breach among my people, I'm sorry to say. Instruct Security to arrest Marbet Grant, currently with me in the anteroom to the prisoner's quarters. The charge is treason."

Marbet looked at him. Her smooth brown skin flushed with underlying color. Her bright green eyes glittered. "Lyle, you don't want to do this. I can read it all over you. The work is too important."

"Don't attempt to move until Security arrives, or I'll restrain you myself."

"Do you know what you're throwing away?"

"Do you know what you've given away to the enemy?"

"He's a prisoner who's never going to be released! What's he going to do with the knowledge, send it by telepathy?"

Before he could answer, two MPs burst through the door. Marbet didn't try to resist them. As they led her away, Kaufman's comlink shrilled and he closed his eyes, trying to think what to tell Grafton, tell Capelo, tell himself.

Later, after difficult sessions with both Grafton and his security chief, Kaufman returned to Marbet's workroom and accessed her session records for the hours after she'd returned aboard ship.

Marbet alone with the Faller, carrying nothing, going through a series of weird, unintelligible postures and gestures to which the prisoner made no apparent response. Apparent to Kaufman, anyway. What was she communicating to him? Reassurance that even though she hadn't seen him in nearly a day, she was back now?

Marbet carrying the model of the artifact, holding it up to the invisible barrier for the alien's closer inspection. Kaufman replayed the first few minutes of this session, over and over. It seemed to him the alien did react. His body weight shifted, there were muscle movements in his face (involuntary?), his free hand curled oddly. What was he thinking? Feeling? Marbet had interpreted his behavior as recognition of the artifact, and Kaufman had no reason to believe her wrong. Or right.

Marbet wheeling in the holostage. Activating it. The simulated beam striking the simulated shuttle, destabilizing all elements with more than seventy-five protons in their nuclei, as clearly indicated by the number diagram along the bottom. Did the Faller react again? Yes, although not as strongly. Maybe he had himself under greater control.

Kaufman listened to her session notes. She described in minute detail every communicable change in nonverbal behavior which indicated to her that the Faller indeed recognized both artifact and its use as a weapon. Kaufman switched off the recorder. Most of what she relied on, he knew, could not be described in words. She was a Sensitive, and she was sure about the enemy recognition.

The Fallers had already found an artifact, or artifacts, and had discovered its property as a shield against proton beams. (That almost made Capelo's projected test irrelevant, although the physicist would never see it that way.) They had either installed multiple artifacts aboard selected ships, or had deduced the principles behind the shield operation and used them to create similar shields. They were using these shields in various theaters of war. Because of that, they were winning the war.

Did the alleged artifact in enemy hands have the same additional settings as the one humans had found buried on World? There was no way to tell. If it had settings prime one and prime three, the destabilizing beam and the destabilizing spherical wave, they would not be very useful. Their range was too limited for long-range ground or space battles, the only kind the Fallers engaged in. Proton beams were far more effective.

That left settings five, seven, eleven, and thirteen. What did they do? Could Capelo find out? If he did, would he be able to figure out any way to use the knowledge to build better weapons or better shields or better somethings? Because if he didn't, there was every indication that humans were going to lose the war, to an enemy that did not take prisoners.

Kaufman stood on the observation deck, which was once more assigned to the project team and their eclectic clutter of equipment. This time, robots for EVAC work augmented the array. They had fixed sensors onto everything within ten thousand clicks: the ship, orbital satellites, tethered probes, and the artifact itself, now in orbit behind the *Alan B. Shepard* like Mary's lamb trailing obediently behind her.

"Now," Capelo said, and Kaufman relayed the command to the bridge, making it official: "Commence firing."

The proton beam shot out from the ship, reached the artifact, and vanished. It looked exactly like the recordings Kaufman had seen, over and over, of beams hitting Faller ships that were equipped with the beam-disrupter shield. In fact, after Marbet's revelation, the scene was almost anti-climactic. They'd all been pretty sure what setting prime two, which apparently activated automatically, would do to the proton beam.

Rosalind, Albemarle, and their herd of techs fell on the sensor data, assessing and interpreting. Capelo stood a bit apart. He looked directly at Kaufman.

Capelo said, "Setting prime one: directed-beam destabilizer, short range," he recited. "Setting prime two: local shield against whatever low-quality energy we can throw at it: laser, proton beam, presumably directed-beam destabilizer, if we had one."

Kaufman said acidly, "A proton beam is 'low-quality energy'? It could blow up this ship."

Capelo ignored the interruption. "Setting prime three: spherical wave destabilizer, short range. Setting prime five should therefore be a longer-range shield. How long a range? Ann Sikorski thinks it affected the whole planet. Maybe that's what it does—shield the planet from any dangerous energy attack. Including the destabilizing wave that resulted from the destruction of Tas, the wave effect that fried Nimitri. That would explain the fall-off at six billion clicks — roughly the radius of an average star system."

Startled, Kaufman said, "A planet-wide shield?"

"The pattern is weapon, shield, weapon, shield. Escalating in strength."

"But a shield strong enough to protect an entire planet? Against a planet-endangering attack? How are you going to test that?"

Capelo said, without a trace of irony, "There's only one way to do it. We have to put the artifact back."

NINETEEN

GOFKIT JEMLOE

When the Terran cart approached the Voratur household gates, Calin Pek Lillifar walked ahead of it.

Enli watched the approach with her neckfur rippling, her skull ridges almost flat. It was a coincidence, of course. Calin would reach the household several minutes before the Terrans. He must have come from Gofkit Shamloe by the capital road, which joined the path from the Terran compound just before Gofkit Jemloe. But why was he here?

Something had happened to her sister Ano or to Ano's children.

Enli dropped her brush—she had been applying a fresh coat of wash to the household gate, because she couldn't stand doing nothing—and ran toward Calin. "Calin! What is it? Ano . . . Fentil . . ."

"No, no, all the soils of your sister's family are rich. Nothing grows crooked, nothing wilts."

"But then . . . why are you here?"

"I wanted to see you."

A little thrill rippled across Enli's skull. She saw that Calin noticed; he grinned and said, "Breathe deeply, Enli, you pant from running."

"And you look a mess." He did, hot and sweating and dirty from travel. To come all that way on foot, not even by bicycle, to see her! Pleasure flooded her, shared with his pleasure at seeing her.

She said, "Where is your bicycle?"

"Broken. And that fool of a mender, Pek Hobbifir, is worse than inept. He cannot get it fixed until tomorrow, if at all. I didn't want to wait until tomorrow."

Again the grin; again the shared pleasure. They stood looking at each other until Enli said, "I can give you a bicycle."

"Give me a bicycle! How could you do that?"

"Much has been happening here. I have much to tell you, Calin. But first, come inside and have a cold drink."

"In a moment. Enli . . . what is *that*?"

The cart had nearly reached them. It was an ordinary World farmcart, its load covered by a blanket, but it was pulled by a Terran servant. Alongside walked another Terran, Captain Pek Heller, frowning as always. Somewhere on Pek Heller, Enli knew, would be a *gun*, and maybe even other strange, deadly Terran weapons.

"Those are Terrans." Calin, she realized, had probably never seen a Terran before. There was only time to add in a low voice, "Don't be surprised if their manners are bad," before the little procession reached them.

Enli plucked a wildflower, a pretty yellow vekifir growing by the side of the road, and held it out. She said in Terran, "Pek Heller, you are welcome to Gofkit Shamloe. This is Calin Pek Lillifar."

Pek Heller shook her head up and down curtly. She offered no gift flower, although surely the cart must be laden with them, nor did she introduce her servant. Terrible manners. All Pek Heller did was say to Enli, "You speak English. Good. These are for Mr. Voratur, from Colonel Kaufman. Trade goods. Where shall I leave them?"

Enli was glad that Calin couldn't know what Pek Heller was saying. Leave trade goods! Without drinking pel with Pek Voratur to water the bargain newly come to flower! Without exchanging hospitality flowers, without ritual wishes for a flourishing garden that rejoiced one's ancestors! But Calin knew no Terran and so confined himself to staring politely at Pek Heller without blinking.

"I will take the trade goods, Pek Heller, to Pek Voratur." Better that than cause more unshared reality between the household and the Terrans.

"Fine," Pek Heller said. "Crewman, transfer cargo to this receiver." Enli could see that Pek Heller didn't really care, possibly didn't approve of the entire bargain. Well, it was not her place to disapprove of a bargain planted between Pek Voratur and the head of her own household, Pek Kaufman. Different realities were one thing, but bad manners quite another.

"Transferred," the servant said.

"Return to base." And the two of them turned and walked away, just like that.

Calin's eyes had begun to pucker and his skull ridges to crease. The beginnings of head pain, Enli knew. To Calin, the Terran behavior must seem like unshared reality, not a different reality. Calin didn't know, as Enli had been forced to know, about different realities. There were many things she knew that he did not.

For just a moment, she was afraid.

Then she said, "Come, let us go inside and get you that cold drink. And I must take these trade goods to Pek Voratur."

"Trade goods? Pek Voratur planted another bargain with the Terrans?"

"Yes."

"For what?" Calin lifted the blanket over the cart and let out a whoop. Masses of Terran flowers, the strangely beautiful flowers Enli had seen in the garden aboard the big flying metal boat. Below the flowers, a neat pile of the square, ugly Terran boxes, containing the other trade goods Pek Voratur had bargained for. Even now, even after so much living with Terrans, it astonished Enli that people who could "make" such wonderful flowers would also make their boxes so ugly.

Calin said, "Pek Voratur planted a bargain for all these Terran blossoms? They are far more beautiful than the rosib he got last time. What did he trade for all this? And what's in those ugly boxes?"

"Let's go inside first, Calin. I must bring this cart to Pek Voratur."

His attention returned from the cart to her. Enli felt her neckfur stir. He said softly, "I missed you, Enli."

"And I, you."

"Gofkit Shamloe was not the same for me after you left. I think it will never be the same, unless you come back with me."

She said falteringly, "Go back to Ano, you mean. To live again with Ano."

"Not to live with Ano."

It was a gift from the First Flower, a miraculous blooming. Enli knew she was plain (not like Ano), too big, too old for a first mating. And there was her history . . . she had once been declared unreal for a great crime, mating with her brother. They had both been declared unreal, Tabor kept from the world of his ancestors after he killed himself, Enli saved from the same everlasting death only by becoming an informant on the Terrans for Reality and Atonement. Enli had earned both their reality back again, hers and Tabor's, and once again shared the sweetness of reality. But Calin knew all this history, and her age, and still he stood there, a man whom any woman would be proud to mate, and he'd said to her . . .

It was a gift from the First Flower, a miraculous blooming, an unfolding beyond any dreaming.

"Enli—" he began, and she said at the same moment, "Not now, Calin. Later. I must take these things to Pek Voratur!"

"I will help you," he said and picked up the cart handle. Practical Calin, turning his hand to the task of the moment, whatever task and whatever moment that might be.

He pulled the cart inside the compound, telling Enli the news of Ano, of small Fentil, of baby Usi and almost-grown Obora, of all the village. Pek Voratur himself, reality having been shared with him by servants, came bustling through the vast courtyards and gardens. "Yes, yes, here they are! Enli, these are the trade goods from the Terrans?"

"Yes, Pek Voratur."

"But where is Pek Kaufman?"

"He did not come." Pek Voratur's skull ridges creased, and Enli explained as well as she could. She introduced Calin, and flowers were exchanged. But Pek Voratur was clearly eager to examine his new acquisitions.

"Enli, ask the others who share in this bargain to come to my personal room. Your visitor can wait for you in the gardens, perhaps, or in your room."

She led Calin to her room, watching his awe at the richness of the Voratur household: the magnificent flowerbeds, swooping curved walls, arched windows hung with the finest fabric from the Seury Islands. Had Calin ever been away from Gofkit Shamloe? Perhaps not. Again Enli felt that prickling of her neckfur. There were so many things she knew that he did not . . .

In her room, a pretty guest room with curving designs painted on the floor and an expensive carved wooden table, Calin took both her hands and pressed them to his stomach. "Enli, I want to say something to you."

"Calin, I must go find some other members of the household, Pek Voratur asked me—"

"I heard what he asked you. You can share the full reality of it with me later. But I want to say this now, before you tell me anything more. I don't understand what you have to do with Pek Voratur's trading. But whatever it is, when it's over, I want you to come back to Gofkit Shamloe with me and unfold in the mating ceremony before the First Flower. I want our gardens to be planted together, our children to dance on the village green, and our petals to intertwine in the land of our ancestors."

Enli listened to the formal words. The head pain started between her eyes—so many things she knew that he did not—but it felt distant, unimportant next to this gift from the First Flower. Perhaps she had become too accustomed to moving between realities that other people could not even see. If so, then that was her reality. She could do that, mate with Calin, and keep to herself the unshared realities the Terrans had forced her to see. To keep Calin, she could do that. She could do anything.

"Yes," Enli said, and placed his two hands on her stomach. "We will unfold in the mating ceremony before the First Flower, and plant our gardens together. Our children will dance on the village green, and our petals will intertwine in the land of our ancestors."

They moved into each other and held on, until practical Calin said, "Now go carry out Pek Voratur's instructions."

She couldn't resist one more bit of information. "The trade goods you saw are one-sixteenth mine. Eight of us, including me, were traders in the bargain that Pek Voratur planted with the Terrans. You are mating with a rich woman, and the first thing I will do is buy you a bicycle."

Calin's skull ridges flattened in surprise, and then his whooping laugh followed her as she left the room.

There was a glass vat of gently bubbling goo, which Pek Voratur said was a potion to cure the scabbing disease. There was a powerful device for seeing things at a very great distance, a *telescope*. There were nine more comlinks, one for each of them. There was a method, shown in careful drawings, for making a stronger blend of metals than existed now. Pek Voratur said that drawing was the most valuable of the Terran trade goods, but it didn't seem that way to the eight others who had ridden on the small metal flying boat up to the larger metal flying boat. To all but Voratur and Enli, the greater value lay in the flowers, amazing flowers with exotic petals and glorious colors, Terran "made" flowers that every great household and every village green on World would want to plant in their gardens.

The nine voyagers sat in Pek Voratur's personal room and listened to him explain how their shared trade goods would be marketed, how the profits would be calculated, what each of them could hope to receive and when. Looking around, Enli saw that few of them actually listened. The woman who was a trade agent for Voratur listened, certainly, and so did the woman who had shrieked on her pallet aboard the flying boat. But the head gardener was more interested in examining the Terran flower he had been given, roots and blossom. The stonemason played with her comlink. The apprentice weaver merely stared around him. And the girl, Essa Pek Criltifor, who had run and laughed and hidden with the Terran child Sudie, seemed more intent on the ugliness of the square-cornered Terran boxes than in the future riches that Pek Voratur described.

And then Enli, who had not been listening because her thoughts brimmed with Calin, saw Ann Pek Sikorski standing in the open archway to the room.

The Terran looked smaller, more tired, more the color of bleached road dust than usual. She stared at the Terran goods being passed around the room. No one noticed her except Enli, who slipped quietly out. A Terran bicycle lay on the ground; Pek Sikorski must have ridden it straight through the household gardens, a breach of manners Enli would never have expected from her. Enli led the Terran to a bench under the shade of a magnificent saj tree.

"Pek Sikorski?" And then, when there was no answer, "Ann?"

"They've gone, Enli. Or some of them have, including Pek Kaufman. The rest will go over the next few days. All of them."

"All the Terrans? Gone where?"

"Back to the ship. And from there, back to Terra."

"Even Pek Gruber? Your mate?"

"Even Pek Gruber," Pek Sikorski said, and her voice throbbed with a sudden anger that Enli didn't understand.

She said, "They left you here? Alone? Why?"

"I chose to stay here. Listen, Enli, I have something very important to tell you."

The scent of the saj blossoms, waxy pink and heavily fragrant, drifted to Enli on the warm air. She had the sudden thought that she would remember that scent the rest of her life as belonging to whatever Pek Sikorski was going to tell her now. The saj perfume, redolent and sweet, spoiled for her forever.

Pek Sikorski said, "Do you remember when Terrans took Tas away from World? Of course you do. There were seven moons, and then there were six."

Enli gestured yes.

"I told you then that Tas was not a real moon. It was a manufactured item, made long ago by people no one now remembers. Well, there was another such manufactured item buried in the Neury Mountains. Smaller than Tas—much, much smaller—but made of the same material, by the same long-ago people. And now Pek Kaufman and the others have dug up this buried object, and taken it away from World up to the flying boat. They will take it back to Terra."

"Why?" Enli asked. Clearly the Terrans should not take things away from World without planting a bargain for them. And nothing at all should be taken away from the Neury Mountains, home of the First Flower. But Enli didn't see why these actions made Pek Sikorski look as she did, so . . . so defeated.

"They'll take it back to Terra because they think they have a use for it there. But there's more. Enli, do you remember what happened when you and Pek Voratur went with me up to the flying boat? Do you?"

She said slowly, "Shared reality went away. Many different realities, one for each person, came instead." She didn't like to think about that. One more thing Calin had not shared.

"Yes. And that is going to happen again. Enli, the buried object causes shared reality. When the object goes off World in the small flying boat, shared reality will stop again, like it did aboard ship. Only this time it will stop forever."

Enli touched Pek Sikorski's head, below the place where the strange headfur began. No, Pek Sikorski was not feverish, even though she looked sick. Nor was she unreal; Enli was too experienced now to believe that. And you could be sick without having a fever.

"It's true, Enli! And it will happen soon!"

"You should lie down. Come with me to my personal room." Too late, she remembered that Calin waited there.

"I have to talk to Pek Voratur," Pek Sikorski said wearily, "and he has to summon a sunflasher. People must be told what's going to happen. There's not much time left."

Enli said gently, "Pek Voratur will not share this reality."

"Yes, he will. Didn't you see him aboard ship? Without shared reality, he was ready to cheat you all. He'll understand."

"Cheat" was a Terran word. Enli didn't know what it meant.

Pek Sikorski's comlink rang. She punched at it, and Pek Kaufman's voice said, "Ann, I just wanted you to know. We're lifting off now."

"Good-bye, Lyle," Pek Sikorski said. "Don't give us another thought." She punched the comlink again and looked at Enli. Her long strange Terran face sagged.

"Too late," she said.

At first, it seemed Pek Sikorski must have been wrong. Nothing happened.

Enli led her to the court she had occupied on her last visit, near the compound wall, with the cool flowerbeds of shade-loving ollinib in bloom beneath the window. Pek Sikorski protested that she couldn't sleep, this was too important, it didn't matter that she hadn't rested in two days. Within three heartbeats she was asleep.

Enli went back to her own room, and to Calin. He wasn't there. She found him in a servants' court, squatting on the ground with two men and a boy, playing clent. The smooth polished stones for the game had been fished out of the pool in the middle of the court. Bright flowers grew around the pool, and a cool breeze blew from it. Watching the laughing group, Enli felt her breath swell in her chest.

Hers. He was hers.

Oh, Tabor . . .

But that thought she pushed away. Tabor was joyous among their ancestors, and he came to Enli not even in dreams. It was time for her, too, to know joy.

She whistled softly, the whistle from a child's game back in Gofkit Shamloe, and Calin looked up. He smiled and beckoned her over. "Look, Enli—I am winning. Already I have won enough to buy us a good evening at a pel house."

One of the men, old Bafil Pek Honimor the jik herder, laughed. The other man, whom Enli didn't know, bristled his neckfur. He took the three dark stones and cast them among the light ones.

"Lil!" the boy called; evidently they were playing the "moons" variation of the game. Despite herself, Enli thought briefly of Tas, the moon that was no more. Did that affect the game?

The surly man cast again. "Obri!" the boy called. "You lose to Calin again, Justafar!"

Justafar's skull ridges creased sharply. He reached for the pile of coins to one side of the stones. The old man laughed; Justafar must be well-known as a poor loser. Good-naturedly Calin put his own big hand over the coins, still smiling. Justafar swung his fist and hit Calin in the neck.

Then the shocking thing happened. Nothing.

Justafar's blow should have set up such crippling head pain in himself that he would drop to the ground without hitting out again. Shared reality meant that you could not strike another without such a consequence: a blow broke the sharing. One person wanted to strike, but the other not to be struck. The three men, the boy, and Enli should all have been clutching their heads, the fight over, until reality was once more shared among them.

Instead, they stared at each other, dazed by not feeling any head pain. The boy cried out in anguish, "I'm not real!" Calin turned to look in bewilderment at Enli. And Justafar struck him again.

The two men fought clumsily; neither had ever done such a thing before. Justafar hit out over and over again because he was enraged, because he was frightened, because the world should not work this way. At first Calin mostly defended himself, but when it was obvious that Justafar was trying to do genuine damage, Calin too fought in earnest. He was bigger and younger. Eventually his fist connected with Justafar's temple, and the other man dropped to the ground and lay still. And Enli saw that no one, not she nor Calin nor old Pek Honimor nor the boy nor the people who had come running from the buildings around the courtyard, felt any head pain.

"Shared reality will stop again, like it did aboard ship, only this time it will stop forever."

"Aiiieeeeee!" a man cried. All her life Enli had heard people make that sound, when the jik stopped giving milk or a child fell ill or a bush failed to flower. But not like this. It seemed to her suddenly that the man's cry sounded strangely Terran, alone and uncertain and desperate. And that the cry would go on forever.

TWENTY

ABOARD THE *ALAN B. SHEPARD*

om Capelo had agreed with that ceaseless inquisitor, Lyle
Kaufman, that thinking about physics was like thinking about
chess: non-verbal, patterned, branching. It wasn't true. Kaufman's statement described a physical world, and a way of
thinking about it, that was neat and well organized and repeatable.
Perhaps some physicists thought that way. If so, Capelo didn't see
how they could be any good.

The physical world wasn't neat, wasn't well organized, wasn't
always repeatable. It hadn't been for roughly two hundred fifty years,
not since a wave became a particle and a particle became unmeasurable in all its particulars at once. And in the last century the physical
world had only gotten more complex: more thread vibrations like
the graviton, more dimensions in the Calabi-Yau spaces, more tiny
but long-range force fields to further complicate the roiling quantum
frenzy. Every time physicists got together and agreed that some phenomenon was impossible, some maverick did an experiment or came
up with an equation that proved it was not. "We shall never understand anything until we have found some contradictions," said the
legendary Bohr. Contradictions were the lifeblood of discoveries:

experiments that contradicted theory, math that contradicted theory, theory that contradicted theory. Contradictions and intuitions.

Capelo's colleagues complained that he couldn't explain how he got his results, and that he insisted on the truth of his results before he had the equations to go with them. Fools, most of them. The point was not to create tidy strings of reasoning—engineers could do that—but to glimpse nature whole for one glorious moment. To catch a fleeting sight beyond the prison of conventional thought, a glimpse out of a briefly illuminated window. And then work like hell to follow that glimpse wherever it led. It wasn't like chess; it was like falling in love. And like love, physics involved obsession, sacrifice, blind spots, enormous anguish. Gazing in delight at some aspects of the beloved and averting your eyes from others, knowing they could not stay averted forever.

That was how he worked, but how could you explain that to a bureaucrat like Kaufman? You couldn't. And Kaufman couldn't understand, although he tried. He was, despite the uniform and authority, a science groupie, and Capelo thought there was nothing more pathetic. Always on the outside, longing to be inside, incapable of doing what he so admired. There were times it was painful for Capelo to be around Kaufman.

But he'd give Kaufman one thing: He didn't try to dictate to Capelo what had to be done. When Capelo said, "We're going to have to put the artifact back," Kaufman had arranged to do it.

Of course, that was only the smallest piece of it. The biggest piece was that glimpse of the whole, that one insight that justified pursuing a line of thought. So far, Capelo hadn't had it. The window was closed as tightly as ever.

"All right," Kaufman said to the assemblage on the observation deck, "Grafton has agreed. We're putting the artifact back on the ring in the meadow."

"I'd love to have heard that conversation," Albemarle said.

Kaufman ignored him. "The techs will retrieve and redirect the artifact. Anyone going planetside should report to shuttle bay in three hours. Tom?"

"Staying here for the test," he said curtly.

"Hal?"

Albemarle hesitated. "Staying here."

Gruber said eagerly, "Then I'll go down." He began to ask technical questions. Capelo didn't listen.

The problem with quantum phenomena was — had always been — that a system goes along one way, particle and wave, for a while. Then it goes along another way, one or the other, after being observed. Why should that be? Why did an observer make so much difference — and why did it have to be an observer who was either sentient or created by sentience? Why should the whole system require an observer, an outside component, at all?

There was another way to think about it, of course. The wave collapses not because of any observer, but because the means of measurement, whatever it is, has somehow forced the curvature of spacetime to exceed some critical, very small value. But what value? Why? How?

The space tunnels transported huge masses — but not more huge than one hundred thousand tons — across great distances, instantaneously. The accepted buzzword for that was "macro-level entanglement," a term which meant exactly nothing. How did anything larger than an electron move from classic laws of motion into the quantum world of entanglement? If the artifact was entangled with something, what was it? Where was it? How did the entanglement work?

A third window to try to catch a glimpse through: probability. Physics itself was probable; it had been clear since the twentieth century that all models of the universe were provisional, and most were partial. Anything that explained anything never explained everything.

On a smaller and more specific level, it was easily seen that certain events were probabilistic: They may or may not occur. In many cases the probability was documentable: We know there is a 17 percent chance that event x will occur under these specified conditions. There is a 53 percent chance that event y will occur under different conditions. Or whatever. What nobody could say yet was *why* event x occurs 17 percent of the time. There were no identified causals for varying probability levels, even when the levels themselves were known. There were no equations.

Yet what the artifact represented was manipulatable probability fields. Had to be. The directed-beam destabilizer: It manipulated the strong force, so that all atoms above atomic number seventy-five emitted alpha particles. Or did it manipulate not the strong force directly, but the probability that a nucleus would emit a more-than-probable number of alpha particles?

How the hell did you manipulate probability? No one could even *explain* probability, let alone direct it. That contradicted every known theory. In fact, Capelo now had reams of experimental data, his own and Syree Johnson's, that clearly contradicted theory. So far, that hadn't led to any progress in his understanding. No glimpses through the window.

"Tom?" Kaufman said, evidently for more than the first time. "Did you hear me?"

"No."

"I said, do you want anything to eat?"

"No." He left the observation deck to find Amanda and Sudie.

They were in their quarters with Jane Shaw. To Capelo's surprise, Jane looked upset. This was serious. Jane never looked upset; she was the bedrock all of them rested on.

"Daddy!" Sudie cried, hurtled herself at him, and burst into tears.

Capelo picked her up and cuddled her. Over Sudie's shoulder he looked inquiringly at Jane. She said, "She's been having nightmares. For a few days now. She's hardly had two hours' unbroken sleep."

"What kind of nightmares?"

"She won't say," Jane said. Sudie's howling rose demonically, making further conversation impossible. Capelo sat in a deep chair and rocked her, crooning wordlessly, patting her back and her springy dark curls. Amanda came to stand beside the chair, and Capelo patted her, too. So grave, so quiet, her pale face way too sad for a ten-year-old.

It took a long time, but Sudie finally fell asleep in her father's arms. Capelo whispered to Amanda, "What are her nightmares about?"

Amanda whispered back, "I don't know, Daddy. She says she can't tell anybody."

" 'Can't'?"

"That's what she says."

"When did they start?"

"Right after the aliens were aboard, and Sudie played with the alien girl in the ship garden."

Capelo shifted Sudie against his shoulder and tried to keep his voice under control. "Jane, why was Sudie playing with an alien?"

Jane said, "I didn't know about it until afterward. In fact, I didn't even know that natives were aboard. I let the girls go to the garden with Marbet Grant . . . you remember that you got them to come aboard without you by promising they would see Marbet again."

Capelo nodded.

"Marbet took them to the garden, and then Ann Sikorski showed up with three aliens, one a little girl."

Amanda took up the story. "Yeah, and I was talking to the nice alien that spoke English, her name is Enli, and Sudie and the native girl were awful. They were running and playing hide-and-seek and dropping leaves and nuts on people from the tops of trees. She always embarrasses me in public, Daddy. It's not fair."

Capelo pushed Amanda back on track. "Did this alien child hit Sudie? Or hurt her in some way? Or give her anything to eat or drink?"

"Oh, no, nothing like that. They just played. Sudie seemed fine, until nighttime when she had her first nightmare. And she's had them ever since. Lots of them."

Jane said, obviously reluctantly, "She cries out, and sometimes she talks. But the only word I can distinguish is 'Mommy.' "

Capelo looked at Amanda. Her eyes had filled with tears. He took one arm off Sudie and put it around Mandy.

Jane said, "I'm sorry."

"It's not your fault," Capelo said, because clearly it wasn't. Still, rage filled him. His girls had been through enough with the death of their mother. Karen's body sliced in two by the sweeping laser weapons from the Faller skeeter, the bastards too cowardly to even land and fight against soldiers. His peaceful wife and his two children . . . Sudie had screamed for her mother for months. Gradually she had calmed down, laughed again, slept through the night. And now the nightmares all over again, set off by *more* aliens even if they weren't Fallers . . .

"Here," he said to Jane, "take Sudie. I'm going to have a little talk with Marbet Grant."

Capelo hoped to find Marbet in her quarters. She wasn't there. Nor was she in the wardroom, the garden, or the exercise area. He glanced into the chapel—her subjective Sensitive art didn't seem to him all that far from mysticism. Certainly you couldn't call it science. She wasn't in the chapel. He headed for the observation deck.

But she wasn't there, either. "Hello, Tom," Kaufman said. "Come to see the show?" Outside the viewport, robots were hauling the artifact back into the shuttle bay.

"It's a routine operation," Capelo said. "Where's Marbet Grant?"

Kaufman turned. Was there tension on that bland face?

"Marbet?"

"Yes. You know, diminutive Sensitive that nobody's seen for weeks."

Kaufman smiled. "Well, not exactly. She did come down to see the artifact, remember. And I've seen her."

"Then where is she?"

Somehow they had edged away from the rest of the group, out of earshot. How had Kaufman managed that? Capelo felt his anger growing. He was being manipulated.

Kaufman said, "You're looking for Marbet Grant."

"A man of insight. You look directly into my soul. Where the hell is she?"

"Can I ask why you want her?"

"No. Where is she?"

Kaufman said easily, "She's indisposed."

" 'Indisposed'? You mean she's sick? In quarantine?"

"I didn't say that. But it might help, Tom, if you could tell me why you want to see her. It might be something I could help you with just as well."

Capelo put his hand on Kaufman's arm. He looked directly into Kaufman's calm brown eyes. He said softly, "I want to talk to Marbet Grant. Not you. Marbet. Now stop fucking around with me and tell me where she is."

Kaufman pressed the door; somehow they had moved all the way over to it. He stepped into the corridor, forcing Capelo to follow, and pressed the door closed. "I can't tell you where she is, Tom. It's a matter of security. Special Compartmentment Information. Believe me, I would answer you if I could. But Marbet is working on a separate project involving the aliens—you knew that much, of course—and she really can't be disturbed."

"Security? SCI? What have those flower-mad aliens got to do with security? They've given us no trouble whatsoever!"

"No, they haven't. Yet," Kaufman said, and Capelo felt that the man was telling him the truth.

"So?"

"Again, I can't explain her project. But she really cannot be disturbed. If I can help—"

"You can tell her to stay away from my kids. She took them into the garden when Ann brought her aliens there, and something happened that's sent Sudie straight into nightmares and screaming."

Kaufman's eyes sharpened. "What happened?"

"I don't know. Sudie's too upset to say. But I don't want it to happen again. Marbet Grant stays away from Sudie and Amanda. And Ann Sikorski does, too."

"I think I can guarantee both those things, Tom. Ann stayed behind on World, did you know that?"

"She did?" So that explained Gruber's uncharacteristic gloom. God, the ways people messed up their lives.

Kaufman said, "She was very opposed to moving the artifact off-planet and destroying shared reality."

"We don't even know for sure if the damn thing causes your so-called shared reality!"

"Yes, I told her that," Kaufman said.

You couldn't get anywhere with the man. He agreed, and smiled, and politely digressed, and all the while he manipulated you and everything else around him. It was like arguing with the wind. Capelo had gotten what he wanted. His kids would be kept away from Marbet, aliens, and upsetting encounters. But he still felt as if he'd lost.

Kaufman's comlink rang. The OOD's voice said, "Colonel, the object is re-secured to the shuttle. Descent in forty minutes."

"Thank you," Kaufman said. To Capelo he said, "Commander Grafton has agreed to your test. Ninety minutes from now is the ideal gunnery position."

"Fine," Capelo said.

"Thanks, Tom," Kaufman said, as if Capelo had done him a favor. Wind.

"You're most sincerely welcome, Lyle," Capelo said, but Kaufman ignored the sarcasm and merely smiled.

Kaufman watched the shuttle leave the ship with its cargo in the net of dislocation-free monofilament cables. In a moment it had dwindled to a dark dot.

He had successfully diverted Capelo from tearing the ship apart looking for Marbet. Which, Lyle was convinced, Capelo was capable of doing. But the larger problem of Marbet remained, twisting Kaufman's gut. He needed to know exactly what she had learned from the Faller, if anything, about the artifact. And he needed to make a decision on how much more might be learned, versus a further breach of security from her.

Not a breach of security. Call it what it was; he'd done so when he had her arrested. Treason. She had knowingly communicated valuable, classified military information to an enemy in time of war.

Kaufman had ninety minutes. He went to the brig.

On a ship like the *Alan B. Shepard*, this consisted of two rooms, an anteroom and a cell. When there were no prisoners, which was nearly all of the time, the anteroom was used for storage. When there was a prisoner, the packing crates became desk and chair for the MP who monitored security, although for petty offenses the formality of a guard was usually skipped. Both anteroom and cell were e-locked. Kaufman had been given the codes at Marbet's arrest, a piece of information he had not expected to need on this expedition.

The MP got to his feet and saluted as Kaufman entered the anteroom. "Sir!"

"At ease, Sergeant. Has Commander Grafton authorized my visit to the prisoner?"

"Yes, sir! The special project team has been cleared for entry, sir!"

Kaufman looked again and saw how young the MP was. A first tour of duty, most likely. The newbies always got the boring assignments.

Kaufman passed into Marbet's cell. It was three meters by two, with a bunk, toilet, and sink. She sat on the edge of the bunk, dressed in green coveralls, writing on paper with a pencil. Not even e-tablets were allowed in the brig. Beside her on the bunk was an untouched tray of food.

"Hello, Marbet."

"Hello, Lyle." Her voice was neutral—a good sign. Kaufman had hoped to avoid hysteria or fury. He realized now that she wouldn't indulge in either one.

"I've come to ask you some necessary questions about your work."

"Am I going to be allowed to continue it?"

Brief and direct. "That's not decided yet." He was lying, of course. Military treason, which giving critical and classified weapons information to enemy personnel certainly was, fell under Grafton's purview no matter who committed the crime. There was no way Grafton would release Marbet Grant to anyone but a Solar Alliance high court.

"You're lying," Marbet said. "Look at you . . . you're lying and you hate it."

"All right." He sat beside her on the bunk, not too close. "You can't resume your work, you can't see the prisoner again, and you're in the brig until we arrive back on Mars. But meanwhile, I need to know everything you've learned about how much the Faller knows about the artifact. This is an official inquiry, Marbet, but it's also an appeal for the good of the project. Will you cooperate?"

"Of course. I never intended anything but the good of the project."

"I believe that. Others won't."

She smiled wanly. "At least now you're being honest. There isn't too much to report. Yes, the Faller recognized the artifact, immediately. He recognized the holo I programmed, too, which suggests to me that they've discovered how to use the directed-beam destabilizer at setting prime one. That was as far as I got. I'd planned on programming a holo to demonstrate the spherical wave-effect destabilizer, too, to see if he recognized that. But you came in before I got to it."

"Was there anything in his nonverbal or sign language that told you anything more than that he recognized it?"

"Yes. He was disturbed that we knew about it, or had it. Very disturbed."

"What else?"

"Nothing else. I didn't have time."

Her nearness was beginning to disturb Kaufman. She looked at him so levelly, without bitterness, seeming to understand his position as well as her own . . . There was no other woman like her. Her scent came to him, distinctively Marbet.

She smiled, and he knew she knew his thoughts. To his intense annoyance, he felt the blood rise in his cheeks.

She said, "It's all right, Lyle. I like you, too. If things were different . . ."

Was it another manipulation? No, not now. Or maybe he just wanted to believe that. He said stiffly, "Anything else?"

"Just one thing. But it's important. You have to convince Grafton to let me talk again to the Faller."

"That's not possible, Marbet. Can't happen."

"It has to. The Faller was *very* disturbed that we have this artifact, Lyle."

"You'd expect that, wouldn't you?"

"Yes. But as far as I can estimate, his disturbance went beyond his discovering our new strategic advantage. He was trying to hide something, Lyle. Something important, that we might need to know about the artifact."

"Could you tell what?"

"Not a clue. But I'm positive I'm right. You shouldn't have had me arrested so quickly. You should have listened to me first, and weighed all the alternatives, and made your usual careful decisions. But you didn't. You went off half-cocked because your personal feelings for me overwhelmed you with disappointment that I did what I did. It was a mistake, Lyle. And if what you say about Grafton is true, I don't see how you're going to rectify it."

On his way back to the observation deck, Kaufman stopped at the secret cell where the other prisoner was being held. In the corridor Grafton's MPs stood guard. Inside the anteroom, Kaufman saw on the viewscreen that the Faller's free hand had again been manacled.

He asked the computer for a five-minute summary of the Faller's behavior since Marbet's arrest. The program didn't need five minutes. It told him that the Faller had done nothing unusual: feed, sleep, stare straight ahead. Analysis of real-time recordings had revealed to the computer no significant body movements or changes of expression.

But, then, the computer wasn't Marbet Grant.

TWENTY-ONE

GOFKIT JEMLOE

Enli sat with Calin in her room in the Voratur household. The door and window tapestries, fully unfurled, shut out the sunshine, and so Enli had lit a lamp. Throughout the household most tapestries were unfurled; people huddled in small groups, as though the loss of shared reality were somehow easier if fewer people were around.

Calin said, "Tell me again, Enli." She had washed away the blood from his fight with Justafar and bandaged his head and arm. Below the head bandage Calin's honest, bewildered eyes gazed at her like a child asking why a beloved pet had died. Occasionally a cry came to them through the tapestries, an outpouring of anguish from someone whose reality had been stretched so far it had temporarily broken.

Perhaps temporarily. Perhaps not.

Enli held Calin's hand tightly. "Once more. Then I must go to Pek Voratur to explain."

"Once more."

"This is what Pek Sikorski told me." Pek Sikorski—was she still asleep in the guest court? Enli must rouse her before she went to Pek Voratur. She spoke faster to Calin.

"Our shared reality comes from something invisible in the air, as the perfume of flowers is invisible. We breathe in shared reality with the air. And like flower fragrance, the shared reality we breathe in comes from an object. Perfume comes from flowers; shared reality comes from a manufactured object that for all of history has lain in the Neury Mountains. It—"

"If it lay in the Neury Mountains, it is a gift from the First Flower."

"Perhaps. But now the Terrans in the large flying boat have taken the manufactured object away in their smaller metal flying boat. And so shared reality no longer perfumes the air of World."

She watched him struggle with this. "But why did they take it? It was our gift from the First Flower! Why do they want our shared reality? Haven't they any of their own?"

"No," Enli said. "They don't. And when the nine of us Worlders went up to the large metal flying boat, we didn't, either."

"If they have no shared reality of their own, then they are unreal! They have no souls!"

"I was not unreal when I went to the flying boat. I retained my soul. So did Pek Voratur and Pek Forbin and Essa Criltifor." Again she saw the little girl running and laughing with the human child Sudie. "We are real, we still have our souls, even if we do not share reality any longer, Calin."

"You're speaking unrealities against the First Flower!"

She was silent. Could he embrace this new strangeness, this blasphemy? Eventually, he must . . . They all must. But if he blamed her for telling him about it, then their mating would not happen. Enli's chest tightened.

He said, "But you're only repeating what the Terrans told you, aren't you, Enli? They're the ones with no souls. They did this terrible thing to us."

"Yes," she said, and could have wept with relief. He was going to blame the Terrans, not her.

He took her in his arms. "How can we get the manufactured object back?"

"I don't think we can, Calin. They took it away from World, out into space. We have no metal flying boats to follow them."

"True. Oh, those filthy unreal soulless people! I would kill them all!"

Pek Sikorski.

Fear clutched Enli. She jumped up and pulled Calin with her. "Come with me. Now. Please, Calin, don't ask questions yet, it's very important . . ." She tugged him up, ran with him through the deserted courts and gardens to the guest court.

Pek Sikorski still slept, unharmed. Few in the Voratur household knew she was here, and fewer still gave her a thought in their own bewilderment. And, Enli belatedly realized, no one but her knew that the Terrans were the cause of the loss of shared reality, of the unmaking of the world.

Except Calin. When he saw Pek Sikorski asleep, his skull ridges creased and his neckfur bristled. "There is one of them! This one at least I can kill!"

"No!" Enli cried, appalled. She should not have brought him here, what was she thinking, none of them could think anymore . . .

She threw herself on Calin, between him and Pek Sikorski. He had little experience of violence. He stopped instantly. "Enli? What?"

"She didn't do it, Calin. She wanted the other Terrans to leave the manufactured object here. For us. She didn't go away from World with them because she hated that they took away our shared reality."

He shook his head like an animal, a jik shaking off water. "I don't understand."

"I know. It's all hard," she said, and something in her voice must have touched him. He was a tender man.

"It is hard, dear one. And especially for you, who had . . . who must . . . who lived with these Terrans. But if you say this one is real, then that is shared reality."

Enli moved into his arms. Grateful . . . she was so grateful. He had held. It was going to be all right.

He said, brokenly as a child, "Enli . . . I . . . don't know how . . . to live like . . . this."

None of them knew. "We'll learn, my Calin," she whispered. "We'll learn."

She saw that Pek Sikorski was awake, quietly listening to them. Enli broke free of Calin and knelt by her pallet.

"Pek Sikorski, it happened. Shared reality stopped."

"Are people locking themselves away in fear? And crying and wailing?"

How had she known? "Yes. But that's not what I came to tell you. Something else, something very important. You cannot tell Voratur, or anyone, that shared reality stopped because of Terrans. If you do—"

"If I do, they'll decide I have no soul and kill me."

Enli said in astonishment, "You know that?"

"Yes. I know."

"Then why didn't you go away with the other Terrans? With your mate, Pek Gruber?"

"I couldn't," Pek Sikorski said, and Enli understood the deep sadness but not the reasoning. She would never grasp a Terran reality whole. Never. Pek Sikorski continued, "I have to explain now to Pek Voratur what happened. He's a rich and powerful man. He can help keep people calm, keep them from *rioting*." The word was Terran.

"Yes, but . . . all right. Tell Pek Voratur that something has happened to the manufactured object that perfumed the air with shared reality, and that we must learn to live without it. But don't tell him the Terrans took the object. Say that the Terrans just saw—" she had an inspiration, "—saw with a big *telescope*, much more powerful than the one Pek Kaufman traded to Pek Voratur, they saw the object . . . die. Say it was a . . . a . . ." What would sound important and strange enough for the First Flower to have created? ". . . a living rock. Not a manufactured object, but a living rock, which the Terrans saw die. And that's why shared reality is gone."

Pek Sikorski said bleakly, "Would you prefer that? Would that be easier for Worlders to accept?"

"Yes," said Enli, and wondered if it were true. She looked at Calin. His skull ridges creased again. "Enli—you are telling this Terran to say unreal things."

"Yes." And there was no head pain—not now, and not when Pek Sikorski eventually talked to Pek Voratur. Enli saw Calin, dismayed, realize this. No head pain. "But it is for everyone's good."

"But anyone can say anything now! Even if it is unreal!"

"Yes," Enli said again.

"I don't want to go with you to Pek Voratur to say this," Calin said abruptly. "I am going back to Gofkit Jemloe. I must see that my sister's soil stays rich, and my mother's."

Enli stood. "I will give you that bicycle, Calin."

"I don't want a bicycle from you." His eyes grew darker. "Maybe shared reality is gone. Maybe anyone can say anything. But people should still say what is real. *You* should, Enli."

He turned abruptly and left. Enli stood rooted to the floor. If she moved, she thought, she would shatter. No pain from unshared reality could have rivaled this one.

Pek Sikorski put her hands over her face.

They told Pek Voratur, deep in his personal rooms with his ailing wife Alu, his children, and an elderly cousin. Pek Sikorski told him the reality she had unfolded, the untrue reality, that the Terrans had seen a great living rock die in the Neury Mountains. Pek Voratur listened carefully, and Enli saw relief spread over his fleshy, well-oiled face. Here was something he could understand. A sacred rock, created by the First Flower—and what could the First Flower not create, having created the World? A sacred rock, now dead as all living things must die, and so the perfume of shared reality gone.

"Yes, we must get sunflashers to tell everyone on World. Yes, yes. I will see to it. Pek Treenifil!" he bellowed for his household steward.

"Shared reality will be gone forever?" Alu Pek Voratur asked falteringly from her sickbed.

"Yes," Pek Sikorski said, and Alu Pek Voratur pulled the blanket over her face.

It proved difficult to find a sunflasher; they, too, cowered in their homes. The village had come to a standstill. No cookfires in the communal hearths, no herders with their jikib, no children racing between bicycle sheds and gardens. But eventually Pek Voratur, walking fearlessly through the stillness, found a sunflasher prostrate before his flower altar.

The sunflasher towers averaged seven cellib apart, circling all of World at the equator, where its principal landmass lay. The towers were constantly staffed on all sunny days. If the weather cooperated, any message could travel halfway around World from dawn to sunset, and all the way around the next day. Branch towers spread to the north and south, after which bicycle messengers took the information to remote villages. Although it was seldom used all at once, the whole sunflasher system could reach everyone on World. Reluctantly, the Gofkit Jemloe sunflasher mounted his bicycle and rode to his tower, set on the highest hill some distance away. Later, Enli and Voratur and Pek Sikorski saw the bright glints from his tilting mirror. Over and over the message glinted. Later still, the sunflasher rode back to Gofkit Jemloe.

"Pek Voratur, there is no answer. The other sunflashers have abandoned their towers, too. I cannot share anything with anybody."

Enli, Pek Voratur, and Pek Sikorski looked at each other. Silently they made their way back to the Voratur household.

The gate servant was not at her post. Someone had broken the delicate wood carving on the gate: smashed it to pieces, senselessly, in rage.

"So it starts," Pek Sikorski said wearily in Terran. Pek Voratur looked at her blankly, but Enli realized, in grief, that she knew what Pek Sikorski meant.

Then, next morning, it was over.

Enli was the first awake, very early, heavy-eyed from poor sleep. There was a foul taste in her mouth. She had slept in Voratur's personal room, along with many others. Pek Voratur seemed to have decided, since the smashing of his gate, that it was better to have many people around him who would not smash anything. Thirty householders crowded together in pallets on the floor. She staggered from the room out to the piss closet off the garden and made her morning stream.

A man waited outside the piss closet for his turn. Enli didn't recognize him; he wasn't one of the people who'd spent the night in Pek Voratur's room. In fact, he didn't wear the tunic of the Voratur household at all. His hands were rough. A laborer who did not belong here.

Roughly he pushed Enli out of the way. She was wearing a neckfur ornament Pek Voratur had given her. He spied it and grabbed it off her, pulling her neckfur so hard it hurt.

Her head pained.

So, she saw, did his. He dropped the ornament, clutched his head, and staggered away. In a corner of the garden, he was sick.

Enli leaned against the wall, gasping. It was back. Shared reality was back. How? Had the Terrans brought the manufactured object back? Why? And what would happen now?

Fifty thousand kilometers above them, Capelo said, "Now."

From the bridge the exec's voice repeated the command to the gunnery officer: "Commence firing."

A proton beam flashed from the *Alan B. Shepard* to the planet. It was aimed at a site in the Neury Mountains kilometers away from where the artifact again resided. A weak beam, to be sure, but it should have resulted in blowing up a lot of rock. Sensors had been affixed to the site, to surrounding mountains, to low-orbit probes, to the artifact itself. Kaufman leaned toward the displays.

"Nothing," Rosalind Singh said. "Hal?"

"Nothing."

From the bridge came the exec's voice, "Colonel Kaufman, the beam did not hit. Disappearance of the beam matches disappearances recorded during failed attacks on Faller ships equipped with their beam-disrupter shield." The words were formal, but the exec's voice betrayed his excitement. They had the equivalent of the enemy defense.

Kaufman said into his comlink, "Dieter? Report in."

Gruber, on the surface, said, "Nothing! I could stand right on the target and not be touched! It is the shield, Tom, as you said. It protects the entire planet!"

"We don't know that yet," Capelo said. "Bridge, fire on increased strength."

"Commence firing," said the exec.

No response on the planetary sensors, orbital sensors, bridge equipment. Gruber witnessed nothing. My God, Kaufman thought, we've got it. The shield that protects the Faller ships, at a setting that protects a planet. That protected World from the wave-effect that killed Syree Johnson and fried Nimitri. We've got it.

"We haven't got it yet," Capelo said.

They spent the next two days firing on the planet. The ship fired every weapon it had, in varying strengths. It fired at the same side of the planet as the artifact, and at the opposite side, and at both poles. Each time the effect was exactly the same: nothing. The planet wasn't touched, and the beam disappeared as if it had never existed.

On the third day, they dropped a nuclear bomb over the great northern sea. Internal sensors indicated that the detonator fired and the chain reaction began. But no energy was released. Nothing happened.

There came to Kaufman a piece of some ancient religion he couldn't identify, or maybe it was a piece of the physics history he'd read so much of: *"I am become Shiva, destroyer of worlds."* No, he thought. No. We have become the savior of worlds, or at least of Earth. An entire planet. He felt himself smiling.

Savior of Worlds.

They threw a party. Everyone came, scientists and techs and officers. Even Grafton showed up, reserved but pleasant to everyone but Kaufman, whom he avoided. Kaufman understood. Marbet was still in the brig, and the POW was still secured in his cell, but Grafton wasn't sure what Kaufman would try next. Neither was Kaufman. He'd told everyone that Marbet was in quarantine with a newly detected version of the Ballinger retrovirus.

He made the obligatory toasts to his team, to the ship, to the unknown vanished master race that had left them both the artifact and the space tunnels. It turned out to be a wonderful party. There were only two unhappy people at it, and they both left early.

Dieter Gruber had not been able to persuade his wife to rejoin the team aboard ship. He would say only that she was still doing research. Gruber drank too much and then retired to his quarters to argue again with Ann by comlink.

The other grim face was Capelo's. Kaufman, who had fences to mend there anyway, waited until Capelo stood alone in a corner. He didn't have to wait long; Capelo was not enough of an addition to the party that people lingered near him.

"Tom. How is your little girl? Have her nightmares stopped?"

"No. They're worse."

"I'm sorry to hear that. But I also want to congratulate you on your brilliant scientific work. This is an amazing find for us."

Capelo looked at him bleakly. "Do you really think it's amazing, Lyle? In fact, do you really think it's science? All we've done is find a black box and try various things to see how it reacts. We still haven't the faintest idea of why. I have no theory, no equations, no models, not even a single worthwhile insight. Somehow I don't think Einstein, Bohr, or Yeovil feel threatened."

Kaufman refused to pick up the gauntlet. "I wanted to ask you something about that. What we have now for the artifact is this: setting prime one: a local weapon. Prime two: a local shield. Prime three: a wider-scale local weapon. Prime five: a planetary shield. Do you think prime seven will be a weapon, following the pattern?"

"Yes. I think setting prime seven will fry an entire planet through destabilizing the strong force."

"And settings prime eleven and prime thirteen?"

"If the pattern holds, prime eleven might protect an entire star system. Prime thirteen will fry an entire star system, like Syree Johnson's artifact fried this one. Except for World."

Capelo said it so quietly that Kaufman felt chilled. *Fry an entire star system . . . I am become Shiva . . .*

"Of course," Capelo said bleakly, "this is all theory. We can't test setting prime thirteen at all, unless you plan on destroying a spare

star system somewhere. Lyle, what are you soldiers planning on doing with this thing? The Fallers have beam-disrupter shields on more
than one of their ships, so obviously they've been more successful
than I have at figuring out how it works, at least enough to build
more. You've only got one. Do you set it up to protect Sol system?
Do you take it to the Faller home star and set it off at setting prime
thirteen, untested, in hopes it will cause their entire star system to
irradiate itself?"

"That's not for me to decide," Kaufman said.

"Right. So you've got no opinion at all, soldiers obey orders not
think them through, nobody here but us chickens."

"Tom—"

"*I* have an opinion. Take the artifact to their home star and blow
the entire system and every bastard Faller in it."

Kaufman realized, for the first time, that Capelo had been either
drinking or doing fizzies. The physicist undoubtedly believed what
he was saying, but under other circumstances he might not have said
it. Or not said it like that.

Capelo seemed, belatedly, to realize this. "Excuse me if I find
this celebration a little flat. I'm going to read my daughters a bedtime
story." He left.

Kaufman stood alone, sipping his drink. Capelo still puzzled
him. So much tenderness in the man toward his tiresome little girls,
so much raw ability, so much clear-sightedness on some things. And
so much blindness on others, along with so much anger and bitterness. Tom Capelo was a man full of too much.

More practically, Capelo regarded himself as the only one capable of seeing the implications of his team's work. But it was Capelo
who couldn't see far enough. The Fallers already had an artifact like
this one, plus facsimiles of at least setting prime two. They could
theoretically do everything Capelo had mentioned, including fry the
entire Sol system. So why hadn't they?

No answer. Unless it lay locked up in the Faller prisoner. If so, Kaufman had disabled Marbet, their only key, and Grafton would make sure she stayed disabled. Kaufman's mistake, and a very bad one. *I am become . . .*

Two of the techs, laughing with drunken high spirits, made their stumbling way toward Kaufman. He put on a welcoming smile.

TWENTY-TWO

GOFKIT JEMLOE

Enli sat outside the village of Gofkit Jemloe, on a hard rock in the gathering twilight, and listened to Pek Sikorski talk on her comlink to Pek Gruber. Enli didn't want to listen. She rose to leave, but Pek Sikorski grasped her wrist and pulled on it, so Enli sat again and stared into the gathering darkness.

It was a beautiful sunset, the red and gold sky seeming to sweeten the air as much as the tiny wild mittib under her feet. She could see the villagers gathered on the green, between the still-glowing embers of the communal cookfires. Children chased each other, weaving among the adults. It almost looked like any evening in Gofkit Jemloe. The difference lay in the way the adults stood in huddles instead of dancing, the reluctant way the huddles changed members, the overly frenzied shouts of the underdisciplined children.

"I asked you how long, Dieter . . . Don't lie to me, please. I can bear anything but that."

On the far end of the comlink, somewhere in the red-and-gold sky, Pek Gruber answered. Enli couldn't distinguish his words.

Pek Sikorski said, "You've finished all the testing you can do while the artifact is back down here, haven't you? Or else you're close to it. When do you lift it off-World again?"

More indistinguishable words, and Pek Sikorski's tense body went still.

Enli watched a figure detach itself from the huddles on the green and stride toward them.

"No," Pek Sikorski said, very low, "I will not. Leave without me. There has to be somebody here to explain to these poor people . . . Don't try to feed me that shit, Dieter! I won't help you murder this civilization! I won't!"

The figure resolved itself into Soshaf Pek Derilin. No, not Derilin—among the great households, it was becoming fashionable for the oldest son to take his father's name, not his mother's. A shift in reality. Pek Voratur, dressed in a magnificent tunic embroidered with flowers, carried a lantern. His bright silky neckfur rippled in a night breeze. A handsome man, Enli thought impersonally, and her heart hurt all over again. Calin . . .

Pek Sikorski said, "Never. Good-bye, Dieter." She broke the link. Immediately the comlink rang again with its peculiar mechanical noise, so unlike a real bell. Pek Sikorski did something that made the ringing stop.

"May your gardens bloom forever, Pek Sikorski, Pek Brimmidin," the young Pek Voratur said. He held out an orange blossom.

"May your ancestors rejoice in your flowers," Enli said, when it became apparent that Pek Sikorski was not going to speak. The Terran's face looked, to Enli, like someone dead: skin even paler than usual, temples tight, eyes flat. Enli saw despair, but she knew Soshaf Pek Voratur did not. Not without creased skull ridges, drooping neckfur, folds of skin around dark eyes. Pek Voratur was not experienced enough with Terrans to see Pek Sikorski's despair, and so was saved the head pain that now pierced Enli. Reality was not shared among the three of them, but only she knew it.

Pek Voratur said to Pek Sikorski, "My father asks the gift of talk with you, Pek."

She looked at him in sorrow and pain. He didn't see it. And that's the way it will be soon for all of us, Enli thought, when the Terrans again lift the artifact into the sky. None of us will know what others feel.

"I will come," Pek Sikorski said listlessly. Pek Voratur smiled and lifted his lantern against the growing dark. Inside its glass, the small deep pan of oil sent up a sudden flame. Then it went out. While Pek Voratur struggled to light it again, Enli whispered to Pek Sikorski.

"When will they take shared reality away again?"

"Tomorrow."

"Forever?"

"Forever."

"There," Pek Voratur said with satisfaction, "it's lit. Just follow me, Peks."

On the green the dancing had resumed, but it was tentative, fearful. Enli could feel the difference. But at least it was shared tentativeness, shared fear. She turned her head away and followed Sochaf Pek Voratur in silence.

"No," Hadjil Pek Voratur said. "Not again. You told me two days ago to summon sunflashers and tell all of World how shared reality had left us forever. And now it is back! If the sunflashers had done as I asked, I would have been called a fool, and rightly so. Perhaps I would even have been thought of as a man who does not share reality. I will not summon the sunflashers again."

"You must," Pek Sikorski said. "Pek Voratur . . . shared reality is going to leave us again. Tomorrow. This time it will not return. The . . . the *telescope* on our metal flying boat saw the great gift of the First Flower, the living rock. It started to die, briefly regained strength—you have seen plants do that, and dying people! And now it is dying again, and shared reality will cease."

"So you said last time," Voratur said. His round shiny face quivered beneath his creased skull ridges. "Not again. No."

Soshaf Pek Voratur said quietly, "Father . . ."

Voratur turned to him. "Yes?"

"We could have the fleet move a little way off shore. Let the agents choose the best men to stay aboard, and give the others the night away. You could tell the agents by comlink." After a moment he added, "When shared reality left a twoday ago, someone smashed the front gate and someone stole several gold goblets."

"It will not happen again," Voratur told his son.

"No, Father."

"I will tell the ship agents. Pek Sikorski, Pek Brimmidin, may your blossoms perfume your heart."

They were dismissed. Enli said, "May your flowers gladden the souls of your ancestors."

Back in Enli's room, Pek Sikorski said, "You felt no head pain at Voratur's change of mind."

"No," Enli said, puzzled. She tried to see what Pek Sikorski meant, and failed.

"Because to the three of you, what Soshaf suggested wasn't a change of mind, was it? You all knew he would not believe that shared reality will go away again, but that he would also protect his trading ships in case it did."

"Of course," Enli said. "Isn't that what anyone would do?"

"Shared reality," Pek Sikorski said sadly. "Enli . . ."

"What?"

"I want you to take my comlink. Here. Hide it someplace. Unlike the links we gave Pek Voratur, it will reach the flying ship anywhere in your star system. If anything happens to me in the next fiveday . . . if I die somehow . . . I want you to link with Pek Kaufman and tell him what's happening on World. Will you do that for me, Enli?"

"Yes."

"Poor Enli, I've made your head hurt."

"No, you haven't," Enli said, and it was true. She and Pek Sikorski shared the reality of what would happen tomorrow. Enli would have preferred the head pain of not knowing.

Shared reality disappeared the next day at mid-morning. Once again, there was nothing to feel. But this time, Enli knew.

Pek Sikorski had been watching her carefully as they ate breakfast, washed in the visitors' bath, sat in the sunshine in a courtyard garden. She said, "It's gone, isn't it?"

"Yes. It's gone."

"We'll go to Pek Voratur now."

Through courtyard after courtyard, garden after garden. Never had Enli taken such a walk. That one knows—look how she hurries toward the kitchen, not meeting Enli's eyes, her basket of larfruit trembling on her arm. That boy, absorbed in weeding flowerbeds, does not yet realize. That man knows, remembers from last time, and will steal something: Look at the way he eyes the archway to that rich personal room. He will violate shared reality. Enli saw it, and her head did not hurt.

Pek Voratur sat in his personal room with Soshaf and his second son, Tebil, barely out of childfur. Tebil looked frightened. They all knew.

Pek Sikorski wasted no words in greeting. "Pek Voratur, when everyone in your household shared reality, anyone would do any task that reality required. But even then there must have been servants who did tasks more reliably, did not quit against difficulties, and shared with you a greater . . ." Enli saw her search for a word. *"Loyalty,"* Enli thought, but the word was Terran, and there was nothing the same in World. ". . . personal responsibility. Was that so?"

Soshaf Pek Voratur answered for his father. "Yes."

"Gather all such servants and agents together here. Now. Explain to them what has happened. Then set them the task of watching the gates and doorways of your household, as they would be watchful against any unreal person who attacked you."

Pek Voratur said, "No unreal person would be allowed to live."

"Make a picture in your mind of a world in which many such live, and many more are in the temporary confusion and fear that may seize anyone if a gliffir attacked them. Make a picture in which people—some people—have become gliffirs."

Gliffirs existed only in story, large dangerous animals who breathed fire and shat knives. Enli realized that Pek Sikorski had rehearsed this speech.

Pek Voratur said, "I understand," and Soshaf Pek Voratur left to find the servants Pek Sikorski had described. The boy Tebil put his face in his hands and cried out. "Stop that," his father said sharply.

The boy did not obey.

Pek Sikorski moved to Tebil and put a hand on his arm. Her voice, with its accented World, was the gentlest thing Enli had ever heard. "He's frightened, Pek Voratur. Even though you are not." She looked steadily at the trader.

Enli understood. Pek Sikorski was showing him how to reach toward Tebil's reality. From Voratur's own. From a different place.

The moment spun itself out. Finally Voratur said harshly, "My son will not be a coward, crying over something as small as a climb up cliffs for birds' eggs!" He turned his broad fleshy back on the trembling boy.

"Pek Voratur," Pek Sikorski said more loudly, "Tebil is frightened. Even though you are not. That is reality now. You can share it with him if you choose. *If you choose.*"

Voratur did not turn around.

At that moment a small figure catapulted through the door and skidded to a stop in front of Pek Sikorski. Essa Pek Criltifor, the girl who had gone up to the metal flying boat and played with Sudie. The girl who had not been afraid when shared reality left them in space. Essa grinned. "Shared reality has left again, Pek Sikorski!"

Pek Sikorski said nothing. Essa turned to Voratur's stiff back. "Soshaf Pek Voratur said you are looking for servants who will still belong to the household without shared reality and will help to protect it. I will still belong to the household, Pek Voratur."

Slowly the trader turned around.

"I will help protect the household. I'm not afraid!"

Voratur studied the girl. Her neckfur was uncombed, her thin face dirty, her black eyes shining. Voratur smiled at her. "I believe you, young Essa."

Across the room, Tebil, still trembling under Pek Sikorski's hand, stared at Essa with sudden hatred in his frightened eyes.

In the late afternoon Enli walked alone to the village. If she had told them she was going there, Pek Sikorski would have advised against it and Pck Voratur forbidden it. Enli didn't tell them.

There was a *guard*—a new word, taken from Terran—at the household gate. He carried a knife and a club, looking worried about both. Earlier in the day three men, brothers from the look of them, had tried to force their way into the household. There had been a fight, a whirling uncoordinated mass of pushing and shoving and hitting out wildly, until the men had run off. One of Voratur's householders had been cut with a knife. Voratur had ordered all guards to have knives and clubs, which frightened half of them so much they told Soshaf Pek Voratur they no longer wanted to be guards. He let them stop, of course. Pek Sikorski had helped Voratur talk to others and choose new guards.

She was very busy, everywhere at once, advising Voratur,

comforting those so scared they could barely move, explaining to the sunflashers, whom Voratur had finally summoned, what to flash from their towers. Half the sunflashers, it turned out, had also stopped performing their duties. In the far distance, visible from the highest Voratur roof, a village was on fire.

Nonetheless, Enli walked alone to Gofkit Jemloe. After the first panic, quiet had descended. The road was deserted. People stayed indoors, barricading their houses. "That won't last," Pek Sikorski said wearily. "They can't hide from it forever. And reality isn't shared within the houses, either. This is only the beginning." She hadn't said what the end would be, and Enli hadn't asked.

Behind her, she heard footsteps. When she whirled around, nobody was there.

Enli's breath tangled in her throat. She had a knife in her hand but knew she could never use it. Not possible. Not on a person.

Panting, she scanned the plentiful bushes, bright with jellitib and canarib. Nothing.

Enli resumed walking. The footsteps returned and she broke into a run. Feet pounded after her. Then Essa threw her arms around Enli's waist from behind. "I caught you!"

"Essa! You . . ." Enli stopped. The girl looked up at her, still clutching Enli's waist, grinning. "Don't you know it's dangerous out here?"

"Then why are you here?" Essa said logically. "I'm fast and I hide good. Nobody will hurt me."

Probably true, Enli thought. Hurting was too new. Hiding came easier to children. There was no comfort in the thought.

"Besides," Essa continued, "I'm Pek Voratur's messenger. He sent me after you with a message."

"What is it?"

Essa's lips moved in rehearsal. Then, in a surprising and wicked mimicry of Voratur's booming voice, she said, "Tell that crazy woman she's too valuable to risk roaming around the countryside!"

Despite herself, Enli laughed. The laugh ended in a gasp for air. Picture a World where people could not go roaming around the countryside!

"You know, Pek Brimmidin," Essa said in her high voice, "I should not say this, but . . . but I like having shared reality gone."

"I know you do," Enli said, and couldn't tell whether her own tone contained more sadness, or anger, or bewilderment. "Why?"

Essa hesitated. "It's . . . I don't know." Another hesitation. "I can think things now. Without head pain."

"What things, Essa?"

The girl said simply, "My things."

"I see," Enli said, and she did. Her mood lifted a little. Maybe it would not be so bad. Maybe Pek Sikorski was wrong, and the worst was over. Maybe—

"Someone's coming," Essa said abruptly, "on a big bicycle. Very fast."

Enli shaded her eyes against the sun. A figure far down the road, speeding along at an amazing rate, much faster than any bicycle could go . . . a big man . . .

"Run!" she told Essa, and then grabbed at her. "No, wait . . . it's Pek Gruber!"

"Who's that?" Essa asked, without fear.

Pek Gruber. Come to take Pek Sikorski away. No, the big ship had already flown away from World forever, Pek Sikorski had told her so after talking to Pek Kaufman an hour ago. Pek Gruber was not coming to take his mate away. He was coming to join her, on World. Because she was his mate, because he didn't want to leave her, because even without shared reality he had *loyalty*.

Not like Calin. Calin . . .

"Who's that?" Essa repeated. "Is his bicycle a machine that goes by itself, like the flying boat?"

"Yes."

"He's very big. Bigger than the other Terrans. Is he coming to help us protect the Voratur household?"

"Yes. He is."

"Without shared reality? To help us anyway?"

"Yes," Enli said, and she walked forward to meet him, Essa following eagerly at her heels.

TWENTY-THREE

ABOARD THE *ALAN B. SHEPARD*

In the military, it can be more fatal to admit you made a mistake than to actually make one.

Lyle Kaufman awoke in his quarters, his head pounding and his bowels watery. Too much celebrating at last night's party. And wouldn't it be nice if he could actually believe that celebrating was the sole cause of the pain in his head. "Head pain"—that was what the natives of World coped with all the time. No wonder they'd never developed a military. The Worlders who had to make its decisions would all die of cerebral thrombosis.

Dieter Gruber had made his decision, shuttling down to the planet at the last possible moment to join his wife. Kaufman didn't expect to see either of them ever again. Most likely they would die on World, probably soon. With them, if Ann was right, would die several million natives, due to Kaufman's decision to remove the artifact from World. But no one at Solar Alliance Defense Command would hold that against Kaufman.

Marbet Grant, a civilian reporting to Kaufman, had released one of the Faller's hands against both direct orders and Grafton's fury. The prisoner might have figured out a way to kill himself, removing the only source humans had for information about the enemy. But the Faller had not in fact killed himself, and so no one at SADC would hold that against Kaufman.

Tom Capelo had discovered what the artifact did—or at least what its first four settings did—without discovering the principles that made the thing work. Capelo was in intellectual despair over that. The military would be unhappy that, without the science, the artifact could not be duplicated. Especially since it appeared that the enemy had duplicated at least the shield aspect. Perhaps a different physicist might have discovered more. Capelo, Kaufman's choice, had not got the job done. But the military had always considered scientists unreliable and suspicious allies, from Los Alamos on. No one at SADC would hold that against Kaufman.

The artifact, the most valuable weapon ever, had been shown to the enemy by Marbet Grant. That was treason of the highest order, and Marbet might well die for it (don't think about that yet). But Capelo's work showed that since the Fallers already had the beam-disrupter shield, they must already have an artifact. So Marbet had revealed nothing, after all. Her act was still treason, but since there were no adverse consequences as a result, and since Kaufman had immediately done the correct thing and had her arrested, probably no one at Solar Alliance Defense Command would hold that against Kaufman.

But if he admitted he should *not* have had her arrested, that it had been a mistake, he would be in deep trouble. He was not supposed to make that kind of mistake: irreversible and carrying adverse consequences. "Irreversible" because now Grafton, the line officer in command, had control of Marbet, who had crossed over from civilian personnel to traitor in time of war. "Carrying adverse consequences" because without Marbet, Kaufman could not learn anything more about the artifact from the Faller.

Marbet might have learned what settings prime seven, prime eleven, and prime thirteen did. Less probable but still possible, she might have learned a hint of the science behind the artifact, a hint to start Capelo in the right direction. Now she could learn nothing, and neither could anyone else without her gift and her accumulated experience with the prisoner.

Solar Alliance Defense Command wouldn't hold Marbet's arrest against him. It was justified by war, by her action, by the book. But if Kaufman admitted it was a mistake, if he brought together again a traitor who gave away military secrets and the "enemy agent" who received them, if he did that against the direct order of the commanding officer, he would be crucified. Certainly court-martialed for disobeying orders. Possibly tried for treason alongside Marbet.

But unless he brought Marbet and the Faller together again, the artifact as weapon remained only partially known and—the critical element—unduplicatable.

Kaufman lay on his bunk, staring at the bulkhead. Play it by the book, or disobey an order. It wouldn't be hard to break Marbet out of the brig. Kaufman already had the first entry code. He recalled the young and inexperienced guard scrambling to his feet and saluting as Kaufman entered the anteroom to the brig. "Yes, sir! The special project team has been cleared for entry, sir!" Newbies always got the boring assignments. And prisoners were so rare on an elite flagship like the *Alan B. Shepard* that the guard room was usually used for storage. Of course, there would be alarms, but Kaufman knew how to forestall their setting off. You manipulated the guard, not the equipment. No, it wouldn't be hard to break Marbet out by force.

Kaufman couldn't do it. He was a soldier.

But neither could he let the mission finish in this half-assed way.

There was a middle ground. Admit to Grafton he'd made a mistake, get Grafton to see the necessity of Marbet's working more with the Faller, convince Grafton to authorize the work. Not a promising middle ground; Kaufman had no reason to think that Grafton would change his inflexible mind, a mind firmly welded to official procedure. But convincing people was what Kaufman did. In military diplomacy, words were weapons. It was worth a shot.

Kaufman rose from his bunk. He had an appointment with Capelo at 0900 to discuss Capelo's non-progress on the physics of the artifact. The meeting promised to be caustic and short. But Kaufman might be able to see Grafton before that.

The middle ground. When hadn't he taken the middle ground? Risk, but not too much. Adverse consequences for failure, but mild adverse consequences (a letter of reprimand in his promotion jacket). An unpleasant encounter, but not really brutal (the one with Capelo would be nastier). Colonel Lyle Daniel Kaufman, master of the middle ground.

He started to dress.

Capelo woke to screaming. Instantly he was out of his bunk, scooping up Sudie.

She thrashed in his arms, still screaming. He pinned her against his chest with one arm, patting her back with the other and crooning. "It's okay, Sudie, it's all right sweetheart, it was just a dream. Just a nightmare, baby, it's all right now, Daddy's got you . . ."

She clung to him, screams changing to sobs, and he went on holding her and murmuring reassuring nonsense. It wasn't all right, it was getting worse. Three, four, even five nightmares a night. Capelo had moved her from the room she'd shared with Amanda and Jane Shaw into his own quarters, jamming a cot into the crowded space. He wanted Amanda to be able to sleep through the night, and he wanted Sudie with him.

"It's all right, sweetheart, it was just a dream. Just a nightmare, baby, just a bad dream . . ."

Her sobs didn't stop. Capelo kicked a chair from under its table/shelf and sat on it. He cradled Sudie's small body, feeling the sparrow-like bones in her back, smelling the sweet childish scent of her dirty hair.

"Maybe if you tell me about the dream, baby, then Daddy can make it go away."

She had always refused to do this, but now she gasped against his neck, her arms almost strangling him. "Mama."

Capelo forced himself to go on. "What about Mama, baby?"

"She's killed dead."

"Yes, sweetheart. Mama's dead." For the last eighteen months, after her first grief had passed, Sudie hadn't talked about Karen's death. Even Sudie's first, violent grief had been mostly wordless; she'd been only three. She had cried and sobbed, but it had been the older Amanda who had needed to talk it out, over and over, until it had taken every muscle in Capelo's soul to go on listening, to hold himself steady to Amanda's need in the gale of his own bereavement. Sudie still refused to be separated from either her favorite blanket or Capelo, she sometimes drew black angry scribbles on her e-tablet, and she developed exaggerated attachments to women of her mother's age, such as Marbet Grant. But nothing like these nightmares, this screaming.

Sudie sobbed, "They killed her. They killed Mama dead."

"Yes, sweetheart." His own throat closed up. Somehow it never got easier. Those who'd said time would heal him were fools, or charlatans, or brutes.

"I don't want them to kill you dead, too, Daddy! Or Mandy or Jane or Marbet! I don't!" The words rose to a wail.

"Nobody's going to kill me dead, sweetheart. Or Amanda or Ja—"

"Yes! Yes, they will! 'Cause the aliens are here on our ship!"

Capelo shifted her in his arms. "There *were* aliens on the ship, baby. Nice aliens. You saw them come up on the shuttle with us, remember, and you played with the alien little girl in the ship garden . . ." He tried to remember the details of what Amanda had told him about the natives in the garden. Marbet had taken the girls there and Ann Sikorski had stupidly let her tame natives wander loose on the ship. Sudie had played hide-and-seek with an alien child . . . nothing that should produce this maelstrom of fear in Sudie.

Sudie was shaking her head against his chest, still nearly cutting off his air with her grip around his neck. "No, no. Not Essa. Essa was nice. The other aliens, the bad ones that killed Mama dead!"

"Sweetheart, there are no bad aliens here. There never are bad aliens near you. Daddy wouldn't let any bad aliens on the ship, and neither would Commander Grafton and all his soldiers."

"No, no, a bad alien is here!"

"Sudie, baby—"

"Marbet said so! She said!"

Capelo stopped patting Sudie's back and went very still. "What did Marbet say to you?"

"Not to me. To Dr. Ann . . ."

"What did Marbet say to Dr. Ann?"

"She said the bad alien was here and Marbet talked to it."

"When did she say this, Sudie? And how did you hear?"

"She said it in the garden. I was behind a bush. Me and Essa were playing hide-and-seek."

Capelo thought very fast. Marbet missing for long periods from team meetings. "In quarantine," Kaufman had said, but there she'd been in the garden with Ann Sikorski. Marbet showing up planetside just once, for a short but intense look at the excavated artifact. Ann, with her exaggerated love for aliens, talking intimately with Marbet, who was a Sensitive, supposedly brought along to bridge communications gaps with the World natives. Whom Marbet had never once gone near until she'd accidentally run across them in ship's garden. A Sensitive, the logical choice to attempt communication with aliens. Any aliens. A scientific mission to the ass end of the

galaxy. A distant, secret place, uncolonized by humans. A place un-
likely to be surprised by a sudden intrusion of the war.

"Daddy, I don't want to be killed dead by the Faller on the ship!
Like Mama was killed dead by bad Fallers!"

"Nobody on this ship going to hurt you, Sudie. Or me or
Mandy or Jane."

"Yes! A bad Faller is here!"

Capelo hated to lie to his children. He never did to Amanda,
and only to Sudie about things for which she was too young to grasp
truth. He lied now.

"Listen to me, Sudie. Listen very hard with your best-hearing
ears on. Are they on?"

Unhappily she pantomimed putting on the ears. Capelo said,
"Sudie, there are no bad Fallers on this ship. There are no Fallers at
all on this ship. Marbet was talking about a holomovie she saw. I
saw it, too. It was scary."

"A holomovie?"

"Yes. A holomovie."

The child considered. Finally she said, "Can I see it, too?"

"No. It's too scary for you."

"Did Mandy see it?"

"No. It's too scary for Mandy. Only grown-ups got to see it."

"Oh."

He could feel her body relax a little. Her small tear-stained face
floated uncertainly on the tide of his barely-checked rage. But check
it he did, for her sake. For now.

"Do you want me to sing the rabbit song? Since you've got your
best-listening ears on?"

"Yes. Sing the rabbit song, Daddy."

He sang her back to sleep, carried her next door to the cabin
containing Jane and Amanda, kicked softly at the door until Jane
opened it. Jane was already dressed. It was eight-thirty ship time;
the night had been so disrupted by Sudie's nightmares that Capelo

had slept far past his usual hour. Wordlessly he handed Sudie, now a limp bundle heavy with the deep sleep of childhood, to Jane.

"Tom—"

"Later." He closed the door, walked back to his own cabin, and dressed. All his movements were controlled and deliberate. Fury gathered in him like a tsunami still far at sea.

"No," Grafton said. "I'm astonished, Colonel, that you would even ask."

"I wouldn't ask if I didn't think the results will justify the action."

"A dangerous tenet."

Kaufman made himself smile. "Usually, yes. But these are unusual circumstances, as I'm sure you'd be the first to understand."

Grafton had not asked Kaufman to sit down. The two men stood beside the polished table of the small conference room adjoining Grafton's quarters. Empty chairs yawned at Kaufman. He could see Grafton reflected in the highly polished metal surface of the table; Grafton looked equally polished and hard.

"Colonel Kaufman, I'm well aware of the circumstances here. More than you are. Those circumstances include information I received only a few hours ago, from a flyer arrived at the tunnel."

Kaufman felt his chest tighten. The mission to World was supposed to be kept as quiet as possible, which meant no unusual traffic through Space Tunnel #438, which effectively meant no traffic at all. Intelligence officer McChesney's warship, the *Murasaki*, kept guard this side of the tunnel but never went through. This meant that for weeks everyone aboard both the *Murasaki* and the *Alan B. Shepard* had effectively been cut off from the rest of the galaxy. If a flyer, the military's fastest small ship, had come through Tunnel #438 and sent lightspeed news to Grafton, the news had to be major. Judging by Grafton's face, it was not good.

Grafton said, "The message comes directly from General Stefanak, inquiring about our progress with the artifact. The inquiry is prompted by a serious war development." Grafton stopped, and Kaufman saw the flesh above his uniform collar work up and down.

Grafton continued, "An entire star system, the Viridian system, has been destroyed by radiation. All five planets, one of them plus its moon colonized by humans, were rendered highly radioactive by destabilizing all elements with an atomic number higher than fifty."

Fifty, not seventy-five. Tin, iodine . . . there would be no life left in the star system. There would never be life there again.

Grafton seemed to be calmed by the recitation of numbers. "Viridian system was ninety-eight percent civilian, with only a small military contingent. No one expected enemy activity so far into our tunnel space. A single Faller skeeter equipped with a beam-disrupter shield evaded all attempts to stop it from going through three separate tunnels, the last of them leading to Viridian. It went through the tunnel and reappeared only a few moments later. By that time, a lightspeed wave had already started to spread outward from the tunnel."

Kaufman said nothing. His mind raced.

"What the report described is consistent with what happened in this system, as I'm sure you realize. The Fallers must have had a large artifact like the one Dr. Johnson tried to take through this tunnel. But why did it destabilize so much more than Dr. Johnson's artifact, and how did the enemy get it through the tunnel to the Viridian system?"

"Commander," Kaufman said, the words rushing out too fast, "we've kept you apprised of all Dr. Capelo's tests and their results. But we have not passed on pure conjecture until we had some experimental basis. Last night at the party, Tom Capelo said . . ."

"What we have now for the artifact is: setting prime one: a local

weapon. Prime two: a local shield. Prime three: a wider-scale local weapon. Prime five: a planetary shield. Do you think prime seven will be a weapon, following the pattern?"

"Yes. I think setting prime seven will fry an entire planet through destabilizing the strong force."

"And settings prime eleven and prime thirteen?"

"If the pattern holds, prime eleven might protect an entire star system. Prime thirteen will fry an entire star system, like Syree Johnson's artifact fried this one. Except for World."

"What did Dr. Capelo say?" Grafton demanded.

Kaufman pulled himself together. "Untested speculation, Commander: Please remember that." He told Grafton of Capelo's hypothesis.

Grafton said evenly, "Do you mean to tell me that you knew of these speculations by our ranking scientist—a scientist who, you've assured me, is brilliant at this sort of thing—and you still asked for Marbet Grant to see the prisoner again? To give away more knowledge of what advantage this artifact may give humans in the war?"

"I made a mistake," Kaufman said bluntly. "I should never have had Ms. Grant arrested. It's precisely *because* of what you just told me about Viridian that Marbet must resume her work with the Faller. We need to know exactly what weapons they have."

"Not by telling them what we have!"

"The Faller is a prisoner, for God's sake! Who's he going to tell?" Kaufman said, and a second afterward knew that he'd lost.

"Colonel," Grafton said, "let me remind you that I am well aware of the military circumstances of the prisoner of war. It is my job to be aware of them. I am also aware that this is no ordinary interrogation situation. There is no way to monitor what Ms. Grant says to the prisoner or he to her because nobody else can interpret his so-called 'nonverbal communication.' Truth drugs, I'm told, are incompatible with the prisoner's biology and may even kill him. Finally, I'm aware—as you seem to not be—that it is precisely for unusual and ambiguous situations that Navy regulations are designed. They—"

The door flew open and Tom Capelo burst into the room.

Kaufman moved swiftly between him and Grafton. Capelo looked demented: wild-eyed, unshaven, his long unknotted hair snaking around his gaunt face. Spittle flew from the corners of his mouth. Kaufman realized he was looking at a man who had lost all control, gone beyond reason.

"Both here. Good. Now you bastards tell me what the fuck a Faller is doing aboard ship with my kids."

Grafton barked, "You're out of line, mister!" at the same moment that Kaufman began, "Tom—"

"Don't 'Tom' me! Do you motherfuckers have any idea what the enemy did to me? To my kids? And you have one here without even telling me! Sudie . . . nightmares . . . nowhere safe . . ." He swung on Kaufman, who stood closer than Grafton.

Kaufman had seen it coming. He blocked the blow and wondered what the hell to do next. He outweighed Capelo, a small man, and Kaufman was trained to fight, as Capelo was not. Kaufman could easily deck the physicist. But that wasn't what needed to be done.

"Tom, listen—"

Capelo swung again. Kaufman countered easily. Grafton had of course summoned security; before Capelo could try for a third blow, two MPs ran through the open door and grabbed him. He fought them with no finesse but surprising persistence, kicking and gouging, screaming incoherently, until an exasperated MP used his tanglefoam and Capelo fell to the deck, encased from shoulders down in sticky strands that could only be broken by dissolving them. His head was still free, and he continued to shout every filthy word that Kaufman, a soldier, had ever heard from experienced combat troops.

Grafton looked down at Capelo in disgust, then at Kaufman.

"Your brilliant physicist. Who you think should determine my military decisions." Then to the MPs, "The brig is occupied. Lock him in his quarters."

Kaufman opened his mouth, and then closed it again. He said nothing.

With that non-action, he knew, he'd just sealed all their fates.

TWENTY-FOUR

THE ROAD TO GOFKIT SHAMLOE

The road leading away from Gofkit Jemloe was wide enough for three bicycles. Enli would have preferred to ride ahead, faster than Ann Pek Sikorski could go, but she did not. Partly this was good manners, partly fear. She was safer riding beside Pek Gruber, and she knew it. Enli wanted to be as safe as possible. She wanted to reach Gofkit Shamloe—to reach Ano and the children—with as little trouble as possible. Pek Gruber, whose bicycle could go by itself even though now he was pedaling it, would have a *gun*. And probably other things as well, things Enli couldn't name. Or even think about. She was glad Pek Gruber was here.

The head pain of shared reality had been better than the living pain of unshared reality. Enli, like most of World, would have instantly traded the new life for the old. Most of World, but not all of it. In Gofkit Jemloe, even in Pek Voratur's household, there were those who seemed to like unshared reality. Those who liked to take from others without head pain. Those who liked to lie to others without head pain. And those who just seemed to like having thoughts that were private from, and different from, the thoughts of others. Like Essa.

The girl rode behind Enli, Ann, and Dieter Gruber. Enli could hear her singing, a faint soft flower song. And she was singing it alone, not joined by the other three, not in any head pain from not being joined. And smiling.

Was it because Essa was so young? Would the young be more comfortable with this new, frightening World? Then perhaps Ano's children—noisy Obora, baby Usi, and quick, grave Fentil—perhaps they would all find it easier to live without shared reality. Enli hoped so. For herself, she wanted only to see her family safe, to be again with Ano. She wanted to be home.

The four rode along the sunny, deserted road through a glory of flowers. Bright yellow vekirib, carpets of gaily colored mittib, trifalitib in cool lacy clouds. No one but Enli seemed to notice the flowers, not even Essa. Would that change, too, and make a World without gardens? Enli didn't think so. Blossoms were too important. They were gifts from the First Flower, they were beauty, they were love.

Calin had given her a vekir flower when he first came to Gofkit Jemloe.

Pek Sikorski broke the silence. She was the least used to riding a bicycle, and the least strong. She panted a bit as she spoke in Terran to Pek Gruber. "You know, Dieter, Terra's past included thousands of wrecked civilizations, all of them decaying over time. This is probably the first time, ever, that a civilization has been wrecked during a single day."

"Yes," Pek Gruber said. He had been very quiet since Enli brought him to Pek Sikorski within the walls of Pek Voratur's household, since he had seen how World was without shared reality. A quiet Pek Gruber was also something new.

Toward evening they passed a farm shed, conveniently nestled between the road and the fields behind it. Worlders all lived in villages and walked to their fields; a farm shed would hold only carts, plows, seeds, implements necessary to help the First Flower bring crops from the fertile ground. But people seemed to be living in this farm shed. The cart stood behind the shed, and there was a crude hearth beside the door, its cookfire still glowing under an iron pot. "Stop," Pek Sikorski said. "There are people here."

Pek Gruber said in Terran, "We should keep riding, *mein Schatz*. After we take Enli to her village, we still have to reach the capital."

"No. Our job is to explain to people. These are people." Through the sweat on her pale skin, Pek Sikorski's face set in stubborn lines. Enli recognized them. The people inside would not, never having seen a Terran before.

"All right," Pek Gruber said, resigned. "Get in place."

At his insistence, they had practiced how they would approach strangers. Pek Gruber first; he carried the *weapons*. Next Pek Sikorski, who also carried something Enli hadn't understood. Enli and Essa would stay back with the bicycles.

"What do you think will happen?" Essa whispered, as if sound could further disturb whoever was inside the farm shed. As if anything could.

"I don't know," Enli said. "Don't sing anymore, Essa."

"All right."

Behind the farm shed lay fields of unharvested zeli. The zeli should have been brought in by now. Enli sniffed the air; yes, the crop was beginning to rot. She stood on her toes and craned her neck to see into the cooking pot. Zeli mush, and nothing else.

Pek Gruber called the stranger-greeting loudly in his heavily accented World, "We first bring our flowers to your home, O friends!"

No response.

"May your blossoms perfume the air, O friends!"

"Go away," a voice called, high and frightened. A terrible thing to say to a stranger.

Pek Sikorski walked up to the door. "We ask water, by the petals of the First Flower, O friends."

No one could refuse a traveler water. No one ever did; it was enough to raise suspicion of being unreal. Enli knew the great struggle that must be going on in the souls behind the farm shed door. Risk harm from strangers (unthinkable only days ago) or fail to share reality and become unreal (but there was no shared reality anymore). The sweet air was painful in her lungs.

Pek Sikorski repeated, "We ask water, by the petals of the First Flower, O friends."

No response. Then, slowly, the door opened.

It was a boy, still a year away from becoming a man, his skull ridges deeply creased and his new adult neckfur bristling sideways. He saw the Terrans and gasped, closed the door, opened it again in terror and compulsion. Enli strode forward.

"It's all right, boy. They are Terrans, not monsters, and they won't harm anyone. I am Enli Pek Brimmidin, from Gofkit Jemloe."

The boy did not look reassured. He thrust a bucket of water out the door and tried to close it again. Pek Gruber's huge foot intervened.

"We must talk to you," Pek Sikorski said gently. "We bring news of the shift in reality and of the First Flower."

From behind the door another voice said, "The First Flower? Open the door, Serlit."

An old woman hobbled out, leaning on a dobwood cane. Enli had never seen her before, but she recognized her with relief. She was a grandmother's mother, revered by every village or rich household lucky enough to have one. Ancient with years, perfumed with experience, the grandmother's mothers had been left on World past their time in order to guide people toward the First Flower. They were usually tough as their canes and fair-minded as only those about to join their ancestors can be. She eyed the Terrans without fear, then Enli, and finally Essa, who had left the bicycles and crept silently forward.

"I am Adra Pek Harrilin. Who are you, and what have you to say about the First Flower?"

Pek Sikorski answered. "We are Enli Pek Brimmidin, Ann Pek Sikorski, and Dieter Pek Gruber. May—"

"And her?" the old woman said, jabbing her cane toward Essa.

Pek Sikorski turned to find Essa beside her, frowned, and said, "Essa Pek Criltifor. May your blossoms perfume the air."

"May your garden bloom forever," Adra Pek Harrilin said. "Now what of the First Flower?"

"Shared reality has gone away. You know this. We are here to tell you why, so you will not be so afraid. Shared reality perfumed the air from a living rock. We Terrans have seen this rock with our flying boat. It lay in the Neury Mountains. But we have seen the living rock die, as all living things must die. That gift of the First Flower is over, and we must all plant new ways to be kind to each other without shared reality. This is what the First Flower wishes."

The grandmother's mother studied Pek Sikorski. "How do you know what the First Flower wishes? Did She tell you?"

"No," Pek Sikorski said, taken aback. Clearly, Enli thought, the speech Pek Sikorski had practiced so carefully had holes in it.

"If the First Flower did not speak to you, then you don't know what She wishes. You saw the living rock die. How do you know when a rock is dead? Did it have petals to wither, or breath to cease?"

"N—no."

"You say that if we know about the rock's death, we will be less afraid. Why should knowing why shared reality stopped make us less afraid of its absence?"

Pek Sikorski stood dumb. Pek Gruber, Enli saw, was grinning. The grandmother's mother eyed him sharply. Abruptly she opened the door wide. "Come in and have some water."

An expensive, very fast bicycle leaned against the inside wall, and three pallets crowded the floor. On one sat a woman nursing a baby. Half-eaten dishes of zeli mush stood beside a pile of the fruit fresh from the field, along with some cari and a bowl of chopped dul.

"My granddaughter Ivi Pek Harrilin. My granddaughter's son

Serlit Pek Harrilin." The old woman of course did not introduce the baby, who was not yet real.

And now never would be, Enli thought. Or else was realer than any of them, born, as they were not, into this strange new reality.

The granddaughter, looking scared, murmured flower greetings, which Pek Sikorski answered in her gentle voice. The boy, Serlit, passed out water. Enli drank hers gratefully.

"We live here now," the grandmother's mother said, "because there is no food in our village. No one will leave their houses to harvest the crops. Fools." She sucked thoughtfully on the inside of her cheek. "Well, they are afraid and it is a very small village. But my family has come here, near the crops, to encourage them back to sense. So far it has not done so. But Serlit here harvests our zeli fruit, and borrows cari and dul from the others' fields, and we eat. Perhaps the others will come soon."

Borrows, Enli thought. Not *steals*. The old woman had accepted the shift in reality without losing her fairness. Enli's spirits bloomed slightly.

Pek Sikorski said, "We are telling people what has happened, so they will not be so afraid. We travel to the capital to seek—"

"Yes, yes," Pek Harrilin said. "Now share with me the true reality of what happened. You, Pek Brimmidin. You share reality with me."

She waited, leaning on her cane, her black eyes bright in her wrinkled old face. Pek Sikorski's face went red. Terrans' faces did that, Enli knew, but she still didn't know why. Pek Gruber grinned again.

Enli said, "What Pek Sikorski said is shared reality, mostly." Unthinkable words, just a tenday ago! "Shared reality has gone away. Shared reality perfumed the air from a manufactured object, not a living rock, that lay in the Neury Mountains. The manufactured object is gone now, and so we must all plant new ways to be kind to each other without shared reality."

"Gone?" Pek Harrilin demanded. "Where did it go?"

"It rose up into the sky far away from World."

The ancient black eyes were shrewd. "You shared this reality? You saw the manufactured object rise up?"

"I did not see it go," Enli said, "but I share the reality that it has risen far away into the sky. Yes."

"It had wings?"

"No. It had . . . some sort of wingless way to fly. Like the Terran flying boat."

The grandmother's mother considered Enli carefully. "Yes," she said finally, "you are sharing reality. All right, then — the manufactured object that perfumed us with shared reality is gone. We will have to make a new reality."

But the enormity was suddenly too great even for the great strength of her old soul. Her skull ridges creased and the cane slid along the floor. Before she could fall completely, Pek Gruber caught her.

"Yes, yes, I am all right," she gasped. "Thank you. I am just very old, and soon I will join my ancestors, praise the First Flower."

Pek Gruber eased her to the pallet. She leaned against the shed wall. "Pek Sikorski, you do a good thing. But you must share reality — the true reality — with people. You must say what Pek Brimmidin has shared with me."

Pek Sikorski's face was still that curious Terran red. "I will. We travel to the capital to seek a sunflasher, so that all on World may share the reality."

Silence hung in the shed. It seemed to Enli that the old woman was deliberately not looking at her granddaughter. The granddaughter pulled the baby, now replete and sleepy, from her breast and laid it on the pallet. She adjusted her tunic and stood.

"I am a sunflasher." Her voice quavered; she was more frightened than her grandmother. Yes, Enli thought, she had so much more to lose. But she was brave. "I will go with you to the capital."

The grandmother's mother said, "You will sleep here tonight, all of you. Tomorrow Ivi will go with you to Rafkit Seloe. Serlit will stay here. You, girl, looking so hard at Serlit and he back at you, will you stay with me, too?"

Essa laughed. "No, grandmother's mother. I go with Pek Sikorski. She took me on a flying boat into the sky once."

"Ah," the old woman said. She closed her eyes. "I am very old. You have all tired me out. Let me sleep."

Ivi Pek Harrilin motioned them outside. Beside the cookfire she said, "Will you eat? We have zeli mush, and I could pound some cari to bake." Her voice still trembled.

"We have food on our bicycles," Pek Sikorski said. "We will all share."

They ate outside, sitting on the ground, four Worlders and two aliens. The sky darkened and the night-blooming flowers unfolded their petals, scenting the air. If she looked away from the Terrans and the farm shed, Enli thought, if she looked across the fields, she could almost think herself back in Gofkit Shamloe. With Ano, with the children, with the people among whom she had grown up. With Calin. Almost, she could think nothing had changed.

Beside her Essa's clear voice spoke to Serlit. "Do you want to go for a walk with me?"

"Yes," Serlit said.

"No," his mother said. "Stay here."

Everything had changed.

Enli watched Pek Sikorski and Pek Gruber walk into the darkness of the zeli field, led by Pek Gruber's powertorch. She knew what they were doing, since they did the same thing every night. Pek Sikorski spoke for a long time into her comlink, describing everything she saw happening on World. Her words, she'd told Enli, went to the large metal flying boat far away in the sky. It took the words longer each night to fly there because they had to catch up with the flying boat, which was speeding away as fast as it could. Sending these words chasing after the flying boat seemed very important to Pek Sikorski, although Enli could not see why.

"Does Pek Kaufman answer you?" she had asked.

"Yes," Pek Sikorski said bitterly, "but not with anything I want to hear."

Enli had asked no more questions. The reality of the Terrans was even stranger than the one that had come to World. Pek Sikorski had agreed to share the true reality in the sunflasher messages, but Enli knew it was not the whole true reality. Pek Sikorski had not spoken a piece of reality: that when the manufactured object rose into the sky, it had been because the Terrans had taken it. And Enli had not said that piece of reality to the old woman, either. Was it a *lie* if what you said was shared reality, but not all of shared reality?

She sat thinking about this, slumped on the rough wooden bench outside the farm shed. Within, the grandmother's mother, Ivi Pek Harrilin, and the baby all slept. Essa and Serlit talked softly; Enli could hear their murmurs through the shed wall. Probably they were holding hands.

Calin . . .

She sat sorrowing over Calin, over unshared reality, over what might have happened to Ano and the children, and so didn't hear the people approach until they were upon her.

"Hit her out!" the woman cried, drunk with pel. Enli could smell it on the man just before he swung his thick stick. She had started to stand and the blow caught her on the chest instead of the head. The pain was astonishing. Enli fell, unable to breathe, against the wooden bench. It scraped along her upper arm but she scarcely felt that pain through the burning agony of her chest.

Essa. Serlit. Ivi and the baby.

"Go in!" the same female voice shrieked. Two large bodies stepped over Enli, kicking in the shed door. Someone screamed.

Something fell heavily against the wall beside Enli's head. Still she couldn't breathe. She heard herself make noise trying: *eueueueu*. The baby began to wail.

"Nothing here but another bicycle," a man's voice snarled out the open door. "Another good one."

"Then take that!" the drunken woman called and laughed, a high horrible sound.

"You, you would try, you're nothing but a *boy*—" Another sickening thud against the inside wall.

Air was returning to Enli's chest. She tried to raise herself on her arms. Essa, she must help Essa, Serlit, and the baby . . . She was a hand's span up from the ground. Someone wheeled a bicycle over her body.

"*Lieber Gott!*"

The bicycle crashed on top of Enli, followed by three more crashes. The drunken woman began to shout incoherently. Enli felt Pek Gruber's massive arms pull her upright.

"Enli! Are you all right?"

She didn't have enough breath to answer. Pek Sikorski pushed past her into the shed. Pek Gruber laid Enli on the bench and rushed after his mate. Everything went dark, but only for a moment. She could hear the others moving round in the shed—how many, O First Flower, how many?—and over all, the high terrified wail of Ivi's baby.

Enli struggled to sit. Essa exploded from the shed, rubbing her shoulder. She stopped short and stared at the ground, so that Enli looked, too.

In the light from four moons lay three people, each wrapped from shoulders to knees in pink mud. No, not mud—some sort of sticky thick stuff, like sap from dobwood trees. They wriggled on the ground like helpless infants. The two men looked terrified, their skull ridges so deeply wrinkled that it drew their eyes higher than

Enli thought eyes could go. The woman had stopped shouting and lay completely still.

"Is she dead?" Essa whispered. "What is it?"

"I . . . don't know," Enli wheezed. Her chest still burned, but she could breathe again. Her arm was scraped raw where it had hit the bench. The pink sap must be one of Pek Gruber's *weapons*.

Pek Gruber and Pek Sikorski came out of the shed, leading Serlit and Ivi. Ivi, carrying the yelling baby, seemed unhurt. Serlit's tunic was torn at one shoulder and his arm hung limply. A great bruise covered one side of his face.

"Your arm is broken!" Pek Sikorski said. She ran to her bicycle to get her healer's bag. Essa forgot the wriggling strangers in the pink sap and hovered around Serlit.

Ivi said to Enli, "What . . . what did the Terran do?"

"I don't know," Enli said. It was getting easier to talk. "The Terrans have many devices. Pek Gruber . . . tied them."

"Tied them? With what?"

"I don't know."

Pek Sikorski returned, and Ivi thrust the baby at Essa so that Ivi could tend her son. Essa, looking startled, took the wailing bundle. Somewhere she had learned to tend infants; she walked up and down, patting the child on its back.

Enli suddenly felt her insides lurch. She staggered behind the shed and emptied her stomach. Leaning against the wooden wall, she took deep breaths of the cool night air until her belly calmed. When she returned, Pek Gruber had dragged the three wriggling and terrified people in pink sap away from the circle of light of his powertorch.

Pek Sikorski looked up from putting salve on Serlit. She said sharply to Pek Gruber, "Did you—"

"No, no," he said in Terran, "I will just leave them in the tanglefoam for the night. Let them think what they do and wonder what I will do."

Pek Sikorski nodded and returned to Serlit. The baby had stopped crying.

"Ann," Pek Gruber said. "No . . . Pek Harrilin, Serlit . . ."

"What?" Ivi said. "What is it?"

"In the shed," Pek Gruber said in his awkward World. "I'm sorry. Your grandmother . . . she is dead."

Ivi said, "She has gone to join our ancestors?"

"Yes. They didn't hurt her. The body is almost cold. I think she just died in her sleep."

"She has gone to join our ancestors," Ivi said, and there was so much joy in her voice and in her face that Enli scarcely recognized her.

They held a farewell burning the next morning. There was no priest, but Essa and Ivi and even Serlit with his broken arm rose at dawn to gather hard woods, plus masses of flowers to burn with the body. Pek Gruber put something from his pack on the fire and it got very hot, consuming the body quickly. They all danced and sang flower songs. Ivi looked radiant. Her beloved grandmother had at last gone to their ancestors, happy and sound and safe.

Afterwards, tired from dragging logs and dancing, they sat in front of the farm shed, eating zeli mush. Ivi looked into her bowl and said to Pek Sikorski, whom she found less strange than Pek Gruber, "Why?"

Pek Sikorski said gently, "Why what, Pek Harrilin?"

"Why did those people come to hurt us—Pek Gruber, what have you done with them? I forgot them completely!"

"They are gone," Pek Gruber said. "I freed them from the . . . the pink ropes and made them run away." The wording was odd; was that Pek Gruber's imperfect World or was he, too, trying to share only part of reality? Enli didn't ask. Ivi appeared not to notice.

Pek Sikorski repeated, "Why what, Pek Harrilin?"

"Why did those people come to hurt us?"

Serlit said, "Because they were drunk, my mother."

"No," Enli surprised herself by saying. "Not because they were drunk."

Everyone looked at her. Enli realized she had been thinking about this for a long time. She said, "They came to hurt and steal because now they can. Without shared reality, they *can*. Just as Essa liked going in the flying boat. And Pek Voratur kept more profits for himself than he agreed to. And Serlit wants to go with Pek Sikorski and Pek Gruber and Essa to Rafkit Seloe. All of them, because they can, without shared reality. People do things just because the things are possible now. Because they can."

Pek Sikorski was looking at her with sadness and love. It made Enli feel strange inside. "Yes," Pek Sikorski said softly.

But Ivi had been caught by a different piece of Enli's words. "Serlit? You want to go to Rafkit Seloe with . . . with these Terrans?"

"Yes," he said shyly, looking at Essa.

"But I want you to go to the next sunflasher with me!"

"I'll come back, Mother. But I want to go. I'm old enough, you know I am."

Ivi looked helplessly at Pek Sikorski. Her mouth moved, stopped, moved again. "How . . . how do you . . . when reality isn't shared, how do you . . ."

"You learn how, mostly," Pek Sikorski said. The love and sadness that had been in her face were now in her voice. "Over time. It's practice, partly. You will learn."

Ivi looked at her son and bowed her head.

"Mother?" Serlit said.

"You can go," Ivi said, very low, and to Enli the words sounded almost like a flower blessing, as if Ivi were not only a farm woman but had, somehow, become also a high priest of the First Flower.

TWENTY-FIVE

ABOARD THE *ALAN B. SHEPARD*

The flyer that had informed McChesney and Grafton of the Viridian massacre had also beamed more routine data to the *Alan B. Shepard*, including the mailbag. The major newsgrams showed holos taken from space of what was left of the colonized planet and its colonized moon. Kaufman looked at the ones with quarter-meter resolution and felt his stomach turn. Human presence had been firmly established on the planet, which, like World, had been fertile and welcoming, so people spent much time outdoors. The holos were horrifying.

Around the ship small knots of crewmen spoke in low voices. Those few with relatives or friends in the Viridian system were excused from duty by their section officers. The chaplain announced an all-faith memorial service in the chapel, and had to hold more than one service because so many off-duty personnel wanted to attend. Kaufman had known the chapel, in this secular age, to be totally empty for weeks at a time.

There was little he could do but wait. He knew what would happen, but not how soon it would happen. He couldn't go to Marbet, or Grafton, or Capelo, not without affecting the outcome.

Maybe this, he thought without humor, was a human equivalent to the Heisenberg Uncertainty Principle. Any attempt to measure the outcome would change its spin or direction.

He told Hal Albemarle and Rosalind Singh only that Tom Capelo had been arrested for attacking two MPs. Albemarle's lip curled knowingly. Rosalind looked grave. "Lyle, we need Tom to finish this project. No one else has a clue about a model for these phenomena."

"Neither does Tom," Albemarle said. Couldn't resist, Kaufman thought with contempt, and then forgot him. Albemarle wasn't important.

Kaufman said to Rosalind, "I don't think he'll be confined to quarters long. After all, he's a civilian. It isn't as if a soldier had assaulted a superior officer. Once Grafton is satisfied that Tom has calmed down and is no longer prejudicial to good order, Grafton will pretty much have to release him."

Rosalind, troubled, said, "He'll be accompanied by MPs, though, won't he? To make sure he doesn't have another go at you or Commander Grafton. Or even try to get to the Faller prisoner."

"Yes, probably."

"Tom's working method . . . you've seen him, Lyle. He roves around. He goes into a sort of other-worldly trance and paces restlessly about. It's counterproductive to restrict him, or have guards constantly hemming him in. He needs to work. *We* need him to work."

"I know," Kaufman said.

"I don't like this, Lyle."

"None of us likes it."

She nodded gravely. Albemarle tried to look as if he were not still sneering. Kaufman left them both and went to his quarters.

To wait.

·   ·   ·

He had lost it. His own fucking fault. The red rage had grabbed him and he'd lost it. No excuse.

Lying helpless on his bunk, wrapped from the shoulders down in tanglefoam, Capelo cursed himself. The red rage was from the time of Karen's death, when it had gripped him every few weeks. Afterward, he wouldn't have been able to remember what he'd done, except that the results lay around him. Broken furniture. A smashed computer. Once, his wedding ring pounded into a flat blob. That scared him, as nothing else had. After that, he worked as hard to keep the red rage in check when he was alone as he did when he was with Amanda and Sudie. And he had succeeded, until now.

One of the motherfuckers that had killed Karen was alive on this ship.

Capelo forced himself to breathe deeply and steadily. It took ten minutes to feel that his breathing was back in his control. Then he started on his mind. Ever since he'd been in graduate school, a favorite relaxer had been to work on the Riemann Conjecture, that piece of unsolved math left over from three centuries ago. He examined various pieces, played with extending the known results, let himself be absorbed by the challenge. Known infinite number on $\times = \frac{1}{2}$ . . . extend to non-denumerable infinity . . . how? He let the Riemann Conjecture massage his brain, and that further massaged his body until his muscles unclenched.

He needed to unclench. The doctor would come soon, and the doctor was strictly military. Grafton's by-the-book military, not Kaufman's slippery PR military. Capelo wasn't sure which was worse. The doctor wasn't going to authorize dissolving the tanglefoam until Capelo showed acceptable skin moisture and temperature, acceptable breathing, acceptable neural-firing patterns.

He thought some more about an infinity of zeros.

·   ·   ·

They made him wait eight hours, through two separate doctor visits, before the MPs sprayed the tanglefoam with the nano-eaters and it dissolved from around Capelo as if it had never been. He sat up on his bunk and rubbed his arms.

"You may feel some circulation slow-down for a brief time. Nothing serious," the doctor said.

"I understand." Keep it quiet, reasonable. Sane.

The Navy officer with the doctor said, "You're now free to come and go as you wish, Dr. Capelo. But you understand that everywhere you go you'll be accompanied by Sergeant Forrester."

Sergeant Forrester, a huge MP with watchful eyes, stared directly at Capelo. Augmented muscles, Capelo thought. And not a fool. Aloud he said, "I understand."

"Good. We're removing computer access from your quarters. When you need access for your work, please use the equipment made available to the Special Project Team on the observation deck."

Under the careful eyes of the MP. Capelo could just picture that: Rosalind's embarrassment, Albemarle's secret smiles, the looks on the techs' faces. Aloud he said again, "I understand." He was sounding like a fucking parrot. *Tommy want a cracker?*

"Do you have any other questions, Dr. Capelo?"

"No. But I'd like to see my children. They're in the next room."

"Certainly."

Doctor and officer left, trailing rectitude. Capelo was escorted next door, where Amanda and Sudie rushed into his arms. Sergeant Forrester took up a post by the door. Jane Shaw discreetly pretended the MP was not there.

"How're my best girls?" Capelo said.

"I'm perfect, thanks to your genes," Amanda said, their old joke, and tossed her hair back from her eyes. God, she was growing up fast.

Sudie said, "Jane said you were sick, Daddy. Are you better?"

"Much better."

"Who's that man?"

"A soldier. He's watching me to learn how I work."

Sudie accepted this; she was used to grad students and postdocs following her father around. She leaned close to his ear and whispered, "We didn't go through the secret door."

He whispered back, "I know you didn't."

"We didn't want the doctor to see."

"Good move."

"And we didn't say nothing to anybody else."

He didn't want her dwelling too much on the door. "What have you two been doing? Turning into space doodles?"

Amanda said, "We're too old for that game, Daddy."

"I'm not," Sudie said. "I'm a space doodle. Look at my holo!"

She danced him over to her construct, a tipsy thing of purple and green light circles, while Amanda went to get her most recent schoolwork to show off.

Over Sudie's head Capelo looked at Jane. She smiled. "Much better, Tom. No nightmares. Almost a different child."

"Look, Dad," Amanda said importantly, "look at this. I can do algebra now. See, you have to solve for x. What you do is, you do this to one side of the equation . . ."

Capelo listened to Amanda teach him algebra and Sudie explain her colorful construct. Jane, who had known him a long time and seen the red rage once before, studied him carefully. Jane was shrewd. Capelo was careful not to meet her eyes.

After Sgt. Forrester escorted him back to his own quarters, Capelo waited half an hour. Then he crawled under his bunk and quietly pushed open Sudie's secret door a few inches. This let him listen as Jane had the girls finish their lessons, pick up their belongings, and get ready to go to the ship's garden. She took them there every afternoon, to get out of their one room. There weren't too many other places on a starship where she could take two children.

"Daddy looks terrible," he heard Amanda say to Jane.

"He had a retrovirus, you know," Jane answered. "That's why he was in quarantine."

"I know. But he looked terrible before the virus, too."

Capelo tensed for Jane's answer. "He has a lot on his mind, Amanda."

"I know. But I don't think it's that. I think he's getting old."

Jane whooped. "Old? Honey, your daddy's thirty-four!"

Amanda said primly, "I think thirty-four is quite old."

Despite himself, Capelo grinned. The grin stretched his mouth painfully, and he realized that he had been clenching his teeth for a long time.

Sudie erupted from the bathroom, there was a fight between her and Amanda over whether or not purple was a stupid color, and then they all left for the garden.

Capelo pushed on the crude metal plate. On its other side, it eased the antique sea chest away from the wall. He crawled through and noiselessly pushed the chest back.

The girls' school computer was, of course, linked to the ship's library. It took Capelo only a few minutes to find what he wanted. The general surveillance recordings were only lightly fire-walled; Amanda could have gotten into them. He instructed the control program to give him the present whereabouts of Marbet Grant.

"Marbet Grant is currently in the brig," the computer said.

In the *brig*? What for? Was the Faller there, too? Capelo didn't dare ask the computer for the Faller's whereabouts; that was undoubtedly deeply classified information and would trigger data alarms that would not be lightly firewalled. Instead, Capelo said, "Show me a map of the ship."

The computer complied. Capelo studied the map.

"Access surveillance file for the brig."

The file was empty until two days ago; apparently nobody had been arrested before Marbet. Grafton ran a tight ship.

He watched Marbet being brought to her cell. The brig consisted of two rooms, an anteroom crowded with storage crates and a single cell, equipped with bunk, toilet, sink. No computer. Both anteroom and cell used retina scans supplemented with non-vocal e-locks. Capelo magnified the picture again and again, but he couldn't see what codes the MP punched in. The soldier kept his body between the codepad and the surveillance camera, undoubtedly as per regs. Capelo instructed the computer to skip to the first visual of Lyle Kaufman and track him.

The MP got to his feet and saluted as Kaufman entered the anteroom. "Sir!"

"At ease, sergeant. Has Commander Grafton authorized my visit to the prisoner?"

"Yes, sir! The special project team has been cleared for entry, sir!"

Kaufman passed into the cell. Marbet sat on the edge of the bunk, dressed in green coveralls, writing on paper with a pencil. Beside her was an untouched tray of food.

"Hello, Marbet."

"Hello, Lyle."

"I've come to ask you some necessary questions about your work."

"Am I going to be allowed to continue it?"

"That's not decided yet."

"You're lying," Marbet said. "Look at you . . . you're lying and you hate it."

"All right." He sat beside her on the bunk. "You can't resume your work, you can't see the prisoner again, and you're in the brig until we arrive back on Mars. But meantime, I need to know everything you've learned about how much the Faller knows about the artifact. This is an official inquiry, Marbet, but it's also an appeal for the good of the project."

Capelo stopped the recording. His breath caught. The Fallers already had something like the artifact themselves; that's where they got their beam-disrupter shields, those copies of setting prime two. So it wasn't just the existence of artifacts in general that had gotten Marbet arrested. It was a specific artifact, the one humans had found. She had told the enemy that humans had it.

Even Capelo, least military of men, knew that qualified as treason.

He restarted the recording.

Kaufman said, "Will you cooperate?"

"Of course. I never intended anything but the good of the project."

"I believe that. Others won't."

"At least now you're being honest. There isn't too much to report. Yes, the Faller recognized the artifact, immediately. He recognized the holo I programmed, too, which suggests to me that they've discovered how to use the directed-beam destabilizer at setting prime one. That was as far as I got. I'd planned on programming a holo to demonstrate the spherical wave-effect destabilizer, too, to see if he recognized that. But you came in before I did that."

My God, Capelo thought, without reverence.

"Was there anything in his non-verbal or sign language that told you anything more than that he recognized it?"

"Yes. He was disturbed that we knew about it, or had it. Very disturbed."

"What else?"

"Nothing else. I didn't have time."

She smiled. "It's all right, Lyle. I like you, too. If things were different . . ."

"Anything else?"

"Just one thing. But it's important. You have to convince Grafton to let me talk again to the Faller."

"That's not possible, Marbet. Can't happen."

"It has to. The Faller was very disturbed that we have this artifact, Lyle."

"You'd expect that, wouldn't you?"

"*Yes. But as far as I can estimate, his disturbance went beyond our new strategic advantage. He was trying to hide something, Lyle. Something important, that we might need to know about the artifact.*"

"*Could you tell what?*"

"*Not a clue. But I'm positive I'm right. You shouldn't have had me arrested so quickly. You should have listened to me first, and weighed all the alternatives, and made your usual careful decisions. But you didn't. You went off half-cocked because your personal feelings for me overwhelmed you with disappointment that I did what I did. It was a mistake, Lyle. And if what you say about Grafton is true, I don't see how you're going to rectify it.*"

Capelo sat stunned. Not only communication with the enemy, but communication about future human weapons in the war. If Capelo had been Kaufman, he would already have had this alien killed, purely for what he now knew. But Kaufman wasn't Capelo. Kaufman didn't think logically. Probably the Faller was still alive somewhere on the ship. A Faller, the bastards who had killed Karen and casually demolished Capelo's life. Alive on this ship somewhere, with Karen's children.

Not for long.

He replayed a fragment of the conversation between Marbet and Kaufman, just to be sure he had it right. The young MP, talking to Kaufman: "*Yes, sir! The special project team has been cleared for entry, sir!*"

Better than he'd hoped.

The far door of the girls' suite opened onto a service corridor. Capelo opened it a few inches and watched. Empty. He snaked into the corridor, softly closing the door behind him. Then he straightened and did his best to assume the look of a man preoccupied with important business.

Several levels of very long corridor lay between him and the brig, located on the ship's lowest level. There was no chance of traversing them unseen. He had to depend on most of the crew's not realizing that he had been arrested, or that he was supposed to be accompanied by an MP. Capelo figured that his chances were good; there was no reason for the crew to be aware, with the exception of the other MPs. They would know about Forrester's special assignment. But the MPs, for obvious reasons, didn't fraternize with officers or crew. They had their own quarters, mess, recreation area, and command structure.

Walking briskly, Capelo moved along what he hoped were the least-used corridors. He passed several crew and three low-ranking officers. The crew ignored him; the officers nodded in a distant way. Capelo nodded back.

He buzzed the antechamber to the brig, and the MP—a different one from the surveillance tape, but also very young—opened the door.

"I'm Dr. Thomas Capelo, here to see Marbet Grant. I am the physicist on the special project team. The team has been cleared for entry."

"Yes, sir. Please step up to the retina scanner to verify that you are Dr. Capelo."

Capelo hesitated. Probably the verification scans were simply stored until someone accessed them. On the other hand, the scans might be linked to a denied-access list, and Grafton might have thought to put him on it. He searched for a way around the scan, didn't find it, calculated the odds, and stepped up to the machine.

It announced, "Dr. Thomas Capelo, chief scientist, special project team."

"You're verified for entry, sir."

"Wait a moment before you open the door, please. Ms. Grant, as you know, was a member of our team. I'd like to ask you some questions about her before I see her in person." Capelo made his voice as authoritative as possible. Maybe the young soldier would even think he was a medical doctor.

"Questions, sir?"

"Yes." He asked about Marbet's movements in her cell, her food consumption, her sleeping habits, her conversations with the MP. There turned out to be none of the latter; apparently it was against regulations. The soldier answered him patiently. He seemed earnest but not particularly bright. Not genetically augmented. As Capelo invented questions, he kept moving slowly around the tiny ante-room. Now here, now there. He kept it up for ten minutes, until the man was used to his restlessness. Finally he said, "Thank you. I'd like to go in now."

The MP turned to bend over the codepad to the cell, blocking it from the surveillance camera with his body. Capelo stood between him and the desk. He waited until the door swung open, then picked up a heavy data-storage cube—the military made everything heavy and sturdy, to last—and hit the MP hard on the back of the head.

This was different from attacking Kaufman and Grafton. You didn't have to be trained to hit a man from behind with a blunt instrument. For a nanosecond shame flooded Capelo—if Amanda saw this!—before he shoved it away. He wasn't going to kill the kid. Karen had suffered worse.

The soldier staggered, tried to recover. By that time Capelo had the taser out of the MP's belt. He pressed it. Nothing happened.

"Shit!" Capelo yelled, and hit him again with the data cube. God, he didn't want to kill this guy! The soldier still moved on the floor.

"Use the tanglefoam. It's not keyed to individual thumbprints," a voice said behind him. Capelo whirled. Marbet Grant stood in the doorway. When Capelo hesitated, unsure if her presence would trip an alarm, she pushed past him, unbuckled something from the MP's belt, and sprayed him as he lay on the floor.

Pink goo formed itself into tight shoulder-to-knees bonds, the same sort of tanglefoam that had bound Capelo for eight hours. Unthinking, he said, "What's the chemistry of it?" and immediately felt like a fool.

Marbet glanced at him, amused. The MP began to sputter. Capelo thought, *Thank God he's not dead.*

"We'll have to gag him," Marbet said. She looked around the anteroom, didn't see anything usable, and took off her socks. She wasn't wearing shoes. To Capelo she explained, "The bedsheets aren't tearable. So that prisoners can't strangle themselves."

She stuffed her socks into the MP's mouth. He glared at her with hatred.

"I'm sorry, Gary," she said softly. "It's only for a little while. And it's not your fault."

Capelo had somehow lost control of the situation. He grabbed her arm. "You're coming with me."

"I know, Tom," she said. "I'm going to show you the way to see the Faller. There's no other reason in the universe you'd be doing what you're doing now. I'm willing."

He took the tanglefoam cylinder from her. She didn't resist. He grasped her firmly by the hand and opened the door to the corridor.

This time, escape was harder. Marbet Grant wore the green coveralls of a prisoner, and there was no other clothing for her in the brig. Her quarters were at the opposite end of the ship. But the Faller's prison, it turned out, was on the same level as the brig, and not far away. Which made sense, once Capelo thought about it.

She led him silently along, stopping at the end of a T-junction to whisper, "It's just around the corridor. But there will be two MPs outside the outer door, and it's possible there could be observers inside. The xenobiologist, the doctor, the intelligence people, even Lyle. I don't know."

Capelo weighed the cost of waiting to see who went out or in, versus the cost of someone's discovering that Capelo was missing, Marbet was missing, or an MP was immobilized in tanglefoam with two nasty lumps on his skull. Waiting lost. "Come on."

"Wait. Let me have the tanglefoam."

Capelo looked at her.

"Tom, I want the same thing you do—to get more information out of the Faller. But I'm more experienced at tanglefoam. You've never used it, have you?"

"No." *She didn't know he was going to kill the son-of-a-bitch.* Or did she, and was this a ploy? "I'll keep the foam. I saw you use it, and it's not exactly a particle accelerator."

She shrugged. "Just make the first sweep over both of them at once, at weapon-belt level, and *fast*. Then do each more carefully. You don't have to avoid the face; the nanos won't go there."

Why? He wondered, but there was no time for science now. He dashed around the corner, already spraying.

It seemed to work. Both MPs went down. Capelo sprayed with a manic glee that should have scared him. What did scare him was his realization that only one MP stayed down. The other was instantly on his feet and charging.

"Antidote-coated!" he heard Marbet cry, and then the soldier hit him full in the stomach. It was the same as before his arrest: astonishing pain and the deep biological panic that he couldn't breathe, wouldn't ever be able to breathe, he was suffocating to death . . .

When enough breath had returned for him to see, it was just in time to glimpse the second MP toppling forward, his face frozen in surprise. *Taser*, Capelo knew. *How* . . .

One MP's body slipped away from Capelo's blurred vision. Someone was dragging it through the door . . . Marbet? He couldn't see her. He struggled to sit.

"Verify identity with retinal scan," the door said. And a moment later, "Marbet Caroline Grant, Special Project civilian personnel. Identity verified." Apparently no one had taken her off the access list. Well, thought Capelo through his blurred pain, that made sense. She was incarcerated and no threat. Although—

But by the time he had this second thought, he was sitting up.

Nobody was left in the corridor, although he could hear voices beyond the door, now partially ajar. He staggered to his feet and through the door . . . and for the second time in nine hours tanglefoam hit him. He crashed back to the floor, rolled over, and saw Lyle Kaufman holding a tanglefoam canister.

"I knew you'd bring her here, Tom," Kaufman said. "Thank you."

TWENTY-SIX

ABOARD THE *ALAN B. SHEPARD*

One of those annoying aphorisms that the Academy fed its cadets surfaced in Kaufman's mind: *There's the right way, the wrong way, and the Army way.* For the first time in his adult life, he was doing none of them. He was doing this his way. His stomach twisted.

He grabbed Capelo by his armpits, dragged him through the door, and closed it. Three bodies lay in front of him on the deck. One tasered, one gasping in tanglefoam, one tasered *and* in tanglefoam. The tanglefoam was what had let Kaufman drag Capelo, unverified by retina scan, through the door: the door "read" tanglefoam as no threat. The MPs, of course, carried automatic pass-throughs for any door aboard ship. Kaufman turned to face Marbet.

"Do I have to restrain you, too?"

"You know you don't. You know you can't."

She was right, of course; he needed her free to work. She added, "Let Tom go, Lyle."

"I can't. He's not cleared to be in here. The room would send code one alarms."

She studied him. "You wouldn't free him anyway."

"No. He's here to kill the Faller, if he possibly can."

He watched her green eyes widen, her body swing to face Capelo. So she had believed that Capelo wanted the physics from the Faller. Even Sensitives could make mistakes about people. The knowledge, obscurely, cheered Kaufman.

Marbet said, "Is that true, Tom? Were you going to try to kill the Faller?"

Capelo tried to speak, failed, tried again. It came out as a wheezing whine: "Yeeeesssss!" The MP must have hit him pretty hard.

Marbet closed her eyes. Visualizing what might have happened, Kaufman guessed. When she opened her eyes again, she said simply to Kaufman, "I'm sorry." Capelo she ignored.

"Doesn't matter now," Kaufman said. "We don't have much time, Marbet. You need to get to work."

"Yes. What do you want to know?"

"Anything he can tell us about settings prime seven, prime eleven, prime thirteen. Or about whatever you think he wasn't saying before. Most of all, try to pick up the location of the artifact the Fallers possess. Is it back in their home system as protection, or on its way to destroy the solar system?"

"Why should he tell us anything?" She was slipping unselfconsciously out of her coveralls, out of her underwear. Kaufman looked away.

"Probably he won't. But anything you can deduce from his behavior . . . can you guess how much he actually knows, Marbet? Is he the equivalent of a front-line grunt who doesn't know anything about weapons or battle plans, or is he their equivalent of a staff specialist, or what?"

"I don't know. Probably something in between. Maybe not. Their military structure is completely opaque to me." She was nude now. Swiftly she moved to a side door, letting it verify her retina print and keying the nonvocal code. The door swung open. "Stay here, Lyle."

"Leave the door open. In case." In case she freed the Faller's hand again and the Faller did his best to kill her. In case Kaufman had to rush through the door with tanglefoam and every second counted. In case.

"All right. But stay out of his line of sight. Watch on the view-screen."

She hadn't needed to tell Kaufman that. He watched her put on a helmet with air supply, disappear through the side door, and emerge moments later from the tech airlock behind the invisible barrier that separated human and Faller atmospheres. She carried a flat package.

The Faller didn't seem to change expression, but Kaufman knew he wouldn't be able to tell if the enemy had. His flat eyes fixed on Marbet. She released the soft manacle on his far right limb. Then she did something Kaufman hadn't expected. Swiftly she unfolded the package, which became a flat marker board on a thin-legged easel. She pushed this close to the Faller, angled to be visible both to him and the viewscreen. Into the Faller's hand she put a frictionless marker before vanishing again through the tech door.

Back in the anteroom, she didn't even glance at Kaufman. She threw off her helmet and assumed the weird posture she used with the prisoner: half crouching, limbs held at unnatural angles, gait strange, face distorted. Kaufman watched her become alien, neither human nor Faller, and pushed down his distaste.

Waddling/crouching, she moved toward the expressionless alien. When she reached the barrier, she went through a series of grotesque motions and grimaces that Kaufman didn't understand.

No response.

Marbet picked up her marker board. The holodeck had been removed, undoubtedly to deprogram it. But blank marker boards offended no one.

Kaufman heard a dragging sound behind him. Without taking his eyes off Marbet, he said to Capelo, "Stop there. If you go into that room, or if you say anything at all, I'll taser you until next week." The dragging noise stopped.

With her marker Marbet sketched swiftly on the board. Kaufman couldn't see her sketch until she turned it toward the Faller and the viewscreen. He changed his corneas to zoom.

Marbet had drawn the artifact: a circle crudely shaded to suggest a sphere, with seven equidistant protuberances around its perimeter.

The Faller began to draw on his board. He copied her sketch exactly, except that beside one of the protuberances he drew a small glyph. Marbet moved her hands, and the Faller moved his one free hand in response. Two strings to her bow: the drawings and the hand signals she had taught him.

A disengaged, analytic part of Kaufman's mind saw the irony of thinking of it like that: *two strings to her bow*. Medieval metaphors in alien weapon scenarios.

What was the flurry of hand signals now? And why was the Faller "talking" to her at all?

That one was easy. He wanted to know how much humans knew. It was possible that the intelligence she might or might not be obtaining consisted of disinformation, lies designed to mislead. With a human subject, a Sensitive could easily discern that. But with a Faller?

Marbet was drawing again. On his side of the barrier, the Faller drew in response; more hand signals. None of it meant anything to Kaufman. Marbet's reflection in the mirrors on the cell wall told him nothing, either. She was too distorted, too alien herself.

Yet more drawings, more hand talk. How much time before someone sounded the alarm? *Work fast*, Marbet, he willed, and his disengaged and ironic mind jeered.

Something happened.

Kaufman could see it immediately. The Faller's whole body jerked. His mouth opened and let out the first sound anyone had ever heard a Faller make: a deep-noted rising roar, not loud but expressive . . . of what? Whatever emotion it was, the Faller felt it deeply. For the first time, his face bore something Kaufman would have called an expression, although he didn't know what expression. It lasted only a moment. The Faller sketched rapidly.

Marbet's expression changed: suddenly she was again human. Her wide mouth opened in a wider, red-tongued O. Her brows rose and her eyes grew enormous. Kaufman didn't have to be a Sensitive to read her surprise.

The Faller ignored Marbet's transformation back to human. His whole strange body seemed agitated, although without obvious fidgeting. He drew more lines, more hand signals, and Marbet sat stunned.

Kaufman could stand it no longer. He stayed out of sight but called out into the room, "What is it? What does he say?"

Marbet half-turned, recollected herself, and turned back to the Faller, but without resuming her Faller body. "He says the entire galaxy will be destroyed. Slowly." She pointed to the alien's last sketch. Kaufman recognized the familiar spiral-armed disk, and over it a huge glyph he did not recognize. Above it were two of Marbet's circle-with-protuberances artifact sketches.

"Does he say why it would be destroyed? How?"

"No. We don't have the communication for that. In fact, I can't be sure whether he's saying it will be destroyed or is being destroyed now. I don't even know how they express temporalities, if they do."

"But you're sure about the galactic destruction."

"Yes."

"It could be a trick," he said to Marbet.

"No. He wasn't surprised—shocked—that we knew setting prime thirteen might destroy a star system. But he was profoundly shocked that we might bring the two artifacts together. I think that's what the drawing means—both artifacts activated at the highest settings in the same star system. This is real, Lyle, he's not faking. I *know* it!"

She didn't know it that positively, he thought. She couldn't. And even if she were right, military intelligence would not see it that way. They would consider that it might be a trick, and then decide it was.

The Faller fumbled at his crowded marker board. Awkwardly, one-handedly, he turned it over to its blank side. He started drawing again, more carefully than before, although his face had returned to impassivity. This sketch filled the entire board. It looked urgent even to Kaufman, although he had no idea what it was supposed to be:

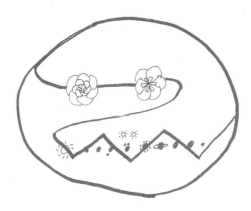

Marbet made a hand sign. The Faller pushed the incomprehensible picture toward her. It shuddered on its easel, fell off, and hit the invisible barrier, ending face-up on the floor.

Kaufman said from the anteroom, "The bottom part is the Solar System."

"Yes."

"Are those flowers in that circle?"

"I don't know," Marbet said helplessly.

"Could he mean flowers because flowers are so important on World, where we took the artifact from?"

"How does he even know we're orbiting World?" Marbet asked, and Kaufman felt stupid. She was right, of course. He wasn't thinking clearly. Although the Fallers in the aggregate did know that humans had taken the first artifact, Syree Johnson's artifact, from World.

Kaufman looked again at the drawing. It meant nothing to him, except for the Solar System covered by the thick jagged line.

"Signal to him—can you do this?—that we need more information." If the Faller would give it.

Before Marbet could respond, the alien raised his face to the ceiling and gave the same sound as before, the deep-noted rising roar. Abruptly, he snapped his head downward to stare at the drawing on the floor.

Behind Kaufman a voice said, "Oh my God."

Kaufman whirled. Capelo had dragged himself into the doorway, either moving noiselessly or else making noise that Kaufman, in his intense focus on Marbet and the Faller, hadn't even heard. Capelo had somehow inched himself up against the doorjamb so that he rested half-upright, a wrapped pink caterpillar helpless as a baby, grotesque as the Faller itself. From that angle, he could see the Faller's drawing lying face-up across the cell.

Kaufman whirled to grab Capelo. The fuck-up, the fool, if his interruption broke off the dialogue between Marbet and the Faller, Kaufman would kill Capelo himself—

"No!" Marbet cried. "Lyle, stop! Free him from the tanglefoam!"

Free him? Kaufman hesitated. Even if she was right, tanglefoam antidote was nano-based; once you sprayed it on, it dissolved *all* the tanglefoam. You couldn't free just arms and leave legs tied, and there was no time for Kaufman to fetch something that would do that, or even to secure Capelo with manacles. Which Kaufman didn't have; he wasn't an MP. More importantly, Capelo wasn't cleared for the secure area.

"Do it!" Marbet said.

"I can't. It'll set off the alarm."

"Do it anyway!" she cried, and Kaufman took the canister from his belt and sprayed Capelo with the dissolvant.

Once free, Capelo raced across the cell and drew something on Marbet's board. He turned it toward the Faller, who did nothing. Meaningless to the alien, Kaufman guessed; the symbols were too different.

"Marbet, give him his fucking board back!" Capelo barked.

She darted into the anteroom and through the tech door, not even stopping to don a helmet. Kaufman saw her holding her breath as she erupted through the airlock. She grabbed the Faller's board, erased both sides, set it back on its easel, and hurried out.

No MPs yet.

The Faller scribbled something, a single glyph.

"That's useless, I don't know what that is," Capelo spat.

The Faller resumed drawing. This time he drew, more carefully, the same drawing that had set Capelo off before. Capelo stared at it, and Kaufman saw his face change, acquire the look of deep thought. Kaufman held his breath.

A long time seemed to pass, although it was probably no longer than thirty seconds. Still no MPs . . . what was Grafton up to? Marbet cried, "Tom . . ." and Kaufman quickly shushed her. Capelo stared again at the drawing. More time. Too long, too long . . . hurry it up, soldier, move it, *move it* . . .

Basic training had been a long time ago, and yesterday.

Finally Capelo's face changed again. Kaufman watched it, and knew what he was looking at. He had never expected to see it for himself, not in this lifetime, not at this height.

Capelo said again, "Oh my dear God." And then, flatly, "The son-of-a-bitch is a physicist." He closed his eyes.

The gas started then, spraying from the walls. Kaufman made himself sniff, and his knees wobbled in gratitude: not lethal. But no, of course not, he should have realized: two MPs lay unconscious in the connecting room and Kaufman's own body blocked the door from sealing off this one. Not lethal, at least not to humans. But to the Faller . . . the sprays were set equidistant in all four walls of the cell . . .

Kaufman had the biggest body. Marbet fell first, landing on her back, the nipples of her small naked breasts like blind eyes. Capelo next, toppling almost gracefully from where he sat. Then the Faller, sagging in his manacles, and the last thought Kaufman had before he succumbed was, *If Grafton really wants the prisoner dead because he knows too much, this appears perfectly plausible. Shrewd choice.*

His mind slipped away.

TWENTY-SEVEN

ABOARD THE *ALAN B. SHEPARD*

Capelo came slowly back to consciousness, and the Faller's sketch came with him. The top figures weren't flowers, as that fool Kaufman had suggested. They were Calabi-Yau spaces, the accepted configurations for the six curled-up dimensions of spacetime. The Faller's drawing was stylized differently from humans' stylizations, and hastily drawn as well. But Capelo was sure. The two figures inside the top half of the circle were two possible Calabi-Yau space configurations.

Including the Calabi-Yau equations in solving the riddle of the disrupter-beam shield had, of course, occurred to him long before. It had occurred to everybody long before. But the equations didn't work, they yielded infinity. There was no way to make them work, no matter how you diddled the data. But that thick circular line leading to the Calabi-Yau—

"Dr. Capelo."

—shapes suggested a connection to something else. And the line extended to—

"Dr. Capelo."

—extended to—

"Dr. Capelo."

He gave up and turned his face to the side. "Who the hell are you?"

"General Victoria Liu, Military Intelligence."

Two stars on the shoulder. Of course, there would have to be someone like this somewhere, a SADA line officer whom Kaufman would have to report to on his unorthodox project. But where had she come from? Capelo didn't care.

"Leave me alone."

"I will. As soon as I inform you of a few crucial points. It won't take long."

Now that he had been jabbed away from Calabi-Yau dimensions and the thick circular line of the Faller's drawing, Capelo took in his surroundings. Not his tiny cabin, not the brig, not the Faller's cell. He lay on a bunk in a room fitted with desk, chair, paper, pencils, and access terminal. Through a half-opened door he glimpsed a bathroom. The other door had two e-locks.

"Am I under arrest?"

"Yes." No hesitation at all. "But as I'm sure you understand, you're a civilian. When we reach Mars, you will be turned over to a civilian court, if the prosecutor deems there to be sufficient charges."

"Or if you tell him there are."

She didn't answer.

"All right, we understand each other. What do you want?"

"The same thing you do. The model and equations for the artifact's functioning. Our aims are identical, Dr. Capelo, and without adversarial intent. You want to understand the artifact because you're a scientist. You're also a patriot, and you know we need that scientific breakthrough to win this war. There is no conflict between us."

"Then why am I under arrest?" Capelo asked.

"Your methods so far have been irregular enough to warrant close supervision. I think you can't disagree with that."

"Very logical, aren't you? Reasonable and agreeable. Are you a scientist, General?"

"I am not."

"What makes you think I can create a 'model and equations'?"

"Colonel Kaufman said you had some sort of breakthrough about the artifact physics just before we penetrated the scene."

"He did? Maybe Lyle can't tell a breakthrough from a break-down. I had been swaddled in unwelcome tanglefoam, remember. Twice."

"I remember."

"Where are my kids?"

"With their nurse, as always. They haven't been told you're under arrest."

"And I won't see them until I cooperate, right?"

"Wrong. You can see them any time you wish."

"What if I just want to see them and the hell with the 'artifact physics,' as you so simplistically and incorrectly label it?"

"That's your privilege."

"But when we get to Mars, I'm in jail until I produce, or until the Big Crunch, whichever comes first."

She leaned forward earnestly. "Dr. Capelo, why would you even hesitate to create those equations? Hesitate to help your race when the enemy just wiped out ten million humans on Viridian?"

"I didn't say I wouldn't 'create the equations.' But I don't like being coerced."

"You did flirt with treason, Doctor. And I think you know it."

"All right, you made your point. Now get out." She rose. Capelo sat up on the bunk. "No, wait a minute. Where are Lyle Kaufman and Marbet Grant?"

"Under arrest."

"For more than a flirtation with treason. They bedded the old girl down and fucked her hard."

"You have a colorful turn of phrase, Doctor. If you need anything at all, there's a comlink in the desk drawer. Preset for certain types of ship access only."

"Including my kids?"

"Of course."

After she left, Capelo said to the computer, "On. Day and time." It said, "Wednesday, four hundred sixteen hours."

He'd been unconscious about six hours. Undoubtedly they'd needed that much time to decide how to proceed with him, Kaufman, and Marbet. Kaufman was useless to Capelo. But he might need Marbet again, to help him check results with the Faller.

Sudden nausea spilled through him. A Faller, one of the bastards who killed Karen . . . Capelo had actually "talked" to that filthy thing, exchanged ideas with it. And forgotten what it was while he did so. That was the part that sickened him. He'd actually forgotten it was a Faller, thought only about that thick black line, as if it could outweigh Karen, outweigh Viridian, outweigh everything . . . Loathing for himself filled Capelo. That thick circular line . . .

That thick circular line.

The marker board with the Faller's last drawing sat propped against the desk. Carefully, as if the floor were a minefield, Capelo got off the bunk. He sat at the access terminal and picked up the marker board. The room disappeared.

He started all over again, from the beginning, as if he had not already worked out anything. The marker board sat propped in front of him. *"Sit down before a fact as a little child,"* Thomas Henry Huxley had famously said, *"be prepared to give up every preconceived notion, follow humbly to whatever abysses nature leads."*

Capelo the Great Crusading Lone Physicist tried to become a child.

A particle stream approaches a ship equipped with the disrupter shield, which is prime setting two on the artifact. Call it a proton beam, although it could just as well be photons focused into a laser, or a half-dozen other possibilities. Call it a proton beam. What happens next?

The beam is actually a stream of tiny oscillating threads. It is also, essentially, a moving smear of probabilities, as are all fundamental particles. The beam passes through the roiling frenzy that is the quantum world, in which particles are constantly deflected, constantly breaking apart and reforming, constantly erupting from the energy of the vacuum and disappearing again. But a proton is a heavy particle, compared to most of this frantic activity, so it speeds on its way without much interruption.

Unless a heavier particle hits it. All right, look again at that quantum agitation. A storm of known and unknown particles: virtual particles existing for a brief moment as well as more stable electrons, gravitons, photons, on and on. And, insists Capelo the Great Crusading Lone Physicist but no one else, also probons. Ubiquitous probons, woven into the very fabric of spacetime as thoroughly as are gravitons, so that gravity operates everywhere. As does probability.

Make the probon heavy, heavier even than Capelo the Great Crusading Lone Physicist had originally thought. Make it heavy because that's why no particle accelerator anywhere in the Solar System can yet reach the energy levels needed to detect it, which explains why we haven't. And make it heavy because the circling line on the Faller's diagram was very heavy in relation to the line on an earlier drawing representing photons.

Each probon, like all fundamental particles, is made of tiny vibrating threads, and each is a smear of probabilities.

The probon is a messenger particle, just as gravitons are messenger particles for gravity and gluons are messenger particles for the strong force. The message it carries, the force it transmits, is probability. In the universe as we know it, probability decrees that the path an object takes *will* be the average of all paths, the path resulting from wave function amplitudes squared, the path that gravity-warped-by-mass makes into the path of least resistance. Mass tells space how to curve; space tells mass how to move.

The proton beam should therefore hit the ship.

But we know, have known for two hundred years, that a particle actually takes all possible paths. That proton beam has traveled directly to the ship, has traveled obliquely to the ship, has reached the ship by detouring first to the Andromeda Galaxy. All possible paths. Including through the six curled-up dimensions of spacetime, the Calabi-Yau spaces. That proton beam traveled through the Calabi-Yau dimensions countless times because the dimensions are so tiny, returning each time to its starting place. But, ultimately, the average of all these circuitous journeys is the least-resistance sum-over-paths integral, because that's the force probons carry and it operates everywhere, just as gravitons make gravity operate everywhere.

Large masses warp gravity, sometimes to extremes, which is why you have black holes. What warps probons? The artifact? How?

By changing the beam's probable path. But no detection equipment anywhere had detected the proton beam the *Alan B. Shepard* fired at the artifact. The beam hadn't merely been deflected, it had disappeared. To where? You can't just lose all that energy; the law of conservation of energy didn't allow it.

He looked again at the Faller's diagram, although it was burned into his brain. From the moment he'd seen the sketch, he'd known. But Capelo stayed with it, worked it out, saw it all as the collection of floating intuitive perceptions that physics had been to him since the age of nine. A child.

The line on the Faller sketch went into one of the six Calabi-Yau spaces. And then the line continued on to a different Calabi-Yau space, with a different configuration. Only it wasn't a different space. That's why the Faller had drawn two "flowers," not six. The "flowers" weren't two different Calabi-Yau spaces. They were the same one, transformed.

The artifact focused probons, shot a huge number of them at an incoming particle stream, just as a laser focused and shot photons. The artifact thus warped probability, in the same way huge mass warped gravity. The energy to do that was certainly available; the strength of the force transmitted by a messenger particle is inversely proportional to the tension on its threads, and Capelo had calculated fairly low tension for the probon, let alone the energy in the protons. All the energy of these tiny vibrating threads brought about a different path, one of low but not zero probability under "normal" circumstances, and now of 100 percent probability. So the proton beam went into a curled-up dimension.

And stayed there.

Why?

Because the energy it brought into the dimension, energy which hadn't been there before, did something else. It effected a space-changing flop transition, changing the shape of that tiny, curled-up dimension into a different shape. Without affecting our larger, three-extended-dimension universe at all. The energy started by making a tiny tear, and to repair the tear, the Calabi-Yau shape evolved into a different shape, which mathematicians had known was possible almost as long as they had known of Calabi-Yau shapes. The flop transition might look something like this:

As the Calabi-Yau space evolves through the tear, what's affected are the precise values of the masses of the individual particles—the energies in their threads. The tiny vibrating threads that made up the protons, always smears of probability, now vibrate at a different resonance. It has ceased to be a proton, and has become a different, unknown particle. After all, matter itself, at the deepest level, was itself a manifestation of probabilities. The probabilities had been changed.

He had never seen it. For ten years he hadn't seen it, Capelo the Great Crusading Lone Physicist. The mathematics of flop-transitions were well established, had been established for a hundred and fifty years. He started to calculate, using the enormous power of the ship's computer.

Hours later, it all balanced, the elegant mathematics, and Capelo felt humbled by the hidden, ineffably beautiful structure he had uncovered.

The enormous energy needed to alter the beam's probable path, to change the vibration of its threads, exactly equaled the net energy of the heavier probons minus the energy lost to quantum agitation. The new vibrational energy exactly equaled the energy needed to effect a space-changing flop transition in a Calabi-Yau dimension of a certain probable configuration. A piece of the dimension was unfolded, and then refolded into a subtly different shape, like refolding a part of a complex origami. All the equations balanced, led into one another with natural rightness.

The probon was real. Now he had its mass, its spin, its thread constant, its neutral charge. Probability could take its rightful place as the fifth force in the universe. Electromagnetism, strong force, weak force, gravity, probability. No, that wasn't right . . . probability had always had an equal place in the universe. It was just that humans hadn't seen it.

Had Fallers? Did their physics start at a different place, perhaps even at probability, and come to the same elegant structure by a different path? There were an infinite number of paths: for particles, for physics, for discovery.

When he finally stood up from the chair, he was shaky from lack of food, lack of motion, uncharacteristic lack of pride. Capelo the

Great Crusading Lone Physicist. Not so Lone, after all. He sat down again and looked down at his printed flimsies, at the beating mathematical heart of his theory.

His critics might say it wasn't even a theory, but a patchwork of intuitions and guesses and borrowed maths. But Capelo knew in his bones, in his testicles that had given life to Amanda and Sudie, that the theory was true, that it did describe reality, even though many details remained to be worked out. Details of theory, solutions to some of his equations, the role of quantum entanglement. And, of course, the entire mass of engineering details that would take this from mathematics to hardware, which the Fallers had already done.

Or had they? A sudden thought occurred to Capelo, but he shoved it aside. Irrelevant to the last major step: the remaining Faller drawing to which its line led: a nine-planet star system, the third planet with one moon, the fourth with two, the sixth with rings . . . the Solar System, with two artifacts drawn within it and a thick circular line canceling the whole thing.

Was it some warlike statement: "We will obliterate you with our artifact and take yours"? Bellicose bragging from a helpless prisoner of war? Capelo didn't think so.

He set about applying his new equations not to the tiny, curled-up dimensions of Calabi-Yau space, but to the large, three-extended-dimensions universe. He already had a few specific numbers to work with, including one for the energy that had fried all of the World star system, except World itself. He worked for more unnoticed hours. Once, when he lay down a flimsy, it encountered a tray of food he hadn't noticed anyone bring in. He made himself gulp down something, he had no idea what, and went on working.

When he finally finished, he sat staring at the results for a long time.

The probability energy focused by two artifacts was huge. It was enough to do what smaller amounts did, over and over, to a small, curled-up dimension of the universe: effect a space-changing flop-transition into a different shape. It did that the same way it did it in the tiny dimensions: by first tearing the fabric of spacetime. But in the tiny dimensions, it was a tiny tear, easily repaired with the energy pouring in at the same time from the entire probability-altering event. In the large extended three dimensions, there wasn't enough energy. The "tear" would spread, and the total dimensional shape of the universe—now a benign sphere extending fifteen billion lightyears before curling back on itself—would undergo a topology-changing flop-transition.

But the vibrational patterns of the threads that make up space-time were intimately dependent on the shape of the dimensions in which they vibrated. Not the size, but the shape. If the three extended dimensions of the universe underwent a flop-transition, its threads would vibrate in different patterns, *giving rise to different fundamental particles*. Extended spacetime itself would be different, the disturbance to its fabric traveling outward at c. And every living thing in it—humans and Fallers, bacteria and grasses, glow-worms and genetically recreated tigers, would die.

That was why the enemy Faller had been so desperate to give humans the physics it knew. Because it knew from Marbet that humans had an artifact, too, and it knew what would happen if the two artifacts were set off as close together as within the same star system.

He had to tell somebody. Some military brass who would understand, somebody not stupid enough to either disbelieve him or to take the artifact to the Faller's home system, where theirs probably already was. Tell somebody . . . Grafton . . . no, not Grafton rigid stupid weapon-pusher . . . Kaufman, then . . . tell somebody . . .

He stood up too quickly, felt the blood rush to his head, and fainted.

*　　　　　*　　　　　*

He found himself back on his bunk when he came to—God, he was tired of coming to, conscious-un-conscious-un-conscious-un, he was starting to feel like a holo persona. A medical patch adorned his arm. Lyle Kaufman sat beside the bunk, studying Capelo's flimsies.

"Don't worry yourself about my privacy," Capelo said. "I'm just Solar Alliance property, like this ship."

Kaufman said, "You did it," and at his tone, reverent as one should be in the face of cosmic beauty, Capelo's mood abruptly changed. He sat up and swung his feet to the floor, and found he could do so easily. Whatever the patch was delivering into his bloodstream, it was terrific.

"I did it, Lyle. Or, rather—" he hated to say this, and his old irritation returned, making him feel more like himself, "—we did it. The . . . the Faller and I."

"Tell me."

"You don't have the math," Capelo said brutally.

"I know. I probably don't even have all the non-mathematical fundamental concepts. But try, Tom. Please."

Capelo studied Kaufman. "You're not asking as a soldier, are you?"

"Later I'll ask like that. Everyone will. But now I just want to know."

Capelo hadn't realized this streak of humility lay in the man. It didn't make him like Kaufman any better, but it made it acceptable to tell him the theory. He explained it as well as he could in layman's terms. Kaufman interrupted with questions, but the questions were intelligent enough that they didn't annoy Capelo too much.

When he'd done, Kaufman sat quietly, his hands on his knees. Finally he said, "The destruction of the fabric of spacetime? If two artifacts are activated at setting prime thirteen in the same star system?"

"Is that the only part you focus on?" The man was a soldier after all, with a soldier's tunnel vision.

"It's a not unimportant point," Kaufman said acerbically. "Why would the makers of the artifacts have permitted such a thing?"

"I have no idea."

"It doesn't make sense. Surely they would have built in safeguards against tearing spacetime."

"Yes . . . no," Capelo said. He was losing the thread here. "Maybe . . . maybe they couldn't control their own technology any better than we can control ours. Maybe that's what happened to them."

Kaufman was silent.

"I suppose this is all being recorded."

"Everything you've done in the last fifty-six hours has been recorded, copied, downloaded, and encrypted. Surely you already knew that."

"I guess," Capelo said, without interest. Fifty-six hours? "What day is it?"

"Very early Friday morning. Oh three hundred hours."

"Where are my children?"

"I imagine they're asleep."

"Did Rosalind win her chess game against Gruber?"

"I don't know," Kaufman said, and from the way he looked at Capelo, Capelo realized that he'd been jumping topics randomly.

"Are we nearing the space tunnel?"

"Yes. Tom, you need sleep. The doctor stabilized you—you were dehydrated, with low blood sugar and abnormal heart rhythm—but you still need sleep. I'm going to put another patch on you. A sedative."

"Don't tell Grafton," Capelo said, which made no sense, even to him.

"Lie back down. There. But before you sleep . . . I'd like to ask one more thing. A favor."

"What?"

Kaufman's speech turned almost formal. "With your permission,

I'd like to comlink Ann Sikorski what you've found. Once we go through the space tunnel, no further communication will be possible. I'd like her to know what you've found, while that's still possible."

"Why?" Capelo said sleepily. The patch was already hitting him.

"So she'll at least know that the reason we took the artifact off World was worth doing so."

"The natives still on your conscience, Lyle? Throw 'em out. But, yes, go ahead and comlink Ann."

"Thank you."

"And in return I want to ask one thing, too," Capelo said. The torpor was coming up on him fast, but this was important. "Tell me the truth, if you're capable of it. What happened to the Faller when the nerve gas immobilized the rest of us?"

"He died."

That fine alien physicist mind, that motherfucking bastard killer. "Good," Capelo said, and there was no time before he slid into sleep to examine how deeply he might or might not have meant it.

TWENTY-EIGHT

GOFKIT SHAMLOE

There were some tall upright sticks in front of Gofkit Shamloe. Enli had never seen such a thing. The sticks were very close together, too close to fly wind toys from, and pointed on the top. A tight row of them blocked her view of Ano's house and then curved around the cookfires to one side.

"What's that?" she exclaimed to Pek Sikorski. "That was never there before."

"It's a fence," Pek Sikorski said, and Enli saw that it was. A fence like the low ones used to keep frebs from eating the tender new shoots of fakimib, and always removed once the fakimib grew tough stems. A freb fence grown tall and pointed, around Gofkit Shamloe. To keep out people.

Enli, Pek Sikorski, and Pek Gruber stood on the road beside their bicycles, staring at the unfinished fence, Essa and Serlit behind them. The adults were dusty and hot. The two youngsters hadn't seemed to mind the heat, or anything else, as they rode along, giggling. Essa would go on giggling if not stopped, but for Serlit, naturally graver, the laughter was a temporary intoxicant due to Essa's presence.

Enli finally said, "Stay here, please, until I've gone to Ano's house. Until I see . . ." See what? If Ano and the children were all right. If Calin had come back to Gofkit Shamloe and told everyone that it was Terrans who had destroyed shared reality. Calin, the only other Worlder beside Enli who knew that piece of reality. If he had told, Pek Sikorski and Pek Gruber, and maybe Enli as well, might not be welcome here. What if while Enli had been on the road to Gofkit Shamloe, sunflashers had told all of World what Terrans had done? Where could Pek Sikorski and Pek Gruber go?

At least the fence would hide the Terrans from Gofkit Shamloe until Enli saw whatever reality possessed it now.

She rounded the last of the tall upright logs. Her breath rose in her throat, bristled her neckfur. *Ano* . . .

Gofkit Shamloe looked unchanged.

No, not completely unchanged. The green, with its hearths for shared cookfires, was deserted, but one would expect that in mid-afternoon. The flowerbeds looked as well-tended as before, a colorful refreshment of trifalitib, allabenirib, mittib. But one house was missing, that of Gostir Pek Nafirif and his family. Where the house had stood was a pile of cold ashes.

Behind the village, its fields stretched to the horizon, gently undulating. Although she strained her eyes, Enli couldn't see anyone working them. But the hills might hide the workers, or the tall larfruit overshadow them, or everyone might be working in the casir grove in the other direction . . .

"May your flowers bloom forever," Enli called, but not very loudly. Afraid, she realized, of any answer, or no answer.

From the other side of the village, where the ground dipped toward the wooded riverbank, came shouting. It drew closer. Enli took a step forward, stopped, waited.

Two men rose slowly above the gentle ridge, their backs to her, dragging something. They shouted to people below, who shouted back. The men kept pulling and shouting, and a large log, most of a tree, scraped up the bank. When enough of it had passed the top of the rise so that the whole thing would not topple back down into the river, the two men stopped dragging and turned, wiping their skull ridges. One of them was Calin.

He saw Enli and stopped dead. The other man saw her, too, and rushed forward. "Enli Pek Brimmidin!" It was Ano's husband, Sparil Pek Trestin. "You're back with us! Back from the household of Voratur and the Terrans!" He embraced her and then stepped back, his thin honest face shining with pleasure and sweat.

"Ano . . ." Enli got out.

"The soil is rich. She will be so happy to see you! She was afraid—so happy to see you!"

"And your children . . ."

A shadow passed over Sparil's face, but before he could answer a small shape hurled itself at Enli. "Enli! Enli!"

"Fentil! By the First Flower, how you've grown!"

Her nephew drew himself up proudly to his full height. His neckfur, as golden as Enli's brother's had been, rippled with health. He smiled even as he spoke. "I've been helping haul logs!"

"And a big help he is," his father said, but the shadow was still there in Sparil's voice. Was it for her? Had Calin told? "Ano is at harvest. They'll come back soon."

Now Calin came forward. He spoke formally. "May your blossoms perfume the world of your ancestors, Enli."

"May your garden bloom forever, Calin." Her eyes questioned him. He saw it, and looked away.

Fentil said eagerly, "You must stay now and not go away again, Enli."

She would have to do it sometime. It might as well be now. "I have visitors with me."

Sparil said, "Are they good workers? We need good workers?"

"Yes." Were the Terrans good workers? Pek Gruber, whom she

still could not bring herself to call by his childname, was at least very strong. "There are two youngsters and . . . and two Terrans."

"Terrans?" said Afri Pek Buctor; she and a man Enli didn't recognize had climbed up from the riverbank. "Are they good workers? We cannot have anyone here who does not work hard, now that reality has shifted so much. You should know that."

So Calin had not told. And Afri Pek Buctor was still a scold. Something broke in Enli, and she suddenly felt close to tears.

"There, Enli, you're tired and hungry," Sparil said kindly, "and so are your friends, I'm sure. Bring them here. O, but . . . what do Terrans eat?"

"They'll manage," Enli said, not up to explaining the foods Terrans could eat, those they could not, those they could but got no good from, those they carried with them along with seeds that grew at an astonishing rate . . . She hated to cry. With a huge effort, she made herself stop.

"I'll get food!" Fentil said, and was off running toward Ano's house. "And water!"

"Where are your friends?" Sparil said. "O, my manners—this is Morfib Pek Chandor, Afri's new mate."

Enli murmured a flower greeting. She had a sudden incongruous hope that Essa would not laugh; "Morfib" was a funny name. If wild Essa giggled, Afri would be affronted.

"Let's go get your friends," Sparil said gently, and took Enli's hand. Calin walked away, toward his house.

Afri said disapprovingly, "I have never seen a Terran before, Enli. Is it true they have neckfur on their heads? Are they very ugly?"

Enli sat with Sparil, Essa, Serlit, and the Terrans on the thick log. Pek Gruber had made himself instantly accepted by dragging it, unassisted, the rest of the way to the new fence. Fentil capered on the green with the few children who had already returned from harvest. The children darted shy looks at the Terrans and giggled among themselves.

So unchanged. So much the shared reality Enli remembered. And so different.

Essa said to Serlit, "Come on! Let's play with them!"

Serlit, more polite, looked at Enli. Had she then become his mother, until his mother returned from sunflashing? Apparently she had.

"Yes, go play." Essa bounded off, Serlit following more slowly. When they were gone, Enli said to Sparil, "Tell me what has happened in Gofkit Shamloe since . . . since shared reality went away." He was the right person to ask, not Ano. Sparil would tell it honestly and austerely. Ano would add too many details, too much feeling. Enli had had enough feeling.

Sparil looked uncomfortable. But it wouldn't occur to him not to share reality, no matter how much his skull ridges wrinkled. Pek Sikorski and Pek Gruber twisted their bodies on the rough log to listen.

"At first," Sparil finally began, "we all stayed inside our houses. Everyone was afraid. And no one spoke much because . . . because we didn't know how, without shared reality. People . . . thought different things. The only one who spoke much was Ano."

Despite herself, Enli smiled. Nothing could shut up Ano.

"We got hungry," Sparil said simply, "so people came out. But some . . . were not right in their brains. They just sat and rocked back and forth. Others were not wrong in their brains, but they wouldn't go to the fields to harvest. They were too afraid. They ate, but they wouldn't work, and other people got angry."

Afri, for one, Ano guessed. No wonder Sparil was anxious that Enli's visitors be good workers.

"One day we went to the fields, except for a few people, and some unreal people came. They were taking things, burning things,

killing things. Gostir Pek Nafirif and his family were in their hut."
His kind, plain face sagged under his agitated skull ridges. "We had
the farewell burning for them all, and then Calin said we should
build the fence."

Calin. With effort, Enli kept her skull ridges smooth.

"Two other families left," Sparil continued, "Udi Pek Giffiliir
and Laril Pek Broffir. They went to other relatives. And some other
people came, who live now in those houses. Plus Morfib Pek Chandor, who mated with Afri."

There was that name again. Enli must warn Essa not to laugh.

"That's all," Sparil said. But Enli knew that it wasn't. There was
a piece of reality Sparil wasn't sharing.

"Sparil—"

He said quickly, "O, and Pek Gruber, you and your mate can
have Laril Pek Broffir's house. It's still empty. Are those youngsters,
ah, yours?"

Pek Sikorski smiled at the mannerly absurdity. Enli realized that
it was the first time she'd seen her smile since shared reality went
away. Pek Sikorski said, "No, Pek Trestin. Essa is in Enli's care. Serlit
is only with us until his mother comes for him. She's a sunflasher.
May I ask, if the petals unfold for your answer . . ."

Sparil looked slightly bewildered. Pek Sikorski had learned her
World in the Household of Voratur, richer and more formal than
Gofkit Shamloe. Her elaborate speech scared Sparil a little. But when
the silence had stretched on, he seemed to realize what he was supposed to say. "You may ask."

"Has Gofkit Shamloe received any messages from your sunflasher about how shared reality went away?"

"Our sunflasher left the village," Sparil said. "He was Gostir Pek
Nafirif."

So no message could reach Gofkit Shamloe, and the chain would
be broken. If Ivi Pek Harrilin had sent Pek Sikorski's explanation
sunflashing from the capital, it might not have gotten very far at all.

World would not hear about the object that had perfumed the air with shared reality and then rose away into the sky. The villages would have to cope with unshared reality on their own, as Gofkit Shamloe was trying to do.

"Look," Pek Sikorski said suddenly, and slowly raised her arm to point at her own face. A lifegiver had perched there, one of the tiny flyers that carried life from blossom to blossom. Sacred to the First Flower, they were revered all over the World. They alit on people's arms, legs, bodies. But never, until shared reality went away, on their heads.

Pek Gruber said in Terran, "You were right. They are sensitive to the altered brain electricity."

"Sparil," Enli said, because it had to be said, "there is a piece of reality you are not sharing with me."

His skull ridges darkened to a dull red. "Enli . . ."

"Please."

Pek Sikorski rose, "We need to control Essa. Come, Dieter." He looked at her blankly. Finally Pek Sikorski said in Terran, "Private family matters!"

"Oh," Pek Gruber said, getting to his feet.

Even Pek Sikorski did not understand all of World. Family matters were village matters. But Enli let the Terrans go. "Sparil?"

"It's Obora," he blurted. "You know how noisy and wild she's always been, Enli, getting into everything . . ." He looked bewildered by this oldest daughter, as well he might, so different from obedient Fentil and placid baby Usi. So different from Sparil himself.

"I know," Enli said. "What has Obora done?"

"She struck Solor Pek Ramul, and he fell into the fire."

Enli gasped. Solor Pek Ramul was the village's ancient piper. He had played music for dancing on the green every evening for as long as Enli could remember. Doddering, sometimes unclear in his mind, he nonetheless played music so sweet it was like the scent of flowers. To strike him, to knock him into the fire . . .

She managed to get out, "Did Pek Ramul join his ancestors?"

"No. In fact, he was only burned a little, on one arm. Calin was there and dragged him right out and threw water on him."

Calin again. "Why did Obora strike him?"

"She wanted him to pipe some song he didn't want to pipe. They didn't . . . share reality about the song. She didn't mean to hurt him, Enli. You know how Obora is. She lost her temper and lashed out, but she caught Pek Ramul off balance, and he's so old . . . her soul wilts over what she did. But some people in the village don't . . . don't share that reality."

"Has . . . has Obora been declared unreal?" If she had, she was now dead.

"That's just it!" Sparil cried. "No one knows what to do! How can you declare someone unreal when there is no shared reality? No one can agree what to do!"

Relief flooded Enli. Obora was still alive, not dead with her body imprisoned in chemicals to prevent its decay and her joyous return to her ancestors. Still alive.

"Where is she now?"

"With Ano at the harvest. No one knows what to do. But tonight everyone will gather on the green to . . . to talk about the reality."

Which always before had needed no talk, had been shared without dissension.

Suddenly Sparil cried, "Everything is different, and no one knows what to do!"

Enli didn't answer. She didn't know, either.

She sat watching Essa chase Serlit on the green, and tried to think what to say to comfort Sparil. Before she could find the unimaginable words, the harvesters burst into the village and Enli was in Ano's arms, and Ano was laughing and crying in that way only Ano had, and Enli was finally home.

•   •   •

The large log had been left (on its side) near the unfinished fence, and
Dieter Pek Gruber, with his enormous strength, had hauled up two
more, less large, from the riverbed. The three logs made a loose
triangle in the darkness. In the middle was a fire, but it was hardly
needed in the night already bright with five of World's six moons.
Enli had heard Pek Gruber say to Pek Sikorski that he wanted to
give his powertorch to the village as a present, but Pek Sikorski had
said, "Wait on that. Don't go too fast."

Everyone in Gofkit Shamloe sat on the logs or stood behind
them. Ano held Usi, asleep in her lap, with Fentil huddled beside
her and Sparil standing with a protective hand on her shoulder. The
new villagers were there, and bad-tempered Afri with her new mate,
and Calin, and the girls Enli had played with as a child, now grown
with mates from other villages and children of their own. Essa and
Serlit crouched, even Essa quiet, on the evening grass. The two Terrans hovered in the background, behind everyone else. At one end
of the log, well away from Ano and Sparil, sat old Solor Pek Ramul,
his burned arm swaddled in cloth treated with healer's salve.

Alone in the middle of the circle Obora sat cross-legged on the
grass.

She had gone there on her own, uninstructed by anyone because
no one knew what to instruct. This had never happened before in
living memory, in the passed-down history of Gofkit Shamloe, in
the history of World. Always shared reality knew what to do with
people who had behaved unreal, as Obora had. Sparil's despairing
cry echoed in Enli's mind: *"How can you declare someone unreal when
there is no shared reality?"*

The villagers of Gofkit Shamloe looked at each other, and
avoided looking at each other, and waited. No one spoke.

Finally a querulous old voice said, "It's getting cold."

Again silence. *"It's practice,"* Pek Sikorski had said to Serlit's mother, Ivi. But no one in Gofkit Shamloe had had any practice.

Finally Afri strode to the center of the circle, and Enli's stomach roiled. Not Afri, mean-spirited even before shared reality went away. Afri said, "Obora Pek Brimmidin pushed Solor Pek Ramul into the fire." But after that, she seemed uncertain what to say next, and so she just walked defiantly out of the center.

But a pattern had been set. A woman walked into the center and said, "She didn't mean to hurt Pek Ramul. It was bad manners, not unreal behavior."

Another long silence. Then a man went into the circle and said, "Obora is a good girl at her root and stem. The petals blow too wildly, is all."

Someone said, "If we only had a grandmother's mother in Gofkit Shamloe!"

"But we have no grandmother's mother to tell us what to do."

More people spoke, some for Obora, some against her, many lamenting the lack of a grandmother's mother. When everyone who wanted to speak was done, everyone sat waiting for whatever would happen next.

Pek Sikorski and Pek Gruber had moved behind Enli. She heard them whisper in Terran behind her, in the dark, Pek Gruber's voice urgent. "Tell them, Ann. Teach them to *vote*."

The word meant nothing to Enli.

"No, Dieter. Let them do it for themselves. They're on the path." More silence.

"I'm going inside," someone said loudly. "It's time to sleep."

"But Obora—"

"Pek Ramul—"

"Nothing—"

"Unreal—"

A stir at one end of the largest log, and Solor Pek Ramul himself hobbled into the circle. He didn't look at Obora. His voice was thin and quavering, a shocking contrast to the full sweetness of his piping. The circle stilled.

"I was burned," he said, paused, began again, a man picking his way over unfamiliar stepping stones in a strange river. "Obora burned me. She is a good girl at her root. I was burned. Some say she is unreal. Some say she is real. Shared reality is gone. I was burned. *I* should say about Obora."

A soft murmur ran over the villagers, who then looked at each other in surprise. The surprise came from the murmurs' being all in agreement with Pek Ramul. They shared this reality, even though shared reality had gone.

"*I* should say," Pek Ramul quavered again, and this time there were shouts of agreement, open elation over the very fact of agreement. Only Afri looked outraged, but she glanced at the people around her and closed her mouth.

Pek Ramul said, "Obora is good at her root. She is real. She should live. She burned me. She must clean my house and cook my food until all six moons appear again together in the sky. And make me two new tunics."

Silence taut as a rope, and then someone laughed. It was Ano, laughing and crying together.

A voice said, very loud and very clear, "It is now shared reality. When someone hurts someone, the person hurt should say." The voice was Calin's.

Obora stood and took Pek Ramul's hand. He smiled at her, his old eyes bright. People laughed and talked, then started toward their houses. Afri went into hers and slammed the door. Ano embraced Obora, which woke baby Usi so that she started to wail.

Pek Sikorski said, under the din, "My God, Dieter. They just invented the town meeting and a code of justice all at once."

"Or the start of one, anyway. *Mein Liebchen*—" Pek Sikorski's comlink shrilled.

Enli heard it, and heard Pek Sikorski instantly cut off the sound. "Not that high tech yet," she said to Pek Gruber. "Not here. At Voratur's was bad enough. Come with me to the other side of the *stockade*." Another new Terran word, but Enli scarcely noticed. Calin was moving toward her through the jumble of people.

"The garden blooms well, Enli."

"The perfume pleases our ancestors, Ano's and mine. Obora . . ."

"I know. I am happy for you."

She blurted, "You didn't tell about the Terrans," and then glanced around fearfully. But they stood alone.

"No. I didn't tell."

"Why not?"

"Terrans took away shared reality. But you said it wasn't these two Terrans, and now people aren't . . . aren't all the same anymore. Not even Terrans . . . like Obora tonight. And Worlders aren't the same as we were . . . as you . . . so you and I . . ."

Through the stammered phrases, Enli knew what he meant. Joy rose in her. "Yes."

"Will you . . . will you drink a cup of water at my house, Enli?"

The joy let her say, teasing him, "Not pel?"

"We have no pel. The traders stopped bringing it."

"They will bring it again."

"Maybe so, maybe not," he said, serious again. "Everything is different now."

"Not everything," she said, and he pulled her into his arms in the sweet darkness.

"Lyle," Ann said into her comlink. "Dieter calculates that you're probably close to the space tunnel. That's the only reason I'm answering you. This is our final conversation, if you can call it that. Dieter, how long is the commlag?"

"Fifty-four minutes." Gruber had his powertorch on low, and it cast eerie shadows upwards on his face. Beside him the fence rose in raw, untrimmed logs.

"All right. Lyle, I'll listen to your recorded message after I send my own. This is the final report of the World anthropological team. Not that I think my report makes any difference to you. The natives of World are surviving, although not without tremendous strain and uncounted casualties. The infrastructure of communication and trade and centralized governance is all gone. There is some looting and rioting, probably not as much as if they were human. They're starting to defend themselves by turning the villages into small forts, with stockades and local justice. The planet-wide civilization is gone along with the biological basis that gave rise to it, thanks to you. What's taking its place is frontier isolation, economically possible without starvation only because this is such a fertile planet. In that isolation most non-practical art will disappear. So will much of the manufacturing that depended on wide trade to sustain it, and the easy exchange of ideas. Religion is bound to fragment. Within a generation, World will be made up of very small pre-Renaissance enclaves, and their own version of the Dark Ages will begin. But don't worry your conscience, Lyle—they're surviving. End of report by the Planet World team, Ann Pek Sikorski, biologist, and Dieter Pek Gruber, geologist."

"*Lieber Gott*," Gruber said softly. "You hacked him to pieces."

"Not him," Ann whispered bitterly. "Lyle is made of unbreakable synthetics." She hit the stored-messages key.

Kaufman's voice rose into the night. "Ann, Dieter, we're going through the tunnel in half an hour. I want to send you this one last report, so you can know at least that there might be sufficient reason for removing the artifact from World. Marbet discovered that the Fallers have an artifact identical to ours. They've already used it to fry the human colonies in the Viridian system. Tom has determined that on setting prime thirteen, the artifact emits a shield that can protect an entire star system from attack. We're going to take our artifact to

Sol, make sure the enemy knows we have it, and activate setting prime thirteen. The sacrifice of World means that billions of people are safe on Earth, on Mars, on Luna, in the Belt, on Titan . . . everywhere.

"And one more thing. Tom has cracked the science behind the artifact. It seems to be the greatest breakthrough of this century in understanding the universe, and maybe of the next century as well. That has to count for something."

"Not enough," Ann said.

"Ann . . . protection of the whole Solar System . . . we are at war, *mein Schatz.*"

"And so may World be someday, thanks to us."

Kaufman's voice grew huskier. "I think that's all I want to say, Ann, Dieter. Except that my heartfelt best wishes go with you both. Always. End transmission, Colonel Lyle Kaufman, SADA."

Into the silence Gruber said, "Ann, you told me something once. You said the human brain has, let me get it right, 'a thousand trillion junctions between neurons.' For Worlders it must be almost the same, same basic DNA. So many neural junctions, so much capacity. Surely they will learn to rebuild, maybe even stronger than before?"

"I don't know," Ann said. "Dieter, I honestly don't know. Have humans? We have better technology than our Dark Ages, but do we have any more morality, any more ethics, any more of the peace and sharing we took away from Worlders?"

Dieter didn't answer. He took Ann's hand, and the fingers were stiff and cold.

TWENTY-NINE

ABOARD THE *ALAN B. SHEPARD*

Space Tunnel #438 led at the moment to Caligula space, a human system with four small, barren, nonhabitable planets. A military base floated there, close to the three tunnels that, inexplicably, orbited out beyond the last planet. When a star system possessed more than one tunnel, the tunnels always orbited close together, but usually only stars with interesting planets rated three tunnels. That Caligula space should be such a crossroads remained one of the mysteries of the tunnel system.

As soon as the *Alan B. Shepard* left orbit around World, a flyer left from the tunnel-orbiting warship *Murasaki* through Space Tunnel #438 into Caligula space. From there it raced with all possible speed through the tunnel system to Mars, carrying classified reports of the artifact to the SADC high command. The *Alan B. Shepard* followed more slowly, after a brief docking with the *Murasaki* on the World side of the tunnel. Commander Grafton had the unenviable job of explaining to McChesney what had happened to the Faller prisoner McChesney had so laboriously captured and faithfully guarded from enemy traffic through the space tunnel.

After that unpleasant interview was over, the *Shepard* flew through another tunnel, and another, and more after that, following the flyer back to the Solar System. The journey proceeded routinely.

Lyle Kaufman knew none of this. He remained under arrest, confined in the brig, waiting for the court of inquiry to convene. The three-person court would make recommendations for or against court-martial, and on what charges. This investigative board could call anyone aboard ship to testify, usually one at a time. The accused had the right to hear all testimony. Commander Grafton had called the court of inquiry, chosen its members from among his officers, and submitted a written statement of special circumstances. Everyone, including Kaufman, considered the outcome a foregone conclusion.

Just before the inquiry began, the *Alan B. Shepard* passed through Space Tunnel #1 and entered Sol System. She then began her journey to Mars.

They had brought him his SADA dress uniform, but without its ceremonial sword. Kaufman pondered this as he put on his blues in the bare cell. Some obscure regulation, created who knew where and for what occasion, dug up and followed by the meticulous Grafton? *The subject of a court of inquiry shall be denied the right to wear his/her dress uniform sword.* Or was the Commander afraid he would stab the MPs, himself, or the entire court of inquiry with the sword's dulled, ineffectual point? For whatever reason, the empty scabbard dangled by his side.

"Ready when you are, sir."

"I'm ready, ensign."

"This way, sir. Follow me, sir," the young woman said, even though Kaufman knew the way perfectly. The court of inquiry would be held in the large conference room. The MPs accompanied Kaufman, one on each side, through the empty corridors.

The conference table was oval. Behind the long side farthest from the door sat three Navy officers in full dress. Kaufman knew only one of them by name, Lieutenant Elizabeth Framingham. On the closer side of the table stood two empty chairs, as widely separated as possible. The ensign led Kaufman to the far chair. The two MPs stood at attention behind him. The other chair, Kaufman supposed, was for witnesses.

Commander Grafton stood, diamond-carbon straight, at the head of the table. When Kaufman had seated himself, Grafton recited formally, for both the sake of the record and the sake of the formality, "This court of inquiry is now in session. Court officers shall be recorded as Lieutenant Commander Carter Campbell Rulanov, SADN, presiding; Lieutenant Antarres L. Ramsay, SADN; and Lieutenant Elizabeth George Framingham, SADN.

"The charge is as follows: 'That Colonel Lyle Daniel Kaufman, Solar Alliance Defense Army, temporarily attached to the Solar Alliance Defense Navy as Special Classified Project Head, on April 16, 2166, aboard the *Alan B. Shepard*, willfully, without proper authority, and without justifiable cause, did assault two Military Police in pursuit of their duties, a charge of "Assault"; did force entry for himself and two civilians into a restricted area of the ship, against prior direct order by the commander of the vessel, a charge of "Conduct to the Prejudice of Good Order and Discipline"; and did commit an act of treason in passing military secrets to an enemy prisoner of war, a charge of "Treason," the Solar Alliance being at that time in a state of war.' Colonel Kaufman, do you understand these charges as presented?"

"Yes," Kaufman said.

"Then this court of inquiry is entrusted with the responsibility of creating a recommendation as to whether sufficient evidence exists for a court-martial of Colonel Kaufman on any or all of these charges. Members of the court, do you understand this responsibility?"

The three officers gave formal assent. Kaufman studied them carefully. Rulanov was clearly genemod, as much a classic—not to say "stereotyped"—military type as Grafton. Tall, erect, clean-boned. Ramsay was about Rulanov's age, early forties (although with genemod it was always hard to tell). Framingham was the junior officer, probably no more than thirty. The three wore identical expressions: a perfect blank, giving away nothing.

Kaufman suddenly wondered what Marbet would have seen on their faces, in their body language.

"I have two additional directives for this court of inquiry," Grafton continued. "First, that because this is a classified matter, Special Compartmented Information, and of great military urgency, all members of the court of inquiry are bound to say nothing of these proceedings, record nothing of these proceedings, and in no way even indicate any knowledge that these proceedings occurred, on penalty of being charged with treason. Is this directive understood and agreed to?"

Three assents.

"Second," Grafton said, and stopped. Three faces waited, expressionless. "Second, I would like the court to remember that the honor and career of an officer with an unblemished military record, including combat duty, is at stake here. That is all."

Grafton turned and left, closing the door behind him. Kaufman felt a dark, angry sadness descend on him. Grafton might think he had a *prima facie* case, but he was still doing everything he could to create as fair an inquiry as possible. It made it that much harder on Kaufman.

"Colonel Kaufman," Rulanov said, "tell us what happened." Direct and simple.

"I arrived at the prisoner-of-war secure area and was given admittance by the MPs and the security equipment. I then waited inside the area but outside the prisoner's cell for Dr. Capelo to break Ms. Marbet out of the brig and bring her there."

"How did you know he would do that? Did he tell you his plans?"

"No."

"When did you last see Dr. Capelo prior to his arrival at the secure area?"

"The day before, when he burst in on Commander Grafton and me to confront us about a Faller being aboard ship." The court would already know this; everyone's movements, plus Tom's tantrum, would have been recorded and those recordings already furnished to the court.

"If he didn't tell you of his plans at any time, how did you know he would bring Ms. Grant to the secure area?"

"I conjectured that he would do so based on my knowledge of his character, including his extreme hatred of Fallers due to his wife's death in an enemy attack on a civilian colony."

"At any time did Ms. Grant aid you in this 'conjecture'?"

"No. I didn't see her between Dr. Capelo's outburst the day before and their arrival at the prisoner's area."

"Did you track their movements on security recordings?"

"I do not have authorized access to security recordings," Kaufman said.

Rulanov repeated the question, more sharply. "Did you track the movements of Dr. Capelo and Ms. Grant on security recordings?"

"I did not."

The court conferred briefly, then Rulanov resumed. "Were you aware that Carpenter's Mate First Class Michael Doolin had cut a hole between Dr. Capelo's cabin and that of his children, a hole hidden under his bunk?"

"Yes. I ordered crewman Doolin to cut the hole."

"No work order or Adjustment to Ship form was logged onto the computer for this work. Did you file these forms?"

"No, sir."

"Why not?"

"I knew Commander Grafton would disapprove them."

"If that's so, Colonel, then why did you have the work done?"

Finally they were asking questions to which they didn't already know the answer. Kaufman said, "I had the hole cut to keep Dr. Capelo and his children happy. His youngest daughter has been in a state of disturbed behavior since the death of her mother. I am—was—Special Project Head of a nonmilitary and highly talented team, and such people are often quirky. Dr. Capelo's irreplaceable expertise was essential to this team, and any quirks I could satisfy made him that much more able to concentrate on his task. A task, may I respectfully remind the court, that is not the equivalent of data entry. Creativity is not like a faucet that one can turn on and off. The more I could do to aid the flow of Dr. Capelo's thinking by removing anxieties from his mind, the more I was advancing his irreplaceable work for the Solar Alliance Defense Council."

Again the court conferred among themselves in low tones. Rulanov said, "Please return to your description of the events of April sixteenth, Colonel. You guessed that Dr. Capelo would break Ms. Grant from the brig and bring her to the prisoner-of-war secure area. You gained authorized admittance to that area. Then what happened?"

Back to known information. "The secure area monitors the surrounding corridors. When I saw Dr. Capelo and Ms. Grant arrive, I opened the door. Dr. Capelo was spraying the MPs with tanglefoam. As per regulations, the senior MP was coated with antidote spray. I don't know why the junior MP was not also coated. The junior MP had gone down in tanglefoam, and the senior was attacking Dr. Capelo. I tasered him and dragged both men inside, with Ms. Grant's help. Dr. Capelo recovered enough to follow us, and I closed the door."

"Were Dr. Capelo and Ms. Grant surprised to see you waiting for them?"

"Yes."

"Colonel, do you habitually carry tanglefoam and taser?"

"No. I brought them with me specifically for this operation."

Kaufman could see that none of the court liked his appropriation of a recognized military term for his escapade. Kaufman had used the term deliberately.

Rulanov said, "Why did you then spray Dr. Capelo with tangle-foam?"

"I knew that Dr. Capelo, given any chance at all, would try to kill the prisoner. That was not what I wanted. I wanted to give Ms. Grant another chance to work with the Faller."

"Why?"

This was the crucial question. Kaufman leaned forward, threw everything he had into his answer. "Ms. Grant is a gifted Sensitive, perhaps the Solar System's most gifted Sensitive. In her last session with the prisoner before her arrest, she had seen a definite, strong, and troubling reaction on the part of the Faller to her indication that we might test setting prime thirteen of the artifact. It seemed to me vital to the welfare of the Solar Alliance—perhaps of the entire human race—that we find out the information that caused such a reaction. And it turned out I was correct: From my intervention came Dr. Capelo's revolutionary understanding of the physics of the artifact, information that may win us the war."

Rulanov said sharply, "You are admonished, Colonel Kaufman, that this is not the place for you to present a defense. This court is merely trying to uncover the facts of this case."

"I understand, sir." But now it was at least on record.

"Did you have any way, Colonel, of knowing or guessing that this illegal meeting would result in Dr. Capelo's scientific break-through?"

"No, of course not," Kaufman said. "But I did think it would yield to Ms. Grant whatever information the prisoner had been try-ing to hide. As it did."

The court now took him, step by step, through Marbet's interactions with the Faller, Kaufman's observation of those interactions, and Capelo's restricted actions while trapped in tanglefoam. All shown in the surveillance data, but they needed him to say it for the official inquiry record, so Kaufman could not claim later that the surveillance data had been tampered with. He answered fully and accurately, his tone cooperative. The entire recitation took over a half hour.

The MPs were called. They testified separately, neither looking once at Kaufman, both exuding contained fury. The senior MP had been made a fool of, and knew it. The junior MP had probably received disciplinary action for not taking the time to coat himself with tanglefoam antidote, which he probably hadn't imagined ever needing aboard ship. Well, he'd been wrong.

The MPs were dismissed. "The court calls Marbet Caroline Grant."

Kaufman's first thought was, *She looks so different clothed.* He had to suppress a grin. Never had he seen so much of a woman's body, over so long a time, with whom he wasn't having sex. War was a strange thing.

Marbet wore green prisoner coveralls. Her red curls were neatly combed above her calm face. The smallest person in the room, she nonetheless looked dignified and competent. Kaufman wondered what she could see about the investigative board members that he could not.

The court took her through her movements on April 16, although these too were all recorded. She answered quietly and firmly.

"Ms. Grant, did you consider not going with Dr. Capelo when he broke illegally into your cell?"

"No."

"Why not?"

"It's the wrong question, Commander. The question should be: Why did I go with Dr. Capelo? And the answer is that I thought the information I could uncover from the Faller would justify any breaking of rules in terms of its value to the human race. Which in fact proved to be true."

Rulanov frowned; this was the second time that subjective assertion had made it into the recordings of what was supposed to be a search for facts.

More questions established that Marbet had not known of Capelo's intentions until he showed up at her cell (indeed, there was no way she could have, being locked up herself). The charge against her of treason still stood but was, Kaufman knew, beyond the jurisdiction of this court. Marbet was a civilian. She would face civilian law.

Lieutenant Ramsay, who had been listening silently, now asked Marbet detailed questions about her work with the prisoner. Kaufman thought Ramsay sounded sympathetic, but he couldn't be sure. All three soldiers kept their faces blank.

Which was not to say that Marbet wasn't reading volumes there.

By the time the court had finished with her, it was well past noon. Rulanov drummed his fingers on the table, the first sign of strain that Kaufman had seen. "We'll break for lunch now. Resume at fourteen hundred hours."

Marbet was led away separately from Kaufman. She smiled at him, a wistful complex smile that nonetheless held a gleam of incongruous mischief. She had undoubtedly been told not to speak to Kaufman, but she did anyway. She said in a loud stage whisper, "After lunch they get Tom."

THIRTY

ABOARD THE *ALAN B. SHEPARD*

aufman noted that Tom Capelo, unlike Marbet, was not dressed in the green coveralls of a prisoner. The physicist wore a dress suit, the tunic a bit shorter than current fashion but the material clearly expensive. Capelo entered the room quietly, his thin dark face no more sardonic than usual. He carried a sheaf of flimsies folded in his right hand. No MPs accompanied him; evidently Capelo, unlike Marbet or Kaufman, had free run of the ship. They were criminals; he was a scientific hero.

"Dr. Capelo, please be seated," Rulanov said. "Will you please start by detailing for this court of inquiry your movements on April sixteenth."

"No," Capelo said.

"I beg your pardon?"

"No, I won't detail for you my movements on April sixteenth. You have them all recorded. I see no point in reiterating what is already known by everybody here."

Rulanov's jaw tightened. "Dr. Capelo, this is an authorized court of inquiry. You are required to answer."

"No, I'm not," Capelo said evenly. "You're an investigative

body, not a court of law—even military law. If you want to force me to answer, convene a formal court-martial and subpoena me. I'm willing to cooperate with you now by answering any real questions you have, but not any bullshit ones."

The three members of the court turned to each other and conferred, Ramsay scowling fiercely. Kaufman tried to catch Capelo's eye, but Capelo stared straight ahead.

"Dr. Capelo," Rulanov finally said, his eyes icier than Kaufman thought humanly possible, "what was your motive for breaking Marbet Grant out of the brig and bringing her to the secure area where the prisoner of war was housed?"

"I wanted to kill the bastard."

"Did Ms. Grant know that was your motive?"

"You'd have to ask her."

"Let me rephrase my question," Rulanov said, and Kaufman saw the effort it cost him to hold his temper. "Did you say anything to Ms. Grant to indicate your intention?"

"No."

"Did she say anything to you that indicated to you that she knew you planned an assassination?"

"No."

"What, in your opinion, was Ms. Grant's motive in going with you?"

"She wanted to talk to the Faller. Or communicate in whatever way she could. Which she did."

Rulanov shifted his weight in his chair. "Were you aware that Colonel Kaufman would be waiting for you in the secure area?"

"No."

"When were you first aware he was there?"

"After I staggered into the anteroom and he sprayed me with tanglefoam."

"And it was the tanglefoam that effectively prevented you from carrying out your plan to kill the prisoner?"

"Yes. Of course, Commander Grafton ended up doing that for me," Capelo said, and Kaufman suddenly saw the conflict Capelo was trying, in his jittery and unintrospective way, to come to grips with. *"I would slay my enemy, and weep that he is dead."*

Poor Tom.

"Dr. Capelo," Rulanov said tightly, "please confine yourself to answering the question asked."

"Only if you answer some in return. Why did Grafton release a nerve gas into the 'secure area' instead of sending in MPs in body armor to subdue us? We weren't heavily armed, even peaceable old Lyle here had just a taser and some slightly used tanglefoam, and we wouldn't have presented any obstacle at all to soldiers who weren't taken by surprise."

"Commander Grafton's actions are not your—"

"Maybe not. But here's one that is: Why is Marbet still locked up and I'm free, when I was the one who engineered getting into your so-called 'secure area'?"

"Ms. Grant is under arrest for the same offense she was arrested for previously. Dr. Capelo, no matter what your scientific stature, you cannot—"

"Let's discuss my scientific stature, shall we? Is that the reason I'm free to roam around without any charges being filed against me? Because I produced the physics theory that's going to win the war for you? Am I free and she's not because I'm going to be a valuable media commodity the second I publish, maybe even a future Nobel winner, and no one wants their scientific savior to be in jail? But a mere Sensitive in a world where Sensitives aren't popular anyway will hardly be missed?"

"That's enough! Dr. Capelo, you—"

"Hypocrisy the size of a warship, commander. That's what we have here."

"—are in contempt of court. One more outburst and I—"

"You'll what? That's your problem, isn't it? You don't know

what to do with me, now that I've produced for you. Oh, and for myself, I admit that. But now I'm an interesting problem, aren't I?"

Kaufman said, because he couldn't resist, "Not as big a problem as you might think, Tom. Haven't you ever heard of J. Robert Oppenheimer?"

Capelo turned toward him, grinning. "So they didn't cut out your tongue after all, Lyle. Or your balls."

"MPs!" Rulanov called. "Remove Dr. Capelo from the court!"

"Lay one hand on me again," Capelo said evenly, not moving from his chair, "and you'll have to kill me to keep from having the worst PR problem the Navy ever saw. And if you do kill me, my daughter and her nanny are prepared to tell the story to what will, I'm sure, be fascinated reporters. Amanda would make an extremely appealing holo witness."

Rulanov was too much of a soldier to be intimidated. He gestured to the MPs, who seized Capelo. Kaufman found himself rising.

Capelo said, still not raising his voice, "The party's over so soon? But I have more questions. What, for instance, are you—" The MPs started dragging him toward the door. Capelo went limp, a dead weight, and kept on talking. "—going to do with this artifact, now that I've explained what it's capable of doing?"

"We're going to use it," another voice said from the doorway.

Kaufman, halfway out of his chair, stumbled up the rest of the way. The court, after a stunned moment, jumped to its collective feet and snapped into salutes. Belatedly, Kaufman did the same. Only the MPs went on with their work, dragging a dead-weight Capelo toward the door. The newcomer said, "Release that man, soldier." The MPs paid no attention.

"Release him!" echoed Rulanov, the most strangled echo Kaufman had ever heard. But Rulanov recovered fast. "Welcome aboard, sir."

Capelo, again free and upright, turned to stare at the doorway, making it unanimous.

Kaufman had never met General Sullivan Stefanak, Supreme Commander of the Solar Alliance Defense Council, but of course he recognized him instantly. The general's face was on every newscast in every media: holo, access, flimsy, newsgram. It wasn't a face anyone could forget, or ignore. Almost all of the SADC top brass were genemod; Stefanak was not. The huge size and strength, easily the equal of Dieter Gruber's, were natural. So, clearly, was the hard face under the bald head, neither one modified by cosmetic treatment. Stefanak's skin was light brown, his eyes deep brown flecked with gold. He had full fleshy lips and a large jaw. He radiated energy, and ruthlessness, and charisma. His appetites, for everything, were rumored to be enormous.

Including for power. Persistent scuttlebutt said that Stefanak was not content with leading the Solar Alliance Defense Council that controlled Army and Navy for the entire Solar System. That he wouldn't even be content to be elected president of the Solar Alliance. That he wanted to be dictator, and that with the war on and martial law always a possibility, it could happen. Looking at Stefanak—even more magnetic, ugly, and dangerous-looking in person than on holo—Kaufman suddenly believed it. A benevolent dictator, perhaps, but dictator nonetheless. This man made his own rules.

Beside Stefanak stood General Tollivar Gordon, who had sent Kaufman on this cursed mission, and Commander Grafton. Grafton looked curiously gray.

Capelo said, "The great man himself," but there was no real bite in it. Even Tom Capelo seemed subdued by Stefanak.

"And you're the great Dr. Capelo. I read your preliminary paper on probons. I didn't understand a single word of it."

Capelo was not that easy to charm. "I hardly expect you would. You're more interested in outcomes than causes."

"Exactly right, Dr. Capelo. And you're interested in what outcomes we plan on creating from your work."

"I am indeed. Are you actually going to tell me?"

"Yes. You have a right to know. Plus, as you so eloquently just pointed out, you represent a problem to us. If you ended up dead, would your not-quite-eleven-year-old daughter really try to tell your version of the story to the holos? Have you really briefed her on what to say?"

"I have, and she would. Would you try to stop her?"

"Difficult to do, I would imagine, if she's like her father. Sit down, or don't, Dr. Capelo, as you choose. I am certainly going to."

Lieutenant Framingham sprang forward with her own chair, and Stefanak squeezed his bulk into it. After an uncertain moment—his first yet, Kaufman thought—Capelo also sat. Everyone else remained standing.

"You have questions," Stefanak said to Capelo. "But before you begin, I have duties." He looked up at Rulanov. "Commander, you have done an excellent job conducting this court of inquiry. Before I relieve you of the responsibility, I want you to know that your thoroughness and professionalism have been noted. Lieutenant Ramsay, Lieutenant Framingham, the same goes for you."

All three officers tried not to look too gratified. Rulanov said, "Thank you, sir."

Stefanak turned to Grafton, still gray. "And you, Commander, have acted completely in accord with the highest standards of the Solar Alliance Defense Navy, correctly following procedure for every action you've taken from the moment the prisoner of war was brought aboard ship. You will receive a letter of commendation, in due time, for your promotion jacket."

Grafton looked less gray, although still uncomfortable. It couldn't be easy, Kaufman thought, having control of your own ship taken away from you as easily as jumping on the moon. Not easy for the court of inquiry, either. Stefanak was now in charge of everything.

"Colonel Kaufman, the charges against you have just been dropped. They were appropriate when filed, but new information, which General Gordon will discuss with you later, has invalidated them."

Kaufman said, "Thank you, sir." He was careful not to look at Grafton. But he risked a question . . . "And if I may ask, sir . . . Ms. Grant? Are the charges against her dropped, as well?"

"Ms. Grant is a civilian; she is beyond my jurisdiction. The matter is still pending," Stefanak said, and everyone in the room knew that the charges against Marbet would also disappear. You didn't aspire to be dictator without extensive political control.

Kaufman said, "Thank you, sir."

"Now. Dr. Capelo . . . your questions. Fire away."

Capelo had had time to regain his equilibrium. "What are you going to do with my artifact?"

Stefanak smiled at the pronoun, which Kaufman knew had been deliberate on Capelo's part, but didn't comment on it. "We're going to take it to the Solar System, install it somewhere secure and classified, and activate setting prime eleven, thereby protecting all of the Solar System from Faller attack."

Somewhere secure and classified. My God, Kaufman thought, Stefanak will control it completely. No one will dare cross him—he'll hold an undefeatable Excalibur, one that could become a doomsday machine if he chose. He *will* be dictator.

And he, Lyle Kaufman, trained diplomat, had not seen it until just this moment. Seduced by the science and the weaponry, he had not looked at all at the politics.

"I see," Capelo said, with shades of meaning. "So you won't take it to the Faller system, activate it at setting prime thirteen, and fry their entire home system?"

"You've told us that's not possible without disastrously affecting the fabric of spacetime itself."

"What if I'm wrong?"

"We hope you'll continue to refine your theory, becoming more sure."

"What if I'm wrong about what setting prime eleven does?"

"Same answer," Stefanak said. He appeared to be enjoying himself.

"What if as I 'refine my theory,' and others do, too—I *am* going to be allowed to publish?"

"Certainly."

"But you know the Fallers most likely monitor whatever of our electromagnetic spectrum they can. They may be able to decipher our breakthroughs."

Kaufman, too, had wondered about this. He listened intently for Stefanak's answer.

"Let them. My scientific advisors are convinced their approach to science is so different from ours that they'll find translation and imitation very difficult."

"Probably true," Capelo admitted. "So what if, as I 'refine my theory' and others do the same, major errors are uncovered?"

"We'll correct for them. Dr. Capelo, I'm a soldier, not a clothing designer. I expect major errors, and I expect to have to correct for them. War is like that."

"And just how do you expect to 'correct' for the destruction of spacetime if two artifacts are activated at setting prime thirteen in the same star system?"

"Don't you think the original engineers thought of that and built in failsafes?"

"I have no idea. And neither do you."

"True enough. But I don't anticipate ever using setting prime thirteen, Doctor. It would constitute an unacceptable risk."

Capelo sat thinking. Finally he said, "You wouldn't have to take any risk. You don't actually have to activate the artifact at all, you know. You merely have to convince people, humans and Fallers, that you activated it. The effect would be the same, unless the bastards are stupid enough to actually bring their artifact to our space and call your bluff."

Stefanak said nothing. He went on smiling, huge legs crossed carelessly at the knee, relaxed and comfortable.

Capelo laughed, the short harsh sound Kaufman had heard a hundred times.

"All right, General. I'm not a soldier. But I have one more question, and it's a soldier's question. I called up all the battle data in the ship's library since the Faller skeeters first turned up protected by disrupter-beam shields. I don't have the classified material, of course, but you know those war correspondents—their robots go practically everywhere and cover practically everything. Then I wrote a program to compare that data to probable tunnel system use and maximum skeeter flying time. And I found something very interesting.

"The two can be made to coordinate such that a single Faller artifact could have been transferred from ship to ship and still cover every place the beam-disrupter shield turned up. They haven't cracked the engineering at all, have they? They only possess one artifact, just like we do."

Lieutenant Framingham gasped. Kaufman could feel his own face stretch in surprise. For the first time, Stefanak looked discomforted. No one spoke; no one dared.

Finally, the general said, "You're a very intelligent man, Dr. Capelo. Pity you didn't choose to become a soldier."

"I'd have made a rotten soldier."

"Perhaps you're right. How good a patriot are you?"

Capelo laughed again. "Do you mean, will I tell anyone about this conjecture? Publish it? Make it part of my daughter's armor? No. I want to see us win the war, General, as much as you do. Maybe more, because I'm not a soldier, and I have nothing to gain from success in battle and even more to lose than I already have. As long as you're not going to prosecute me for treason, or breaking-and-entering, or any other stupid charge, you have my silence on everything that you tell me is classified. I already have heavy-duty security clearances, you know."

"I know."

"And Marbet Grant?" Capelo asked.

"Much lighter security clearances. But I suspect she, too, will remain silent about anything that happened aboard this ship."

"In return for her freedom."

Stefanak had resumed his easy smile. "I told you—Ms. Grant is a civilian. All I can do is present her case as I see it to the proper authorities."

"Yes," Capelo said sardonically, "only that."

"Are we finished here yet, Doctor?"

"As finished as something like this can be."

Stefanak stood. Capelo rose, too; it was impossible to stay seated when that overwhelming presence did not. Stefanak held out his hand. "Good-bye, Doctor Capelo."

"Good-bye, General Stefanak."

"Colonel Kaufman," Stefanak said, "General Gordon will stay behind on this ship to debrief you. I must leave immediately. Gentlemen, madam." He saluted the officers, who responded with the hypercorrect fervor of Academy cadets. Stefanak left, trailing Grafton behind him like a flyer behind a war cruiser.

Rulanov, Ramsay, and Framingham seemed eager to leave as well. They marched stiffly out the door. Capelo followed, saying, "I have to tell my girls I'm not going to jail. They'll be glad to get home to Earth, I think. Good luck, Lyle, you deserve it."

In a few moments the room contained only Kaufman and Gordon. The silence felt unnatural to Kaufman, after so many jolts. Like the suspended moment after a Marsquake.

Gordon grinned. "I told you that you were the right man for this job, Lyle."

"The . . . *right* man?"

"Certainly. It doesn't matter that you got everybody connected with it arrested, and the prisoner of war killed. Oh, it does matter, actually, you know that. Your career in the military is over. You know too much. More important, Stefanak will need a scapegoat for those closed, classified SADC sessions in which he explains how we lost the alien POW we never officially had. He'll be grateful to you, Lyle, and a bit nervous about you, and he'll stick you behind a desk way out on some remote battle station served by one space tunnel and hope to never lay eyes on you again. Probably after first sweetening the assignment with a promotion and a medal. And if you ever move against him in any way, you'll be dead."

"I know," Kaufman said.

"I'm sorry. But you were still the right man for the mission. You got the job done, Lyle, and done as well as anyone in the galaxy could have done it."

"Thank you, sir. I'm just another casualty of war, is that it?"

"Yes. Capelo and Stefanak will get the glory of protecting the Solar System. But because of you, the war may yet be won. Is it enough?"

"No," Kaufman said, but he knew, as did Gordon, that it would have to do.

EPILOGUE

LUNA CITY, JULY 2167

While he waited for the elevator that would take him down to the living levels of Luna City, Kaufman studied the park. He hadn't seen it since he'd recruited Marbet Grant for the World mission well over a year ago. The park hadn't changed. It still looked dark to him compared to Martian parks. On Mars, the sky had a pinkish light, its intensity depending on the day's dust count. Here, the only light was artificial, unless you counted either the stars shining coldly through the piezoelectric dome or the earthlight from the monstrous blue-and-green world suspended above. Or maybe, on Luna, this was the world and Earth qualified as a moon. It all depended on how you looked at it.

As in his last visit, the fenced play yard held squealing toddlers and their caretakers, toddlers who could jump almost as high as the top of their very high slide. The scientific experiments under clear plastic domes still dotted a restricted area, which was still not restricted very much. There was little crime in Luna City's carefully pre-selected population. On benches set between beds of flowers genemod for the low light, people talked or star-gazed or kissed.

The flowers didn't remind Kaufman much of World. These were

too small, too subdued, to evoke World's riot of glorious blossoms.

The elevator came, and he stepped inside.

At H Level, he stepped into a wide corridor curving away at both ends. A small tram said cheerfully, "Hello! I make a circuit of this residential level every ten minutes, stopping whenever you instruct me to do so. Or, if you prefer, you can walk. All entrances to residential clusters are found on or just off this main circular corridor."

"I'll walk," Kaufman said, and the tram fell silent.

The corridor was utilitarian, except for soft patterns of lights playing over the walls. The doors opening directly off the corridor, numbered consecutively, were as plain as the walkway. Evidently Lunarians saved their decoration for their residences.

The tram passed him, carrying an elderly lady. Two walkers nodded to him pleasantly without interrupting their conversation. In fifteen minutes he reached Marbet's cluster. In another five he stood in front of her apartment door.

She opened it even before he signaled; she'd been watching for him. "Lyle! Hello!"

"Hello, Marbet," he said, and wondered if it had really been more than a year, and then how he had let it be more than a year. Not that he'd had much choice. She looked as unchanged as the park above, no older, her auburn curls as bright and her genemod-green cat's eyes as startlingly vivid. She wore a long tunic of some fine, ivory-colored material that floated around her, and a dramatic gold necklace.

"Come in. What can I give you to drink? A fizzie? Some wine? I have wine from Chile."

"Sounds expensive. A fizzy is fine. You look wonderful, Marbet."

"Thank you. You look tired."

"I am."

He'd forgotten how it felt to be with her: that strange combination of ease and stimulation, laced with discomfort about what she might be reading from his face, his body, the tone of his voice. Had she decorated her home to offset that discomfort, making it as welcoming and reassuring as possible? Large comfortable pillows, bright floral fabrics, soft lighting and minimal clutter. A room to relax in. In these surroundings, his dress uniform felt stiff.

He said, "What have you been doing?" She hadn't appeared lately in the newscasts; he'd had a search program scan Mars's central library.

"A few small jobs on Earth, mostly private businesses wanting intelligence during negotiations. Nothing very compelling lately, I'm afraid. Have you heard about Tom?"

"Capelo? No, what?"

"He's back at Harvard, expanding his probon theory, and his papers are making all sorts of waves in the physics world. But you already knew that. The news is that he's getting married."

Kaufman almost sputtered into his drink. "*Tom?*"

"Yes. It seems he met her at some sort of physics conference and fell like a ship into a black hole. He comlinked me last week. I was as surprised as you look."

"I thought he'd mourn his dead wife forever."

"Nothing as unpredictable as people. Quantum particles are nothing compared to us. Although actually, I think something else happened with Tom. I think he exorcised something out there on the World mission. It made him open again to caring for someone else besides his daughters. Who apparently are delighted with their new stepmother, Tom says."

"I wish him all happiness," Kaufman said.

They sat quietly, drinking their fizzies, each contemplating the strange places in the human soul. Kaufman was more at home with such contemplations than he'd once been, he thought wryly. Although not as a result of any exorcism. Kaufman said finally, "The artifact's been a great success. Hidden somewhere in the Solar System, 'safeguarding the cradle of humanity,' as the flimsies say."

Marbet said, "Do you think it's actually activated at setting prime eleven?"

"Who knows? Tom showed us that if it is, it's undetectable unless someone brings in another one and tries to fry Sol. Unless that happens, we'll never really know if it works or not. It's like that old joke about the witch doctor who gives the explorer a charm against ferocious man-eating tigers. The guy says, 'But there aren't any tigers on Mars,' and—"

"—and the witch doctor says, 'See? It's working already.' Lyle, that joke's *ancient*."

"But applicable. All you can do is figure the probabilities that the artifact is guarding Sol."

"Probability sun," Marbet said.

"Exactly."

"What about you? What have you been doing?"

He said, "I've resigned from the military, Marbet, effective next week. I'm on my way to debriefing on Mars."

"I know."

"How? How could you know I'm on my way to debriefing?"

She laughed. "I didn't know that part. But I did know you've resigned. It's in the way you wear your uniform now . . . I can't explain in words."

"They stuck me out in Ariel System, at the ass-end of the galaxy. You think World was isolated . . . I commanded a space station."

"And you hated it."

"And I hated it. So I've resigned, honorable discharge, out as soon as I debrief."

She set down her fizzy on a small table woven of some strong grass, or of something that looked like grass. "Mars is between here and the space tunnel. You've taken a long detour for somebody who's on his way to a debrief on Mars."

"Yes. I was hoping I could persuade you to go with me."

"To where?"

He breathed deep. This was it. Although being Marbet, she might already know. "Back to World. A private expedition, privately funded. To search for Ann Sikorski and Dieter Gruber, if they're still alive, and bring them home. If they want to come."

"To bring home Ann and Gruber? Is that really the reason?"

He said, "It's a reason."

"Lyle," she said softly, "it isn't your fault. Whatever has happened to World, it isn't your fault. You had no choice."

"I know. But it's odd, isn't it? Most of the world's Prometheuses have destroyed worlds by bringing new technology: fire, bombs, whatever. I destroyed one by removing technology."

"But, Lyle—"

He didn't want to talk about it any longer. He interrupted Marbet. "Will you go with me? To Mars and then back to World?"

"Yes. I'll go with you."

He sipped his fizzy. Eventually he said, "Did you know I was going to ask that?"

"Lyle, a Sensitive is not clairvoyant. No, I didn't know you were going to ask that."

"Good," he said, put down his drink, and took her hand.

Enli and Essa sat outside their house in the cool evening air. Enli was cross. How had she become responsible for Essa, anyway? And why? The girl would wilt anyone.

"Essa, did you hear what I said? His mother is taking Serlit away from here because of you. He's too young for . . . for that kind of mating play, and you know it, and you did it with him anyway."

"He liked it," Essa said, unperturbed.

"I'm sure he did. But he's still too young, not even past his youth-planting ceremony. Shared reality . . ." She stopped. The words had just slipped out. Even after so long.

Essa ignored Enli's crossness. "Look at the stars come out, Enli.

They're so bright 'cause Ral is the only moon up and it's only part curvy. Look at that bright one just above the top of the stockade."

"Essa—"

"I'm going to the stars one day. I am. Pek Sikorski says there are other Worlds out there, and she saw them in a big metal flying boat. I will, too."

"You won't go anywhere if you don't behave."

"Listen! Pek Ramul's starting!"

The sounds of the pipe drifted in from the green, signaling the start of the dancing. Essa leaped up and ran off. Enli scowled. Such a girl! And O, Enli was too tired to go after her tonight. Calin was on guard duty—there had been some more threats from Gofkit Firtoe—and Enli had cooked for both her family and for Ann, who had a flower sickness and was isolated in her hut in atonement. Since trade with the capital had stopped (Gofkit Shamloe had nothing to trade), there was no more antihistamine. Dieter was off on a foraging trip and Ann was worried about him, and worry only made flower sickness worse. Added to all that, the little one kicked hard inside Enli's belly, and her back hurt.

Nonetheless, she lumbered to her feet and went after Essa. It *was* a lovely night. Enli stopped to sniff the sweet warm air. Slowly, a blossom unfolded inside her, its petals delicate and perfumed and blessed as a perfect allabenirib. She felt the blossom bud, open, fully flower.

Happiness.

Enli stood a moment longer, and then she continued along the path, into the deep shadow of the stockade and then out again, walking off-balance under the emerging stars and the one small, waning moon.